HELLO,

WITHIN THESE PAGE
IDENTITY, AUTHEN:
MEASURE, MISCHIEF AND CHAOS.

I HOPE THAT YOU ENJOY OPHELIA O'LEARY'S
STORY. I HOPE THAT YOU CAN IDENTIFY WITH
SOME OF THE CHARACTERS, AND THAT PARTS
OF THEIR JOURNEYS RESONATE WITH YOU.

IF YOU ENJOY YOUR VISIT TO NOLLAG, IT
WOULD MEAN A LOT IF YOU SHARED YOUR
EXPERIENCE IN THE FORM OF A RECOMMENDATION
TO A FRIEND, A REVIEW, OR POST ON YOUR
PREFERRED SOCIAL MEDIA PLATORM USING
THE HASHTAGS #CHRISTMASBITCH,
#OPHELIAOLEARY, OR # WELCOMETO NOLLAG.

THANK YOU FOR YOUR SUPPORT. IT MEANS
SO MUCH.

ALL THE BEST,

JACK

P.S. WHEN DONE, PLEASE RETURN THIS COPY
TO A LENDING LIBRARY OR PASS IT ON
TO AN INTERESTED PARTY.

Christmas Bitch

A Novel by Jack Lelko

Nollag Bookery and Bindery

First edition July 2022

Edited by Ami Maxine Irmen

Book design by Jack Lelko

ISBN 978-1-7374566-1-2 (paperback)

ISBN 978-1-7374566-0-5 (hardcover)

ISBN 978-1-7374566-2-9 (ebook)

Library of Congress Control Number: 2022910145

Published by Nollag Bookery and Bindery

Tacoma, WA

www.neurdotically.wordpress.com

To Kevin: for cooking up this wonderful, quirky story.

To Butler: thank you for being my best friend many lifetimes over and for being in love with this story before it was even written.

To Ami: thank you for being a friend and editor.

Table of Contents:

By JACK
11/25/15

Christmas Bitch

A Glimpse

In Which Ophelia O'Leary Gets Ready for a Con of Sorts

At the plea of one Ophelia O'Leary, Clarence Smith had come to fit her for a wire. In truth, this step was unnecessary. Anyone on the Nollag Police Force could have done it, but that's what lifelong friends were for, and he sensed a friend was exactly what she needed right now. Pep talks were always needed when taking down dirty dealings from the inside. It may have actually been in the Nollag Police Manual. He made a mental note to check the index later.

With the task now completed, Clarence found it increasingly challenging to keep his eyes open. He attributed this sudden onset of fatigue not to the stakeout he had just completed that had lasted twelve hours, thirty-one minutes, and seventeen seconds, but to the fact that he had sat down. It, of course, did not help that his chosen place to rest his posterior was on the soft, plush sofa. He should have opted for one of those hard stools, the ones without a back that were, quite possibly, structurally unsound.

But no such thing existed in Ophelia's apartment. He could have cursed her had he not been distracted by the knitted blanket slung over the couch. *Is this cashmere?* he wondered absentmindedly, and gently caressed the light gray blanket.

A sound came around the corner from Ophelia's closet, which had once been a bedroom, but, well, Ophelia had a penchant for clothes. The sound of Ophelia's voice was indistinguishable at first, the stage left rumbling of a French horn. Fatigue peeled away, and the "wa-wa-wa" noise became structured with syllables and enunciation. Noises turned to words, eventually stringing themselves into sentences.

"Thanks again for fitting me with the wire, Clare," Ophelia said, poking her head out of the door to her closet, a cascade of red curls soon following. "Are you sure you don't want coffee or tea?"

"Naw," Clarence yawned, his hand holding the blanket moving to cover his mouth. "That'll keep me up. I should go home to bed." When he looked down, he was surprised to find he had a lap full of cashmere.

Ophelia hummed back sarcastically. Her left eyebrow arched in disbelief, and the right corner of her mouth pulled up at the side for balance. "You should just crash on the couch," she replied, retreating into the cavernous closet again.

Clarence blinked back, drawing a large throw pillow closer to him. *So fluffy*, he thought. *Possibly stuffed with cumulus clouds.*

"Okay," Ophelia stood in the hall, "help me rehearse for today. I don't want to let Copper down, and, you know, this is the first time I'm flying blind." Ophelia's left thumb and index finger wrung the pinky on her right.

Clarence had known Ophelia for lifetimes. Seeing her so unsure of herself, well, it had never happened before. Anxiety made his stomach complete a floor routine that would certainly guarantee a gold medal in fretting. Lately, he found himself trying to ease both their minds with the consolation that this would pass as all things inevitably do, but, this time, that comfort was not easily forthcoming.

"Ophie." He tried to make his smile reassuring. "You've hatched and juggled far more complex schemes than a sting operation."

Ophelia tried to hold back a slight grimace. "You're right," she finally said with a nod. "I have, haven't I? I have." She said the last part to herself. "The Deal and Steal will be under new management when I'm done with them."

"Considering 'Steal' is directly in the pawn shop's name, I'm surprised none of us figured this out sooner," Clarence frowned. "Anyway, when you get to the Deal and Steal, you're picking up…."

"A book," Ophelia replied, pointing a finger from Clarence to her head as if to indicate exactly where in her cranium that piece of information was stored. She walked to the coat closet by the front door. She stood back from the opened door, surveying her options.

"Which book?" Clarence followed up.

"Hm?" Ophelia hummed. *Basic black? No. The navy one with the silver buttons? What coat should one don when visiting a pawn shop? Tsk. Of course. The bright red swing coat with the capelet. It has nice motion to it. Beautiful lines….* "Oh!" Ophelia exclaimed, remembering Clarence was in the room. "*Alice's Adventures in Wonderland.*"

"And?"

"Aaaaand a lamp."

"What kind of la—"

"Honestly, Clarence," she huffed now in her familiar confident tone. "I've got this. Oh! But what I don't got—have," she corrected herself, running back to her closet, the big one.

"What are you getting?" Clarence called after her, but her reply was lost amongst the sounds of shuffling boxes and the scraping of old dresser drawers as they were opened and shut again.

Clarence squinted at his watch. When the blur was mostly gone, and his vision finally aligned, he read the time as 10:47 a.m. She was cutting it close, a luxury she could not afford. This situation wasn't like all the others before when time offered Ophelia spoilers to the consequences of her actions. He rolled his hazel eyes to the back of his head, his face pinching at the peak. He had overextended the roll. "Ow," he said under his breath, rubbing each eye with the heel of his right hand.

"Besides," she echoed her friend's encouraging words from earlier, "it's not like we haven't pulled cons before." She stepped back into the living room and took a seat next to Clarence, something small clasped in her left hand.

"True," he conceded, slumping against the back of the couch, sinking farther into it and feeling his eyelids struggle to hold themselves up. It took him a moment to register that things had gotten quiet, which was rare when the two of them were together. Ophelia, he noticed, was off somewhere in her thoughts again, her thumb absentmindedly stroking the thing in her hand.

"Whatcha have there, Ophie?" he asked, pulling her from her reverie.

She opened her hand to show Clarence a small black velvet covered box.

"You kept it."

She nodded. "What was I going to do with it otherwise?" she shrugged, opening the little box, the hinges sounding like cracking knuckles. She made a face, eyes widening almost as if in horror at the contents. "Calum has terrible taste. No other woman should have to be put in that position."

"Not even Bailey?" Clarence asked, jumpstarting the conversation again.

"Shockingly, no," she laughed. "Besides, now I have something to pawn." Ophelia securely placed the box into the front left pocket of her coat.

"Mm," was all Clarence said. Within that "Mm" came a question only a best friend could pluck from the sound: *Not even Delaney?*

Ophelia exhaled audibly, then stood up and walked over to the dish where she kept her keys by the door. She picked up a pin in the shape of a poinsettia and fed it through the lapel of her coat. "I know everything with Dee is done. Squared away. All neatly packaged and tied up with a bright green bow." She caught a half-lidded look from Clarence. "Well, not 'neat,' but it had to get messy. You know this." She said this with conviction where many would have expected, at the very least, a tinge of regret. Delaney was her sister, after all.

"I know," he confirmed. "Things with family are always messy. I turned my parents in to the police when I was ten, remember?" He plopped onto his side, embracing the very large pillow, the faux fur of its slipcover getting caught on his stubble.

"I'm going to meet her over at Beatrice's after I'm done at the pawn shop. She said she wanted to talk about something. I'll stop by your place later to drop off your coat and the gift for Mynah."

"I can take them now," Clarence offered. He snuggled into the pillow.

"I still have some finishing touches to add," Ophelia replied. "Besides, I wanted to see Gin and Olive's new baby." Also, Clarence was so tired, and Ophelia knew that any directions she left him would surely get lost in the Wonderland that was Clarence's impending dreams.

He didn't hear her response; his fatigued mind moved to another topic.

"After we help Copper pull off his fairy tale evening with Mynah, we'll be done. Mission accomplished." Clarence was now cocooned in both the light gray knitted blanket and in his thoughts. He meditated on their process: coming into people's lives, working their brand of charm (in the case of Ophelia, *charm* was used loosely), and then disappearing. Onto the next thing. It never failed. "It always feels strange," he mused to his friend. "Although, this time is different, huh?" A sadness crept into his words. Ophelia chose to ignore this last part.

"Well, we've been Ophelia O'Leary and Clarence Smith for twenty and twenty-five years, respectively," Ophelia said to the gray mound that was Clarence reflected in the mirror as she played with her hair and pulled on her gloves. *It may feel strange, but it doesn't come as a surprise*, she said to herself.

The reason for that off kilter feeling, at least for Ophelia, was due to the emotion that she usually felt every time she left behind the life she had assumed once she helped someone, like Delaney, find their footing with happiness. Sadness usually did accompany happiness, sometimes riding on its coattails and lingering long after the party was over. This time, however, things were different. This time, Clarence was going to move on without Ophelia all because she had been, let's say, a *little* too helpful.

Her shoulders drooped another half an inch when her thoughts moved to her meeting at the café with her sister. Delaney hadn't said one word to her since last Christmas, when Ophelia put Bailey Barrymore in the hospital, who, by the way, more than deserved it. Reconciliation seemed improbable. Perhaps she shouldn't go at all. Still, she couldn't help but be curious as to why her sister had invited her.

Clarence half-yawned, half-spoke, bringing Ophelia out of her tangled emotions, not unlike a recently unpacked box of Christmas lights. "Course, it's always a bit exciting…getting to figure out who we'll be the next time around," he said sleepily.

Ophelia hummed in agreement. She felt a slight ache when she heard Clarence's sleepy words. Ophelia had no choice but to remain Ophelia O'Leary. This would be the rest of her, what she speculated to be, mortal life. "Hey, Clare?" Ophelia asked, her face and tone serious once again.

"Yeah?" Clarence picked his head up off the pillow. He made a face, spitting out some of the faux fur that mixed with the drool at the corner of his mouth.

"Can you see the wire?" She came closer and gave a twirl.

"Nope. You're good." He gave her a drowsy smile.

"All right then. I'm off. Wish me luck."

Whether she was referring to her dealings with the pawn shop or with her impending meeting with her sister, even Ophelia could not be certain.

"Enjoy the nap," she said, stepping out into the apartment hallway. "I'll come by you sometime this afternoon," she reminded her friend. She caught a glimpse of a hand limply waving as she closed the door behind her. Muffled snoring followed while she turned the key in the lock.

Ophelia synched the belt of her coat a little tighter and began to make her way down to the street where she was meeting Copper. "Mrs. Beezle," she said in salutation to the old woman who was fumbling with her keys in one hand and balancing a parcel of groceries in the other. An orange had escaped and was rolling down the hall. Ophelia stopped it with her boot, picked it up, and took five steps forward to toss the fruit back into the paper bag. "Merry Christmas." She pinched her mouth into a smile that could best be described as toxically polite.

Mrs. Beezle scowled back at the now retreating young woman before resuming her task of getting back into her apartment. "I really don't care for her," she said to no one in particular, shuffling into apartment 7A.

Chapter 1

In Which We Start at the Beginning of the Beginning of the End

The city of Nollag was beginning to resemble a town you would find on the annual greeting card received from your second cousin twice removed who you have never actually met. Ever. Yesterday, the weather had drenched the downtown with heavy rains, and the following night yanked the tolerable temperature of thirty-eight degrees to a teeth-chattering, knee-knocking ten degrees…with a wind chill of negative two.

The shops that lined the main street of Nollag, strangely enough not named Main Street but rather Athas Avenue, were now encased in a thick sheet of ice — a quarter of an inch to be precise. If that were not enough, all of Nollag was getting a gentle dusting of fine snow.

The confection shop, Salty N. Sweets: Sweets and Baked Goods, was making the best of the abysmal winter weather by marketing their new Holi-Glazed Donuts and Cookies. The iridescently glossy treats sold like hot cakes while the hot cakes failed to rake in even a modest amount of dough.

That, thought Ophelia gleefully, *was ironic*, more pleased with herself that she was able to recall her word of the day. She pushed her way past the throngs of marshmallow-shaped Salty N. Sweets' patrons in their vibrant down coats with their equally harsh and itchy-looking wool knitted hats and mittens. She squinted through her fogged breath at the line that spilled out the confectionary's doors leaving little room for passersby to fit comfortably on the slick sidewalks. Her squint transitioned to an overemphatic eye roll, trying to save her vision from being accosted by a lemon-yellow coat with a pea green and purple scarf. "Oh, yay, it gets better," she muttered just loud enough for the woman behind the yellow blimp. She was wearing a herringbone black and white coat topped with an obnoxious crème and orange houndstooth knitted cap. The pompom nestled atop the pile of pattern was almost enough to work Ophelia's gag reflex. Try as she might, Ophelia struggled to understand not everyone knew the proper etiquette of dressing for occasions where the public would see them in daylight. The woman in yellow returned the snarky remark with an equally acidic smile. Ophelia made it a point to stare back as she passed by.

As the crowd began to thin and the wind picked up, the town hall's clock chimed its last of the eleven chimes, jarring Ophelia back to her reality that was riddled with brazen colors and mismatched patterns. Her date with her sister, Delaney, at Beatrice Clark's Caffeine and Bean Coffee Café on the corner of Slumber Lane and Jazzed Avenue was to happen in exactly twenty-nine minutes and fifty-eight seconds. For the twenty-third time that morning, give or take a fragmented thought in between a toothbrush stroke here and the middle of chewing this morning's waffle there, she again considered not going.

She pondered for a minute as her chilled fingers stopped fidgeting with the loose thread that threatened to open up a hole in her front left pocket and instead coiled around the small box currently taking occupancy in there, as well. *No, I made a promise. How long will the pawn shop thing really take, anyway? Twenty minutes?* She shrugged at the plausibility of her guess. *Besides, when am I ever punctual? Dee is used to it.* She had convinced herself, and so she pointed the tip of her black leather boot due northwest.

She swaggered down the smoothed cobblestone street toward the small shop that lay at the point where Droch Boulevard curved sharply to the right. The building was older, and shorter, than the two structures on either side of it. The foundation had settled faster on the left side, causing the flat roof of the shop to slant by four point three degrees. The large brick slabs of the Deal and Steal Pawn Shop had a permanent black tarnish on them from the big fire fifty years back, which had decimated the whole northern portion of the city… save for this little hovel.

Ophelia's walk said a lot about her person. It said that she was someone important, that she was not to be tangled with, and that there was precisely a ninety-two point seven percent probability that you would lose should you even attempt to, give or take a tenth of a percentage point. And that very tenacity and backbone was what would serve her well in the next fourteen minutes and thirty-seven seconds.

The sleigh bells banged clumsily against the door of the Deal and Steal Pawn Shop announcing the arrival of another mark, er, perspective client. Ophelia noted that the discolored bells on the shedding red velvet ribbon were not the only pathetic holiday touch in the equally drab establishment. The storefront window displayed a shabby looking miniature Black Hills spruce that not even Charlie Brown would have given a second glance at. The limescale-crusted water pan indicated it had gone without water for about two and a half days, turning the tips of the needles a sickly brown, some of which obscured the faded cardinals that adorned the tree skirt. The lopsided sprinkling of tinsel and chipped resin ornaments of cherubs only added to what could best be categorized as a holiday mishap.

Ophelia gave the rest of the shop a quick once over as she began to tug at the fingertips of her left glove. The shop was mostly clean, save the corners, which horded their own antiques of cobwebs and dust bunnies. As Ophelia's thumb and index finger pinched the tip of the third finger of her glove, her gaze settled on a particularly large tumble comprised of matted fur and crumbs. This unsightly collection of debris was evidence enough that not having her hand touch anything directly was the wisest choice for the time being, so the glove was pulled snuggly back onto her hand. Simultaneously, she forced back her conjectures of what exactly contributed to the composition of the dust boulder.

The light that managed to get past the smeared front windows showed the expected cornucopia of eclectic thingamabobs, doohickeys, and plain junk. Near the front of the establishment, on large heavy tables painted in flaking teal and tangerine, lay a veritable timeline of appliances and electronics: mantle clocks, a phonograph, televisions, a crank washing machine, and a miniature jukebox. Beyond this lay a few clusters of antique furniture that

12

hid the finger smudged glass cases that harbored the true bounty of watches, grandmothers' pearls and broaches, and the near mint condition comic books and baseball cards of yesteryear.

Ophelia heard the muted purr of a cat on the bookshelf on the west wall. Cuddlebum, a longhaired black domestic feline, watched the woman with his seductive yellow-green eyes as she approached the back counter. He sat on a shelf, propped up against an autographed copy of *Horton Hears a Who*. His tail gently tickled the spine of a leather bound first edition of *Alice's Adventures in Wonderland* on the shelf below. *Alice*, she mentally noted. *Check. Oddly shaped lamp? Isssssomewhere, I hope…*.

Ophelia felt the tear drop and hummingbird-shaped crystals of the wind chimes graze the top of her auburn red hair. She looked above her. The wind chimes hung on an ornate golden chandelier that had been precariously hung from the ceiling. At that moment, she finally understood the phrase about slapping makeup on a pig. The golden filigree, strings of pearls, and the delicately etched goblets that encased the candles on the fixture made everything else seem cheap and depressing.

"Can I help you?" Ophelia heard a smoker's voice come from behind an old slot machine. A haggard-looking woman leaned into view; the work stool she sat upon creaked under her shifting weight. Adele Swinde was the owner of the Deal and Steal Pawn Shop. Ophelia looked her up and down and decided in three seconds that Adele was not a pleasant person. That, and she had no style to speak of.

Heavily grooved lines had contoured themselves around her mouth, the result of years of frowning and only fleeting seconds of smiles sparingly sprinkled in between. Her eyes showed no remnants of sparkle. They had been eclipsed by her heavy purple lids and further obscured by the matching set of dark bags beneath them, making her eye color that of old guacamole. She had tied her brown and silver hair into a knotted mess that would have made a nice sanctuary for a church mouse who had suddenly experienced a crisis of faith.

Oh, what is that? Ophelia deliberated in puzzled horror.

What "that" was specifically was a sweater coat that Adele had shrouded herself in, comprised, Ophelia was willing to bet a sizable sum, of eighty percent dryer lint and twenty percent rayon. The sagging mess was mostly a heathered oatmeal speckled with bits of red, blue, and green. Ophelia resisted the compulsion to count all the pills that had formed on it, especially a rather nasty cluster along the right cuff. Reminded she had come with a very important purpose, Ophelia struggled to suppress analyzing the yellowed "I Heart Athas" t-shirt underneath that she was sure sported at least one hole somewhere.

Adele, too, had made up her mind about Ophelia. She labeled her a skinny bitch. She was accosted by memories that could not be held back by her mental dam. Ophelia bore a remarkable resemblance to the dime-a-dozen girls that had teased Adele all through her adolescence, and even a little bit through her early twenties. Each had the standard 36"-24"-36" measurements, satin hair that always caught the right light, and unblemished, smooth skin. Regardless, she was also more than well aware that this perfect package usually incubated a putrid attitude and a cruel and cunning desire to persecute anyone not manufactured out of the same mold.

14

"Actually, yes, you can, *ma'am*," Ophelia responded, putting a little too much emphasis on the last word.

Adele tried to work the muscles in her face into a convincing smile, one that conveyed having the client's best interest at heart and a genuine notion that she was happy Ophelia had chosen her establishment to do business. Rather, however, her mouth only managed to contort into a sneer. What was the point in smiling when humanity rarely proved itself worth the effort? She cleared her throat to push down the frustration that was beginning to curdle amidst stomach acids. She did not like this girl.

"Are you looking for anything in particular?" she queried Ophelia in a deadpan tone.

"Perhaps, uh…" she trailed, still trying to locate the lamp. *What did it look like again?*

Adele's gloomy eyes rolled in the back of her head as if to check a roster of the inventory tacked in the far corner of her occipital lobe. "Um, a bauble of some sort? I'm without a doubt that you'll be inevitably attending some fabulously fantastic soiree soon." Her last four words dripped with bellicosity so hot it burned the thin passive aggressive veneer Adele had halfheartedly tried to disguise them with.

"Well, thank you, ma'ma," Ophelia said, this time making Adele's right eye tick. "While I appreciate your suggestion, I could never buy a bauble, a trinket, or a trifle from this particular establishment. It…wouldn't suit my taste."

"Not even a gewgaw?" Adele surprised herself by actually managing to pose her question in a sweet tone while successfully ignoring the girl's last comment.

Ophelia simply wrinkled her nose in response.

Adele released an exasperated exhale, making her phlegm vibrate menacingly, like the end of a rattlesnake's tail. Furiously, she wiped at her oil-stained fingertips. She did not have time to play a tedious game of wits with one she was ninety-nine point three seven five percent sure was dim like the clearance bin of light bulbs at What's the Bright Idea Light Bulb and Lamp Outlet that only lit on one side.

"I'm here to do some business," Ophelia said with a gentle lilt at the end of her request. She tilted her head ever so slightly to the left, letting the light showcase her rosy cheeks. The spectacle left her looking rather doe eyed.

Adele no longer needed to work to maintain a small smile. "Will you be selling or pawning then? What is it that I can do for you?" Adele rolled her stool to the left of the slot machine. Surreptitiously, she folded her hands and leaned over the counter with hungry eyes that darted all over Ophelia's person, searching for treasure the young woman had brought. This would be more satisfying than a glass of eggnog with a little too much brandy. Try as she might, though, Adele could find nothing, save for the friendly smile Ophelia adorned on her pink lips. But that smile harbored something else – perhaps a pinch of smug.

After a long, thoughtful pause, Ophelia drew in a breath to speak, never taking her glistening green eyes off the drab mess of the woman before her. "I'm here to sell –"

Fireworks excitedly exploded in Adele's subconscious. She was one step closer to discovering what she hoped was something expensive from someone whom she had very little regard for.

"– but not to you," Ophelia impishly said, her cheeks pulling up ever so slightly in a conniving smile. The fireworks fizzed to sputtering sparks. Toying with Adele was not explicitly outlined in the plan she had reviewed with Clarence or Copper, but when it came to improvising, Ophelia never hesitated with an emphatic, "yes, and."

Adele was suddenly taken back to her thirteen-year-old self after just being denied the privilege to sit at the same lunch table as Angela Treetopper, the most popular girl at school. Angela had worn the same smoldering smirk that now rested on the lips of the young woman before her in the present.

"I'd rather handle my business with someone else at this… establishment. Clearly, you are threatened by me, and, to be brief, I want to make sure I receive an accurate appraisal that is not tainted by your bias." Ophelia punctuated her thought with a broader smile that stretched from ear to ear, a smile she only wore when she knew she had won. "Your frown lines were a dead giveaway," she said to the woman, adding, "They got deeper when I walked in."

Adele glowered back darkly.

"Like that." Ophelia waved a gloved finger in the air about the shopkeeper's expression, indicating the glower. "Maybe try and bury that…hmm…I'm guessing childhood trauma, just a smidge deeper."

Adele sucked in her lips as the words she wished to say built up to a dangerous pressure. Her face had turned an embarrassing shade of holly berry red. With all her might, she managed to suppress her temper and pretend that she and Ophelia were civil to one another, and that she was far too busy to help her at this particular time. Memory suppression was one of her mastered skills…most of the time. Adele had found this cultivated skill imperative when dealing in customer service.

"Oh, Woody," Adele crooned, which came out sounding more like a menacing growl. "Can you please come out here?"

Woody Hinklehimeriner was a giant of a man of equal parts fat and muscle. He could not quite clear the white doorframe that led to the back office that doubled as a storage room, height wise or widthwise. The tarnished bronze hinge at the bottom of the door shrieked loudly. The newly replaced gleaming silver hinge on top only whispered.

The display case's glass shuddered with each of the man's massive steps. Ophelia stood there unflinching. Where it would have taken an average person approximately five steps to make it to the front counter from the office, it took Woody exactly four steps plus a shuffle.

He had a square head with an angular jaw dotted in a five o'clock shadow. The creases on his forehead slanted from the left to the right. A red button nose ironically punctuated the wide face, which indicated Woody was nursing a cold. His charcoal gray and silver hair was neatly buzzed on the sides of his head but left slightly longer up top. Last, but not least, two dark eyes were set beneath thick, groomed eyebrows. Ophelia observed the eyes and the man they were set within, which both seemed quite kind. For that was what Ophelia had done in her line of "work." She noticed people.

An inconspicuous smile danced from one corner of her lips to the other. The dimple in the lower right quadrant of her face struggled to remain concealed as she fought to suppress her grin. *Piece of cake*, she thought. Some of the tension eased in her shoulders.

Woody failed to gently lay his hands across the countertop, making the glass panes shake from the force. Ophelia looked annoyed. "Sorry," Woody said with a faltering smile. Neither lady was sure to whom he was directing the apology.

"How can—"

"Woody, comere for a sec," Adele gruffly said to the gentle giant.

As Woody lumbered over, Ophelia leaned to her left, pretending to be enamored with the faux ruby earrings but was really giving Woody the once over. It truly was a habit that she had no intention of kicking in the near future.

Initially, she thought the heavy steps Woody took were causing the bells at the front to jitter and jangle. Turns out, he wore red and white stripped knee-highs with bells along the cuff – four on the left, five on the right. How did Ophelia ascertain the socks were knee-high, one may wonder? Or how she knew there were bells lining the tops of them? Simple. You would notice, daresay could not help to, as Woody was wearing a kilt.

The kilt was a plaid of dark green with small traces of yellow and pale moss green. It came to just above the knee, exposing bulky, pink, hairy legs. Ophelia found herself missing the woman in the yellow marshmallow coat from earlier that day. On the other hand, not really.

Whatever instructions that needed to be relayed to Woody did not take long on Adele's part. Forty-three seconds of heated whispers were all that was required. Ophelia could not hear what was said and wore a vacant look on her face. Woody wore a grimace, his lower jaw jutting out a little. It made him look a little doltish. On the contrary, Woody was no doofus, but in order to be able to afford more than one measly lump of coal this year, he needed to keep his job and therefore work for the Scrooge that was Adele Swinde.

Two hefty steps later, and Woody was back in front of Ophelia.

"Now," he said with a rattling in his throat, "what can I do for you?" He beamed genially back at Ophelia. Through his thick, chapped, purple lips, she could see he was missing his right lower canine.

"I," she began as she dug into her pocket, "would like to sell." She paused again for dramatic effect and to make sure Adele's eyes were on her. Ophelia presented the small hinged box. The velvet on its top still had the remnants of adhesive from the ruby red bow that had been affixed to it last year, now replaced with flecks of red pocket lint.

Ophelia's fingers unfurled from around the small package, holding it forward for Woody to take.

His index finger and knobby thumb gingerly plucked the box out of Ophelia's hand. Gently, he lifted the cover to see the treasure within. He had learned from past experiences to be careful doing so. Many a lid and hinge had snapped like dry twigs from the sheer force of his strength. The door leading to the backroom had not been the same since his first day.

The first to let out a gasp was Adele. She was not struck by the beauty of the thing inside, more or less by the disappointment of how well she could have cleaned up had she been the one to work the sale. She swore under her breath, very unbecoming for the holiday season, but this was the exact response Ophelia was hoping for, like whenever she managed to prove her sister incorrect.

Woody gazed at the ring in the box, taking up about an eighth of the surface area on the palm of his hand.

"Miss—"

"O'Leary," Ophelia finished the salutation for him.

"Are—are you sure, my dear?"

Adele menacingly cleared her throat.

"Yes," Ophelia said, not missing a beat.

Woody now pinched the ring between his thick fingers. It looked like a fragment of glitter in comparison. He inspected the cut, clarity, and color of the diamond, even employing an eye loupe, which magnified the rock's details by a power of ten. The ring was the very real deal.

"All right," Woody said in a tone that could have been misconstrued as skepticism by nine of out ten speech pathologists. Ophelia kept her cool, looking complacent. Cuddlebum saw a kindred spirit in her and wished to grace her with his presence. He hopped from his perch to the shelf below, then to the floor. In the process, *Alice* fell to the ground with a slap. The cat sashayed over to Ophelia, meowing his arrival, before completing a figure eight around her legs and jumping onto the counter to get a better look at her.

"What is the story behind this little gem?"

Adele exhaled, wishing for the business to be wrapped up and for the girl to be out of her shop. She left a bad taste in

Adele's mouth, like a candy cane with too much peppermint in it.

Ophelia raised an eyebrow in response, not anticipating anyone would be interested in the ring's history.

"Everyone and everything that comes through that door has a story behind it. Like this…." Woody set the ring box down and led Ophelia over to the other end of the shop. He grabbed a nutcracker that had been carved from a gnarled piece of wood; the paint could not conceal the warps in the figure. "It's a historical piece," he said excitedly. "Sold from Nick and Jack's Tchotchkes and Toys Treasure Trove. This particular piece was carved by Jack Knack at the grand opening of the store fifty-three years ago. You can see the date and initials carved into the base. Only five were made. Which is actually amazing being they were all made by hand on that very day. I know because I had spoken with Mr. Knack when I was verifying the authenticity of the piece."

Woody, evidently, was not so much a pawn shop clerk as he was a historian.

"So why did its owner give it up?" Ophelia queried with genuine interest.

"Ah," Woody began, his face falling. "It gave the owner nightmares."

Ophelia took a closer look at the face. "Yeah, I can see why." The right eye was drooped two centimeters compared to its left counterpart. In some spots, like the knobby knees and the sharp elbows, the grain of the wood could be seen through the faded single coat of paint. There was some splintering at the base of his now gray boots and around his jacket, giving it a frayed look.

Woody was about to go into the funny story about the old washing machine but was cut short by another of Adele's curt throat clearing sessions. Back to business.

Woody and Ophelia returned to the counter where the ring box sat. Adele had deposited a small slip of white paper covered in scrawled handwriting, an offering she felt was fitting, not for the ring but its soon-to-be previous owner. Cuddlebum batted at an upturned corner on the sheet.

Placing a pair of small gold eyeglasses on his nose, Woody squinted through the bifocal lenses to read the message. "Uh, I can offer you $600.00," which was a price he knew to be unfair. The ring was worth more than four and two-thirds times the offer. Atop the 950 Platinum band rested a 1.3 carat round cut diamond with undeniably exquisite symmetry. (Usually, "perfect" would be a sufficient descriptor, but in this instance, it would not cut it.) Two other diamonds flanked the larger stone. They resembled pure ice and were precariously affixed with spindly prongs of glossy platinum. One would have to be a fool to take the present deal.

"All right," said Ophelia without a hint of hesitation. In fact, she said it with earnest, like a child offered the opportunity to peak at one of their presents on Christmas Eve. Adele was too far into a state of euphoria to pick up that Ophelia's reply was a bit too forced and overacted, like most of the actors at the Nollag North Star Community Theater. (Tickets currently available for their rendition of Irving Berlin's *White Christmas the Musical* at the box office today!)

Fool, Adele chuckled to herself.

"O—okay," Woody said. He went to grab the necessary legal documentation.

"Actually," Ophelia said to Woody, "I wouldn't mind picking out a few items now that I think of it," she fibbed. "Christmas poking its head around the corner and all. I'm afraid that I won't be able to get all my shopping done before the department stores close." Her eye zoned in on something cat-shaped in the southwest corner of the shop.

"Of course," Woody said with a smile, not unlike the one pulling at the corners of Adele's lips. This was almost a two-for-one special: underprice the ring but overprice whatever Ophelia would purchase.

Ophelia swept from corner to corner of the shop with precision, her red locks dancing and swaying about. In a matter of thirty-one seconds, Ophelia had found the items that would make suitable gifts. (Excuse me, I mean "gifts.")

Adele was not surprised in the least. Pretty girls such as this were experts in shopping, practically an Olympic event to them.

Ophelia had grabbed two items. One was the first edition of *Alice's Adventures in Wonderland* that she plucked from off the floor. The second was a peculiar-looking lamp, Tiffany in style and pieced together to look like a slumbering cat. The bright blue, green, and purple shards of the lamp battled with the crystals of the grand chandelier for the fragments of dwindling light from outside, being ushered behind blue-gray snow clouds. The cat rested on a box made from a Vermont Maple tree, giving it the appearance that one could not lift the lid to see what was contained inside. A gold keyhole clashed against the dark varnished wood.

Cuddlebum moved to sit in front of the cat lamp, flicking his tail in its face, not wanting to be upstaged by the faux feline.

"These two items, Mr. Woody," said Ophelia. "Oh, do you do gift wrapping?" she added as an afterthought, intentionally sounding vapid.

"I'm afraid we don't," was his reply. He tried to soften his tone as much as he could. He hated to deliver bad news, no matter how insignificant.

"Oh, that's okay."

"That will be $580.00…plus tax," Adele butted in. She wished she could have charged the even $600.00, but it would seem too suspicious.

"How lucky that the ring will cover the cost," Ophelia said. Adele finally picked up on the sarcasm. That statement sounded a bit too incredulous. "I hadn't realized how hefty the price tag would be. You wouldn't mind me taking a closer look at them, do you? To make sure they are in a condition befitting the price?"

"Not at all," Woody interjected this time. "The customer is always right."

I've always hated that motto, thought Adele.

As Ophelia began to appraise the cat lamp from all angles, Woody could not help himself. "Ms. O'Leary, I'm still curious."

Ophelia looked up at him, eyes wide and expectant.

"What is the story behind the ring?"

Woody's imagination worked in overdrive, trying to decide if its story harbored one of tragedy or revenge, perhaps even a happy ending. To him, that was where the real value lay: the story he would potentially share with its new owner.

"Ah," she exhaled, sounding slightly pained. "Yes, the story."

Ophelia could have made up a lie and made it up quick. Instead, she chose to tell the truth. Granted, she left the details vague, knowing that Woody would eat up the mystery of it all.

She wetted her lips and drew in a breath to begin the tale. "I can't divulge too much detail, but, basically, the man who bought this engagement ring was making a big mistake. And you know how it is. You can't re-gift an engagement ring to someone else. There's a bad memory attached to it. Simply put, it would be tacky."

Woody let out a gasp. He couldn't wait to tell the cryptic tale and pique another's curiosity of the beautiful ring with a dark past. He would have to share it when Adele would be out of earshot, though. Bad memories, she had said, tended to kill sales, but he was sure he could put a fairy tale spin on it. Perhaps the ring spared the lovers a doomed life of unhappiness? He'd work it out over his lunchbreak.

"So—so you never saw him again?'

"Huh?"

"The man? The one who gave you the ring? I'm amazed he let you keep it." Woody secretly hoped that Ophelia would confess to 'neglecting' to return the ring. She seemed like that sort of a person.

Adele swore under her breath (a problem, indeed), a crass way of reminding Woody to make the sale.

Ophelia wore a wry smile, the one that had greeted Adele earlier. "I never said I was the one who was being proposed to, Mr. Woody. I am the one who saved him, though. Writers always need saving." Ophelia noted the puzzled look on Woody's face. "Oh, the man is a writer. Wasn't then but is now. Always living in his head

26

or on a page, oblivious to what's actually happening in front of him." (Never mind the aforementioned writer was now dating her sister, which was fate. Good thing she liked Calum.)

This only made the giant of a man want to know more. Who was Ms. O'Leary in this story, really? Was she a friend of the man's? Maybe a jealous lover made bitter by unreciprocated love? Or was she lying and really was the bride-not-to-be?

Adele said nothing. She just nudged the paperwork closer to Ophelia. Cuddlebum rested on them and posed seductively.

Ignoring the papers, and Cuddlebum to his dismay, Ophelia had moved onto the book of *Alice's Adventures in Wonderland*. Thinking back to the instructions Copper had shared with her, she quickly flipped through the yellow tinged pages, careful to catch any that might be marked, torn, or dog-eared. At the back of the book there appeared to be a large ink blot. In small letters, no taller than one thirty-second of an inch, was an inscription: *Look Behind the Rabbit Hole*. (You would have thought the note should have said *DOWN*, but I assure you this was not a typo.)

Ophelia's index finger began to scratch at the corner of the paper lying against the leather-bound cover. "I'll be taking this one for sure," Ophelia said to the wide-eyed Woody and Adele as she was finally able to pinch the corner between her fingers. She pulled, and the adhesive gave way with a quick POP!

There was a metallic THUNK against the glass counter. A small gold key was before the young woman now. Without one beat missed, not even half of one, Ophelia picked it up and slipped the key into the cat lamp's box, turning it.

The box was not a box, but a drawer that Ophelia slid wide open. Adele's jaw went slack emphasizing her underbite. Ophelia reached in and pulled out two rolls of $2 bills, comprised of fifty bills each, along with a slip of parchment folded and sealed with a dot of blue wax. The intricate image of a snowflake had been pressed into it.

Ophelia beamed. Woody was gobsmacked. Adele was still in shock and beginning to attract flies. Cuddlebum was perturbed. No one was paying attention to him after all.

"This must be my lucky day," Ophelia said as she finished dotting the "i" on her flourished signature. "Thank you very much, Mr. Woody, and…you," she referred to Adele. "A pleasure to do business with you. Sort of. Oh! By the way," Ophelia said, peering deeper into the drawer and pulling out the parchment, "it looks like you have a message."

Adele's eyebrows knit together, and she took the envelope. Indeed, it did have her name printed on it. She made no sound, save for the air that whistled in and out of her left nostril. Cracking the seal, she pulled a single sheet of paper from it and read the one-word note. At first, her face went ghastly white and then bloomed into a candy apple red, her anger solely focused on Ophelia.

*   *   *

Copper Lawson raced across the cobblestones of Droch Boulevard. He was only five foot four, which did not help to cover a large span of ground in a short time, nor did it help in the department of intimidation. Regardless, he was a good cop. There was no need to check his name twice on any list.

His barrel chest sucked in the cold air, along with three snowflakes, each entirely unlike the other. He was going to get her this time. It had taken him almost two years, but he had all the evidence he needed. Her wit could not, and would not, be able to help her disguise her guilt as the thief she so clearly was.

Copper's eyes twinkled as they anticipated how the inevitable victory would play out. He could hear that satisfying click of the handcuffs, the clank of the jail cell door closing behind her, and the hopefully grotesque mug shot—one of her in mid blink.

He looked over his shoulder to make sure that officers Marcus and Douglas were still with him. He puzzled why he even needed back up, but the chief was adamant. *Oh well,* he consoled himself. *They're rookies. It's like I'm practically doing this by myself, anyway.*

The ball of his black dress shoe hit some black ice conspicuously hidden where the curb rose up to connect with the sidewalk. His expression faltered for one point two seconds, images of sweet triumph momentarily flashing to those of him spread eagle and skidding to a stop with a mouthful of snow and rock salt.

As he skated across the sidewalk, the slush washed over the tops of his shoes, depositing itself into the cuffs of his pants. In a flash, he recovered his balance, and his hand clasped the doorknob of the Deal and Steal. With a flourish of his wrist, he swung the door open. Copper slid across the gritty planked floor coming to a stop six inches past the threshold. The wind blew at his open trench coat, making it ripple like a superhero's cape. Officers Marcus and Douglas soon followed, stepping into the Deal and Steal and flanking Copper on either side. A silent sigh of relief escaped past his lips. He had saved face and looked pretty damn good doing it.

Adele and Woody's eyes grew wider than before at the unexpected entrance. Ophelia and Cuddlebum could not be bothered to register a reaction.

Copper was out of breath now. His lungs burned as they acclimated themselves to the warmer air inside the pawn shop. He raised an index finger to point to the woman who had given him so much trouble until he remembered he was wearing mittens…with little reindeer crocheted into them, a gift made by his hopefully soon-to-be fiancée.

In a flash, the jolly reindeers flew out of sight and deep into his right-side pocket. "You—you are under arrest!"

Chapter 2

In Which We Learn About Octogenarian Erotica

That took longer than anticipated, thought Ophelia as she walked away from the Deal and Steal Pawn Shop. She relished the image of Adele, mouth still agape, as she was being carted out while a very confused Woody Hinklehimeriner, Cuddlebum cradled in his arms, and a very priggish Ophelia looked on. Adele squawked and screeched about the handcuffs pinching her wrists, how she could not begin to fathom what was going on, and of her innocence in this whole mess. Two truths and a lie.

The lie being Adele's innocence. With the help of a silent partner, who was not Woody Hinklehimeriner, Adele had been pilfering valuable objects from some of the elderly citizens of Nollag, the *Alice's Adventures in Wonderland* and the cat-lamp among them. When enough time had passed or the owner had moved on in one way or another, the object would somehow appear on the Deal and Steal's shelves or in one of its display cases. Adele would have continued to get away with it had her silent partner not begun to sing last year like a ruffled Grey Partridge. Woody remained a sort of confused Horseman Thief Pouter in all of this, slightly bug-eyed and tilting his head from side to side, unable to believe that his boss was capable of purloining others' possessions.

Ophelia glanced at the town hall clock as she quickly swaggered onto Jazzed Avenue, noting the time to be 11:34 a.m. She knew that Delaney would be most displeased with her, but whatever would be would be just that. She had performed a civil duty. One which no one would know about as most of her good deeds went unbeknownst to others. Ophelia may be considered overly confident, even slightly smug, but she was no braggart.

Beatrice Clark's Caffeine and Bean Coffee Café was across the street, a mere ten feet away. *Almost there*, she reassured herself.

A little wisp of a woman was power walking towards Ophelia. Her pristine white gym shoes outshone the snow that crunched beneath their soles. Her hair was in loose curls of a pale yellow. She was decked out in a cranberry jogging suit with the word "DUPA" stitched and bedazzled in large baby pink letters across the backside of her pants.

She was hard to miss. She was Mrs. Fulgencia Wick, a prominent figure in the community as one of the three founders of Nollag's thriving business association. There was also Mrs. Vitla Slaughter who opened a butcher shop and later expanded her business into a full-fledged grocery store complete with farmer's market from May to October. Mrs. Forina Baker was the owner of Salty N. Sweets: Sweets and Baked Goods before she turned the business over to her daughter, Cookie, upon her retirement. Mrs.

Wick opened and still operated a successful taxidermy shop on the east side of the city and tried her hand at writing bestselling octogenarian erotica novels. Such titles included *Past Visiting Hours, That's Not Rigor Mortis,* and *The Breath of Life.*

Ophelia had played muse to Mrs. Wick nineteen years ago, back when Ophelia was Jucinda Jorgenson. Since her foresight had left her after helping Delaney last year, Ophelia could not read the futures of new prospects. However, she couldn't help but wonder if she could see into the fates of past clients. *Doubtful,* she said to herself pessimistically.

She stared intently at the powerwalking elderly woman, who had caught sight of her and was now excitedly waving to her in salutation. An abrupt, and somewhat unexpected, thought jumped into Ophelia's head like an attention starved Kindergartener. The thought was an image of something that had not yet happened but could: a flash of yellow hair and a floating rectangular sheet of ice. She stopped in her tracks, placing a hand in the air as if to ask time to hold on for a minute, which Mrs. Wick took as a subdued hello.

The flashes of what could be did not used to knock her for a loop. *I was pretty sure these weren't going to happen anymore,* she puzzled.

Apparently, unbeknownst to Ophelia, she had one more task to complete.

Her premonition told her that she had a brief meeting only eight feet away from the café in front of Auntie Pasta's Negozio di Specialitá Italiane. *Don't worry, though.* She reviewed the now fleeting portent. *It'll happen forty-eight seconds after 11:35, or in approximately one minute and twenty-eight seconds…I hope,* she added, her intuition, after all, not being what it used to be.

"Well, hello, young lady," the pint-sized woman greeted Ophelia. "Hello, Mrs. Wick."

Ophelia was met with a wagging index finger, not two centimeters from the tip of her nose. "Call me Gen. Mrs. Wick was my mother-in-law." Her tone was sour.

"So sorry, Gen, and why do we not speak of Mrs. Wick?"

"Because she was the devil!" Mrs. Wick piped up, before muttering under her breath, "May God rest her soul." Clearing her throat, she continued, "Why bring down the holiday festivities with such a solemn topic? How are you, my dear? How is Gregory?"

"Wouldn't know, Gen. We haven't been together for almost three years." Ophelia wished people would drop the topic of her and Gregory McGregor, but when one would let it go, another was around the corner stooping down to pick it up once again. Clearly the Nollag gossip mill was not churning out any new juicy stories, but instead had come to a grinding halt, been shut down, and was condemned. "How about yourself?" Ophelia interjected before Mrs. Wick could reminisce about how perfectly the two of them complemented each other.

"Oh, the usual, dear. I just finished a kick boxing class over at the Senior Center." She motioned Ophelia to lean in, all the while pursing her lips to suppress a toothy grin from spreading across her face. In a low voice, she shared, "The pole dancing class was canceled." She attempted a demure giggle that progressed into a loud cackle.

Ophelia knew Mrs. Wick was looking for a very specific reaction and was more than happy to oblige to register a surprised expression on her face.

"All the girls ask about you and Gregory." Mrs. Wick still had an ironclad grip on the failed relationship.

"Mm," Ophelia hummed politely in response, her smile only faltered but once. "Uh, do you have the time?"

"Yes, dear." Mrs. Wick looked at her watch. "It's 11:35."

Ophelia's eyes widened. "Oh! Mrs. Wi—Gen, I would love to chat a little more, but I am incredibly late to meet my sister for coffee. I hope you don't think me rude." She wore worry across her brow.

"No, no, not at all. I best be going now, too." She studied her watch, which was also a heart monitor. "My heart rate is dropping, and I still have another two point three miles to finish. Then I need to get the feast a rollin'." She smiled. "Cuthbert cannot be trusted in the kitchen. He couldn't stuff or truss a turkey to save his life. In fact," she recalled, "it nearly killed him fifteen years ago, ironically enough. Take care, dear. It was nice to catch up with you. Merry Christmas."

Forty-one seconds after 11:35 a.m., Mrs. Wick turned to cross the street right at the moment when a parcel truck passed by striking a deep pothole in the road, causing it to shudder and groan on top of its suspension.

"Gen," Ophelia said a little too loudly as she grabbed her arm to stop her. "Before I forget, I had a question."

Right on the forty-eighth second, the sound of silk flying off a smooth surface zipped through the cold air, shortly followed by the sound of shattering porcelain. Before Ophelia and Mrs. Wick lay what used to be a six foot by four foot sheet of ice, three quarters of an inch thick.

"Gracious," Mrs. Wick said in exasperation, accompanied by a mixture of holy names and expletives. "One more second…." She blinked her eyes three times to clear away the unpleasant picture her imagination was compositing. "Sorry, you had a question?"

Ophelia pulled her gaze from the shards of ice. She seemed to have lost her cool expression, it now replaced by a more confounded look. Her mind willed her to table the shock of the premonition and incident to actually ask her query. "I wanted to know if your husband had received the gold wrapping paper I requested. He was out of it last week." Mr. Wick ran the Cockles of My Heart Greeting Card and Candle Cache.

"He may now, dear. Shipments do come in on Thursdays."

"Fantastic!" she sang gleefully. "A Christmas miracle!" Ophelia stepped off the sidewalk to cross to Beatrice Clark's Caffeine and Bean Coffee Café.

"You're telling me," Mrs. Wick responded with a deep, "Phew!"

"Oh, and, Gen," Ophelia said, spinning around in the middle of the street, "Merry Christmas to you, too."

Mrs. Wick waved and decided it more prudent to stay on her current side of the street; that and the rest of her walk could wait. After all, she had a turkey to stuff and truss and a husband that needed a kiss. The kind of kiss one would find in her latest work, *A Night to Try and Remember: Passion So Intense, Not Even Senility Could Make Them Forget.*

Ophelia puckered her mouth to the left side of her face, something she did whenever she was deeply puzzled. *Way too close,* she chastised herself, ruminating over having asked her question at just the right time before Mrs. Wick's near-death experience, and wishing she had had more time to prepare. *Still, the fact that I had one has got to be a good sign, right?*

Not wanting to get her hopes up, she tempered her fresh excitement with well-aged lamentations over that night, one year ago, that changed everything between her and Delaney, to the event that threw everything out of whack. The night she ruined a Christmas party, an engagement, and may have even weaponized a fruitcake. She had no one to blame but herself. Regardless, she would not have changed a thing. *It was for the best. It still is*, she reminded herself, thinking of her sister.

Chapter 3

In Which Delaney O'Leary Sips on Cold Tea and Ophelia Receives a Chilly Reception

Delaney O'Leary was glad she had ordered the chamomile tea, checking the time with every sip she took. The second hand made another lap to make it exactly four minutes past her and Ophelia's agreed time to meet at Beatrice Clark's Caffeine and Bean Coffee Café.

I don't know if I have the patience of a saint or if it's the tea, she thought. *I should be furious.* But she knew that there was not a tea in the world strong enough to sedate her now-winded patience that had been pacing back and forth, wearing thin the strands of thought that concerned Ophelia.

Delaney was lying to herself. She was furious. While four minutes was usually nothing to get worked up over, this was not the first, nor thirty-first, time Ophelia would arrive fashionably late. It did not matter that Ophelia always did come; all the waiting added up to approximately two hundred thirty-six hours and forty-two minutes over the past decade. She was mindful to omit her usual fifteen-minute early arrival to order her drink, get herself settled, and allow her beverage to cool, knowing it wasn't fair to count this time against her sister. Plus, being the first to any meeting or appointment always made her feel slightly superior.

Looking out the window, Delaney could see her sister sashaying onto Jazzed Avenue and then stopping to chat with Mrs. Wick. With a huff, Delaney picked up her tea in the turquoise cup with the glued-on orange handle and sipped her now tepid tea, praying the chamomile would douse the monster that roiled inside her.

Deeply sighing, Delaney tried her best to let go of her animosity, it being Christmas after all. One was not supposed to be anything but cheerful during the holiday season. Ophelia was her sister, adoptive not biological. Delaney was the one who, for lack of a better term, picked her out. *Besides*, she resolved, *I'm used to it. Push it out of your mind. That's what families do for each other when one bugs the living daylights out of the other.* "It's Christmas," she quietly reiterated to herself while pretending to study the pattern of the area rug beneath her feet.

"Yes, it is," a voice replied matter-of-factly. Timothy Dickens stood by her blue velour dining chair and set a small plate on the glass-topped, white wrought-iron garden table. "Christmas special. It's a vanilla cookie half dipped in a white chocolate and nutmeg ganache."

"Thanks, Tim," Delaney said, looking up at him with her big mocha eyes. Her cheeks rounded as she gave him a sweet smile. The cookie was one of her favorite treats. "But I'm perfectly content with my tea. Why don't you, uh, give it to the girl sitting over there?" She glanced to her left without moving her head.

A corner of Timothy's mouth twitched. "It's from Mr. Clark. It's a sort of thank you for being a regular," he explained. "That and it's your recipe. Says they've been rivaling the holi-glazed donuts over at Salty N. Sweets."

"I know, and I really appreciate the thought, and you can quote me on that, but, seriously, Tim, give her the cookie."

Timothy stood rooted to one of the green linoleum tiles.

"You've been staring at her the whole time she's been here."

Panic opened Timothy Dickens' eyes to thirty percent larger their normal size.

"Yes," Delaney said in a hushed tone, "it's that noticeable. Any more obvious and your pupils would be shaped like hearts. Go. Give her the cookie."

The "her" Delaney was referring to sat at the back of the café within her peripheral line of sight. Her chestnut hair was done up in a knotted mess, all kept at bay with an orange headband. She concealed her curves beneath an extra-large College of Nollag hooded sweatshirt when a large would have been more than sufficient. The large orange C and N block letters were almost completely lost in its folds.

She sat cross-legged at a heavy walnut table. Her papers and textbooks covered up the dents and dings the square slab top had sustained during its forty-five and three-eighths years of existence, after its initial seventy-five years as a tree.

Delaney continued to stare back at Timothy. If she could have moved him telepathically from where he stood, she would

41

have. Timothy was relieved to get a moment of reprieve when a loud shattering sound from outside caused the café window to shudder, pulling everyone's attention in that direction. The patrons of Beatrice Clark's Caffeine and Bean Coffee Café would only find Mrs. Wick and Ophelia staring at a mess of shattered ice in the street.

"You go over there now," Delaney said, returning to the matter at hand.

Timothy limply shook his head in reply wishing to keep as much attention off himself as possible. Mrs. McKibbins briefly looked over the top of her *Nollag Blow-By-Blow Bugle*, no doubt trying to scavenge any shred of gossip, and that was all he could stand.

"Oh, Tim, who in the—" Delaney began to say in an elevated tone, but she never finished. For one, Timothy began to jump in the girl's general direction. For another, Ophelia stepped through the café door. The silver bell at the upper right corner jingled jubilantly to announce the café's latest patron.

"Tim!" Ophelia called to him across the room. The six-foot lanky boy stopped mid-step toward his crush. "Can I please get an espresso macchiato with a lemon biscotti?"

Timothy swallowed hard, a little relieved. His personal challenge would have to wait. "Sure," he said happily. He looked back at the girl who was now flipping through flashcards of derivatives and integrals. She looked up trying to recall the derivative of x to the nth power and unintentionally locked eyes with Timothy, who then made a swift retreat to the back of the café counter with his back to the rest of the establishment, feverishly grabbing the coffee beans and milk to make Ophelia's drink.

His impressive split-second dash across the café was made all the more spectacular given the seating area was clogged with a collection of mismatched garden, patio, and living room furniture. Some were crafted from metal. Some were overstuffed. Still others were covered in leather or draped in cashmere and fleece throws. Ottomans dotted the room like marshmallows in a big cup of cocoa. Pillows of various sizes, jewel-toned colors, and eclectic patterns were sprinkled about the floor and seats. Even on Timothy's best day, he managed to spill something. The better of those days would be on the carpet and not on someone's lap. He would never live down the nickname "Hot Pants."

"Ophelia!" Damodar Clark boomed from the kitchen. He leaned over the serving hatch and waved. "How in the hell have you been?"

"How in the hell have you been?" his Eclectus parrot, Basil, repeated over by the cash register.

"Quite well, thank you. And yourself, sir?"

"Oh, the business is doing phenomenal thanks to your sister, so I'm terrific!" He punctuated his observation with a hearty laugh that made his belly dance up and down, a clear sign to the patrons of Beatrice Clark's Caffeine and Bean Coffee Café that Mr. Clark not only made the treats that were stockpiled in the display cases up front, but regularly indulged in them, as well, which was a good enough selling point for them.

"How's Greg? Doing well, I hope?"

Ophelia let out a breathy laugh at Mr. Clark. It would be Mr. Clark in the café with the disarming salutation who would resurrect the topic of Gregory and Ophelia reuniting once again that day. "Fine…as far as I know."

"Great," Mr. Clark yelled back, returning to kneading a pile of sourdough.

Delaney smiled to herself. Someone able to catch Ophelia off guard was a rarity, but when they did, it felt like…well, like Christmas. She quickly stuffed her smile behind her cup of now cold tea, knowing she had enjoyed what had transpired a little more than would be considered socially acceptable. Then again, thinking back to last year, and really any other Christmas in the last half-decade for that matter, she felt a little more justified.

Ophelia swept into the chair across from Delaney. The folds and pleats of her coat eloquently falling about the wired chair that complemented the table. She swept her hair out of her eyes, which were now regarding the subtle smirk that hung on Delaney's lips.

"Just laughing at my writer's block," she fibbed to Ophelia.

That was another reason Delaney did not allow herself to be perturbed with her sister. You see, Ophelia's chronic tardiness had taught Delaney to come prepared to their meetings. For this particular occasion, she came armed with the foreword her publisher over at Comestible Collective Publishing Culinary Co., an imprint of Nollag Bookery and Bindery, had requested her to compose for her cookbook, *Seasons Servings*. He had requested that it be in his hands by the first of the New Year. On the surface, the task was simple. *Why isn't it simple?* Delaney had bemoaned to herself earlier that day while a page with scribbled failed attempts taunted her.

What inspired you? What drives you today? What impression do you hope this book leaves with your readers? Delaney let her publisher's queries cycle through her mind. The only answer that came to mind was she hoped her readers would be left full. Well, that's not entirely true. She wanted them to think that her recipes were good, that they did not think they had wasted their money, and that her book would not become the top white elephant gift being passed around like a decade-old fruitcake from disappointed recipient to disappointed recipient. All this she was able to summarize vocally to her publisher with "Um." She knew she would have to expand and expound on this. Therein lay the challenge.

"Who even reads the foreword of a cookbook, Ophelia?"

"Um…." Ophelia turned to see how Timothy was doing on her order. "It'll come," she finally said to her sister in a rather feeble voice. It bothered her that she did not have the perfect words to say.

"That's what Mom said," came the reply in a flat tone.

"Write from the heart?" Ophelia shrugged.

"Publisher said the exact same thing last week."

"Stop whining," Ophelia huffed.

Delaney let out a deep exhale at the brash, yet honest, advice, choosing to reply by looking past her sister to stare out the wide-paned front window. Five seconds passed before she spoke once more. "You're late…again." Her tone did not reveal a hint of surprise nor a pinch of anger.

"Looks like the extra time served you well." Ophelia glanced across the table at the scribbled pages resting on top of a chocolate brown portfolio.

"Beside the point." Delaney scuttled away the papers instantly from sight.

"Some errands ran late. My time management is atrocious. Why did you ask me to meet you anyway? Clearly not to read your foreword. Am I in the acknowledgements?"

The glass tabletop made a light "plink" as Tim set down Ophelia's order. "Thanks so much, Tiny."

Timothy frowned and looked back at the girl still nose deep in her flashcards. He hoped she had not heard Ophelia's nickname for him, one she had given him when he had still enjoyed Saturday morning cartoons and action figures. He quickly fled to make sure the other tables were well stocked with the usual condiments of butter, sugar, and cream.

"Don't call him that," Delaney snapped, her patience all but consumed, save for a couple of crumbs. At this point, Ophelia breathing through the wrong nostril was enough to set her on edge.

"Why exactly? Is it because no seventeen-year-old boy wants any form of association with the word 'tiny'?" she said, sarcastically replying to her own question.

"You and I both know that question doesn't need positing, let alone answering."

"I'm only teasing, Delaney. I babysat him for four years. He knows. It's fine."

"Not a phase boys grow out of, Ophelia." She shook the petty argument out of her head, moving to the next item on her mental agenda. "I invited you here to invite you."

Ophelia's eyebrows raised. She began to nibble at an end of the biscotti, trying to anticipate the forthcoming clarifying details.

"Come over for Christmas Eve, Ophelia. I think enough time has passed that the wounds have healed. I acted childishly. I want to put it behind us." Delaney's words were meant to be liberally spiced with good intention, but seemingly lacked even the tiniest pinch of Grade A organic sincerity.

Ophelia fixed her gaze upon her sister, trying to see if she could get a preview of Delaney's holiday gathering. She sat in stunned silence, unblinking, for three and a half seconds without so much as a speck of a hint coming forward before finally answering with a question. "Who's gonna be there?"

"Uh, Calum, Petunia, me…Greg," Delaney added hesitantly.

Ophelia squinted at her sister. Still nothing. "Can't."

Delaney's brow furrowed. "Well, why not?" she asked, assuming it solely had to do with Ophelia's ex.

"I have other plans tonight," she said but didn't offer more details. Ophelia really did have plans, well, maybe, which made it easy to turn down the short-notice invitation. Clarence had asked if she would come to the Nollag police department's Christmas Party that night, but she had yet to officially accept. Unable to glimpse into Delaney's future, and she did try, it seemed logical that Ophelia wasn't needed by her sister anymore. It would be better for everyone if she cut ties now.

"Oh, well, I understand. What about tomorrow? Are you free then?"

Ophelia looked into her sister's eyes. She could only find apprehension, further confirming her choice to stay away. Truthfully, she wanted to say "yes."

Ophelia knew her sister. The invitation was not genuine, simply done by the book. After all this time, Delaney still did what was "right," not what was right…if that makes sense. Growing up, Ophelia had tried so hard to help her break that habit, but she had managed to only crack it a little.

Ophelia had built a case against herself over the last four Christmases, what with blabbing secrets that were not hers, dumping

Gregory out of the blue, de-bearding that mall Santa, and, the pièce de résistance, electrocuting Bailey Barrymore at last year's Christmas party. On the surface, these were, undeniably, horrible things. But these events *needed* to happen. They needed to happen to spare Delaney and her friends.

Ophelia sipped at her coffee, wishing she had not taken the invitation to come today. But how do you say "no" to someone you have that much history with? Simple. You don't.

"Maybe," was all she offered Delaney.

The two sisters sat in silence and let the clatter of cups and saucers and the chatter of customers overtake their conversation. Delaney stewed over her olive branch, more or less, being treated like some knockoff from the clearance aisle at the Buck Bazaar. She had hoped Ophelia would have attended tonight. Mostly to let go of Christmases past, but also because Gregory was invited. Delaney would be fibbing if she didn't admit seeing her sister squirm would be a bonus…but just a little one, barely the size of a dust speck.

"I have to go," Ophelia said, finally breaking the quiet between them. "I have a few errands to still get through before tonight." She pulled seven dollars from her right pocket and slipped it under the plate.

Delaney looked down at the three quarters of biscotti and five eighths of a full cup remaining. "Okay," was all she said, swallowing the rest of her words.

"I'll let you know," she answered Delaney's silent question. Ophelia stood and resisted the urge to embrace her sister. *It will make things too hard*, she thought.

48

With a "See you, Tiny," Ophelia was gone, heading toward Poetry Parkway.

Tiny—er—Timothy stood in shock by his crush's table, finally having worked up the courage to edge his way over to her, pastry still in hand.

"I'm not tiny," he rambled to the girl. "There's nothing tiny about me. I mean, I'm tall. Well—but—also—I'm no—you know—uh. Enjoy a cookiehappyholidaysit'sonthehouse."

The girl watched as Timothy cleared three ottomans in one point three seconds before he turned the corner and slid into the kitchen.

"I think he likes you," Delaney said, raising her cup up as if to toast Timothy's speech.

The girl smiled back without one bit of pity and resumed studying her derivatives. She would thank him later for the cookie.

Delaney tugged at the corners of the white sheets protruding from the portfolio, ready to face her foe once more. She groaned as she picked up her pen. It had managed to become two hundred times its actual weight.

Chapter 4

In Which We Learn What Ophelia Was Like as a Child - Hint... She Was Quite the Scamp

Am I in the acknowledgements? Ophelia's question reverberated and festered in Delaney's brain. How brazen, but not unexpected, of her sister to ask such a query! There were a few reasons why she did not deserve a mention. Delaney was not alone in that thought.

But one memory managed to make it to the forefront in support of Ophelia: the first day the two of them had met. There were not many memories that stood out among Delaney's recollections as a little girl (the initial ones were all on the uneventful side, you see), but this particular memory was poised to be one of the exceptions.

Delaney had been five at the time and was the daughter to two very logical parents, Éamon and Alicia O'Leary, both mathematics teachers. Mr. and Mrs. O'Leary had arrived at the conclusion that their daughter needed a sibling in an effort to expand her mind. This was attributed to their own lack of imagination and the promise Mrs. O'Leary was still making good on that Mr. O'Leary would never touch her again after the thirty-six hours, twenty-seven minutes, and fifteen seconds of labor it took to bring Delaney into the world.

Delaney was a bright girl but was exhibiting similar traits as her parents when it came to not being able to believe in something unless there was sufficient research and evidence to back it up. This made for quite a hurdle come time of most major holidays. Mr. and Mrs. O'Leary also noticed the other children were pulling away from Delaney, them finding it challenging to explain the proof they had of fairies and dragons when they asked if she would like to play Knights and Princesses. Perhaps a new brother or sister would help Delaney exercise her suspension of disbelief.

"I suppose," Delaney had told her parents after they had posited their idea to her and presented their research. "I wouldn't want to grow up socially deficient."

"We'll even let you pick your new brother or sister out," they offered.

"Well, that seems a little crude. I'm looking for a sibling, not a puppy. But, a puppy wouldn't be turned down…." She had attempted, and failed, to wink at her parents, it looking more like an awkward blink or an eye twitch.

The date on the calendar had read December 12th when the O'Leary family had arrived at the doorstep of Mother Mary Claire Brog's Haven for Nippers, Toddlers, Tykes, and Children. The house was very large, spanning four stories. The slats of wood were painted gray, accented with white trim. Delaney remembered it almost blending in with the cloudy winter sky.

A frazzled looking young woman opened the door to greet them. "Please do come in Mr. and Mrs. O'Leary, Ms. Delaney. I'll be with you in a moment," said Mynah Moriel. She scooted off in a flash, leaving the O'Learys in the large high-ceilinged front entryway, the clip-clop of her heels disappearing down the hall with her.

"Whoa!"

Mr. and Mrs. O'Leary found their daughter with her jaw on the floor and her head craned upward. They followed suit and assumed their daughter's flabbergasted expression. An "oh my" slipped past Mrs. O'Leary's lips and bounced off the walls in the big empty room.

What lay before them would have been nothing special. Merely the east wall, eight feet high by five feet wide, flanked by a hallway on each side. Well, at three o'clock that morning, the wall would have been perfectly pedestrian.

Now at ten o'clock, the wall contained the portrait of a seven-and-a-half-foot tall woman. She was drawn in profile with a wide grin and her short blonde hair pulled behind her ears. The gown she wore was a simple yellow and gold. The way the fabric had been drawn gave it an ethereal quality, seeming to dance about the woman.

While words such as "eloquent," "beauteous," "awe-inspiring," and "gorgeous" ping-ponged about in Mr. and Mrs. O'Leary's heads to describe the artistic production before them, Delaney beat them to the punch with a short and to the point "cool."

"I'm glad you like it," replied Mynah. "Sorry for running off. I'm sure you can appreciate how hard it is to get twenty-six children under the age of twelve to behave, what with Christmas break a week away." She smoothed her bob cut and pressed the wrinkles out of her thin houndstooth skirt.

Delaney squinted at the young woman. "It's you. The painting, I mean," she said, her voice starting very quiet and growing to something braver and more convicted.

"Hmm?" Mynah had moved on to adjusting the amethyst and diamond broach on her royal purple sweater, the one with the three-quarter length sleeves. Her blue eyes roved over the girl and up to the wall. "Oh, well, I didn't do that," she laughed.

"No. I mean the picture *is* you."

Mynah took her turn, squinting up at the picture. "I don't think so," she blushed back at the girl. "She's much too pretty."

"Who did the painting? It seems a little out of place at an orphanage," said Mrs. O'Leary.

Mynah let out a deep sigh, one that any parent could pick out a hint of frustration from. "Ophelia." She changed her tone to add, lovingly, "One of our kiddos."

"I want to meet her!"

Mr. O'Leary suppressed a gulp as he looked back at the painting with fresh eyes. They had repainted the house not three months ago, but the love he had for his little girl would always make apprehensions such as these inconsequential. He tripped over his scuffed oxfords as Delaney, led by Mynah, excitedly dragged him by the scarf up the stairs to the third floor.

"Please understand, Mr. and Mrs. O'Leary, Ophelia really is a good girl. Her imagination sometimes gets the best of her," Mynah explained in her most genuine tone, so as not to sound as if she

54

secretly wished to get this mystery child out of her hair. That was the furthest from the truth if we are being absolutely transparent.

"How old is she?" Delaney interjected.

"She's a very mature seven years old."

Delaney pondered how a seven-year-old could be mature and then, realizing the notion was not entirely impossible, scrapped the thought.

"She's creativity personified," continued Mynah. "Last Halloween, she made her own Snow White costume. Not only did she manage to get seven of our toddlers to be her dwarves, she made all the costumes from scratch. The bedsheets were never the same. On the bright side," she back peddled, "they all looked very authentic." This did not seem to quell the worried looks written across Mr. and Mrs. O'Leary's faces. Suddenly potty training a puppy did not seem so bad.

"What's her favorite color?" Delaney tried to match Mynah's stride.

"I think it's purple." Mynah's tone was sweet but not patronizing the way other adults chose to speak to children.

"Like the color you're wearing? Or a light purple? Or does it matter?"

"I think," Mynah pointed to her sweater, "this color purple."

"That's my favorite color!" Delaney shrieked, not able to contain her excitement or her newfound knowledge on color theory. "Did you know that purple is the color that means you make good choices?"

"I did not know that. You are a very smart girl, Delaney."

"And—and did you know—"

"So sorry," Mrs. O'Leary interjected, "she's excited. Delaney, dear, calm down."

Mynah gently shook her head, barely perceptible, as if silently communicating how little of an inconvenience her conversation with Delaney actually was. "It's nice to be taught something for a change."

Mynah was the second in command at Mother Mary Claire Brog's Haven for Nippers, Toddlers, Tykes, and Children, and the early education teacher for the children not old enough to go to elementary school. But she was so much more to all the children.

Mynah held a paramount belief that each of the children should be instilled with a healthy sense of creativity because through creativity would spring forth ingenuity and a hunger to look deeper into the workings of the world and life itself. This same belief made Mynah feel responsible for Ophelia's actions. Most recently, the one that had the little girl sitting atop a ladder coloring in the last of the dress at 6 a.m. this morning.

Mynah had not let Ophelia explain herself and made her stay in her room for the rest of the day, bathroom breaks and meals being the exceptions. It pained her to do it, but she needed to set a boundary on grand scale artworks, a boundary she had never thought she would need to impose on a seven-year-old child.

"Ms. Moriel! Ms. Moriel, one more question! Can I ask one more?" Delaney bounded and pranced on the third-floor landing.

Mynah nodded.

"What does Ophelia look like?"

"Delaney," Mynah replied. She had the little girl's undivided attention. "See for yourself." She turned a large brass doorknob on a pastel green door covered in stickers of fairies, dragons, unicorns, and rainbows.

A little girl with a wild mound of bright orange hair sat in the middle of a slumped mattress. Her feet swung to and fro as she pulled a needle through some red fabric.

"Delaney, meet Ophelia. Ophelia, this is Delaney."

"Hi," Ophelia grinned a large grin back at the girl. She was missing her front left tooth and her right mandibular central incisor. "How're ya?" She hopped off the bed with a BANG!

Mrs. O'Leary was the first to notice Ophelia's skirt was made up of different pieces of patterned fabric, some floral, some stripped, and some checked. She could not help but wonder what things all the scraps of cloth and textile had originally belonged to.

The initially animated Delaney now hid behind her mother's leg and peered back at the hand that Ophelia extended in greeting; dried, pale-yellow paint still clung to the grooves of her fingers.

"Are ya shy? Or afraid of germs or somethin'? Oh!" she exclaimed, looking down at her hands, "One second." And she strode off through another door to the connected bathroom. In twenty-nine exact seconds, she was back. "Better?" She waved freshly-scrubbed, pristine hands for everyone to see, save for the flecks of yellow that still clung to her cuticles.

"Delaney, you can say 'hi'," her mother coaxed.

"I like your name," Ophelia said. "Come over to m' bed. I wanna show ya somethin' I made."

Big brown eyes darted from Mrs. O'Leary to Mr. O'Leary to Mynah and finally over to the bed. "Okay," she replied feebly in answer, giving in to the peer pressure.

"We'll leave you two alone to play for a little bit," Mynah said to Ophelia as she walked over and pulled a granola bar from her pocket and handed it to her.

"I told ya the purple would look pretty on you." Ophelia impishly smiled, the left corner of her mouth pulling a little higher than the right.

"Thank you, Ophelia," Mynah said as she turned to walk out with Mr. and Mrs. O'Leary.

"Yum," Ophelia squealed as she unwrapped the treat, snapped it in half, and threw a portion into her mouth. "Mmmm cho'lat!" she squeaked while doing a little happy dance sitting on her bed. Delaney noticed the yellow bedspread had what appeared to be funny shapes sewn into it, like a skirt and a night cap.

"Here," Ophelia said, shoving the other half of the treat into Delaney's hands. "So good," she said as she sucked the melted chocolate from her fingertips.

Delaney hefted herself up onto the foot of the bed and gingerly munched at the granola bar. Her eyes were wide as she began to wonder if meeting Ophelia was a good idea. She was pretty loud and made quick movements. She eventually shrugged it off as nerves but still wondered if Ophelia could smell fear.

"Isn't this fabulous?" Ophelia shoved a small red thing she had been working on earlier into Delaney's free hand.

Delaney placed the cloth in her lap and unfolded it to reveal a very petite dress. "Oooo, pretty," she said smiling at it. "Did you make it?"

"Yup," Ophelia beamed her gapped grin again; some chocolate dotted her front right tooth. "I made it for Corlis." She plucked a doll that sat on the windowsill next to her bed.

Delaney liked how Ophelia's messy red curls bounced and changed color from auburn to orange in the light coming though the frosted panes.

"She likes to look out and let me know who passes by. She's a bit of a gossip," she whispered while covering Corlis' ears. "I indulge her to be nice. Uh, could I have that back, please? I want to put it on her."

"Oh, sure," Delaney replied, handing the little garment back. She paused, screwing up her face, stopping to ponder over the alleged busybody that was Corlis. "Uh, you said she tells you what happens outside? How?"

"How?" Ophelia echoed.

"Well, yeah," but Delaney did not pursue the subject further. This was exactly why the other children did not play with her — lack of imagination. "Hey, I think I have the same doll, but the package said her name is Ima."

"So?" Ophelia said as she concentrated on pulling the black yarn hair of the ragdoll through the top of the red dress. "Is there a rule that says I can't change her name? She *is* my doll, and I think Corlis suits her better."

Delaney frowned. "I—well…um…."

Ophelia waved a hand at Delaney's verbal sputtering. "Ms. Moriel says stuff like dolls names an' art an' stuff is, like—um—guy lines or somethin'."

"Guidelines."

"She says that toy companies are takin' away kids' imaginations. Isn't that horrible!?" Her eyes gave a knowing glance over to Delaney.

Delaney panicked being put on the spot, choosing to finish her granola bar and chewing slowly in lieu of an answer.

"Ms. Moriel gives us reminders! Reminder number one," Ophelia said sternly, her index finger pointed toward the ceiling, "a doll, once bought, needs its own iden—ident-ate-y. Like, what's the fun if there're three hundred twenty-three Imas all doin' the same thing? Also, um, reminder number eight: You define the toy. The toy doesn't define you. Or—or, oh! Reminder number three: Fun is not necessarily found in rules. Sometimes the fun is found in breaking the rules. I added that last part," Ophelia said proudly.

The logic of reminder number three crossed and frazzled the wires of poor Delaney's mind. However, before she could even begin to untangle the rule, she had to unsnag her thoughts from something else Ophelia had told her. "Wait. How are toy companies stealing imaginations?" Delaney wondered how this had not made the front pages of the papers or the evening news, which was how she started and ended her days.

"They keep coming up with more and more toys with all these rules attached to 'em. Um, they—they don't work unless you follow all the instructions."

"Oh," Delaney gasped, grateful her eyes were opened to the conspiracy. It seemed to go hand-in-hand with the concerns her parents had presented to her over dinner three nights ago.

"It's a real problem. What do ya think?"

"I think you're right. I may have that!" Delaney ran her fingers through her black locks as if checking for places where her imagination could be leaking out.

"No, not that, silly. The dress. Isn't it fabulous?" Ophelia tipped the doll back and forth as if to make Corlis dance. The dress had perfectly straight seams and fit her like a glove.

"Yeah!"

"I can make one for your doll if you want. Here." Ophelia handed Corlis to Delaney so she could get a better look at the dress again. "What's your favorite color?"

Delaney set the doll on her lap. With her treat all gone, she bought herself some time by pretending to ruminate over the question. She found herself wanting Ophelia to like her, really like her, and placed more pressure on herself than was necessary to answer the question "correctly." The burden, however, proved to be too much for the little girl, so she defaulted to honesty instead. "Hmm...I like purple," she offered, hoping that Ophelia might exclaim that purple was, in fact, her favorite color, too. Except she was all business and did not.

"Okay, I'll make a purple dress for your doll. I'm thinking of trying a sweetheart neckline."

Delaney turned Corlis over in her hands, admiring the stitch work of the dress as best a five-year-old girl could. "You are very good," she said, unable to take her eyes off the shiny red fabric.

"Thanks. I want to be a fashion designer when I grow up. I'm good at it. I even help Ms. Moriel look nice. You know," Ophelia leaned in with a rumor on her pink lips, "Ms. Moriel—" But Delaney would have to wait to hear how ripe and juicy the gossip really was.

BOOM! The heavy bedroom door banged against the interior wall, hitting the door stop at such an angle and with such force that it spun across the dusty hardwood ten feet and hissed to a stop beneath Ophelia's bed.

"What's your problem, Clarence?"

"Gregory is such a little tattler," said the little boy. He shuffled over in worn Converse high tops and did a body slam on the bed next to the one the girls were on. He exhaled a muffled groan into a pillow. He may have said, "I'm getting too old for this," but that seemed a rather odd thing to be said by someone who appeared to be around the same age as Ophelia.

"Why did he tattle on you?" Delaney asked.

Without lifting his head, Clarence waved a small tattered cerulean blanket into the air.

"You stole it back...again?" Ophelia rolled her eyes. "Klepts," she muttered.

Delaney was not absolutely sure what that meant. It hadn't appeared on her Word of the Day calendar yet.

"You don't even know what that means," he said in a whining tone, spitting out a feather and shoving bleach blond hair out of his hazel eyes.

"Do, too. Lucy told me so." She stuck out her tongue as if that would drive her point home.

Clarence's retort was a spooked look on his face, followed by him hopping to the floor and clambering under the bed he had just sprawled out on, pillow and blanket still in hand. As Delaney was beginning to conclude that Clarence was lacking in his argumentative skills, she was met with the slight tapping of footsteps coming up the stairs and a whispered, "Quiet," from under the bed.

"Okay," Delaney said, unsure if they were now in the middle of a game no one decided to include her in on.

"Shhh!" the bed hissed again.

"Is he in here?" said a small boy with black curly hair. He rolled up his navy and white stripped sleeves in an attempt to look intimidating, only to have them collapse down like two accordions. He scowled.

"No, Gregory, he isn't here," Ophelia droned in an exhausted tone.

"How do you know who I'm looking for?"

"Because you always ask me!"

"Because you're the one he tells everything to. You're closest to him—" Ophelia said in unison with Gregory.

Gregory was stamping his way from the bathroom to the closet, shuffling through the technicolored skirts, plaid jumpers, and mounds of stuffed animals.

"And who are you?" the boy inquired at Delaney; her eyes became round with surprise.

"Gregory! Don't be rude to my friend!"

This made Delaney smile slightly.

"I'll tell Ms. Moriel that you're bothering us." Ophelia put her hands on her hips and gave them an authoritative shimmy.

"Okay," he said with a pout. "Sorry." He lingered in his spot between the two beds, gently twisting back and forth. "Ah ha!" His body banged against the floorboards, shoving an arm past the curtain that was the green bedspread, which was much too big for the twin bed it covered. Gregory was clearly not afraid of monsters under the bed…at least not during daylight hours.

Delaney and Ophelia could tell he had gotten ahold of something. That something was soft, sliding instead of scraping against the floor as Gregory reverse army crawled away from the bed. His prize did not struggle. Bringing himself to a kneeling position, he dragged…a pillow from under the bedframe.

"Rats!" He stuck his head underneath the bed this time. Nothing was there.

This was the second time Delaney had been surprised that day. She wore her confusion on her face; her eyes silently begged for an explanation from Ophelia. The girl shook her mop of red hair, clearly fed up with the game of cat and mouse that played out before her. *"I'll tell you in a minute,"* her eyes seemed to communicate back.

"I'll find him," he huffed from under the bed again. The sheets billowed as his amplified voiced bellowed. "You'll see. I always get my man," Gregory said resolutely as he stood up once again, fists on his hips like a superhero. Present company included, all would agree that this was 'damn cute' instead of ominous or intimidating.

"Uh-huh," Ophelia laughed at the staticky hair atop Gregory's head. Her infectious giggling soon turned to unbridled mirth.

Delaney did her best to be polite, but the hand she held in front of her face could not contain her giggles.

Gregory sheepishly smiled back as he unsuccessfully tried to push the strands back into place. He said something else, but by this time, both Ophelia and Delaney were grasping their sides as they began to ache from a lack of oxygen due to prolonged bouts of laughter. "Phooey!" he shouted before stomping out of the room and slamming the door for dramatic effect.

"Between you and me, I actually think Gregory is upset that he won't be able to tell on Clarence anymore. He actually likes Clare, he just doesn't show it." She looked to the ceiling; the right corner of her mouth downturned, clearly frustrated with the boys' dynamic.

"He's been adopted?" Delaney deduced.

Ophelia nodded in confirmation. "Gregory gets to go with his new family tomorrow. His dad is a wizard. He made a quarter come out of Mother Mary Claire's ear. His new mom is an actress. She does a lot of funny voices. He's excited, but maybe nervous, too. Change can be hard but good."

Delaney considered this but was interrupted after only seven seconds by a "bump." (Some may argue the sound was more of a "thunk.") This was followed by a choice of words that would not be appropriate to write down in this tale because, well, what if a child were to read such expletives?

After a moment, fifty-four seconds to be exact, of quiet crying, Clarence emerged from behind the bedspread covered in a fine layer of dust. He sucked in air and made a whistling sound through the space that had been occupied by his left lateral incisor until December 9th. He greeted the girls with a whispered, "Ow."

Sympathy was the last thing taking up space on Delaney's mind. Astonishment and curiosity tussled to be at the forefront. "How did he not find you under there?" she asked with the enthusiasm of an apprentice asking a magician to reveal the secret to their best illusion.

He wore a smug smile. "He wasn't supposed to move the pillow," he said, taking a seat on the bed next to the girls.

"He cut a hole under the box spring and squeezed inside between all the springs. Been working on it for five months and three days," Ophelia blabbed.

Clarence now wore a long frown accessorized with a smoldering glare.

"Don't worry." Ophelia displayed her doll, her hands pressed to the sides of its head. "I kept Corlis' ears covered the whole time."

"So why did you steal the blanket, Clarence?" Delaney asked.

But the voice that came out of Clarence when he opened his mouth was not his own. Ophelia had beaten him to the punch, filling Delaney in on his story. She brought to light how her best friend wished to become a police officer when he grew up. His career aspirations justified his rationale for all his time outs and the subsequent losses of his security blanket. He needed to get all the wrongdoing out of his system in order to be an upstanding citizen as an adult. (This was kind of like a teacher wanting to get all the stupid out before managing a classroom of impressionable minds.)

What Mother Mary Claire and Mynah did not realize was how much actual mischief Clarence could get into. He was caught almost on a weekly basis, usually a distraction from a number of bigger shenanigans he had in the works. "Forty-seven this month," he chimed in when Ophelia took a breath. He looked down at his well-worn blanket that he had sprung from the locked second-from-the-top drawer of the filing cabinet in Mary Claire's office. "Soon to be forty-eight," he smirked. One of his ten upcoming capers could possibly involve sneaking into the orphanage's records to "borrow" a file, but Clarence would never tell. Nor would Ophelia mention her intention to return it…in about eighteen years. "Wait.

No. Forty-nine? Forty-nine." he amended, "Getting my blanket back was number forty-eight. Forty-nine will be—"

Ophelia cleared her throat and peered at Clarence through her mess of hair.

"Ya see, it's more than that," Clarence said, steering the conversation back to his career aspirations. "Ya have to know thine enemy. To catch the bad guy, ya need to think like one."

Delaney leaned in, intrigued.

"I want to be like Officer Lawson. He's my idol."

Copper Lawson was the one who had found and brought Clarence and Ophelia to Mother Mary Claire's, Clarence when he was only a couple weeks old and in the dead of winter. Ophelia, last year, wandering aimlessly at the Nollag Harvest Fest. In both cases, there was not a crumb of a clue that could trace the children back to their parents. Both cases had gone cold, but their love for the policeman who found them, as well as having a chance at a happy future, still burned white hot.

"Aww. That's so sweet," Delaney cooed, warm fuzzies percolating within her heart.

The muffled clicking of heels and light banter wafted through the hallway and began to resonate clearly. Clarence sat bolt upright and mumbled a very low "Uh-oh" as he was supposed to be in a time-out. (Instead, a stuffed monkey wearing his clothes was doing his time for him.) The comforter made a high pitched woosh against his burgundy corduroy pants as he scooted himself off his perch and made a mad dash for his box spring foxhole.

"Ms. Moriel is coming!" Ophelia announced to Delaney in an urgent whisper. "Clarence was never here, okay?"

Delaney nodded emphatically and offered an awkward thumbs up.

"I can tell he liked you," Ophelia said. "Clarence can tend to be a loner. He doesn't stick around new kids." She beamed a big smile.

The footfalls and conversation out in the hall had fallen to silence as Mynah and the O'Learys hovered outside the door, out of view.

"So, you wanted a purple dress, right? Are we talking an orchid, a mauve, or a heliotrope? I also should have some indigo and some phlox. Uh, right here," she said pointing to some fluorescent-looking swatches on her skirt.

"That one's nice," Delaney said of the phlox. "Can we do a combination of colors?"

"No problem. I can make anything." There was not an iota of self-doubt in the statement. "I like you, Delaney," Ophelia added without a hint, dash, or pinch of artificiality. Now both took a moment of silence to enjoy the warm fuzzies. "Do you want to be friends?"

Astonishment changed the lithe U-shaped smile to an O. To Delaney this was a most exclusive offer. "You want to be my friend? Why?"

With a crinkled nose and one eye pinched shut, Ophelia examined the dust caught in the filtered sunlight. "Because you're different, and I like things and people that are different."

Again, Delaney's pink lips turned upwards into a U. Her mind screamed, "Yes!" a million and three times, but her mouth worked out something different. "Would—would you wanna be my sister?"

The bed next to them gasped.

"Yes, she just up-ed and went to Aruba for a holiday," Mynah enunciated a little too clearly, and said a little too loudly to be deemed believable, before entering in from the hall. The same could be said of the rigid and emphatic nodding that made Mr. and Mrs. O'Leary look like bobbleheads. Copper had joined the group.

"How are you girls doing?" asked Mr. O'Leary.

"Fine, Daddy."

"That's good." There were a couple extra o's added in as Mr. O'Leary rocked back and forth on his heels.

"Copper! Copper! Guess what?"

"Officer Lawson," Mynah corrected Ophelia, but Copper chuckled.

"What is it, Ophie?"

"I'm gonna be someone's sister! Wait. Someone's big sister! Hers!" She pointed at Delaney and continued to bounce. "You're younger than I am, right?" But she didn't wait for an answer. "That's okay, Mr. and Mrs. O'Leary, right? I would be a really good big sister. Promise. Can I call you Mom and Dad?"

"Please," both girls said, adding thirty-seven e's to the word. There may or may not have been some sugar, gum drops, and a cherry mixed in there somewhere. The extra accoutrements were, at best, implied.

"Under one condition," Mrs. O'Leary said in a rather serious tone. "The walls and linens remain off limits for further works of art."

"Can I get some canvases and fabric out of the deal, then?"

"Ophelia!" Mynah crossed her arms in disapproval.

"Yeah, Mom. You don't need to get me any Christmas presents this year," Delaney offered.

"I think we can work something out."

With that, the deal was sealed with a family group hug…plus one.

"Thanks for letting me be here," Copper leaned over and whispered to Mynah.

"Pleasure is all mine," she replied softly.

"I like your sweater. Purple is a good color on you," he said in an even more hushed tone. If words could blush, his surely would.

"I told you so," Ophelia said.

Copper, now sporting bright red cheeks, unsuccessfully tried to suppress the goofy smile that was contorting on his freshly shaven face. He wanted to say more to the dainty blonde with the bob, but his nerves took an almost unanimous vote to hold it in.

"He totally likes you," the little girl said and then puckered her lips.

"Uh-huh," Mynah replied through a breathy laugh, "Ophelia, remember, don't push it…."

*   *   *

Ophelia was given a suitcase, so the girls could collect her things while the adults moved to the office to take care of the necessary paperwork. They had finished with putting away the skirts when they heard a strange noise.

It started as a low whine and then exploded into full sobs.

"Oh my gosh, Clarence, I completely forgot you were under there," Ophelia said, sticking her head under the bed to find her friend.

He emerged with dust bunnies clinging to his tear-stained face.

"What's with the long face—I mean mug, Clarence?" Ophelia was quick to correct herself to speak in delinquent lingo. Her own was drawn with concern. A mist clung to the corners of her eyes and at the tips of her long lashes.

"You're going a—" but synapses would not accept the message for his mouth to work out the last word for fear of complete meltdown. Tears already went against his rules of being a criminal. They were supposed to be saved for his hero years.

Delaney pouted out a sympathetic lower lip and tried to calm him by placing a reassuring hand on his shoulder. "You can come and visit us anytime," she reassured.

Clarence rubbed at his eyes furiously so he could see Delaney a little more clearly — to glare at her. It was all for show, a request Ophelia had made of him before Delaney had arrived.

"Yeah, you know, you can come over for a slumber party."

Attempts to cheer the boy were falling flat on the floor with an almost audible kerplunk. With a gulp, Delaney went back in for another try. "Of course, we wouldn't tell my parents? You could sneak in, like a breaking and entering."

If one looked hard enough, a glint of mischief could be found at the back of Clarence's eyes.

"Aw, Clare, I'm gonna miss ya so much." Ophelia swept the boy, blanket and all, into her arms. It could not be denied she had freakishly strong upper body strength for a girl of seven point six years of age.

"Don't call me that, Ophie," Clarence choked out. "That's a girl's name." His little chest heaved as his arms wrapped around

71

her a little tighter. They quaked as he fought to decide if he could hold onto her forever or if he would have to let go.

Seventy-eight seconds plodded by. Silence was only interrupted by some intermittent sniffling.

Little arms and fingers relaxed as Clarence touched the ground again. The calm smile that stretched across his cherub cheeks began to inflate, turning his face a shade of cranberry. "Bye," he quickly said and sprinted noiselessly out of the room.

"Tsk." Ophelia shook her red locks here and there and with a low chuckle said to herself, "Cry baby." Three sweaters were tossed into the suitcase on top of her crumpled mess of fabric shards and a small jar of sequins.

Her new sister's head ticked to the side. With an eyebrow raised in curiosity and left eye wide and round with skepticism, she scoured Ophelia's face for any hidden signs of sorrow, not unlike how an expert would examine a counterfeit painting. All indications proved her mood to be authentic. "Aren't you gonna miss him?" she queried incredulously.

"What's to miss?" she replied.

"Well, I suppose he does steal…." Delaney muttered to herself.

"Silly," Ophelia tsked again. Some brown boots, bedazzled ruby red Mary Janes, fuzzy lavender and aqua polka dot slippers, and sneakers laced with sapphire blue ribbons were crammed into the inside perimeter of the case. "We're best friends," she explained with a huff. The brown boots were a tight squeeze. "Best friends are forever and ever."

"How do you know? I mean there are so many factors that could change that."

"Yeah, we're gonna have to work on that." An index finger zig-zagged in Delaney's general direction.

"What?" she sputtered.

"Thinking."

"Thinking is a good thing," Delaney said defensively.

"I know. But overthinking isn't. And don't worry about Clare and me. I just know."

Delaney could find no rational reason to doubt Ophelia's words. So, she didn't.

"Don't call me Clare," he declared from the hall.

Grinning, Ophelia hefted Delaney onto the suitcase and quickly snapped it closed.

"I can be your best friend, too." Ophelia gave her new little sister a knowing look. "You're allowed to have more than one."

Pensive features could not completely conceal the worry Delaney had harbored behind it. "Oh," was all Delaney said and flashed a genuine, grin.

"Sisters are natural best friends."

Delaney opened her mouth to point out the relation was through adoption but decided against it. That would be overthinking. Thus, progress was already being made. For despite her not having any hard data, quantitative or qualitative, a small light bulb went off in the frontal lobe of her brain that concluded Ophelia was right. Confirmation was registered with the tingly feeling she usually got telling her all was right with the world. She would file this conversation, along with the associated tingles, away in her hippocampus for later.

*   *   *

Delaney would retrieve this exact memory eighteen years, eleven days, and twenty-three hours later, on the dot, as she sipped her chilled tea. The problem was the tingling feeling was not as prevalent as it once was. Doubt now made that reassured feeling from years gone by shaky, like a toy that came with too many parts and an instruction sheet with three languages, none of which the buyer could decipher. The time that had passed from that day to the present had collected and crowded many tarnished recollections into the suitcase that was Delaney's memory. Sighing heavily, she collected her sentence-worth of a foreword, dropped a two-dollar tip for Timothy, and left Beatrice Clark's Caffeine and Bean Coffee Café on Jazzed Avenue and headed for her grandparents' house on Partridge Parkway. Well, in truth, it had been hers for almost a year, but her mind still struggled to see it that way.

Chapter 5

In Which Opehlia Is Caught in the Middle of a Business Meeting, an Awkward Chat, and a Love Story

Ophelia let out a long exhale after picking up her supplies from the Cockles of My Heart Greeting Card and Candle Cache. Mr. Wick had said the gold wrapping paper was on the house. She pretended not to have noticed the note stuck to the register that clearly had the word "FREE" heavily bolded in Mrs. Wick's scrawl.

Why was it that the to-do list never got any shorter even when you seemed to be making a respectable amount of progress? A nagging feeling pulled at the bottom of her stomach as she neared Fabulously Festooned Frocks and Alterations Dress Shoppe on Twin Street, the neon light from its sign staining the bricks pink. She ignored the sensation, no longer trusting in her intuition. One new vision in almost a year was not enough to convince her to get her hopes up.

"Ophelia, I need your help," Grey Terne said, bursting out through the shop's doors, neglecting the obligatory pleasantries of "hello" and "how is your day?"

She let out a barely audible groan from the back of her throat before saying, "Grey, what's the matter? You know not to disturb me on my day off." Her shoulders drooped, the bottom of the bag containing the wrapping paper lightly grazing the snow that lined the sidewalk.

"I sign your paychecks," he reminded her, coaxing her in with the very hand that did, in fact, sign her paychecks. "Sorry, that was uncalled for," he amended. He cocked his head to the side and turned his chin up, indicating to Ophelia that she should turn right and proceed through the double doors in about two feet and four inches to arrive at her new destination.

Ophelia stepped out of the cold, which was being obnoxious with its constant nipping at noses. Blinking the garish light of the brazen neon pink sign of the shop from her eyes, her vision came into focus on Grey standing in front of the store's two largest display windows. He nervously gnawed on his left index finger, his right arm cradling the left's elbow. Mannequins were lined up on the raised stages in front of them. The large glass panes were covered up with brown paper. Even from the inside, one could read "New Display Coming Soon!" scrawled on them in big backwards letters.

"Mr. Terne." Kitty Cloissone, a new and overeager intern at the shop, did her best to keep her tone firm and professional. "If you would hear me out for an iota of a sec—" She cut herself off, her lavender eyes darting toward Ophelia for a quarter of a second before snapping back to Grey. She began to wring sweaty hands.

"No discussion needed, Kitty. We are not carrying menswear," he addressed his employee.

76

The woman was awash in tweed and pinstripe swatches, a measuring tape wrapped around her neck like a scarf and a row of silk ties in deep jewel tones evenly displayed on her right forearm. Her jaw was set on edge, and she seemed to be holding her breath as if frozen in mid-sentence. "But you're—" A thought came to her, overriding her protest. She quickly walked back to her desk, shedding the ties amongst the notes and invoices that cluttered its top. Kitty momentarily vanished under her workspace, resurfacing with some colorful looking bar and pie charts on projected sales. The large visual aids barely made it to their easels when she caught Grey's eyebrow had lifted two centimeters. This subtle tell was a warning. Another point three and she was dangerously close to having some damask chucked at her.

"No men's clothing." Grey shuddered slightly.

Kitty looked back at him crestfallen and deflated, some swatches sloughing off her slumped shoulders, not unlike a melting snowman on an uncharacteristically warm December day. She shoved the charts and graphs underneath her desk and excused herself to the backroom where no one would hear her whimper.

"Ah, the whole inseam thing," Ophelia recalled with curled lips, offering a sympathetic glance to Kitty. "Too close for comfort?"

Grey gave another shudder. "The windows," he began, choosing not to delve into the issue, "what are your thoughts on the New Year's layout?"

Ophelia smirked and shook her head. Grey had no desire for Ophelia's actual opinion, merely reassurance that what he had put together, so far, was better than good enough. She would oblige… on her terms.

"You're gonna have to confront your family on this sooner or later," she sang.

"I don't see what they have to do with the windows," he said back flatly.

Grey kept a secret from his family, or, more to the truth, he *thought* he kept a secret from his family. The Terne name was synonymous with impeccable tailoring in men's suits. It had been stitched in the stars that Grey would follow in the footsteps of his father, grandfather, and every other great grand-relative in his lineage, just as his younger brothers had. And that was exactly what his family believed he was doing in Nollag, two cities over from his hometown, Glory.

The skinny on the big, fat, pinstriped elephant in the room was that Grey was a good tailor from the waist up. Anything below the Italian leather belt left him in crippling cold sweats or a fit of uncomfortable giggling. That last one only happened one time. Needless to say, but it will be stated regardless, gowns were easier due to their definite lack of having to get close and personal to measure a client's inseam.

His fear, in its own way, was a blessing, for Grey loved what he did and had managed to harness his passion into a successful business.

He waved Ophelia over to his left ear, which signaled to her that he really needed her honest opinion. The right ear harbored an inner ear problem, rendering its functionality little more than to help balance out both sides of his head. "What do we think of them?" This translated to, "Are the colors okay?" Among his other hurtles, Grey was also colorblind and unable to discern the difference between the colors red or green. As a result, he always found Christmas particularly drab.

Ophelia tilted her head thirty degrees to the left and screwed her face into deep contemplation, her eyes ticking and tocking from the left window to the right and back again.

The body form on the right sat hunched atop a large box wrapped in newspaper and was surrounded by other variously sized boxes in brown paper and twine. She was clad in a crisp taffeta khaki floor-length gown synched at the waist with a skinny chocolate brown ribbon with an hourglass dangling from the end of it. The wire framed form on the left waved her arms in the air and seemed to be dancing amidst a sky of dangling multicolored star ornaments. Her one shouldered mini dress was nothing but large silver, red, and shiny black sequins. The small slit on the side exposed a peak of red silk.

"Yeah."

Grey sucked in some air and held it as if he tried to figure out if the "yeah" was genuine or sarcastic. He hated it when Ophelia toyed with him, which was more often than not; seventy-one point three percent of the time to be exact.

"No. Yeah. Definitely. Uh-huh. Hmm…."

"Specifics, Ophelia."

"I really like how the mannequin on the right symbolizes the old year with the beige tones and how the one on the left has the flashy pizazz with the silver, red, and black. A classic made new again." She punctuated her critique with a "Fabulous," and Grey exhaled a sigh of non-imitation relief. "Can I go now?"

Grey tapped his ear. "Say it in the right one." He grinned slyly at Ophelia who looked back at him with half-lidded eyes. She made an audible sigh, slowly shaking her head.

Hoisting her bag over her shoulder, only to have it slide down her arm six seconds later, she proceeded to the backroom where she plucked a spool of gold thread off the wall. She gave a sympathetic smile to Kitty, who was licking her wounds and pretending to take inventory.

"Borrowing," she said waving the thread in Grey's face as she passed by him on her way out.

"Fine."

"Going now."

"Bye now."

"Oh, and Grey?"

"Yes?"

"You know it will come out," she said with sincerity, eyes roving over the store and back to him.

Grey swallowed hard and glared at her, unconsciously fidgeting with his lapel. Every time Ophelia uttered this, the words sank in a little deeper. One could not simply stow away an entire store in the inside pocket of a jacket or hide it behind one's back.

Outside, the pink light made the fluffy snowflakes look like cotton candy, which started Ophelia's mind working on ideas for the next display layout.

"Ophelia?" she heard a familiar voice say.

Well, this was inevitable. This city needs to be bigger.

With a deep breath to prepare herself, she straightened her back and spun around with as much of a dramatic flair as she could muster. "Gregory," she said with a forced smile that looked exactly that, forced. This was the first time she had spoken to her ex since they had broken up. The one or two times they had almost bumped into each other, Ophelia had been fortunate enough to happen upon Gregory first and took the necessary steps to remain unseen.

As with everything she had done, Ophelia had a very calculated reason for breaking things off with Gregory almost three years ago on New Year's Eve. It forced Gregory to make a change for the better.

The thing was, Ophelia's brand of helping usually left one feeling, well, quite frankly, melancholy or ireful. In Ophelia's experience, the best outcomes from her interventions always came after things had gotten much, much worse, inclining these individuals not to want the perpetrator of their emotional trauma to hang around. This, Ophelia assumed, was how Gregory still felt.

Ophelia was not good with damage control, mostly because once her good deed was done, she was off to a whole new existence, ready to stir the pot of someone else's inner turmoil before turning the heat down to a simmer and checking to make sure her intervention was not too salty. *But because I went rogue and helped not only Dee, but Gregory and Petunia and…*but the thought faded away when she noticed Gregory smiling at her.

Gregory took a deep breath, beginning to say, "I wa—"

"Gottagobye." The words came too quickly for her mouth to say them clearly, but with that, she was off in a flurry of snow, leaving poor Gregory McGregor sputtering in the late afternoon chill.

Ophelia did not look back. "You have nothing to worry about," she heard herself say with less than genuine reassurance. Rounding the corner on Tangtooker Thruway, past Grandma and Grandpa's Mom and Pop Kiddie Toy Storehouse, onto Miracle Street, Ophelia sucked in the cool air to dull her unfounded worries. Home was two blocks over on 34th, also called Crosby Lane. A good thing, too, since her feet had decided they would keep quiet no longer, especially after their two point six mile roundtrip trek. Shoving all remaining remnants of Gregory away, Ophelia called forth an image of her purple fuzzy slippers, and her feet found their second wind.

Ophelia resided at Vermont Village, an older building with a white brick façade, and had called it home for almost six and a half years. Most of the memories that occupied the nooks and crannies of the sixty-eight-year-old building were happy ones for Ophelia. Its sixty-seventh year was another story; one which will be saved for later.

With a tug on the tarnished brass handle, Ophelia was able to pop the front door open just enough to squeeze herself through. A west-northwest wind blew the evergreen door shut with a BANG! Apartment doors 1A through 1C quaked as the force reverberated through the first floor.

CLICK. BANG. Shhh.

A small woman by the name of Violet Wikershamson poked her head out of apartment 1B, her comically large eyes scanning the hall to see who might be paying a visit to Vermont.

"Why, Ophelia, dearie me," she cooed, pushing her pink tortoiseshell glasses back up the bridge of her nose. "How are you? Merry Christmas. Oh, my, that is lovely wrapping paper you have there. So pretty."

"How are you, Mrs. Wikershamson? You are looking quite the picture."

Violet giggled throwing a shaky hand over her mouth to conceal her flattery. "You're too kind, sweetheart." She gave a twirl to show off her lavender housecoat with the pink and yellow rose print.

"Are you still drawing, my dear?" This was a question that was almost as frequent as the salutation she always gave Ophelia.

"Yes and no," Ophelia answered.

"Aww…." In an instant, Violet looked to be on the verge of tears.

"I sketch the dresses I design. I make dresses," Ophelia reminded her.

"And you enjoy it?"

"I absolutely love it," Ophelia said truthfully. Most would not use the word 'love' as their first choice when describing their profession, erring on the side of 'like' but dancing a thin line into 'tolerate' territory.

"Well, I'm glad you're still able to do it. You have such talent."

"Yes. Thank you. How is Mr. Wikershamson?"

Violet flashed a toothless smile. "Honey, he has never been better. My prince charming is taking me to the ball."

The look of adoration would stay with Ophelia for the rest of her existence. It almost made Violet more youthful; her eyes sparkled eight watts brighter, and the apples of her cheeks grew firmer and rosier.

"We've gone every year to the library gala since we met. I love it," she added sweetly.

"Well, if it ain't broke, don't fix it."

Violet giggled again, smiling wider.

"Mrs. Wikershamson, do—do you know you don't have your dentures in?"

"Yes," she leaned in, her eyes narrowed to slits, darting from left to right, and raised a hand to conceal the movement of her lips from anyone who may enter the hall. "I'm going commando," she whispered.

Ophelia desperately wished they were still discussing teeth and thought it best to not press further.

"Well, dear, I must be going and finish getting ready. Being my age, it takes a lot longer to put everything back where it should be. Take care."

"You, as well," Ophelia said from halfway down the hall, making her way to the stairs.

"Get your dancin' shoes ready, Charlie. I wanna try some stuff I read in Flugencia's new book," Ophelia could hear Violet say before the door to 1B closed shut.

I hope they're still talking about the gala, Ophelia thought with a shiver as she made her way up to the seventh-floor landing.

*   *   *

Prince Charming was exactly who Charlie Wikershamson was to Violet. Back in the day, Violet had resigned herself to a life as a spinster librarian, convinced that love would only be found in the books she reshelved day in and day out. Little did she know, the short spindle of a man with a sweater vest for every day of the week pined for her behind his collection of legal pads and journals at the back table of the reference section. Unbeknownst to him, the feeling was mutual.

While most would have written coy little notes disclosing their true feelings, this would simply not do; he was an aspiring writer, after all. Well, an aspiring writer by night and an accountant by day. So, between bouts of tax research and balancing books, he created his own story: *It All Balances Out to Love.*

Of course, like any great boy meets girl story, something must be thrown into the plot to gnarl the path to Happily Ever After. That particular hiccup came in the form of the dedication: "To my favorite keeper of the books. I wrote this for you."

Certain Charlie could not be writing about her, Violet thought it more logical that the beautiful bookkeeper he referred to was her identical twin sister, Indigo, who worked alongside Charlie at Checks & Balances & Then Some Accounting Firm and Financial Consultation Co. The misguided twists and turns of her logic dashed the then young Violet's dreams.

The facts were clearly laid out, or so she thought, as she had decided to twist the proverbial knife a little deeper and park herself in front of the extensive love letter with a pint, or three, of triple chocolate mousse ice cream. As she read and gorged, she became more and more convinced. The dazzling green eyes with a dark amber ring surrounding the pupil, the red luxuriant hair that made the very flames of the sun look like waning light, and the very ample bosom: the description was practically a painted picture of Indigo. A lack of self-esteem often makes one forget some key details.

As she was about to give up and set the book aside, page thirty-four grabbed her attention with a chapter entitled "The First Meeting." It described how Ms. Cutter and Mr. Dewey shared an intimate, but awkward, pause in the book stacks, and how Dewey, at that moment, knew the keeper of the books would be the keeper of his heart. That and he wondered what it would feel like to kiss her. Charlie would find out later that night.

The poorly veiled nonfiction piece in a fiction dust jacket never did become a great seller. In actuality, the opposite—a big flop as the saying goes. It did not matter, though. Charlie got what he desired out of the book deal, and Violet got her Prince Charming.

What neither would know was that Ophelia had a hand in their matchmaking. Sixty-two years ago, Ophelia was Beatrix Bartholomew, who preferred to go by Trixie, a volunteer librarian and friend of Violet's with a penchant for romance novels…the more torn bodices and waxed chests the better.

She was the one who planted the idea that Charlie, as he took fleeting glances of Violet from behind his accounting books, pledge his devotion to his clueless crush in no less than fifty thousand words. She would also borrow from Violet's appearance for when she would return to Nollag as Ophelia: the red hair, the green eyes, and ample bosom. Although, not so ample as to provoke poor posture and the literal pain in the neck, among other places.

Years later, a then seventy-six-year-old Violet would see Ophelia through the window of the Bookend Bookstore, be taken back to her youth, and feel compelled to go up to Ophelia and tell her precisely that. (Actually, her exact words were, "You're a dead ringer for my sister if she were fifty-three years younger.") This would lead to a conversation where Ophelia would mention she was taking a break from the exhausting task of apartment hunting. To which Violet would excitedly share there was a recent vacancy at the Vermont Village and how Ophelia should look into it and what a coincidence this all was! As one might imagine at this point, this was no coincidence, but a very well-choreographed and executed plan that resembled something like luck.

The happenstance was not only so Ophelia would acquire apartment 7H, but also so she could see her old friend, Violet

Wickershamson, on a regular basis. She relished having a regular reminder that not all fairy tales remained relegated to the pages of a book, and that happily ever afters could, in fact, be obtained.

Chapter 6

In Which an Empty Room Is Used as a Metaphor for the Hole in Ophelia's Heart

She ran through her mental checklist as she quickly clicked her way up each step. *Pawn Shop. Check. Dee. Check…sort of.* Ophelia grimaced, thinking back to those stilted moments she shared with her sister back at the café not even two hours and seventeen minutes ago. *Gold paper,* she continued. *Check. Dress and jacket. Almost done. Just a few finishing touches left. Party. Undecided at the moment…would love to see my handiwork though. Oh! Clarence! That's right. Stop over at Clare's.*

Ophelia gave a heaving sigh, rolling her shoulders back to release the strain of the day thus far. She was finally back home, and all of the craziness of the day was about to be left outside her door, along with the empty milk bottles from this week.

The brass key clicked and clacked, begrudgingly passing each of the lock's tumblers. The heavy oak door only gave a short groan as it swung open, almost banging against the wall if not for the small cast iron doorstop fashioned into a mouse. The pictures of abstract lavender flowers tilted a little more to the left now. Ophelia quickly scooted out of the way before the door swung back and shut.

After locking the deadbolt, Ophelia placed the apartment key in the rectangular teal tray on the table to the immediate left of the door and tossed the bag of gold paper and thread into the curved armchair in her small front room. It did not fit with the purple and gray décor of the rest of the room, but Ophelia was able to explain away the true green chair with a pattern of circles and parallel lines as a statement piece. Most accepted the explanation, given the eye-popping flare Ophelia managed to carry off in her own attire.

"Water," Ophelia muttered as she hopped five hops to the kitchen, releasing another relieved sigh when she managed to get her second boot off. "Better," she told herself, flexing her toes and unbuttoning her coat.

She paused at the fridge, grabbed the pitcher, and poured the contents into a clean glass on the counter. Before she drank, though, she glanced down the hall behind the kitchen. Forgetting she had a thirst to be quenched, she shuffled six feet down the hall, taking the glass and pitcher with her, to stare into a dark and sparse room, now only known as the second bedroom. Most days, she was thankful to forget the little room even existed. Delaney's room. Well, it *used to be* Delaney's room. Her recent rendezvous with her sister, however, forced Ophelia to peak behind the curtain of her mental block.

*   *   *

During a late afternoon on Christmas Day one year ago, Ophelia had come home to find the front door propped open by a cardboard box that had been labeled 'Books' in faded black marker, though it actually contained shoes. Delaney had not anticipated her sister returning from Clarence's so early, and had Ophelia still been able to prognosticate, she would have stayed away.

Upon entering, she saw Calum Dooley standing in the kitchen as if frozen, holding a box marked 'Sweaters.' This one actually did contain two cable knits, five cardigans, and a turtleneck with a nasty snag in the stitching, a gift from her departed grandmother that Delaney couldn't bring herself to throw away. Calum gave Ophelia a sympathetic smile before breaking eye contact and making his way out of the apartment.

Ophelia puttered where she stood, pulling at the fingers of her gloves and yanking at the scarf that was suddenly too tight on her neck. She could hear the tearing of packing tape and the footfalls of her sister and her friend, Petunia Perkins. When the two entered the hall, laden down with boxes and bags, they met Ophelia with cold stares.

In that moment, Ophelia wanted to explain everything to Delaney. Why she had done what she had done the night before. Why it had been necessary to break up an engagement. Why Bailey Barrymore needed to be in the hospital with a broken wrist and a possible concussion. But that was not part of the plan. Because Ophelia wasn't normally around for this part, usually already having moved on to a new life with new circumstances and a new person to help, her past personas either having moved away or, if she was feeling dramatic, disappearing without warning. (There was also that time she faked her own death.) It just so happened, this time, she was still Ophelia O'Leary, sans premonitions, which left her completely and utterly flummoxed. So, Ophelia said nothing. Delaney and Petunia did the same, their mouths working into hard lines.

The sound of the box of shoes being kicked into the hallway, followed by the slow eek of the door's hinges as it sought its doorframe, brought Ophelia out of her anxious reverie. She was alone, save for the ghost of Christmas past.

*   *   *

A small whimper escaped into the silence as her eyes roamed over the last couple of dusty cardboard boxes that sat in the center of the room, their contents unknown. The edges of the tape had begun to yellow. Delaney was supposed to have come back for them, but she never did. *She doesn't live here anymore*, Ophelia reminded herself. She swallowed the painful memory along with her glass of water, switching her focus back to her to-do list yet again. Moments were sparse to spare on this particular day, and she needed to help pull off a miracle.

Quickly swinging back to the kitchen, Ophelia replaced the pitcher into the fridge and left her empty glass on the counter, before picking up her boots and swaggering down the other hall to her room to change.

No more than three minutes and forty-seven seconds had passed when a knock came at the lower half of apartment 7H's door.

"Coming," Ophelia yelled as she finished tying her locks up atop her head in a pile of tangled red ribbon, not unlike her former seven-year-old self. Gone was the simple cotton black dress with the royal purple band that wrapped under the bust line. Instead, the maven of style emerged in baggy lavender sweatpants and an oversized lilac sweatshirt, a green strap from a tank top peeked out over her left shoulder. The outside world only saw her in her best, but home was all about comfort. A select few knew and kept her secret. Delaney, Clarence, and....

Chapter 7

In Which There Are Gifts of the Unexpected Variety... and By Unexpected, We Are Referring to the Annoying and Misfortunate Kind

Nigella Gellar rocked back and forth on her black and white saddle shoes in front of apartment 7H's door, waiting for her friend to answer.

She cast her eyes downward as the creaking sound of floorboards grew louder and a shadow slipped beneath the door.

"What?" came a muffled voice. The door's thickness made it difficult to tell if the tone was playful or annoyed.

A forced, exaggerated grin spread across Nigella's face, making the volume of her chubby cheeks increase by twenty-one percent. She raised and proceeded to shake a package of Miss Fit's Dollies Peppermint Cookie Crumblies that Ophelia had ordered.

The cookie delivery was an excuse to see and spend some time with her friend. Her mother, who did not approve of Ophelia, would not have allowed it otherwise. Ophelia was a bad influence, she would lecture to her daughter, which all stemmed from her own poor interaction with "that woman from 7H." This made Nigella want to have a friend that was exclusively hers and one that made her feel as dangerous as any eight-year-old could feel.

Ophelia was more than happy to fill the role of disliked neighbor, all part of her grand plan while she was Ophelia O'Leary. She did not need to be liked. In most cases, she did not *want* to be liked. What some forgot was that miracles, big and small, tended to emerge from the worst situations. As it just so happened, Ophelia could be found to be the common denominator in some of the more unfortunate circumstances Nollag had seen recently. However, what most failed to see was how she had helped them, choosing to focus on how she had wronged them instead, her cosmic sleight of hand.

"Hey!" the muffled voice said over the symphony of cookie and cellophane. "Stop or all that'll be left will be crumbs." The deadbolt popped from its locked position, and the door edged open just enough to let Nigella through. She sucked in her round stomach and slid inside.

"Thank you much," Ophelia said as she eagerly grabbed the box of cookies from Nigella and produced a five-dollar bill.

"Pleasure doing business with you," Nigella replied playfully snapping the crisp bill and looking at it through the light.

Ophelia opened the box and popped half of a Crumblie into her mouth. "Mmmm," she purred, shutting her eyes to concentrate on the melting concoction of peppermint and fudge currently entertaining her tastebuds. "Orgas—Euphoric," she said, quickly changing her word choice, realizing Nigella was still there.

"I've never heard that word before," Nigella said curiously.

Ophelia offered her the other half of the Crumblie and asked, "How are you doing?" She prayed the fragment of the new word might be forgotten in the shuffle of their ensuing conversation.

"Mm-well," the little girl smacked and spat.

"Please, sweetie, not on the white carpet. Come by the kitchen table, and I'll get you some milk."

"K," she said, dancing to a chair. It had seemingly not taken long for the sugar to hit her bloodstream.

"You were saying?" Ophelia placed two, tall, chilled glasses of skim milk on the table. Nigella needed to use both hands to hold her glass.

"Well," started Nigella with a dramatic flip of her wispy hair as she came up for air from her milk, "Ebony is at it again."

Ophelia bristled. "Is she picking on you?"

"Exactly. She said—um—she said that—on purpose—that she thought my Dollies sash was stupid." Nigella puffed out her little chest to proudly showcase her handiwork. While all the other Dollies of Nigella's chapter had simple purple cotton sashes to display their badges for their various community services and learned skills, Nigella had decided hers was too bland and spent the better part of her weeknights for the past three weeks adding a layer of sequins over the top. Ophelia was inclined to agree the addition vastly improved the look of the uniform.

"So, then what did you do?" Ophelia licked away her milk mustache.

"I told her that her face was stupid and that she wouldn't know fashion if it hit her. And, you know, she didn't? I threw Anita Fashionista's Guide to Modern Trends at her, and she didn't like my sash any more than she did the first time." Nigella frowned, whether due to Ebony's distaste or a lack of another Crumblie was up for debate.

Ophelia leaned over to Nigella and whispered, "Good girl." The frown was turned upside down and then some. "But what did your mother say? There is no way she didn't hear about this little spat."

The smile remained intact but a little worse for wear. Through tight lips, Nigella confessed, "Uh, she says it's because I'm around you too much."

"Of course, it's my fault," Ophelia resigned.

"It's only because she doesn't like you."

Truer words were never confessed. Mrs. Gellar turned her unnaturally straight nose up at Ophelia and made no effort to be pleasant about it.

"I don't know why. I never did anything to her." This...was a slight understatement.

"You ruined her tray of cookies she made for the school bake sale. Something about sa-bo-tage?" Nigella was not confident in her understanding of the last word but, nevertheless, was pleased that she could mimic the string of syllables successfully. "My dad doesn't really like you, either."

Ophelia gawked at her disclosure, an expression that betrayed the fact that she already knew this.

"You made him late for his boss' party. He said his boss yelled at him." She locked a hard stare onto Ophelia and stressed the next two words "Really. Bad. If he had been late one more minute, he would have been fired. Fi-er-d."

"How was I supposed to know that? And the cookie thing was an accident."

The cookie thing was no accident. Knowing her window to look into the future would shut tightly after she had finished helping Delaney, Ophelia decided early on, she would add the odd good deed here and there to her already full to-do list. If her ability was going away, what harm could further bending the cosmic rules really do?

"You sneezed on the cookies. Like, all of them."

"Allergy to nutmeg," Ophelia said curtly, throwing back the rest of her milk like a shot of, well, something a lot stronger than skim milk.

A moment of fleeting silence passed between the two. Nigella swung her legs back and forth, the heels of her shoes occasionally connecting with one of the legs of her chair with a low thunking sound. Ophelia stared out the large window behind her couch, checking if the snow had started up again. Indeed, it had.

"So, who else is there?" Ophelia asked, referring to the running list of her 'fan club.'

"Mrs. Beezle."

"That nut!? Why?"

"You kept her up all night that one time you were remodeling."

"Whatever," Ophelia said with disgust. "If it weren't for me, she would have—" Ophelia stopped herself. "How do you know all this?"

"Adults don't think I remember any of this stuff they say when I'm in the room." Nigella paused for a second or two. "I guess it's kinda good and bad," she mused, with a little nod of her head. "Good 'cause sometimes what they say might be handy for later, but bad because it's an insult to my intelligence."

Once empty milk glasses were placed in the sink and Miss Fit's Dollies Peppermint Cookie Crumblies were safely stowed out of sight, Ophelia collected her gold paper and thread and led Nigella to her closet.

Most of the apartments in Vermont Village had very small cubicles for closets — a fact to keep in mind. But Ophelia, being Ophelia, could not stand the thought of a tiny closet crammed full of her fantastical one-of-a-kind and dry-clean-only pieces. One could argue they were simply clothes. One could also tell their grandmother that the Christmas sweater she painstakingly knitted with a Rudolph on the front, complete with an actual glowing red nose, was bombastic. If one had a soul, however, one did not do such things to one's grandmother. Truthfully, either scenario would result in a sneaky uppercut and a black eye, possibly a bruised rib, too. Grandmothers and Ophelias were not meant to be trifled with.

Ophelia had essentially turned her ten by eight master bedroom inside out. She had divided the area by erecting a wall with a door that led to a four by eight room with enough space to cram her bed and a tiny table for a nightstand. The remaining eight feet by six feet had been transformed into what could be best described as a showroom where "the magic happened." (Ophelia's words.)

"Wow," Nigella exhaled when the light clicked on. She never got tired of seeing all the pretty garments, dresses, accouterments, and Sunday bests glitter, glisten, and look plain fancy as they tightly lined the double racks that ran along most of the perimeter of the room, save for the back wall where the door leading to the bedroom, one of two chests of drawers, and an armchair were.

"Make yourself at home, kiddo." Ophelia laid the gold paper on top of a large white cube of a table in the center of the room. On the tabletop were a pistachio-colored sewing machine, a Word of the Day calendar that Ophelia propped Corlis, her old doll, against, and a large white box. The left side of the cube contained compartments with bolts of fabric in a variety of colors, textures, and patterns. None of that synthetic stuff, though. Ophelia was not a fan of fabrics whose fiber content she could not pronounce.

Nigella skipped over to the old pine chest on the western wall. As she had routinely done, she pulled out the first two drawers, the bottom one farther than the other, and quickly clamored to the top of the weathered teal furniture. "I love this place," she said more so to herself than to her hostess. She scanned the jewelry box, ring dish, and necklace stand next to her. Slipping a large padmaraga yellow sapphire cocktail ring on her index finger, she watched as the angles of the gem played with the light. It had belonged to Ophelia's grandmother and, unbeknownst to Nigella, had been worn on one of Bailey Barrymore's sticky fingers for the briefest of moments.

"What's in the box?" Nigella asked, joining the world yet again, only to have her attention diverted back to the ring and then to a long rope of pearls looped on the necklace stand. She delicately picked up the strand of opulent orbs and placed it around her neck, which, due to its length and her short stature, collected in her lap.

"Ah, I'm about to get to that part," Ophelia said; a small smile crept across her face as she pulled the spool of gold thread from the bag as if it were a hint. "See, I thought it was done, but there was a part of me that said it might be missing something." With a little drama, and a dash of mystery, her fingers slowly and gently gripped the lid of the large white box. The suction from the lid gave way to a gasp as if it were a thousand-year-old sarcophagus being opened for the first time.

With a symphony of rustles, Ophelia pulled out a pile of yellow and gold fabric and carried the mess over to the dress form situated on the other side of the table and started to chase the creases from its skirt. Nigella's jaw relaxed and waggled at the beauty of the dress. The dress was a soft yellow with little cap sleeves and a modest neckline. A layer of pale yellow barege, accented with winking golden thread, came from beneath the waistline forming an hourglass shape and pleating at the center. Ophelia double checked the length of the dress, making sure the hemline would kiss the ankles of its intended recipient.

"Do you like it?" Ophelia asked.

There was silence, but the seamstress knew it was of the complementary variety.

"I thought so," Ophelia said, pleased as pudding, the figgy kind. "Anyway, what do you think of adding a gold ribbon right about here?" She lightly ran her index finger along the bateau neckline.

Nigella shrugged. Her lower lip protruded in a frown. "I guess," she said, "you're the designer, and you have awesome taste." Her big brown eyes departed from the dress to once again scan over the veritable rainbow of jewelry that spilled from the three displays next to her. Her fingers nimbly tickled the air as she decided what to don next.

"Both things are true," Ophelia replied without a hint of playfulness in her voice. "The wonderful thing about art, Nigella, is that it gets better when it evolves. Art only evolves with new ideas, which are a result of inspiration. And inspiration doesn't like to be caught wearing the same outfit twice. I need your help to find it again. Said inspiration sometimes hides in other pieces of art or in the everyday, like in the conversation we're having right now. Now, let me ask you again, what do you think of this?" She held up a metallic gold ribbon about three inches wide.

"I don't know. I'm eight."

"Ideas aren't reserved for people eighteen years and up," she said, quoting one of the reminders Mynah Moriel had taught her as a child. She crossed the room and placed the spool of ribbon in Nigella's tiny pink hands. "Reminder number six," she said under her breath to herself.

"I. Well. I'm not in love with the idea because I think it makes the dress too…" Nigella gritted her teeth, "flashy. But—" she quickly added, "but I think you should add something." She gestured to indicate the neckline. "What if…." Ophelia's eyebrows crept up. "What if you added a shade of yellow that's close to the yellows in the dress? You know, more mon—cram—matic."

"You mean monochromatic."

"I said that."

Ophelia pondered, taking a step back from the dress form and scrunched her face, trying to envision Nigella's suggestion. Nigella appeared to have stopped breathing.

"I can't quite see it. What do you have in mind?"

Shedding her baubles and finery, the girl hesitantly descended from her shabby chic teal perch and headed over to the large worktable. A few beats of silent deliberation, fifty-one seconds to be precise, and Nigella returned with a bright satin yellow ribbon, slightly bolder than the yellows of the dress, and, depending on how the light caught it, there was a hint of gold for shine.

"This?"

The girl nervously nodded.

"I love it," Ophelia said, quickly grabbing a box of small pins to attach the ribbon to the gown's neckline. She would run it through the sewing machine later. "I wish I had thought of it." (And Ophelia truly wished she had.)

"Yeah," Nigella said. A wide grin stretched over her face, pushing her cheeks up high and making her eyes resemble little glittering crescent moons. Nigella proceeded to confidently explain her thought process, her tone implying her vast, yet unfounded, knowledge in color theory.

"I see you've found your voice again."

"I wasn't sure if you would like it," she admitted, sounding slightly embarrassed.

"Well, what do you think would happen if I didn't?"

"I don't know. Um, maybe, youuuu wouldn't bemyfriendanymore." Nigella's voice hid under her breath as if Ophelia would take this hypothesis into consideration and accept it as reality.

"Aw, sweetie, you need to redefine your definition of what makes someone a friend. Let me ask you this," Ophelia posited as she finished the pinning. "There. What kind of a friend would you describe me as if I kicked you out for offering a constructive piece of criticism, which," she added, "I asked for?"

"Not a very good one?" Nigella admittedly was not all that used to being treated like an adult and was still chewing on how construction was playing into the conversation.

"Or?"

"Not a friend at all…."

"Nigella, never let what you think other people expect of you to shape you. Trust me when I say it is very hard to fit into a mold someone else has made for you because, ultimately, they don't know you, not completely. I've seen it happen with so many people."

The girl's eyebrows pulled together, trying to process the moral of the little life lesson.

"I like you exactly the way you are," Ophelia said, helping the girl to the point of her little monologue.

Nigella's young mind could not fathom why this conversation had transpired right at this moment. She was glad it had, though. "Nigella Gellar," Ebony Zer had sneered, "you are such a freaky little elf. Nothing matches." The memory of her nemesis' criticism stuck in the webbing of her subconscious. The little girl, who was no less than four inches shorter than the other girls her age, pretended it did not vex her, but it actually predisposed her to a thought that crippled the unique and eccentric. *What if Ebony's right?* The record player in her mind repeatedly jumped back to her fretful question after every Dollies meeting and stayed with her for at least one day, eleven hours, and thirty-one minutes.

Ophelia's kind words moved the needle off the scratch in Nigella's record of thought and set her attention to a smooth cheerful carol of self-actualization, complete with an original score and lyrics performed by the Nollag Community Choir, the Tannenbaum Tenors. (You might be interested to know they are available for office parties and weddings.)

"Thanks," Nigella squeaked back. She made her way over to the bolts of fabric. "Can I take a few of these fabrics? The purple and tan? Do you mind? I want to try and update the Miss Fit's Dollies uniform."

"Sure," Ophelia said.

"Thanks. The one I have now is kinda on the Monday side."

With a 'here you go,' a 'do you need a sewing needle and some thread,' and a 'I think you mean mundane instead of Monday' followed by a 'are you sure you've got it all,' the little girl, overloaded with tweed and cotton bundles, tottered her way back down the hall to apartment 7D.

*   *   *

"Hi, sweetheart, how was your—dear Lord what is all that?" Gabby Gellar's voice drifted out into the hall.

"Ophelia gave it to me. I'm gonna make a new uniform."

"Nigella, are you sure—"

"Yes, Mom. It will go toward a creativity patch."

"You already have seven of those."

"One can never be too creative...or crafty," Nigella quipped, another one of Mynah Moriel's reminders Ophelia had taught her.

Her mother sputtered for three point five seconds until finally saying, "I don't care for that Ophelia. You know she ruined my Christmas cookies that one year."

106

"She has an allergy to nutmeg, Mom."

"They didn't have any nutmeg in them," Mrs. Gellar pouted. "Nigella…" she added.

"What, Mom?" Nigella turned her tone to one with a little more innocence to it. She may have only been eight, but she was able to read her mother on an eighth-grade level.

"I got the most interesting call from Miss Fit about Ebony and an unfortunate collision with good taste. Care to fill me in?"

"Uh, well, as always, Mom, you may want to take a seat." The kitchen chair gave a drawn-out groan as Nigella dragged it across the tiles. "It was my fault. Ophelia had nothing to do with it," she said to try and immediately squash her mother's ensuing argument and to save her friend.

*   *   *

For the record, Ophelia had caused all that trouble: the ruined Christmas cookies, Mr. Gellar almost being fired, and Mrs. Beezle's night of insomnia. It all boiled down to who was recounting the event.

Truth be told, Ophelia was not allergic to nutmeg, real or phantom varieties. What Mrs. Gellar had not surmised was that she had in fact used salt in place of sugar when she made those cookies. Long days of shopping, wrapping, and decorating, all while managing a three-year-old Nigella, had made her a little careless even on the big details.

Ophelia could have told her the truth, sure, but Mrs. Gellar had a bit of an ego. Not to mention that in order to tell her the cookies were made with salt, Ophelia would have had to taste one. Why hang both Mrs. Gellar's baking reputation and Ophelia's tastebuds out to dry when both could have been spared thanks to a little glimpse into the future?

For Mr. Gellar, what he had forgotten was that the suit jacket Ophelia had intentionally accidentally doused with red wine was missing the invitation to his boss' benefit. The jacket he ended up wearing instead had harbored it all along. He had placed it in there for safe keeping when he first received the invitation and, like many, soon became preoccupied with life's more pressing matters.

Had Mr. Gellar come to the benefit without the invitation, he would have been turned away. His boss, best described as a grinch, would have fired him over such a petty thing, but you probably already deduced that. It had been easier to run up the dry-cleaning bill than try to explain how Ophelia had known what she had known.

Concerning Mrs. Beezle, well, shortly after Ophelia had moved into the Vermont Village, she immediately began framing a wall and installing hanging racks for her wardrobe. This racket would carry on late into the night. Mrs. Beezle could vouch for this as she heard every bang, clang, and thwack through her walls. As one might imagine, this generated a lack of sleep.

One night, at 3:32 a.m., Mrs. Beezle became fed up with the sound of hammering. Throwing off her covers, and feeling lightheaded and fatigued, she stomped to the kitchen to call the police and complain about her disturbed peace. She was halfway through dialing when she happened to notice one of the stove's red dials set slightly askew, yet the burner did not emit even the faintest of electric blue flames. She must not have completely turned it off after removing the kettle for her evening cup of tea.

Seven minutes and thirty-one seconds more and her goose would have been, unfortunately, cooked. She quietly turned off the gas and then proceeded to finish dialing.

There was a brief moment later, in her sleep deprived stupor after she had cracked a window to drink in the fresh cold night air, that a thought began to form. Perhaps Ophelia's raucous renovations that night were not a happenstance. The rumination, however, was fleeting, chased away by her already long laundry list of grievances she harbored for her neighbor. Every now and then, this thought would try to emerge again, only to be squashed once more because, as was already stated in the prologue, she really did not like Ophelia O'Leary.

Nigella thought Ophelia had some sixth sense she kept cloaked in misfortunes and bad luck, like some sort of magic. (Sometimes the fanciful stories concocted out of a child's imagination can be spot on, you know.) Most others wrote it off as dumb luck. Be that as it may, whether a coincidence of clashing misfortunes and luck or something a little more, it all boiled down to how each individual chose to see the situation and its respective outcome. Mrs. Gellar saw Ophelia as a bad influence, Mr. Gellar as a klutz, and Mrs. Beezle as a rabble-rouser. Ophelia could simply not give a flying fig. Those closest to her, like Delaney, couldn't help but think of Ophelia as self-centered and petty, for it seemed that she did as she pleased, even at the expense of leaving others in emotional shambles. These assumptions, Ophelia would admit to herself, did smart maybe a fig or two.

Chapter 8

In Which We Look in on a Couple of Block(ed) Heads

The house just isn't the same, Delaney thought glumly. She burrowed herself deeper in her oversized sweater, a mix of deep red and dark magenta stripes flecked with sparks of fire-engine red. Drawing in a deep breath of the thickly knitted cowl neck, she was still able to pick up the faintest notes of vanilla and lily, her grandmother's perfume.

Yes, indeed things were not the same in the house with the address of One Partridge Parkway. Gone were the frilly white-lace curtains that had hung about the windows all around the front room, replaced with sleek roman shades and ninety-six-inch long tan drapes. Decades-old floral furniture had moved on to make room for a warm charcoal-gray couch with matching loveseat and dark denim wingback chair, Delaney's favorite spot to sit and ponder.

Unfortunately, the powers of inspiration seemed to be on the fritz, most likely drained by all the lights carefully woven about the balsam fir. Delaney sat with downcast eyes at the open folder and its strewn papers, each containing no more than a fragment of a thought or two.

One more snowball, and I'll be good to go, she lied to herself, picking up the cookie and popping it into her mouth. It left a small speckled trail of powdered sugar from the plate to the lower right corner of the leather ottoman.

Okay. Aaaannnnd GO!!! She commanded her brain, but only a couple useless thoughts trickled out, redundancies of what she had already written and something about remembering to buy fabric softener.

"Why is this so hard?" she whined, quickly popping snowball number fourteen into her mouth.

"You're thinking about it too much is all," replied her boyfriend, Calum Dooley. He pulled his gaze from the back window, having momentarily allowed himself to be mesmerized by the snowflakes pressed against the panes, admiring their intricate patterns of crystallized water. His expression was relaxed, always giving people the impression he was not getting enough sleep.

He clicked and clacked as the wooden heels of his suede boots connected with the cherry wood floor. "Let me see what you have so far," he said, seating himself on the right arm of the denim chair and reaching toward the scrawled-upon papers.

"Nooooo…" Delaney said in a feeble voice and quickly scooped up the papers, clutching them to her chest. "It all sounds stupid. Do it for me," she pleaded, employing a damsel in distress pout while adding a batting or two of her eyelashes. "You're the writer."

"Del, y—Jeeze it is sweltering over here! How are you not a puddle on the floor!?" Calum exclaimed. Nimble fingers unbuttoned the light gray, double-breasted admiral's sweater, hands shedding it to reveal his slight frame. "Phew!" The navy and red plaid shirt was discolored near the armpits. Calum fanned his underarms furiously, the musk of his deodorant working overtime.

"Del, this book is yours, and I think it should be all yours, from start to finish. If I wrote the intro, it would never be good enough. I'm not privy to what it meant to you to learn your family's recipes or invent new ones." He eyed one of her newer creations on the cocktail table, a snowball cookie, half of it dipped in white chocolate with a hazelnut and candied cranberry filling.

"Sales would be lackluster because of it. Then you would resent me for my good-natured, but rather valueless, attempt." Calum's gaze focused off into the room, nowhere specific, urgency flooded his voice like that of a child who had been caught sneaking a peek at their Christmas present a day and a half too early. "Then we—we would grow distant, tension boiling and roiling between us, because that's the nature of tension, you see. Oh, and then you would kick me out, fulfilling my dad's prophecy of me becoming a starving artist. And you, *you* would despise yourself for your rash and callous decision and gorge yourself on platter after platter of these tasty, tasty snowballs until you ballooned out and sported a permanent powdered sugar mustache." He popped an aforementioned cookie into his mouth. "Mmmm. Scho, you schee," he concluded betwixt and between chews, "mmm good. Um…where was I? Oh! It would be a very bad thing."

She looked back with skepticism punctuated with a raised eyebrow. The left corner of her mouth twitched up and down until she could no longer keep the smile at bay. "Ha, a very convincing argument. You paint a vivid picture," she said, a chuckle mixed with her words. "I can't believe you came up with that entire story off the top of your head. Soooooo, why don't you put it to good use and write my prologue?" she beamed back at him, eyebrows waggling up and down.

"Apparently, the picture I painted wasn't vivid enough," Calum said. "Let me start from the beginning. If I wro—"

Delaney playfully pushed Calum on the shoulder but misjudged the force she put behind it. Calum went down to the floor and sprawled about like a pile of matches.

"I'm so sorry." She checked over the arm of the chair to make sure her boyfriend was okay. Seeing only his ego and the lower quadrant of his tush were bruised, she let out a belly laugh.

"I'm still falling head over heels for you," Calum said.

"Pfft!" Delaney sputtered, taken aback at how cheesy the line was, wanting to hand him a cracker but fearing he wouldn't catch the joke.

Calum drew himself up from the floor to kiss Delaney. His knees comically wobbled and knocked. His scrawny legs appeared unable to bolster the one hundred and thirty pounds and two ounces of man atop of them.

"Do your intro. The inspiration will come to you." He punctuated his advice with a peck on the lips.

"I know," she said sweetly. "I was playing with you," she half-lied. "I needed a break from all the thinking of bad ideas." She smirked back at him a little defeated, realizing literary gold had not taken up occupancy in her mind during Calum's melodramatic performance. She was eighty-four point seven-two percent sure that very incident would wind up in his column in the not-too-distant future.

Delaney buried her face in her hands and heaved a heavy sigh. Blinking past her fingers, she brushed her hair away from her face and smiled back up at Calum. A nonverbal fib that she would be okay.

He reciprocated with a similar smile that seemed to say he believed her.

"How is the column coming?"

He sighed as he haphazardly folded his sweater, it now being his turn to half-lie; the first part being the lie, and the second part being the boldfaced truth. "Uh, almost done. I just have to work on the conclusion…and the middle…and the beginning. I'll let you see it when I'm done," he said, answering the question that danced in Delaney's chocolate brown eyes. He was not always so keen to have her read his work, fearing she would tell him his writing was no good. (This never actually happened, but the anxious part of Calum reminded him daily that there was a first time for everything.) In truth, Calum struggled to take a compliment, assuming Delaney was being polite to spare his feelings. "Which better be soon because the deadline is in two days." He put on a pained smile complete with gritted teeth.

Calum had recently been promoted with a new column at the *Nollag Blow-By-Blow Bugle*. Some would say he was living the dream, almost twenty-four and moving up on the journalistic ladder, not unlike the spry squirrel that did gymnastics for nuts at the Nollag Public Park. Many tended to forget, however, that every accomplishment comes with its own backstory.

Calum's journey was random and sporadic. Instead of a natural progression from grunt work newbie to covering an uneventful event piece to journalist to column writer, Calum went from a degree in accounting to substitute teaching to a corporate job in advertising to covering uneventful events and accidentally tripping, stumbling, and concussing his head on the miraculous opportunity to write a column. Accidents, good and bad, tended to happen to Calum relatively often.

Delaney was another of these accidents, and he loved her with everything he had. It had taken long enough for them to get together. That blame or credit, depending on who one asked, could be attributed to Ophelia. But that did not matter now as the journey, and the wait, had been well worth it all.

"If you'll excuse me, I'm going to change into something a little drier," he said, giving up on folding the sweater and balling it up in his hands. "You know, Petunia and Greg won't be here for another half hour. Try to take another crack at it," Calum suggested as he entered the front hall to go up the stairs. "Or…." He stepped back into the room and attempted to seductively drape the sweater over his left shoulder. "We could make out or whatever. I don't know," he said in a deadpan tone accented with a grin.

Delaney made a sound that was part laugh and part snort. "Go write."

"Alright," Calum said melodramatically, followed by a heavy sigh. "But…your loss." He turned, shoulders slumped, and head hung low to punctuate his disappointment.

After Calum was out of the room, Delaney kicked back in her denim chair and stared around the room. So much had changed since her grandfather had turned over the keys to her at the start of the year. The house had simply become too big and empty for Edwin to see the logic of one man residing in it. Though Delaney and Calum had offered, asked, and then begged him to stay, he declined, saying the Elegant Arbors Residence for the Elderly and Active would be better suited for him. "I need people my own age to play with," he had joked. Delaney and Ophelia still visited him every other week…on separate, opposite weeks, of course.

History and moments could still be found about the home, despite its updated decor. Case in point, the long table along the wall had been built by Grandpa Edwin. Its espresso color and brass finishings still looked like new. It still had Edwin's 1:32 scale model of a Sopwith Camel displayed on it.

A collection of Charles Dickens' works rested on the seat of a chair near the back window adjacent to a fully stocked bookcase. This was one of several. Delaney's grandfather was an avid collector of classic literature and stories. Many first editions were kept in the small library upstairs, what used to be Delaney's father's childhood room and now served as Calum's office. Grandpa Edwin had scoured the world in search of the editions. Most, however, had been gifts from his now late wife, Mildred. Given that his new space was significantly smaller, he rotated a portion of his collection from the house to his apartment every three months.

With every reminder of her grandfather, there was an equal representation of her grandmother, from her favorite painting, a simple autumn scene using vibrant pops of color, to the red wool coat that still hung in the hall. Even the stockings that Mildred had knitted fifty years ago, which now hung off the mantle, were a reminder of her. It both warmed and hurt Delaney's heart, eighty-nine percent and eleven percent respectively, for Delaney, like many, had lost her grandmother too soon.

A small, four by six framed photo was perched on the cherry wood mantle. It captured Delaney at the age of five. She was placing an ornament of an angel on the tree. Her grandmother was bent over to Delaney's height, her hand lovingly placed against her granddaughter's back. Both wore beaming smiles that rivaled the brilliant lights that had been draped on the tree's branches.

Now, it is said that a picture is worth a thousand words. If one were to appraise the photo, some of those aforementioned thousand words may be "Christmas," "Love," or "Touching."

Depending on who you ask, "Misdirected Frustration" with a sprinkling of "Favoritism" were also in the mix. A picture only captures one moment in time. This particular snapshot was altogether unlike the events leading up to what ensued after....

Chapter 9

In Which There Is a Rattle and a Rattled Angel

Seventeen years, eleven months, four weeks, two days, and twenty-two hours ago at One Partridge Parkway, the same grandfather clock that resided against the east wall in the front hall chimed to let the household know the time was 6:45 p.m. on Christmas Eve. A very small five-year-old Delaney O'Leary plucked a delicate looking angel from a box of ornaments comprised of silver, gold, and red mercury glass sphere and spindle ornaments. Her pudgy fingers lightly cupped the angel, and her wide eyes watched as the white lights on the tree created a glow against the face and halo of the bisque porcelain ornament.

"All right, sweetheart, now be careful, and gently, *gently*, put the angel on the tree," Mildred O'Leary instructed.

"She's so pretty, Grandma," Delaney replied, still in awe. The ornament was perfection to her, from the sweet blushed expression of its face to the shiny black hair that was like hers.

The angel was clad in a robe made of a heavy cream fabric with touches of gold accents along the cuffs and base of the skirt and was sinched at the waist with a gold chord. The rest of the garment was covered in a delicate filigree design with a hair-fine gold thread that resembled several symmetrical snowflakes. The folded wings were also sculpted in porcelain, nearly as long as the angel herself.

Mimicking the angel's pose, Delaney raised her arms to reach a branch higher up, a place she deemed dignified for the ornament. Mildred did the same, her hand acting as a net (just in case). As the angel had found her place amongst the winking lights, both wore ear to ear grins, Delaney because she was tall enough to decorate the tree this year and Mildred for the memory the two of them were creating. Mildred moved her hand away from the ornament to lovingly rest it on Delaney's back.

Click. FOOM! Clink.

The camera flashed abruptly, momentarily startling and blinding grandmother and granddaughter. Once vision was restored, the angel was no longer in Delaney's hands nor on the tree. Instead, it lay on the floor…in several pieces.

"Oh, no!" Delaney cried, her lower lip pouting.

"Ophelia!" Mildred glared at her newly adopted granddaughter over the tops of her spectacles, which had slipped almost to the very tip of her straight thin nose, giving her a severe look that bordered along bothered librarian and ticked off teacher territory. "Look at what you've done!" She splayed her arms out to encompass the area the thirteen pieces of the angel now occupied on the floor. "Just…just." Her words were reduced to sputters.

"Calm down, Millie," Edwin O'Leary chimed in, removing himself from a Sherlock Holmes mystery, his fifth within the hour.

"But, Edwin," she blustered. Her right hand moved to fidget with one of the charms on the bracelet she wore, a heart that was missing a bit of its gold plating.

Having become well-tuned to Mildred's tones and inflections, Edwin knew Sherlock's big reveal would have to wait. He picked up a small five and a half by five and a half piece of cardstock from the side table to mark his page. It read "Marriage Certificate" on one side and contained an official-looking announcement of Edwin's and Mildred's nuptials on the other. Mildred found it sweet. Edwin found that it helped him remember their anniversary, which kept him out of the doghouse.

"But nothing." He gently set his book down and stood up. "First, it's Christmas," Edwin explained, crossing the room toward Mildred. "Second, she didn't do it on purpose, and third, you're sixty-five and she's seven and a half. Think about it." He looked into her russet brown eyes and massaged the back of her neck with the least of his arthritic hands. (The left if you're curious.) Mildred being a statuesque six feet tall and Edwin measuring five foot five and seven sixteenth inches proved to make it a bit of a reach for him.

"Actually, I'm seven point six," Ophelia offered a correction, still clutching the camera. It partially covered the image on the front of her sweater.

"You're not helping, my dear." Edwin made a feeble attempt to bottle up a chuckle as he come over to Ophelia and ducked down to give her a one-armed hug. The lines around his mouth pulled back to reveal a broad grin. His forehead crinkled and creased simultaneously. "You better hope you got one heck of a picture there, kid," he whispered into her left ear. His words conjured a coy smile on the girl's face.

"Don't worry. I did," she muttered in, what many would consider, an overly confident tone. "Sorry," she added audibly.

Mildred stifled a grumble because Edwin was right — ill-feelings had no place during the holidays. Instead, she made her way to the closet for a brush and dustpan to collect what remained of the fallen angel.

The fact was not that she disliked Ophelia, not in the least. Who could dislike an orphan? *Orphan was the wrong word*, Mildred remedied her thought. *She wasn't one anymore. Not since a few days ago.*

Adoption was not the issue, especially if her son and daughter-in-law did not want to try and bring another child into the world. Mildred could not blame them. Once had been enough for her when it had come to childbirth. There was a sliver of her that would always resent her son for putting her through forty-six hours of labor. The same would go for Edwin. Arthritis had set in shortly after those almost two days of experiencing his wife's iron-grip, for which he harbored no ill-will.

The reason stemmed from the unconventional dynamic her presence created within the family. *Ophelia was older than Delaney*, Mildred had argued to herself. *Shouldn't Éamon and Alicia have chosen a baby instead? Wasn't that the way it should be done? That seemed like the natural progression of things if there was going to be a sibling for Delaney – my sweet and innocent little angel.* She didn't want to think it, but Ophelia was unconventional. She wasn't *really* an O'Leary. She was, well, to put it lightly, she was unexpected.

Never mind the fact that Delaney had told her grandmother how she had been allowed to find her new sibling. The idea of a five-year-old having that sort of responsibility was absolutely outrageous to Mildred. Older children could be very mean. Older children could take advantage of her granddaughter.

Ophelia's presence, in a certain sense, rushed things. Here was this little seven-year-old girl with her own mannerisms and thoughts that, at most times, clashed with her own sensibilities. For instance, Ophelia's need to taste test the cookie batter. "The creative process is all about the journey, not the end," she had said, quoting number seven of Mynah's reminders, before explaining she had merely been making sure there was an appropriate ratio of three parts dough to two parts chocolate chips – the golden-brown ratio with respect to chocolate chip cookies…apparently not everyone knew that.

The little red-headed spitfire was a jumbled puzzle of favorite foods, colors, activities, hobbies, and random trivia that needed to be carefully fitted together to form a cohesive picture. But the pieces did not fall into place so easily, and Mildred had decided that she was much too old for this. (What she really meant was that she did not want to.)

And when she did try, she would catch herself forcing pieces together that clearly did not make sense, such as the dress that Ophelia wore today. It used to be a pristine emerald velvet dress that came to the knee. It came with a little cardigan that had a thin gold ribbon running through the white yarn and was adorned with small star-shaped buttons. "Used to be" were the operative words.

Now, in Mildred's opinion, it had become an arts and crafts project gone awry. Ophelia had pushed the envelope when she decided to modify the already perfectly lovely dress. In fact, it appeared she had pushed the envelope over a cliff into a bucket of glitter and colored cotton balls.

When Ophelia showcased her updates to the dress, Mildred's lungs momentarily forgot how to draw breath while her heart lodged itself somewhere in the vicinity of her throat. The frilly skirt now sported extra frills of varying green felts cut into triangular shapes. The cardigan and top of the dress popped with fluorescent pinks, oranges, and yellows from small cotton balls and were accented with metallic red, blue, and gold sequins. Ophelia had removed the star buttons and threaded them through the extracted gold ribbon to tie up a portion of her hair into a loose bun. Mildred took the whispered advice of her husband to "grin and bear it."

The dress had been a quick save a few days prior, purchased in the nick of time before Frankie's Fancy Frilly Frocks, known as the department store with the best dresses for your dainty darling, had closed for that day. Her jaw had slammed hard into the floor of the front parlor, leaving a figurative dent, when her daughter-in-law crossed the threshold with a little bundle of joy that was considerably bigger than twenty-four inches tall and twelve point six pounds. It prompted a conversation of urgent whispers in the dining room between Edwin and Mildred, leaving Edwin mere minutes to go and exchange the dress, originally purchased in size three to six months.

"Here ya go, Gramma? Mildred? Millie? Mrs. O'Leary?" Ophelia said, placing a small trash bin in front of Mildred, so she could empty the porcelain shards into it.

Mildred stopped mid-sweep to ponder this. "Grandma" would make the most sense, but all her prior thoughts had occluded a quick answer.

"Yes. Grandma," Mildred finally piped up, dropping the bits of ornament into the can. She began to feel ashamed about her feelings toward Ophelia, though they would still hang about in the corners of her mind for years to come. They would become slightly less audible, at least. Slightly.

"Mm-kay, Gramma," Ophelia said meekly, which, despite Mildred having only spent a collective twelve hours and fourteen minutes in the same room with her new granddaughter, seemed rather out of character. Ophelia scooped up the canister and waddled it back into the kitchen. Edwin took the brush and dustpan from his wife and replaced them back in the closet.

"Grandma, can we open a present tonight? Pleeeease?" Delaney begged using her full arsenal. She batted her eyelashes, simultaneously willing her eyes to sparkle and twinkle. She accompanied this first blow with a pouted lower lip and a chubby cheek pressed innocently against her raised shoulder. Mildred never stood a chance.

She smiled back sweetly, unable to suppress it. "Okay, but only one, and the rest tomorrow with the ones Santa will bring you." She actually would have let her granddaughter open more, but, thankfully, one was all it took for the little tyke to count herself satisfied and lucky.

"Santa," Delaney laughed. She was willing to play along with the idea that St. Nick, centuries-old by now, would travel the globe in one night, dispensing gifts to good children, whether by choice or because of veiled threats of coal. She didn't say anything to the contrary because she didn't want to hurt her grandparents' feelings. Also, presents were presents.

"Don't tell your Dad, okay?" Edwin said to Delaney. "Your Grandma and I never let him open presents early. So, you better do it now, before your parents get back from their holiday party."

Delaney pulled an imaginary zipper across her lips to indicate they were securely sealed.

Ophelia poked her head from around the entrance to the kitchen. "Wait. We get to open a present now!?" she asked incredulously.

Mildred and Edwin nodded together and then grimaced when the same realization hit them too late. They had been so fixated on exchanging the dress that it had slipped both their minds to switch out all the presents they had purchased and wrapped for their assumed infant granddaughter.

The girls were already digging underneath the expansive tree for a gift to open, little Mary-Jane clad feet kicking about. Brightly colored ribbons and paper with Santa Clauses and glitter flew about, settling in an explosive mess on the floor.

"A kitty!!" Delaney squealed, taking in all of its glorious cuteness. She wrapped the toy in her arms; the yellow ribbon around its neck creased from the overly enthusiastic embrace. "Thank you, thank you, thank you, thank you, Grandma and Grandpa!"

"Oh," Ophelia said, stopping short after she lifted the lid off a silver and blue box. She tilted her head to the side and peered down at its contents. Ever so gingerly, she reached down to pull out a small silver rattle. There were tiny purple flowers around the circumference of the bulb, Forget Me Nots were Ophelia's best guess. Below the rattle, a thin purple ribbon held in place a jingle bell. Ophelia gave it a good shake. "Hmm…" she thought aloud. "Well, it works."

"Ophelia," Edwin began.

The little girl blankly looked in his direction, eyebrows pulled up in expectation.

"I'm sorry, dear," Mildred interjected. She stepped forward, awkwardly wringing her hands together. "We—we honestly thought you would…be…smaller." She looked back at her husband quizzically, shoulders shrugging a little. She was unsure if such an explanation was satisfactory for a child of seven point six years.

"No," Ophelia said, a smile pulling at the corners of her mouth. "It's the thought that counts. Really. Besides, I think I can make this work." She gave the bell one more jingle with her left index finger and looked at it as if it were already one of her most prized possessions.

Edwin gave a silent sigh of relief, oblivious to the fact that the gift Ophelia had selected had been buried beneath the rest of the parcels. What's more, it had no tag attached, having become dislodged when he had carried the gifts from upstairs and deposited them under the tree earlier that day. The label was now peeking from the bottom of the heel of his right loafer. These were details that did not escape Mildred's keen eye, though. In her carefully constructed world of bisque porcelain, the mishaps weren't quite buffing out. In the presence of such a chaotic spirit, Mildred wondered if something else was at play.

Indeed, Ophelia was unconventional and unexpected. What some tend to forget is that unconventional and unexpected can also come with its own magical agenda.

Chapter 10

In Which Mildred O'Leary Offers Some Parting Gifts

"Hey, angel," Calum said, coming downstairs. He held up a small ivory colored box.

"What?" Delaney said pulling her focus away from the photograph and out of the memory of Christmas way past.

"Oh, uh, not you, Angel, but angel, angel." He walked into the room and set the box on the coffee table between a small plate of peppermint fudge and a bowl of freshly baked everything bagel chips with extra caraway seeds and garlic flakes. Delaney kept this box on her nightstand, having shared its origin story and its significance with Calum the first day they moved into One Partridge Parkway. "Not that you're not an angel, Del. I was talking about the actual angel for the tree. And then when I initially said 'angel,' and you thought I said 'Angel'—as—in—" he sputtered to a stop and attempted to reboot. "What are you thinking about?

"Grandma," Delaney said, looking back forlornly at the picture. "I miss her." She punctuated her thought with a heavy sigh, and the corners of her eyes started to glisten with tears.

"I know you do, but…you have a lot of happy memories with her. I know that it's not the same." Calum kneeled beside her chair and gave Delaney a comforting hug.

"Then why do I only remember the sad ones the best?" She pulled Calum closer to her, burying her face against his shoulder as the day of her grandmother's passing flickered on in her mind like an old movie projector.

"Hey, Del, don't cry," Calum said. "I mean, you can cry if you want," he amended.

Delaney lifted her face to meet Calum's. "I'll be fine," she sniffled, chasing the unhappiness from her face and redirecting her focus from the movie in her head back to Calum. "Sorry. I got your shirt wet." She pointed at the darkened spots that dotted the right shoulder of his heather gray shirt.

"Eh," he said nonchalantly, shrugging it off and making a face that was supposed to say, 'No big deal' but instead came off as 'I had some bad fish.' "Do you want to be alone?" Calum finally asked.

Delaney did not immediately respond. Her attention was back to the photo on the mantle. "Hm?" she hummed.

"That would be a 'yes?'" He got to his feet. "I'm gonna finish changing" was all he said before kissing Delaney on the forehead and making his way upstairs again. Delaney quietly listened to the sound of his steps fading away with each of the thirteen stairs leading to the second floor.

Delaney blinked three times, tearing her eyes away from the photo. She brushed her hair out of her face and caught sight of the box patiently waiting on the table.

Picking up the little package and setting it in her lap, she lifted its lid. The box exhaled stale air that faintly smelled of last year's Christmas tree. Within the folds of buttery, pale-green satin rested an angel. She was wholly unlike her predecessor from the photograph, handcrafted from a block of sturdy maple. The wings were painted an opulent pearl. The wavy, flowing hair was jet black, accented with fine traces of navy blue. The gown she wore was made of silk and was almost identical to the original angel's, down to the gold filigree snowflakes stitched onto the skirt. The face was different. What had amazed Delaney was the resemblance it had to her grandmother when she was younger, about twenty-seven.

"How did she do that?" Delaney wondered out loud, holding it up by its ribbon and watching the ornament slowly turn in front of her; the baby blue glitter twinkled along the etchings of the carved feathers. As if by magic or miracle, the wooden angel had appeared the year after the tragic demise of the porcelain one. She never admitted it, but Delaney would not discount the possibility that Ophelia, even at seven or eight years old, had the ingenuity to fashion the ornament.

Silently, Delaney left her denim chair and her unwritten introduction. Her thick socks muffled the thuds of her feet as she crossed the room to the tree. The balsam fir tree was set in the exact same place as where her grandparents had set up their trees for the last fifty-seven years. She hung up the angel with care.

As Delaney stood back to admire the tree, her mind loosened its grip on the memory it tried to hold back. She had a bad habit of unpacking this particular memory from almost six years ago. Without hesitation, the switch to her mind's projector was flipped. Roll film….

*   *   *

The memory was set six years, ten days, twenty-one hours, and thirty minutes ago. It had been an abnormally mild winter, and Nollag was lacking that certain sprinkling of magic. Delaney would have been the first to express her displeasure at the possibility of a green Christmas.

A city without its customary blanket of snow, however, was the furthest thing from her mind that night. She sat in the small lobby of the hospital's fifth floor in the east wing. Absentmindedly, her fingers plucked at a stray string that had come undone on the seafoam green upholstery of the seat she occupied. The chair was uncomfortable, the foam of the seat having lost its resiliency from hosting many a worried and fretting family member or friend of the hospital's patients over the years.

The room was a cool, sky-blue color. A twenty-four by thirty-six gold framed picture of a white sand beach and a palm tree hung behind her. In the three weeks that Delaney had sat in that lobby, she found it did very little in inducing a sense of calm. Of course, it wouldn't have, would it? Not when Delaney knew her grandmother was dying. Not when she was not permitted to see her.

That ordeal alone was all she could take, and even that may have been a lie. She was seventeen and juggling several crises at once. She was losing her grandmother, the Christmas traditions she

132

shared with Mildred turning from cozy to empty. She might also be losing her home and the future she thought she had somewhat figured out.

Delaney was a senior at the Bells of St. Mary's Catholic school that year and had initially looked forward to graduation. Her plan had been to go to the College of Nollag in the fall. This way she could still be close to her family. Delaney was by nature the quintessential homebody. Her family, on the other hand, had different plans.

Éamon O'Leary had received an opportunity of a lifetime from Bing University, home of the Leaping Lords – a tenure track position with a significant pay bump at one of the most prestigious schools in the country to do what he was most passionate about: teach mathematics. The job wasn't his quite yet. He and his wife, Alicia, were currently visiting the university for Éamon's second interview.

Alicia preferred the notion of living in the smaller city of Glory, located two hours southwest of Nollag and where the university was located. It offered a little less of the hustle and bustle. Should Éamon accept the position, which started the next academic year, she planned to do some adjunct work at Clooney Community College until a full-time position opened up. She, for the time being, kept these feelings and plans to herself, so as not to add any unnecessary pressure to her husband's decision.

Delaney, in a way, did the same. She did not want anything to change, but it seemed that life was dragging her to a crossroads that forked and fragmented itself into an infinite number of paths. Her mind obsessed over how she could control the uncontrollable fate that time seemed to be accelerating towards, playing a game of mental hopscotch between her family scattering and her ailing grandmother.

"But, Grandma, I'm here. Why can't I come in to see you?" Delaney recalled herself saying not eleven minutes ago at the hospital payphone.

There was a hesitation on the other end as Mildred drew in an audible breath before speaking. "Honey, I don't want you to see me like this. I know it doesn't seem fair, but I want to protect you." Since the cancer had worsened, Delaney and Ophelia had been barred from seeing Mildred, only able to check-in with phone calls.

In an effort to relieve the tense emotions of frustration and sadness that coursed through her, Delaney scrunched and flexed her fingers and toes, silently counting to ten during the bouts of awkward silence in their conversation.

Delaney wanted to tell Mildred her way of protecting her granddaughters was cruel, that it wasn't fair. Actually, what *wasn't* fair was Mildred had relented and was permitting Ophelia, *just* Ophelia, to come in that night, who at that moment was rushing down to the hospital. Mildred had said it was to have a serious talk, but that didn't sit well with Delaney. Mildred and Ophelia had never been close. If anyone deserved to have a face-to-face heart-to-heart with Mildred, it most certainly was her. Instead, she was still viewed as a child who needed to be shielded from the harsh reality of things. These thoughts were nocked like arrows against her vocal cords, ready to spew her truth her mouth. But she held her fire for fear of upsetting her grandmother. *One…two…three…four….*

134

The truth was, Mildred could not reconcile that Delaney was capable of handling the heaviness of the situation and the fact that she was seventeen and not simply seven. Not unlike her granddaughter, fear prevented her from seeing just how unreasonable she was being. "Sweetie," she said to Delaney, breaking the lull in the conversation, "I'm afraid I have to go. The doctor just walked in. I'll talk to you later. I love you."

*   *   *

She didn't remember hanging up the phone, nor could she recall walking back into the waiting room and taking a seat, her mind too preoccupied with trying to rationalize Mildred's choices. She began to go deeper and deeper into herself, not hearing the click clacking of black leather boots against the linoleum tiles in the main hallway.

"Dee?" she heard her name called as if from far off in the distance. "Delaney," the voice said again, punctuating it with a couple finger snaps in front of her face.

The world rushed back, and Delaney was still without a satisfactory solution to her dilemma. Sounds amplified and clarified. Blurred colors and images came back to crisp shapes and detail.

Ophelia stood in front of the girl; a look of concern overlaid with annoyance was drawn upon her face. For a split second, Delaney compared her own appearance to her sister's. Without fail, not a thing about Ophelia was out of place. Her face freshly washed. Her long trench coat without a crease. Her hair was pulled back into a neatly knotted ponytail of thick red curls. *So much for rushing down....*

"Are you okay?" Ophelia asked, knowing full and well the answer to her question.

"She said she wanted to see you…and not me."

"I know," Ophelia said, treading lightly, "that's what she said on the phone. Delaney, for what it's worth, I don't think that she doesn't want to see you. Not really."

Delaney stared at a worn spot on the carpet. Her eyes squinted and lips scrunched to the left side of her face, her mind in confounded thought, unwilling to accept Ophelia's offering of consolation as anything but worthless. Her own words "not me" reverberated about in her head and fueled irrational emotions. *Why does she want to see Ophelia? Why won't she change her mind? Doesn't she love me? Why?*

Before she departed the waiting room, Ophelia tried to let her sister know that their parents were on their way back from Glory. "They should be here in forty-six minutes."

If Delaney heard her, she did not respond.

"Dee, did you…," but Ophelia let the question dissolve.

Seeing that her sister was otherwise engaged, Ophelia knew that she must not dawdle. She adjusted the bag slung over her right shoulder and began to walk down the hall. Time was not going to grace the O'Leary family with its company for much longer.

When Mildred had called, asking her granddaughter to come to the hospital, Ophelia had been ready to depart the moment she picked the phone up in the middle of its second ring. She had just finished making a sandwich for a then eleven-year-old Timothy Dickens, whom she was babysitting. (In actuality, the snack had always been intended for her grandfather once she arrived at the hospital.) Once she had hung up the phone, she played out a convincing scene for young Timothy, calling a taxicab, rushing around the apartment, throwing on her boots and coat, and nearly "forgetting" her bag full of necessities for that night, which included a tape recorder she had pulled from storage that morning. Still, hearing the gravity and the sadness in her grandmother's voice spurred on her performance. In under two point two minutes, she had gathered her things, swept her hair up into a ponytail, and ushered Timothy down the hall to Mrs. Beezle's residence with a stern, yet cryptic, implore not to let her make him any hot cocoa on her stove.

After rapping on the frame of the door to Room Three, Ophelia walked in without waiting to hear the usual "Come in" from either of her grandparents. She had taken two steps into the room before being taken aback by the state of her grandmother. Mildred had kept Ophelia and Delaney from visiting for three weeks and a day. From then until now, in Ophelia's mind, it felt as if Mildred's statuesque frame had withered to a fragile shell of her former self overnight. Something cringed in the pit of Ophelia's stomach as she took in the beeping machines, the nasal cannula, and the IV that left a purple bruise on her grandmother's forearm.

"Why don't you go get something to eat?" Mildred said to Edwin in a low purr of a voice. He blinked his droopy eyelids, confused. When the question had finally churned through the wheels and cogs of his brain, he solemnly shook his head back and forth in answer. He seemed to root himself deeper into the chair by Mildred's bedside, cupping her tiny, frail hand in his large, chapped ones and pulled it closer so he could kiss it. His hands trembled.

"Ophelia. Make him go," Mildred tried to suppress the wet that threatened to rain from the corners of her eyes.

"I'm not hungry," Edwin choked out in what could best be described as grumpy old man voice.

Never one to shy away from an argument, especially when she was given the rare "Grandma Said So" card to play, Ophelia simpered and drew in a breath. Instead of backing Mildred up, however, she produced a liverwurst sandwich with one leaf of lettuce on seeded rye along with a hard bound collection of *The Brothers Grimm Fairy Tales*.

Never one to pass up a good read, Edwin took both sandwich and book from his granddaughter. "I'm not going anywhere," he said to Mildred with a weak smile before moving to the rocking chair over by the window. He placed the sandwich on top of the heater to warm it and cracked the book open to the table of contents.

Mildred sported half of a grimace. What she had wanted was to have a private conversation with her granddaughter. She knew, though, the next best thing was to have Edwin's bump of a nose buried in the pages of "Sleeping Beauty" and "The Pied Piper." He would be swept away by the fairy tales, practically oblivious to the world around, and he would not be tempted to go against her wishes and try to sneak Delaney into Hospital Room Three.

In truth, she knew he would not have left her side; not now, not when it really mattered. Edwin loved his wife and respected her wishes even if he did not fully agree with them. Although, deep down, even unbeknownst to her, she secretly wished he would rebel against her request. Her grimace changed directions to reflect the smirk Ophelia still wore across her own face, silently saying "good work" to her.

"Is she upset?" Mildred asked, her fingers tracing the dips and rises created by the folds in the scratchy sheets.

Ophelia took a deep breath. "Why?" she said, knitting her eyebrows together. "Why won't you let her come in?"

"Because," her grandmother gave a huff, "I told her it's because I don't want her to see me like this. Sick and weak." Her voice choked and faded. Mildred frowned and the wrinkles around her mouth deepened to darkened sallow lines. "Can't bear to see her sad."

"Only about half of that makes sense."

Mildred's sunken eyes looked back into the bright green of Ophelia's. There was worry in them that mirrored her own. There was fear. Her frown pulled at the corners of her lips a little more. She cast her gaze back down to her hands, cringing at how much of the fat and muscle had wasted away from them. Mildred began to feel ashamed. She was losing the battle. She should have tried harder to beat back this thing.

"I know it doesn't make sense. At the time, I...I called you because you're strong, Ophelia."

Ophelia was not sure she wished to take the complement. In the twelve years that she had been an O'Leary, she and Mildred had kept each other at arm's length – Mildred making little progress in accepting Ophelia as a member of the family and Ophelia unwilling to yield to her grandmother's expectations of who she should be and how she should act.

She sat with Mildred's words, only the flip of a page interrupting her silent examination as she turned them over in her mind. Ophelia could not, and would not, argue that she was tenacious when it came to getting what she wanted in life. When she had decided that she wanted to go into fashion, the questions about the stability of her career choice merely rolled off her back, impervious to her resolve. When she decided to move out of her parent's home, she asked for no help. Instead, she balanced working two jobs to make her very meager ends barely touch while continuing to complete her degree and hunt for an internship. Yes, her own opinion was held paramount to others, and if her mind and heart were set on something, and worked in tandem, that goal would be obtained.

But this was a different scenario, was it not? She was asked to be strong for something she did not want. She was asked to be prepared on a whim, to console her sister and help to pick up the pieces in the aftermath. Ophelia was not sure even she had the strength to weather this death. Experiences from her previous lives had proved loss of a loved one baffling and overwhelming. Was anyone that strong? Would it ever get easier?

Ophelia waited three more seconds, until she was sure her vocal cords had stopped quivering, before speaking. There was not a hint of inquiry in her tone when she asked, "What did you want to talk to me about, Gramma?"

"It's more that I need you to do something for me." Mildred made to reach toward the small bedside table but thought twice when her joints refused to bend. Her arm, thin as a pin, strained to lift her hand as she pointed at the top drawer with a shaky index finger.

Without missing a beat, Ophelia went to the little table and withdrew the drawer's only contents. The small pine box was simple in appearance, flat on all sides with plain tarnished brass hinges. There were faded images of purple and pink hearts and swirls that Ophelia and Delaney had painted on as children, a gift they had given Mildred on Mother's Day a decade ago.

Mildred took the box from her. The weight of it seemed to decuple as it exchanged hands.

Ophelia's stomach dipped as the past recounted itself. No one had seen the signs then, but everyone now blamed themselves for not being more perceptive. Being who Ophelia was, she of all people should have seen it coming. But even someone like her has limits. This particular moment in time that she found herself now had only become available to her three and a half days earlier. Not all sadness and misfortune can be sidestepped.

At first, Mildred had started to lose a little weight, her clothes becoming slightly loose about the waist and middle. Then, as the months passed, she began to eat less and less, not bothering to sample from the plethora of holiday sweets and treats she had made. It progressed to her not finishing her meals, to eating even less than that. Sometimes she would complain of a slight stomachache. Other times, she would simply state, "I just don't have a taste for anything anymore," not accepting any counterargument or protest to go see the doctor. It all came to a head when she had collapsed a month ago. Initially, the O'Leary family worried it was fatigue brought on by old age, not wanting to believe that it was something more ominous.

Pancreatic cancer had devoured the illusion of the impenetrable woman, leaving a frail, emaciated Mildred that only continued to evaporate before the very eyes of her beloved husband without a chance to resist or fight back. The doctors had informed her and Edwin that her case was aggressive and had already spread to other areas of her body.

Mildred was not the only one the disease had left powerless. The doctors, in defeat, admitted that the cancer had moved too far along for any treatment to be successful in anything but completely depleting an already weakened Mildred. She was informed that she would be released to go home tomorrow. A nurse would accompany her to make sure she would be kept as comfortable as possible. Deep down, a part of Mildred sensed that she would not make it home, hence her need to speak with Ophelia that night.

Ophelia wished she could refute her grandmother's feeling, but knowing what she knew, she could not.

"Ophelia?"

The sound returned to the room as Ophelia became aware of where she was once again. She wished she could retreat back to the realms of her mind as she had found Delaney doing in the waiting room.

Her grandmother cleared her throat and withdrew her charm bracelet from the heart speckled box. It played with the poor fluorescent lighting that illuminated the room. It tinkled, jingled, and jangled lightly. "I want you to give this to Delaney. It will mean a lot to her." Mildred gulped the air and willed the tears to retreat from her eyes.

"You could give it to her yourself," Ophelia suggested.

"Please, Ophelia, now is not the time for that." She placed the delicate charm bracelet in her granddaughter's right hand. "It's a veritable timeline of my life with Edwin and our little family."

Ophelia had seen the bracelet growing up, but she had never thought to inquire about its history, focusing her attention on drawing Delaney out of her shell, which had proven harder than originally anticipated. She sat silent for a minute studying it. She held a charm of a tiny rattle between her thumb and index finger. It rested next to a sizeable pewter heart charm that was also a locket, its gold plating flaking off. "She will have to tell you the stories behind all the charms," Mildred added.

"Um, yeah," Ophelia replied slowly. "I—I will ask." She lightly placed the bracelet on the bedside table, only hesitating one point two seconds as her fingers relinquished contact with it. The bracelet would go missing in sixteen minutes and would not return for almost five years. It had to if Ophelia's plans for Delaney were to unfurl rather than unravel.

Mildred took notice of Ophelia's slight stammer and the waver of her hand as it let go of the bracelet. She had never seen her granddaughter ever be the slightest uncertain before. Mildred smiled as her mind altered its perception of her adopted granddaughter, and her heart warmed to her a few degrees more.

"Now," she continued, pulling something else from the little box, "I have something for you."

This time, what rested within the palm of Ophelia's hand was a small brooch fashioned into a poinsettia.

Ophelia looked back at the thing, befuddled. Edwin stealthily peaked over the pages of fairy tales. Mildred waited for a readable expression on the girl's face.

"But," was the first word that slipped out of Ophelia's gapping mouth, followed by some others. "But I gave this to you, Gramma. This is yours. I can't take it back. I made it for you."

"It's too pretty for a dy—a woman in my condi—" Mildred's lips formed into a tight sealed line. There were no words that could sensibly and gently soften the blow of what she was doing and why she was doing it, not without dragging the reality of the situation into some harsh light. She simply put her hands up to decline Ophelia's attempt to hand it back to her.

"It's your favorite flower," Ophelia continued to protest.

"Take it," Mildred said, firmly this time as if to say, under Grandmother Law, her strict order was not to be disobeyed.

Ophelia let out a huff along with her frustrations with everything.

"Gramma, why did you have me come here when Dee has basically been living in the waiting room for the past twenty-two days?" Truth be told, she already knew the reason, and what her grandmother needed from her could not wait until tomorrow, for it would be too late.

"I already told you, and don't you make me feel guilty about it, young lady."

"There has to be more to me giving her a bracelet," she pressed. "I'm sure you have some things you want to say to her."

"There are, but you already knew that…." Mildred mouthed what appeared to be the name 'Jucinda.' Edwin, who was currently hiding between the pages of "Chicken Little," was perplexed, not by how a chicken could mistake an acorn as a piece of sky, but by his wife's words.

But Ophelia did not allow her grandmother the opportunity to divulge her theory. She rummaged through her black bag to find a recorder with a small microphone, which had become tangled in a silk scarf and some wadded-up receipts. "Then luckily you'll be able to."

There was no huffing or puffing from Mildred, understanding her granddaughter's plan when she laid eyes on the recorder, just a simple "Okay" followed by a kind of smile someone gets after receiving a pleasant surprise.

"Excellent," Ophelia said as she opened her bag a little wider and dug deeper. "Let's get you ready."

"You're only doing a voice recording, aren't you?"

"Yes," Ophelia said picking up a compact of blush.

"Well, then why the—" Mildred looked at the contents of the bag now splayed about the bed, "—the scarf, the blush and lipstick, the spray bottle, and the comb?"

"Don't take this the wrong way, Gramma, but you could use a bit of sprucing up," Ophelia said, sweeping the blush on the apples of her grandmother's cheeks. Edwin gave a small chuckle, and Mildred did take it the wrong way.

"It's a little hard to do the day-to-day upkeep when you're not feeling well, but if it's a recording, I don't…." She patted at her frazzled fly away white tresses and nursed her bruised feelings.

"I heard about this study that found if you feel like you look good, then it permeates into other parts of your life," Ophelia explained as she leaned back to make sure the rose color she applied to her grandmother's cheeks was even. "Dee doesn't need to hear you sounding tired and ill. That's the whole reason you won't let her in here, right?

"So, you think a little make-up will make me better?"

145

"At least sound better," Ophelia corrected, now spraying a little water and combing back the wild brittle hair before wrapping the scarf around it and tying it in the back. The scarf was dotted with bright red poinsettias on a jewel-tone green satin background.

After applying the balm to Mildred's cracked lips, Ophelia took a step back, tilting her head thirty-three degrees to the left. "It needs something." Then, picking up the brooch she had fashioned together when she was twelve, she affixed it on the right side of the scarf, so it looked like a crystalline flower tucked behind Mildred's ear.

"I think you look pretty," Ophelia said approvingly and handed Mildred a small mirror.

"You look swell, my dear," Edwin said, looking over the top of his book.

Mildred only gave a soft grunt as she examined her face in the mirror. A careful observer would have noticed the corners of her mouth twitch upward for a quarter of a second. Ophelia did. As if by the power of suggestion, Mildred did feel a tad more energized. Maybe the reason was a Christmas miracle or a factual scientific finding. The jury was still out.

Edwin adjusted the bed and helped to ease his wife into a seated position. Despite her weakened state, she now exuded strength, maybe the last bit she had, along with perfect posture. Some extra pillows helped to prop her up. Clearing her throat, Mildred said, "Press record."

As the tape began to spin and spool itself to the other reel, so began Mildred's heartfelt message to her granddaughter, not in the feeble defeated voice she could not stand to hear emanating from the back of her throat, but the warm tone she thought the cancer had stolen away and claimed for its own. And because the recording was a surprise intended for Delaney, so too must the reader of these words wait for the unveiling of it in subsequent pages.

When Mildred had finished, Ophelia stopped recording and placed the recorder, microphone, and reel back into her large bag. Mildred was breathing shallowly as if unable to catch her breath. She tapped the brooch, indicating Ophelia to take it back. Managing to work out a "Thank you," she lightly touched her granddaughter's hand, adding an "I love you." Those words were the next to last that Mildred would speak.

Her breathing began to accelerate. Edwin abandoned his tales and rushed to his wife's side. He clung tightly to her hand, and Mildred reciprocated tenfold.

"Gramma?" Ophelia asked with rehearsed yet genuine shock, for she knew that this would happen at 9:13 p.m. on the dot. "I'll go get help."

"No need," said Edwin, holding up the nurse call button he had illuminated. "Go be with your sister." There was more to his sentence, but he could not bring himself to speak the words because it would bring reality crashing down upon him. Denial was all that Edwin had left, and not even it could stave off the impending sorrow or save the life of his true love, entirely unlike the potions and magic talismans found in his stories.

Ophelia simply nodded. Her heart broke feeling the helpless despair resonating off her grandfather. As she turned to go, a hand caught the cuff of her coat. Eyes filled with tears met with her own misty ones. Mildred looked up at Ophelia and saw her granddaughter surrounded in an aura of violet and silver. Her expression was a mixture of shock and amazement, like she was seeing Ophelia for the first time. Her lips pulled into a placid smile, and she whispered, "You're an angel." The last word was softer than an exhale.

Ophelia was touched by the words and yet unable, for once, to determine how to reciprocate. She just stood in her quandary.

"Back at ya, Gramma. I'll see you tomorrow," the girl lied to herself, the words finally coming to her. Ophelia moved Mildred's hand to rest by her side as Edwin reclined the bed.

She exited out of the hospital room where she bumped into a candy striper named Bailey Barrymore. "Please make sure my grandmother is made as comfortable as possible. Now," Ophelia said to the wide-eyed girl before she took powerful strides back down the hall to the tackily decorated waiting room.

The audible popping sound of her heels striking the floor began to soften as yards shrank to feet and then inches. *So, this is what fear feels like*, she reminded herself, very rarely entertaining the emotion.

*   *   *

Delaney was hunched forward in her seat with the deflated cushion. Her raven hair had come forward, shrouding her face and shielding her tired eyes from the harsh fluorescent lights.

She did not hear her sister approach, but she could sense her standing in front of her. Shaking the hair from her face and blinking furiously to adjust her eyes to the light again, she asked, "How is she?"

A simple question, with an unequally difficult answer.

Ophelia stood motionless and silent. She could only stare back at Delaney. Even if she had the courage to speak, her words would have been blocked by the coal-sized lump of emotion lodged in her throat.

Delaney was the first to break in the staring contest. She wrapped herself in her wool sweater coat and gently rocked, gulping the air. The tears began to pour from her eyes once she felt Ophelia's arm curl around to her right shoulder and gently lead her into an embrace.

Éamon and Alicia would arrive at the hospital to see Delaney unabashedly weeping into her sister's shoulder. Ophelia was composed, sitting rail straight and casting a glare to anyone who dared peer in their general direction. She did not break her role as emotional rock, not when Alicia took a turn to hold Delaney, not when Éamon wrapped his arms around her as he, too, started to cry, and not even when Edwin came in to deliver the news that Mildred had passed away. She kept herself together by avoiding eye contact and counting her inhales and exhales because her family needed her. What good would she be if she succumbed to her sadness?

After tears had been exhausted and the fog brought on by grief had lifted just enough, about one hour and forty minutes to be exact, the O'Leary family would depart the hospital. Delaney, Éamon, and Alicia returned to their home, and Edwin would drop Ophelia back to her apartment. Grandfather and granddaughter didn't say a word for the entire ride. Ophelia stared out the passenger's side window, looking at nothing in particular, clutching the poinsettia brooch in her coat pocket.

*   *   *

At 12:01 a.m., Ophelia arrived back at the Vermont Village. The stairs leading up to the seventh floor groaned under her feet, and the center hinge on apartment 7H's door emitted a slight squeak as it opened.

Ophelia stepped across the threshold of the apartment and took a deep breath. *This is how it has to play out*, she reminded herself, replacing her keys back into the dish next to the door and dropping the bag next to the table. *She's gonna need me.*

The events of the evening buzzed about Ophelia's head. Visions of sugar plums would not be dancing in her dreams that night. After pulling off her boots and draping her coat over the green patterned chair, she stood in place, briefly unsure what to do with herself. Her eyes scanned the dark apartment, looking for nothing in particular.

With a sniffle, she walked over to the window where a small pine tree, only about a foot in height, basked in the moonlight. Its crown was decorated with tiny royal purple ornaments and lavender ribbons that wove in and out of the branches. On an outstretched limb, a tiny jingle bell hung on a worn ribbon. It gave out a crisp clear jingle as Ophelia plucked at the decoration.

"That was for you, Gramma."

The last words she heard her grandmother say to her were impossible to quiet down. They warmed her to the core yet caused her great sadness. The time in the hospital room was the first moment Mildred had let her know how she really felt about her, and that could never be taken away. *But it's also the last time*, Ophelia couldn't help to remind herself.

Sleep would not come quickly to Ophelia. It was a good thing, she thought, that she had one more thing to take care of that night. She stepped into her soon-to-be closet, and walked over to some lumber and a toolbox, selecting a hammer and nails.

Yes, the city of Nollag had a silent night, save for the raucous banging of the hammer that covered Ophelia's sobbing as she worked on the wall framing. Mrs. Beezle would wake up shortly after the second nail had been driven in to notify the police of the disturbance.

Chapter 11

In Which Delaney Has a Chat with Grandpa Edwin

The phone clattered to life, pulling Delaney back to the warm living room all decked out with white light and the scent of pine mixed with cinnamon and vanilla. On the third ring, she checked the time on the large face clock that hung on the wall across from the exposed brick chimney. The time was 6:15 p.m. On the fourth ring, she picked up the phone's black receiver.

"Hello?" she said into the phone.

"Hello, my darling girl," an aged voice chortled over the line.

A smile danced to her lips as her round cheeks pulled up making her eyes squint a bit. "Hi, Grandpa."

"Merry Christmas," they both said in perfect unison.

Edwin gave another joyous chuckle that almost sounded like a cough. It emanated from deep within his throat. "How are you, sweetheart?"

"Oh, I'm fine. Doing good."

"Oh? What's the matter?" Edwin immediately pressed. 'Fine' was a lie that Delaney inadvertently used whenever things were, in fact, not good…or going well. In recent years, the reason for Delaney using the F-word was due to Ophelia — usually a combination of something she had said and done.

"What do you mean?" Delaney asked, feigning a poorly rehearsed tone of confusion. She instinctively bit at her thumb and pigeon toed her right foot.

"You only use improper grammar when you're hiding something," he chuckled.

"Well. I'm doing g—well. How are you doing, Grandpa? Are things still okay at the home? You know you can always move back here. Cal and I wouldn't mind at all."

"Don't call it a home. Makes me feel old, but, yes, I am having a wonderful time here. And as for how I am, I'm busting my buttons. My granddaughter's going to be a published author!" he exclaimed with childish glee so loud that Delaney could hear the sound of a nurse hushing her grandfather. "It's a big deal!" Whether he directed this exclamation at Delaney or the nurse was not clear.

Delaney's face flushed with color, and she sported a broad toothy grin that her grandfather was able to pick up in her reply. "Why thank you very, very, very much," she replied, "but it wouldn't have happened without Grandma's recipes."

"Now wait a second, Sweets," his nickname for Delaney, "some of those treats are yours."

"Yeah, but they were inspired by Grandma."

"Not all…" Edwin said in a melodic tone.

"Grandpa," Delaney sang back. "Don't go there." She desperately wanted to sound serious but instead broke into stifled laughter.

"Young lady, I'm eighty-one years old. I can go where I please these days…mostly because senility passes for an excuse. And before you protest, yes, *I'm* going there. But first a detour…embrace this accomplishment. You found your grandmother's recipes and had the creativity and ingenuity to make your own culinary masterpieces alongside them. You folded in the stories and history with each recipe. Then—oh my stars, there's more?" he said incredulously, interrupting his own train of thought. "Why, yes. You. You alone had the gumption to go to every café and restaurant and grocery store in the city limits to get them to try and pick up your treats. Why, it seems like one minute you were telling me Damodar Clark agreed to sell your cookies and muffins, and by the end of the day, you had a book deal. It's as if—as if, I don't know…it was your birthright." Grandpa Edwin always had a flair for the dramatic.

"It was good timing, Grandpa," Delaney blushed. "Dumb luck."

"Point is, Sweets, that you not only took your own path, against the wishes of your overly practical parents, but you also fulfilled a dream of your grandmother's."

Delaney felt a giddy tingle run up and about her entire being.

"She never found the confidence to see if it would take flight," he concluded.

"I miss her, Grandpa."

"Me, too, kiddo…every day."

Grandfather and granddaughter shared in a moment of silence, allowing a slideshow of memories to run through their minds.

155

"But back to our final destination," Edwin interrupted, a bit trepid. The many images of Mildred's smiling face in Delaney's mind's eye became staticky and hazy, much like her television on a snowy day with temperatures below twenty degrees Fahrenheit. Instead, they were replaced with other images that left her seeing red…hair. Her uplifted spirits numbed.

"I invited her here," Delaney quickly pipped up, answering Edwin's question before he could ask it directly.

"When?"

There was another brief moment of silence. This one taking on more of an awkward feeling.

"To-today."

"Delaney," Edwin said to her as if she were four again and had been caught completing a linear regression problem on the dining room wall in orange crayon. "You know your sister. She's going to think the offer was an afterthought. It shows that you haven't forgiven her yet."

"Uh-huh," Delaney said through gritted teeth that held her thumbnail fixed in place.

"You have forgiven her, haven't you?"

"I don't know if I can, Grandpa. I mean, she crossed an enormously thick line."

"Sweets, why? Things turned out fine, didn't they? I know the whole thing with Ophelia and that Bailey girl was messy, but, all things considered, it's partly the reason Cal is with you."

"Things could've also gone very awry," she glowered. "Nothing good comes from someone getting tased."

Edwin chose to ignore the taser comment. "You can't live in hypotheticals, Delaney, especially the ones that end up never coming to pass."

"Why do we have to talk about this? It's just the way it is."

"Because I hate to see my girls fighting on Christmas…or any other day of the year. It breaks an old man's already weak heart," Edwin said, playing a well-executed guilt card.

"She put a woman in the hospital," Delaney answered flatly. Moving the receiver to her shoulder and crossing her arms across her chest.

"Eh." Edwin shrugged off Delaney's point. The sound of rustled wool came through the telephone. "She deserved it," he sniffed.

"Grandpa!"

"She was a thief, and you got something out of it. If you really think about it, a someone *and* a something. Don't forget that."

"Touché," Delaney said in a meek voice. She looked down first at the charm bracelet secured around her left wrist before moving to glimpse at a photo of her and Calum next to the phone. "But, if *you* remember, Ophelia started the whole chain of events leading up to the fight."

"Do this for me. Forget about all that and focus on the good Ophelia has done for you…in her own way," he amended. "Your sister has always had your best interests at heart. Do that for me tonight, okay?"

"Yeah, I'll try." Delaney rolled her brown eyes, following the perimeter of the ornate crown molding.

"Don't roll your eyes. That's right, Grandpa knows all."

Delaney muttered a timid apology.

"All right," Edwin chuckled, "I love you, Sweets. See you tomorrow."

"Love you back, Grandpa."

"Delaney?"

"Yeah, Grandpa?" she asked timidly, wondering what else she could be potentially guilted into.

"Congrats."

"Thanks, Grandpa." She smiled and blushed, her cheeks burning hotter than a four-hour lit Christmas tree light.

After Delaney confirmed what time she should pick up her grandfather tomorrow, followed by another exchange of "Merry Christmases," the line clicked off.

Chapter 12

In Which Delaney Is in a Very Bad Mood and Is Being Quite the Sourpuss

Delaney hung on the line until she was ushered off by a noticeably pushy sounding operator. "Merry Christmas," the operator had said in an acerbic and nasal voice.

"Same to you," Delaney replied with a grimace before setting the phone back onto the receiver with a 'clunk' and a 'clang.' While always a joy to speak with her grandfather, more recent conversations always settled on the same unpleasant topic: Ophelia.

Delaney did love her sister, but even love could not manage to erase all the mistakes Ophelia had made. These mistakes, after all, had had a ripple effect on Delaney. One could only wipe the slate clean so many times before permanent smudges and marks made themselves at home, no matter how hard a scrubbing they received.

Still…there was always a "still" to give one pause. Love did exist. And with love, happy memories were able to take root and germinate. And happy memories bore blossoms for the potential of forgiveness where needed. That was exactly where Delaney was at as she held on to the phone not three seconds ago, plucking at the petals of her proverbial flower, a poinsettia given the current festive season. *I forgive her. I forgive her not. I forgive her. I forgive her not....*

"Focus on the good Ophelia has done for you," her grandfather had told her. Being the good granddaughter that Delaney was, she did just that, summoning a recollection that took place precisely one year and twenty hours after her grandmother's passing....

* * *

Christmas that year felt wrong to Delaney. All of it. She could count the things that were going well on one mittened hand with at least a thumb to spare. While most of the citizens of Nollag were filled with cheer and goodwill toward others, brought about by the season, she felt only animosity toward anything red, green, or twinkling.

Every day seemed to get progressively worse for Delaney O'Leary. Her heart still bore the ache of her grandmother's passing as it wrestled with her mind to unsuccessfully find peace. Her parents' departure only compounded these feelings of loss. Delaney had had the option to go with them, of course, when they had moved away to Glory for Éamon's new job at Bing University, but she had only applied to the University of Nollag as had always been her plan ever since the very mature age of eight.

She could have waited a year and gone to Bing University, but that would mean leaving a city she knew like an old friend, as well as her actual friends, and all the little reminders strewn about the city that ignited some of her most coveted memories. There was Jack Frost's Ice Cream and Soda Stand on the corner of Nipping

Street and Srón Boulevard where she had learned the concept of combination and the fact there were one thousand twenty-seven different sundaes to try. Currently, she had only tried two hundred thirty-seven of the possible frozen delights amongst the ice creams, gelatos, frozen yogurts, sherbets, and toppings.

Then there was the Spinning Yarn where a freshly adopted Ophelia had taken Delaney to find fabric for the new doll dress Ophelia had promised to make for her the day they met at the orphanage.

She had met her best friend, Petunia, on the first day of Kindergarten at the Nollag Public School, District 12. They bonded over their shared personality quirk of being painfully shy…not right away, obviously. Their teacher, Mr. Kratchet, helped initiate their first conversation during snack time that day.

Calum was there, as well, only a secret crush back then. She would remember him as being so cute, but also so very, very melancholy looking. Their first meeting had taken place at the Come Write On Inn, a trendy little bookstore that doubled as a recruiting agency for the next great authors.

Last, but actually first and foremost, was the large gray-blue house with the address One Partridge Parkway. Like a chest of priceless heirlooms, it contained all her fondest memories of one of her "bestest" friends, her grandmother.

Its kitchen was where she had discovered her fondness of baking as it incorporated the tools of precise measurement, unit conversions, and ratios. She had preferred it to cooking, which would call for "a pinch of this" or "a dash of that," along with the occasional "smidge" or "touch." The fact that these subjective directions did not drive her grandmother up the wall made her believe she had a superpower.

Every Friday, Delaney would make her way over to her grandparents' home to help make a dessert, and the occasional side dish, for dinner. Her most adored memory was from when she was three months and nine days shy of her tenth birthday. Mildred, after having tasted her cranberry and pear tort, a confection Delaney had created on her own, ran out of the kitchen and returned with a recipe card and pen in hand, demanding Delaney neatly write down the recipe for "the box," which housed all of Mildred's favorite recipes.

Logically, Delaney knew time was not kind to the mind, and memories faded and distorted like a favorite t-shirt washed thirty-two times. They would never be the same as they were the moment they happened. She needed to keep her mind sharp and her cherished memories in mint condition. While time could not be stopped, she still had some control over her proximity to the places that served as reminders to these mental mementos.

But her decision had come with repercussions. With her parents gone, Delaney had lost her childhood home and, with it, her room with lemon yellow walls and blue and white striped headboard with gold studding that faced the east to greet the rising sun. That room would belong to a new little boy or girl, she hoped.

"It's for the best," Ophelia had said, consoling her sister for the 'I've lost count' time. "I heard some study found that if a child doesn't rebel a little, they become too dependent on their parents. Sad." She had emphatically punctuated her final comment.

Mr. and Mrs. O'Leary had reacted poorly when Delaney told them she would not be going to Glory with them. She learned that parents can sometimes have double standards, especially when they did not get to choose the change that is being imposed on them.

"What study?" Delaney had asked.

Her sister had only shrugged, saying, "Don't know. Some psych guy was telling me. The things you learn when boys out of your league try and ask you out," she recalled to herself with an absent-minded chuckle. "I hate to say, 'Come on,' since it makes me sound like I'm being insensitive, but come on, Dee, it's been over six months. I'm sure Mom and Dad have adjusted to your staying here."

"It's not that," Delaney replied in a whining tone that left a bad taste in her mouth. She cleared her throat of the potential tantrum before continuing. "Mom and Dad aren't even coming for Christmas. They can't!" she amended.

Where weather conditions had been excessively mild last year, Mother Nature was making up for it with interest. The little city of Glory was bundled up with five feet and three-eighths inches of snow, practically shutting down the city and forcing everyone and their families to stay put. This would result in most Glory residents cracking open their bottles of "Holiday Cheer" after the fourth consecutive day of family togetherness. (As a side note, Glory also saw a spike in the birthrate more or less nine months after that blizzard.)

"It's coming this way, too," Ophelia said matter-of-factly.

"Expect the heavy wet stuff to come up from the southwest with harsh winds and temperatures close to zero," the weatherman on the television interjected. Ophelia frowned at the television screen.

"Guess that means we won't get our Christmas presents until the thaw…Brightside, I can get the rest of my shopping done at the after Christmas sales."

Delaney glared back.

"Oh, calm down." Ophelia rolled her large green eyes to glance up at the antique tin work on the ceiling. "You're taken care of already." She received a huffed exhale in response.

With another eye roll, Ophelia excused herself and disappeared into to her closet. Delaney could hear rummaging sounds as drawers were opened and banged shut, shoes clattered, clicked, and scraped against the wood floors, bracelets and necklaces and jewelry clinked, and the sound of hat boxes and bins whispered on and off the shelves.

An insane idea, really. How could Ophelia call that a closet? The very question festered in Delaney's mind like the sound of nails on a chalkboard. It did not make sense. It simply was not practical to need an eight by six-foot room for clothes, and then to only need a matchbox of a room for sleeping with furniture crammed up next to each other like an ill-fitting puzzle.

Don't think about it. Delaney shook the thoughts from her mind. She bundled herself on the oversized, purple sofa pulling her knees closer to her body and swaddling herself in another knitted blanket, her favorite, crocheted from sunny yellow, white, and gold yarn by her grandmother.

She worked her hand through the folds of the blankets to retrieve the remote. *Snap out of it and watch some TV.* But Delaney's type-A personality could not leave well enough alone. With every channel change and ensuing image of hugging families, glistening

Christmas trees, one-horse open sleighs, and dancing gum drops and sugarplum fairies, Delaney grew more and more sour.

"Gloria! You're home," the man on the television exclaimed, throwing open the door and sweeping his daughter out of the thick falling snow into a warm sweater-clad embrace.

"Oh, Daddy, it's so great to be home. I wasn't sure if I was going to make it," Gloria said, fighting back faux tears and throwing a hand up to delicately rest on her forehead.

Because at least every eight out of ten Christmas movies uses this tired plotline, thought Delaney, completely disgusted by the ham acting.

"It's a Christmas miracle," her father said in a choked-up tone, flashing too-white veneered teeth.

Puke. 'Click!'

"We're all unique," explained the giant cartoon snowflake now on the screen, gesturing to the reindeer, Christmas tree, menorah, and handful of children in Technicolor coats, hats, and mittens. The stop animation made each one glitter. "That's what makes this season so…so…."

"Magical," Delaney said flatly.

"Magical!"

"Hey, he's right!" said a bucktoothed freckled boy, most likely named Bobby.

Ugh. Change before they sing. 'Click!'

"Ho. Ho. Ho."

No. No. No. 'Click!'

"What's the true meaning of Christmas?" queried a round-faced boy.

With a decisive click, the screen went black, leaving Delaney to stew in silence.

What was Christmas all about? Delaney could rattle off the socially acceptable answers to that question, but she did not believe in them now.

She pulled herself up to a sitting position and kicked away the blanket from her now blazing hot legs.

Placing her chin in her hand, she surveyed the scene outside framed by the seventh-floor apartment's living room window. Whatever was out there had to be more interesting than all the holiday movies she had seen approximately seventy-one times a piece before. But, really, there wasn't anything of note. Like channel four: snow, only without the static soundtrack.

"Are you planning to come with me?" Ophelia asked. She hung out into the hallway from the entrance to her closet wearing three hangers around her neck that contained the same dress, each a different color.

"Huh?" Delaney said, not bothering to conceal her agitation. She knew exactly what her sister was referring to. How could she not, after all? She had had the displeasure of hearing about it for the past two and a half weeks. And while she was on the topic of her sister, and her grouchiness was at an all-time irrational high, why did Ophelia have to have red hair today?

"Dee," Ophelia pressed. She narrowed her eyes and relaxed her jaw, letting her smile fall into a grimace. Ophelia missed the Delaney who let her in and shared what she was thinking, who laughed with her, and who, at least every now and then, would point a toe outside of her comfort zone. Before Life so rudely upended Delaney's world, Ophelia had a sister. Now, it felt like she just had a roommate.

"Ophelia, drop it."

"Why don't you want to come?" She came out into the main area, red, black, and yellow skirts of the dresses swished about and either complemented or clashed with the crystal studded belt or satin sash she had slung around her waist. Her right foot clicked in a black ankle boot while the left clopped in a tan leather chukka boot.

"It'll just be you and Greg. Not a fan of being the third wheel. It's practically a white out," she gestured to the picture window, "and it's Christmas Eve. You shouldn't be going out. Frankly, it's cruel to have people working today. They should be allowed to be home with their families. I, for one, will not contribute to the capitalization of the holiday."

Ophelia's eyes darted back and forth, not quite sure where whatever her sister had said had come from. Her best educated guess was left field.

"Ookaay…all valid reasons, but we both know none of those is the real reason."

"They're not?" Delaney restated skeptically.

"No. Clearly, they're decoys. Decoys strategically placed within the conversation and disguised in a fairly convincing delivery to throw me off from what's really bothering you."

Delaney hated it when her sister became matter-of-fact.

Ophelia paused, biting her lower lip, a way to make it appear she was not sure if what she would say next would diffuse the underlying tension or generate a tiny emotional explosion. The red wire or the blue wire? "Sweetie, it's been a year. You…you need to let go a bit. Relax a pinkie, at least."

Delaney's nostrils flared as her eyes bulged out of her head and her lips formed into a single razor thin line.

Shoulda cut the blue wire, Ophelia thought. "What if I ask Grey to tag along?" she suggested. "You like Grey, and I'm pretty sure he doesn't have any plans." Ophelia's smile broadened. She leaned forward and shrugged her shoulders anticipating her sister's mood to break with this addendum to the evening's plans.

It did not.

"Dee, look, if you don't want to come out, that's on you. I thought it would be good for you, is all." She removed the hangers from around her neck, tossed the dresses to the side, and stood there awkwardly staring back at her sister. She desperately yearned for a reaction, any emotion. Delaney had worn her solace to the point of it, well, becoming pretty sad. It weighed on Ophelia to see her little sister ache from this loss still. Regardless of what her sister thought of her, Ophelia did understand loss. In this life alone, she had seen many a newcomer to Mother Mary Claire Brog's Haven for Nippers, Toddlers, Tykes, and Children become inconsolable, be it due to a misplaced toy or the over family they had lost or never had. It should not be forgotten that she had lost a grandmother, too, after all.

The main point was that just because someone was gone, it did not mean your life ended with theirs. As Delaney had given a life and a family to Ophelia back at the age of seven point six, Ophelia was determined to do the same of sorts for her; only in Delaney's case, Ophelia knew the alternative was a dire looking future.

"I don't like Chinese food," Delaney finally said.

With defeat further pulling down Ophelia's sagging shoulders, she turned taking uneven steps back into her closet with an over exaggerated grimace across her mouth. "Fine," she called back, "but I still think you need to do something with yourself."

Delaney rolled her eyes again. She made a mental note to stop since she had done it so many times that the room was starting to spin. "Like what?"

"Uh," Ophelia puzzled, "how about you cook something? You know, you bake and stuff…you're pretty good at it…" Ophelia continued on, dropping hints like a trail of breadcrumbs.

"Like what?" Delaney repeated, half listening and clearly not interested in helping move the conversation along at anything but a snail's pace.

Emerging from the closet this time with a confident stride, Ophelia glided toward her sister, holding out two index cards in her hands. They were worn around the edges, speckled with small stains and decorated with little pot belly stoves about the lower right corner.

Delaney's eyebrows pulled up and together in a quizzical fashion as her thumb and index finger finally decided to accept the cards after a prolonged beat and a half. They still smelled of cinnamon. They were recipes written in a very tidy flourished hand for orange ginger cookies and a cashew and pistachio bread with a black cherry glaze. They were Mildred O'Leary's recipes.

Curiosity simmered away to something that resembled an unappetizing mixture of fear and a dollop of blue funk.

"Nuh-uh. Nope," Delaney said with a slight shake of her head, her loose tresses trembling. She practically shoved the cards back at her sister. Edwin had told her months ago Mildred had wanted her to have them, but Delaney always seemed to find a reason to put off picking them up.

"Wh—why not, Delaney?" Too much urgency came through in Ophelia's tone.

"It wouldn't be right."

"What are you talking about? It wouldn't be right? You make them every Christmas."

"I made them with Grandma, Ophelia." Delaney's tone chastised her older sister.

"So, because Gramma's not here, you're not allowed to make them anymore? That's—that's like—uh, what's it like?" She pinched the bridge of her nose, concentrating hard. "Oh," she snapped her fingers in victory. "It's like keeping a vintage piece under glass. It's meant to be worn, enjoyed, and shone off. Same with these," she regarded the recipes. "Don't let them go to waste."

Delaney made to reply, but Ophelia talked over her.

"I guess I could make them," Ophelia said. She looked down at the cards as if trying to decipher the meaning of a 'smidgen of orange zest' and whatever the exact meaning was for a 'healthy handful of dried cherries,' which Delaney equated to a teaspoon and forty grams respectively. Ophelia was indeed creative…except when a whisk or an oven was involved. "You remember what happened five Thanksgivings ago? And those were just the rolls. The only thing everyone was thankful for was indoor plumbing and several bathrooms."

Delaney and Ophelia both shuddered from the recollection.

"I—" but Delaney did not finish her thought. Instead, she shook her head and pulled the blanket tighter around her.

"Fine," Ophelia said, defeated. She picked up the clothes and returned to the closet to finish changing.

Not two minutes passed, and Ophelia danced out in a simple teal dress with vibrant orange stockings, caramel ankle boots, and a matching belt synched at her natural waist. She had pinned her mane of auburn and red curls so that they spilled over her left shoulder.

After she collected her coat and a deep turquoise colored bowler hat, she gave a fleeting glance toward her sister. Abruptly, she whirled through the door of the apartment; her hand held the knob at mid-turn. "I left the recipes on the table, next to the sewing machine."

Her sister wore a stretched grimace on her face that made her resemble a disgruntled toad.

"Okay. Just wanted to plant that seed. Bye. Love you. Make good choices." She picked up her keys from the dish by the door and a bag that was festively decorated with red and white striped tissue paper.

The door clicked shut and the confident pounding footsteps of Ophelia O'Leary began to fade. Quietly and quickly, Delaney snuck up half-crouched to the peep hole. There was no one on the other side of the door. Only the muffled murmur of voices could be heard out in the hall. Her sister was sneaky, and it seemed odd she had given up so easily.

"Ahchoo!" The sneeze came from out in the hall, followed by something like fingers drumming a table.

"Oh! Dear!" came the muffled voice of Mrs. Gellar.

"Oh, no," Delaney could hear her sister say. "I am so sorry. I'm frightfully allergic to nutmeg."

"There is no nutmeg in them!" Mrs. Gellar yelled on the verge of sobbing.

"Do you think any can be salvaged?"

Delaney waited for the ruckus to die down before she finally straightened her posture and began to survey the apartment. Of course, nothing had changed since Delaney had moved in five months ago. *Why was everything so purple?* she wondered to herself.

Living with Ophelia was interesting to say the least. There was absolutely no sort of structure or schedule living with her sister, one hundred eighty degrees from how life at the O'Leary family home ran. Delaney felt a little lost and anxious leaving the regiments of her parents. It made her lightheaded and caused her stomach to yo-yo with the occasional lindy loop.

Ophelia craved the potential for spontaneity, for a life that was truly her own. She was bound and determined to carve adventure into her life even if it killed her, seeming to intrinsically understand that chances and their uncertainties were a necessary evil.

So true was this point: Ophelia, when not attending school for fashion design, worked around the clock to earn money to pay for her rent and fund her sewing projects. She came and went from the apartment sometimes ten or twelve times a day, only stopping in for a wardrobe change or to drop another bolt of fabric off. Delaney was convinced there was a ninety-seven point four percent chance her sister would have a meltdown with school, work, friends, family, and all the other bits and pieces crammed into her impossibly claustrophobic schedule. However, she thrived in the two point six percent of downtime. It all seemed improbable, almost like Ophelia had somehow rigged the system.

The truth of the matter was Delaney harbored a mild jealousy of her sister. Ophelia managed to do what many believed to be an impossibility, the ultimate outlier. She enjoyed her life down to its most mundane responsibilities with such finesse, without compromising who she was, unwilling to spare even a zeptosecond of her time to entertain the petty judgments others were all too willing to lavish upon her.

Enough of that, she resolved, directing her attention toward the closet door.

After a few tentative steps, she loitered within the doorway to the closet off the main hallway. She aimed her gaze at the small silver box that rested on some shiny scraps of silk in front of Ophelia's calendar, an annual stocking stuffer from Delaney, whose word of the day, appropriately enough, was "Snook."

The promise she had made to herself to never make her grandmother's holiday recipes, some of which she had helped concoct, buzzed inside her head. Her mind considered revising this new law. Perhaps a loophole could be conjured?

Yet it had seemed poetic and a fitting tribute to Mildred that the recipes "rest" with her, for another set of hands would never be able to replicate them – not exactly. Yes, it made sense. Loads of sense. So much sense, the idea of breaking her promise, even the notion of bending the self-imposed rule, was inconceivable to consider, downright ludicrous even. Yes, so much sense was made when that vow was silently sworn in a swirling vortex of grieving and sorrowful emotions that Delaney had donated a portion of that sense to charity so that others might share in it.

Still…each three by five card containing a dish or a treat had a special story attached to it. Should these memories be left to spoil? That would be a waste and counterintuitive to a fitting tribute. The "sense," it appeared, had gone cold and was starting to rot into nonsense.

Besides, Delaney liked to bake. The genuine kind of like; not that kind of like where you like to finish all of your vegetables before you can have dessert or where you like to be your sister's body form and stand still for four hours and seven minutes being pinned and pinched. *Note to self,* Delaney thought, *get Ophelia a body form for next Christmas.* Maybe that feeling isn't like. Maybe it's love?

With the mental note filed away for later, Delaney concluded perhaps she had been too rash before. Baking was her passion, and why should Ophelia get to be the only one with an overabundance of happy?

Delaney stepped into the room.

Chapter 13

In Which Delaney Receives a Present from the Past

Crossing the threshold, the word "boggled" conjured itself forward in Delaney's mind, eyes sweeping over garments of every different type of color, pattern, and fabric. Ophelia's wardrobe was, in Delaney's opinion, excessive.

She silently scolded herself for being unnecessarily judgmental. *It's not my place*, Delaney thought while stifling a criticism when she noticed the veritable bounty of bracelets, rings, and pendants that would make a pirate begin to uncontrollably salivate right before burying it under a very large "X."

The distinct scent of cinnamon directed her attention back over to the table in the center of the room. Nestled between a stack of jeans running from light to dark and a pistachio green sewing machine lay a priceless treasure. The two cards Ophelia had wafted under Delaney's nose were set on top of the recipe box. With a touch, the memories of a four-year-old Delaney cutting out gingerbread cookies in the shapes of stars and angels began to slowly rise to the forefront of her mind, much like the soufflé she had first made with Mildred at age eleven. Mildred had used some of those cookies Delaney had decorated as ornaments that year. She used a couple of Ophelia's, too, but Delaney knew whose Mildred had preferred.

Delaney craved more, wishing now to indulge in the sweet, happy reminders the other cards contained. No longer able to deny herself, she opened the lid of the little box.

With recipes in hand, what Delaney felt was uncanny. With each recipe she flipped to, the potato pancakes at age nine, the black and elderberry crumble at thirteen, and the honey glazed roasted salmon with a warm red potato salad at fourteen, she was not only able to recall the image, but the smells and tastes of each dish. Best of all was the sense of pride her grandmother had lavished upon her with each new skill Delaney picked up. She could feel it radiate from the tiny silver vessel.

Like an overbaked cookie, Delaney found herself beginning to crumble. Perhaps shelving Mildred's recipes was not the best way to honor her.

No, she had it reversed. Her recollections were not the source of sorrow and pain. That, as it turned out, was caused by self-denial to revisit them. They were actually comforting, like a belly of warm homemade chicken noodle soup. Delaney lifted and embraced the small box as if it were a long-lost old friend. Then it dawned on her….

Crap, she thought, her half-smile faltering due to the weight of her new concern.

Ophelia knew what this was about all along. She hated it when her sister did that thing where she was right. Partly because she figured out the situation first, like she always seemed to do, but more so because that meant a good six months of "I told you so"s. She shuddered at the thought of all those "I told you so"s.

Looking down at the little box of recipes, she decided it wouldn't matter. She could keep Ophelia quiet by filling her pie hole with her favorite cupcake that Delaney and Mildred had created, an orange and vanilla cake topped with too much lavender meringue buttercream and purple sprinkles. It was a little much, but it was inspired by Ophelia, after all.

She nodded to herself, decidedly committing to her plan of action, and unwittingly began to dance a small jig out of the room. Inspiration and motivation bubbled over in her mind yielding potentially tasty new treats to concoct. (As some can attest, these moments of creative illumination have been known to lift even the heaviest of spirits, not unlike the combination of pixie dust and happy thoughts.)

Five and a half steps remained to the doorway leading back to the hall when something shiny caught Delaney's attention mid-twirl. All her thoughts were hushed as if her subconscious already knew that that the large box she saw protruding from under the gold tassels on the royal purple armchair was significant and meant for her.

She approached the box, which was only partially wrapped in a shimmery baby blue paper, and knelt down next to it. Its lid was slightly ajar, allowing the red tissue paper to peek though. *To: Delaney. From: Ophelia* was written on the large

177

white tag with a golden filigree border hanging off the side of the parcel.

Two or three minutes slowly passed by, each lingering a little longer than the one before, as Delaney looked at the tag's calligraphy until its words lost all meaning, devolving to pretty swoops and curls.

She scooted closer to the gift, pulling her sleeves over her hands, deliberating with her proverbial devil and angel. What did this large box contain? It would be wrong to look inside, but this would be the first time she would open a gift before Christmas without permission. Everyone was entitled to at least one freebie in their lifetime, right? Was she a good enough actress that she could fake surprise? Ophelia would see through it. Still…she had never felt so drawn to a box's contents like she did with this particular parcel. It caused an excited spark in the pit of her stomach that she had not felt in over a year. She had to know. The current circumstances couldn't be more perfect even if one had staged it. No one was around, and she would hear Ophelia unlocking the front door. She could be off the floor and into the bathroom just down the hall in five point six seconds. Easy. To be safe, though, she did test her time estimations, noting she should flush the toilet and run the faucet so as not to draw her sister's suspicion.

Oh, just go for it, she heard the devil and angel sing in unison. The devil was a little flat and off-key, but the message was clear all the same.

She grabbed and donned a pair of gloves Ophelia had left on one of the chests of drawers. *Best not to leave fingerprints,* Delaney thought. She settled back on the floor and slowly dragged the gift from its hiding place. The sound of the hissing paper against the floor sounded like metal on concrete to her. Delaney gritted her teeth and looked about the empty room, knowing full and well Ophelia had not returned home. That did not stop her paranoia from telling her she was being watched.

She took a mental picture in an effort to remember the exact angle the lid had been placed atop the box. Taking a deep breath, she used only the tips of her fingers to slowly lift the lid. Peeling back the tissue was like unwrapping a Smacky Snap's Deluxe Dark Chocolate Raisins bar during the most crucial part of a movie, the part where everyone was holding their breath in anticipation of either the final culminations of a murder or a reunion of lost lovers.

Shhhh!!! Delaney cautioned herself.

But the hardest part had been done, and now she was able to see her Christmas present was…an old tape recorder?

Surely there must be more to this than a hand me down recorder, Delaney wondered, peering deeper into the box. There was. It appeared to be something cylindrical in shape, three inches in diameter and about one-half inch thick, wrapped in white paper, resting against one of the sides of the box. A recording? *Damn. This is gonna take some effort,* she thought, throwing caution to the wind and rolling up her sleeves to tackle the single piece of tape that stood between her and what was contained on the recording. Six minutes and forty-seven seconds later, armed with a cotton swab and some rubbing alcohol, the strip of tape holding the paper closed came away.

With the perspiration wiped from her brow, Delaney gave herself a literal and figurative pat on the back. The unwrapped reel was in place, its magnetic tape threaded over to the empty take-up reel on the other side of the recorder. Delaney wore the headphones slightly askew so she could keep an ear out for her sister's return. She pressed the play button, not prepared for what she was about to hear as the white noise was pulled away like a theater curtain.

"Hello, Delaney. Merry Christmas, sweetheart. Um…I'm sorry that we haven't been able to decorate the tree or make cookies this year. This holiday has been a little rough, huh?

"Oh, dear, I'm not sure what to say. What can I say, Sweetie? I can imagine that you're disappointed in me for not letting you come into this room to…to see me. I hope you'll let me explain.

"The reason is…this isn't easy to say. I'm dying, Delaney. I can feel that I've lost this battle. And…I didn't want your last memories of me to be pathetic ones, seeing me waste away more than you already have. I couldn't break your heart, but maybe I already did. I haven't let you come in to see me because I'm trying to protect you. Maybe I got it wrong. Can you forgive me?

"If you haven't shut this off yet…I hope you haven't—that is…I wanted to bust my buttons over you. You have grown up so much from that awkward little girl who acted more like an adult—haha. I remember when you tried to determine the lung capacity the Big Bad Wolf needed in order to successfully blow down a house of straw, but then got upset when the fairy tale neglected to stipulate the dimensions of the house. You were, and still are, a beautiful girl. You've brought so much joy, so much *life* into my own….

"Ahem, sorry, dear. I got lost for a bit. Um…yes…but you've grown and changed so much. You have straight As and friends, so much love, and you have great things waiting for you to discover them.

"I know your parents want you to be a math teacher like they are, but as your Grandma, I have seniority and, therefore, a little more weight to my vote. I say that you do what you want. Maybe—and, please, take this as just a suggestion—maybe do something with our recipes? You always seem so, so at peace when you're in the kitchen.

"Anyway, you're young, and I know you still haven't necessarily discovered what really excites you. Ignites your passion. Grandma knows. And as your Grandma, I want that for you, and you should want that for yourself, too. Do you understand?

"Life happens when you make plans, and I know how much you love your lists and schedules. Take my advice, though. Life doesn't operate on a schedule or feels the need to check all the boxes in a predetermined order, not a life that is full and happy. It just doesn't, and you have to exercise some bravery in those times.

"Listen carefully. If something comes out of left field, and it doesn't mesh with what you expected your life to be, or what others think your life should look like, consider it anyway. It may be exactly what you need, and you will be better for it. Embrace this life and let it take you places. Don't contain it in some preconceived mold.

"I know this because I did exactly that. When I was your age, I tried to control every detail of my life, what I expected of it, and it limited me. You think I'm Type-A now?

"Anyway, even when we try to color outside of the lines, us control fanatics will find ourselves panicking and taking an eraser to things, bringing the picture back to how it's 'supposed' to look.

Something tells me, though, your sister won't let that happen to you. She will do for you what Grandpa did for me.

"I don't want this message to end. I love you so much, Delaney. I'm giving you a hug right now. Can you feel it? I hope you can. I pray that you do. Take care. Be you. Live your life. Find your passion no matter what. I—I love you. Will miss you. Miss you already. Bye-bye, Sweetie."

The recorder clicked itself off when Mildred's message finished spooling itself onto the opposite reel. Delaney sat on the floor of the closet in disbelief, pressing the part of the headphone that was over her ear closer as if it would help her better understand what she had heard.

She was stunned and angry, her chest rising and falling from quick shallow breaths. Her brain still weighing the options between crying or screaming into a pillow.

Why? Delaney wondered. Why couldn't Mildred have told her what she had to say a year ago? If only she had let her into the hospital room. The sadness that she kept bottled up deep inside was leaking, drop by drop bobbing to the surface, like oil in water.

But Ophelia knew! Delaney frowned, staring at the recorder. She removed the headphones and quickly packed everything up, precise order be damned, and shoved it back under the armchair. Picking herself up, she moved back into the hallway and began to pace.

Delaney pondered over many things as she moved up and down the hall. Why had Ophelia waited until a year later to give Delaney the recording, and as a gift of all things? Was it some sort of cruel joke? "I don't know," she said to herself after completing a full lap.

She fantasized about confessing to finding her gift right as Ophelia walked into the apartment. The look of shock on her face would all be worth it. Delaney stopped and stood in the middle of the hallway. She realized that she couldn't remember a time when her sister had ever looked surprised. This added to her already agitated state.

Back to the plan. She'd ask Ophelia why she had kept the recording of Mildred from her for all this time. She'd do it before Ophelia even had a chance to take her coat off. Or should she wait until Ophelia had changed into her comfy clothes, thus reducing the probability of her storming off before Delaney could give her a piece of her mind?

Ophelia would probably try to say something slick in a soothing tone. *She always does that.* Delaney scowled, mostly because she knew from experience that this tactic usually worked. *But not this time*, she thought with conviction, albeit wavering.

Waver she did, plus a little wobble, both in thought and in reality; Delaney's socked foot slipped on the kitchen floor. She grabbed the back of the kitchen chair to steady herself. The jolt of her near tumble was enough to move her thoughts from boiled over rage to lukewarm logic.

It's Christmas, Delaney heard her grandmother's voice echo through her mind. Mildred would say these words several times during the holiday, usually to herself and under her breath, a reminder to push down any sort of frustrations she was feeling toward anyone, more than likely Ophelia but not always. Uttering this mantra would become a habit that her granddaughter would internalize, too.

"It's Christmas," Delaney said. She continued to pace the kitchen, all the while backtracking her plans of confrontation and dramatic accusations. Her thoughts bounced back and forth about how she had been wronged, and how the gift was almost callous, to her feelings of guilt for having snooped around. *Maybe Ophelia really did have good intentions, but why wait until now? Maybe…maybe I wasn't ready to get this gift until now.* She hated herself for turning the blame for her anger back on herself.

Delaney stopped in her tracks, her mind drawing a blank on the appropriate course of action. So, Delaney did what she always did when she couldn't pick apart an emotional problem to uncover its solution. She shoved her feelings of frustration toward her sister into a mental junk drawer, along with the little speck of anger she still harbored against her grandmother for leaving that was tangled in her grief and barely recognizable as a result. The metaphorical key was turned clockwise to lock the drawer, leaving the unprocessed emotions to fester.

It's Christmas, she thought, then went to collect her shoes and coat.

*   *   *

The bell that hung over the door of the Wǔ Yàosù Restaurant rang loud and clear as Delaney entered. After a short eight second scan of the dining room, she found Gregory McGregor and Ophelia sitting in a corner booth. Gregory was holding up and admiring a faire isle sweater. Ophelia smiled back at him. "I'm glad you like it, Greg," Delaney heard her sister say sweetly as she slowly approached the table. "There's more."

Gregory pulled out two tickets to the Nollag Cinema's Celestial Saga Saturday, the movie house's all-day marathon of classic sci-fi flicks. "Whoa! I love it!" Gregory replied before giving Ophelia a kiss in gratitude.

The public display of affection made Delaney feel a tad awkward, conjuring up the desire to take another lap around the floor.

"You came," Ophelia said without even a hint of surprise in her tone. The sly smile precariously dancing on her lips contrasted with the toothy grin Delaney sported.

"I did," she replied.

Ophelia scooted over in the tiny red pleather booth, almost causing Gregory to pop onto the floor in what would have been a very funny sight of splayed limbs. Thankfully, or unfortunately to those with more of a grim sense of humor, he was able to quickly reclaim his balance. With a sheepish grin and muffled chuckle, he replaced his arm around Ophelia before casually saying "hi" to Delaney.

"Sooo…what changed your mind?" Ophelia rested her head on Gregory's shoulder and touched the arm wrapped around her.

"Ummm…hmmmn," Delaney purred, pretending to be more interested in the restuaruant's specials, which were not printed on the menu.

"Really? Uh-huh. You found your present then? You rule breaker! You rebel!" Ophelia smiled back, not even attempting to disguise her enthusiasm. "Honestly, you're out of Mom and Dad's house for only a few months…."

"You know, I hear the Gongbao Chicken is really great here," Gregory chimed in and signaled their waiter, Jian, over to the table.

"It is good," Ophelia added, sitting up and sliding over to sit closer to Delaney and look at the menu with her. "I'd recommend crow, but, ya know, it must be out of season."

"Is crow used in Chinese cuisine?" Gregory said in a comically vapid tone and screwed his face into a confused mask of perplexment. Both sisters looked back at him annoyed. "Joke," he said, hands raised in surrender. "Tough crowd." He took a swig of baijiu and stifled a cough, unaccustomed to the one hundred twenty proof.

"Are we ready to order?" Jian asked.

"Yes, we are!" Delaney said. "Wait. What are your specials?" She leaned forward, staring intently back at the waiter.

"Five minutes please, Jian," Ophelia said. "Dee, got something to say for yourself?"

The younger of the O'Leary women relaxed back into the booth. The seat emitted an uncomfortable noise that made the boy at table three shoot his Fish in Sour Soup from his nose.

"Um...." Delaney scrunched her nose and puckered her lips. "Sorry, Ophie. I shouldn't have snooped."

"No. That's not what I wanted to hear," she said seriously.

"Give her a break, Ophelia."

"Sweetie, sisters are talking," Ophelia said over her shoulder.

Delaney paused for a moment, trying to read her sister's expression to come up with the correct response. She pulled her eyebrows together and squinted her eyes as she worked out the words. "Thank you? Thank you," she said with sincerity on her second try.

Ophelia took her sister in her arms with a tight embrace. "You're welcome."

Gregory exhaled a sigh of relief and finished his baijiu in celebration...using gentler sips this time.

And with that, all seemed to be right in Delaney's world, or at least back on the right track. Christmas was something to love again. And despite the small pang of sadness she felt knowing she would never spend another holiday with Mildred, the joy that came with her memories of her grandmother overwhelmingly numbed the pain. Oh, and Gregory was right - the Gongbao Chicken was tasty, bordering on scrumptious.

∗   ∗   ∗

Delaney must have listened to the tape another twelve times before noticing the clock on her nightstand read 12:16 a.m. She gently replaced the recorder on her dresser before crawling under the two fluffy comforters on her bed, one with small pink peonies and the other of a marigold and turquoise paisley pattern.

Merry Christmas, Grandma, Delaney cheerfully thought as she clicked the lamp off. *Please watch over Ophelia. I love you both so much.*

Her own even breathing and gentle warmth of flannel and fluffy pillows had Delaney lulled into a peaceful slumber in five minutes and forty-four seconds.

Within the girl's subconscious, her grandmother's voice came to life with a click of PLAY.

∗   ∗   ∗

Like the recording, the memory had reached its end, and Delaney was back in the present, sitting in her chair in the living room of One Partridge Parkway, left as conflicted about her sister as she was after last year's incident.

Ophelia was capable of very good and sweet things. Ophelia was also capable of very catastrophic epic debacles. One never knew what was coming, and that was the source of the queasy unease in the lower pit of her stomach.

She could not help but wonder what Ophelia was up to that evening, but only for a mere moment. For just as she was pondering the whereabouts of her sister, the formulated thought was disrupted by the approach of a slender silhouette outside the living room window gliding through the gently falling dust bunny sized snowflakes.

But before we welcome this new guest into the story, why should we be left to hypothesize and conjecture the whereabouts of Ophelia O'Leary?

Chapter 14

In Which There Are Stool Pigeons and Sport Coats

In that same moment that Delaney puzzled over what her sister was currently up to, Ophelia was rummaging through her closet. Parting the curtain of dresses and slacks on one of her racks, Ophelia exhaled in triumph. "Here," she said to herself as she unzipped a taupe garment bag, checking to make sure the dress's red fabric did not require a quick steam. Marking her satisfaction with a nod and a smile that all was in order, she zipped the bag back up and moved it to her pile of things she would be taking with her.

She was eighty-six percent certain she would be attending the Nollag police department's party that night. A small part of her, only four percent, still toyed with the idea of showing up to One Partridge Parkway to see Delaney. The remaining ten percent entertained the thought of going home after she dropped off Mynah's gift and Clarence's coat. In any case, she wanted to be prepared for whichever decision she landed on. *Times like these, I wish I knew what the right answer was.*

"Okay," she said to herself, twirling in a small circle about her closet, checking her mental list twice. "Yes."

Throwing on a deep plum three-quarter-length coat over her skinny, dark blue jeans and chunky turtleneck, the light orange one, she quickly glanced over to the mirror, only taking but a moment to straighten the poinsettia brooch affixed to the sweater's collar.

The clock ticked on five-fourteen and tocked on thirty-six seconds past. Not wasting a speck of time, she slung a full hunter green, leather duffle bag over her right shoulder, draped the garment bag over her left arm, and gave a bear hug to the broad box, its top and bottom separately covered in gold paper. A yellow ribbon with glistening five-pointed stars and tiny twinkles was secured to the upper left corner of the lid. A tag with a crumpled corner just beneath the ribbon read *To My One*. The intended message was supposed to say *To My One & Only*, but Ophelia had misgauged the font.

"Oh!" Ophelia said as she passed through the threshold. She shifted the box under one arm, gently pressing it to her side to make sure the lid didn't come loose, and stooped to pick up a small black suit bag that was hanging on the closet door's crystal doorknob. "For Clarence…."

The clock clicked into place quietly letting her know the time was 5:15 p.m. Another ten seconds, and Ophelia would respond with the click of a closing apartment door and a clack as she locked the deadbolt and a jumbling sound as her box and bags all tumbled to the floor. Sigh. This was going to be a long walk over to the Wallace and Davis Flats on Green Street.

To Ophelia's surprise, the temperature felt slightly warmer than the projected thirty degrees Fahrenheit, more like thirty-seven, give or take a tenth of a degree. She found herself better able to juggle her cumbersome cargo as the air neither nipped nor outright bit at her nose or earlobes. Except for the unanticipated dance across some black ice, Ophelia managed to reach the front of the Wallace and Davis Flats without any mishap.

She proceeded inside and was welcomed with a tip of a top hat from the doorman. "Miss O'Leary, Merry Christmas. How are you doing? Here to see Mr. Smith?" Harvey Feedle continued without waiting for a reply from Ophelia as these questions were merely practiced pleasantries and did not really require answers.

As Harvey continued chatting with no one in particular, he pushed past his mahogany desk with pristinely white gloved hands. Ophelia took in the lobby's welcoming décor, clad in warm creams, deep maroons, and rich golds. The pair passed a plump circular couch complete with matching, round, throw pillows with braided golden accents. The walls contained heavy tapestries of firefighters and police officers in heroic poses in front of dramatic scenes in modern clean lines and encased in chocolate wood frames. The Wallace and Davis Flats were a predominant haven for Nollag's law enforcement and fire protection.

Over the chatter of the soles of their shoes against the intricately tiled floor of maroon and beige squares, triangles, and tiny diamonds, Ophelia sensed Harvey was wrapping up his thoughts with neat little bows complete with cute curlicues in the form of a punchline. "Needless to say, Mack is no fan of fans. Haha."

Ophelia followed suit with a chortle that did not leave Harvey completely convinced, but that he would acquiesce to buy.

"Anyway, what's in the box, Ms. O'Leary?" Harvey asked as he pulled back the cast iron elevator gates, so Ophelia could step inside.

"Harvey, you can call me Ophelia. I've only told you two hundred fifty-three times."

"Two hundred fifty-four now." His deep brown eyes crinkled as apple cheeks rose with his smile. "You okay gettin' up there by yourself?" he asked, watching Ophelia continue to precariously balance her things on trembling arms. He was deliberate in leaving off the "Ms. O'Leary" part.

"I'll manage, Harv. Thanks."

"Let me at least get—" Harvey made sure both of the elevator's gates were securely closed and tipped his hat to Ophelia.

Pressing the button for the ninth floor with her elbow, the elevator whirred to life. Ophelia was slowly on her way. The lift creaked, and the tarnished arrow overhead slightly shuddered as it moved clockwise, wavering a bit as it pointed to each floor. Three… four…five…. Even as it shuddered to a halt, having reached its destination, Ophelia's expression was unflinching. It may have seemed rickety, but the elevator was reliable. She gave out a "tsk," realizing she would have to set part of her load down in order to move the gate aside and exit the cramped cube.

The sound of paper sliding against the checkered tile whistled across the hall, gently stopping against apartment 9D with a tap, stop number one. The clatter caused from Ophelia closing the elevator gates drowned out the inhaled whisper of 9D's door opening to greet her.

"Hello there," a woman with wavy, butterscotch-colored hair said. Her deep-blue eyes complemented the ill-fitted, pale blue, pinstriped shirt she wore and the thin, marigold towel slung over her right shoulder. A small baby boy, twenty-five days old, wiggled in her arms and drooled on the spit up rag.

Dazed for only a moment, Ophelia looked pleased to see her friend Gin Flic. "Hey," she said in a gentle whisper and giving Gin a light embrace, careful not to disturb little Dalton. "How are you?"

"I'm good. Yeah, really good," she replied with a strained smile that revealed all her teeth. "A little on edge from a significant loss of sleep, but how can I be mad at this guy?" She regarded Dalton with a nod of her head. The little almost month-old baby nestled further into the blanket and brought a tiny pink fist up to shield his chubby face from the hallway's bright lights.

"Freakin' adorable."

Gin gave a muted laugh and then mouthed an "I know, right?"

"So, no sleep, huh?" Along with the gold box, Ophelia shed her bags in a pile by the door, save for a small package she plucked from the green leather bag, a gift for little Dalton.

"Oh! Thank you!" Gin exclaimed. "Don't worry. You can still sleep easy. No criminals are getting away with shi—uh, crime on my watch. Sleep deprivation be…darned. Darned? Is that a word? I am so tired."

"What about Olive? How is she holdin' up?"

"Maternity leave is making her batty." Gin gently rocked Dalton, who was beginning to make little groans. "I think she wants to get back on patrol with Clarence. Can't blame her, though. Dalton here is not big on conversation so much as he is on pooping."

"Hi, Ophelia," a groggy voice croaked from behind Gin.

"Olive, looking fabulous as always," Ophelia lied.

"You're lucky I just woke up, or else I might take that as an insult. But thanks," she laughed, sweeping some stray hairs away from her puffy eyes. "You visiting Clarence?" She looked across the hall.

But Olive was not interested in the answer, still not fully equipped to assemble her thoughts, let alone coherent ones, into anything that even mildly resembled adult conversation. Instead, she kicked into mommy-mode and reached for Dalton. Dalton pumped his legs and arms and took quick breaths, unsure if now was a good time to cry.

"Oh, is he ready to eat?" Olive asked.

"Yup," answered Gin, handing over their son, who changed course from his almost tantrum to gurgling and blowing little spit bubbles out the corners of his plump lips, which could barely contain the little pink tongue sandwiched between even pinker gums.

"Are you ready to eat? Do you want nom-noms?" Olive cooed at him.

Gin accepted the gift Ophelia was holding. "Thank you so much!" She balanced the present in her hand, as if to determine its weight, then gave it a gentle shake, listening intently. The tip

194

of her tongue pokes out of the corner of her mouth. "I'm going to guess...rattle?"

Ophelia smiled and shrugged. Memories of her first Christmas with the O'Learys momentarily danced through her mind. "The tag says, 'Don't Open Until Christmas.' Looks like you have a few more hours before you can find out."

"Thank you. Ophelia, always a pleasure," Olive said with an absentminded smile and swept back into the bedroom.

"Happy feeding," Ophelia called after her. Her expression faltered for a beat, reconsidering how awkward that salutation had sounded.

"Maybe for one of us. This little bambino has such suction on him. I'm still feeling it in my right boob from earlier."

They all laughed. Ophelia shuddered, trying not to think about what that must actually feel like.

"How's your day been so far?" Gin asked as she transferred freshly folded laundry from the couch to a basket.

"Um, ran some errands today," Ophelia replied simply. "Dropping off a suit coat and a surprise for the party tonight." She indicated the box. "You're going to be there?"

Gin answered the question with an amused glare, but then switched her expression to genuine excitement. "Oh! Wait! Copper's thing! That's tonight!" she gasped, doing a little hopping dance in her striped woolen socks. "Can I see it? Olive! Come here for a minute!"

Ophelia grabbed the large golden box and carried it into the apartment, placing it on the kitchen table after Gin had cleared away the stacks of junk mail and the dirty dishes from lunch.

Peeling back the tissue paper, Gin took in the sight of the yellow and gold gown and let out a gasp that ended in a high-pitched squeak. "Ugh, she's going to love it! Copper's going to love her in it! I wish we could be there," she cried, looking back at her wife, who was supporting Dalton's head as he suckled. If only she could be in two places at once. "You'll be there, though? You'll have to let us know how it goes!"

"Clarence will fill you in tomorrow," offered Ophelia as she replaced the lid on the box.

"Aren't you going?" Olive asked, now a little more awake. Nursing had that effect on her.

"Uh, nah—not really a cop." Ophelia's resolve to attend quickly plummeted to forty-four percent, the idea of returning home becoming the slightly more appealing option at fifty-two percent. The option of going to see Delaney still held at four percent.

"Accurate, but you're kind of an honorary one."

Ophelia squirmed, for once not comfortable in the spotlight and wishing to talk about something else.

"You helped with that illegal resale scam those two at the Deal and Steal were carrying out, didn't you? Take me through what was going on again," Olive asked, gently swaying Dalton as he continued to nurse.

"Swinde was the mastermind behind all those thefts. Wasn't hard for her to go about the richer part of the city and five-finger discount some new merchandise from the more senile residents. I mean, her partner did all the heavy lifting. They were the one scoping out the hospital and visiting patients after they were discharged under the guise of wellness checks when they were really there making a list of potential things to purloin for Swinde to review.

"Swinde doesn't have those kind of people skills. I doubt anyone would have let her through the door." She frowned, recollecting Adele's customer service skills from that morning.

"Yes, Copper was saying that all this started over at the hospital," Olive added.

"Mmhm." Ophelia shook off her coat and fanned herself with her sweater. "They were a candy striper. The partner, not Swinde." Ophelia conjured an image of Adele in her mind wearing that pinstripe pink and white uniform. *No*, she said to herself, preventing the image from taking any further detail.

"Makes sense," Gin mused. "Patients are hopped up on drugs, taken in by someone offering them some sympathy. I'm guessing they wouldn't notice a couple things missing here and there, let alone remembered they still owned them."

"Sorry," Olive addressed the two women. "The other guy at the Deal and Steal was the candy striper?" She frowned, the idea like a square peg trying to fit into a triangular opening.

"Innocent," Ophelia corrected her. "Nice guy, actually. Nice legs, too." She thought back to the kilt.

Gin decided to leave that one alone, unsure if she had actually heard Ophelia correctly.

"After her partner got nabbed, Adele started to work alone."

"Okay. No more shop talk. Really, though, you should go to the party." Gin's tone was stern.

"I'll think about it." And this time, Ophelia was honest.

"Well, we won't keep you from Clarence. Merry Christmas."

"Don't be a stranger," Olive said brightly, sitting Dalton up against her shoulder to be burped. He ripped a magnificent one.

"I won't," Ophelia said. "Enjoy that baby boy." With a hug and help collecting her cargo, Ophelia was off to Clarence's apartment, which was across the hall and a little to the right.

Laden down, she walked the width of the hall to stand in front of apartment 9C, which was now C9 since the landlord absentmindedly inverted the letter and digit when he had replaced the tarnished numbers last year. Clarence had never bothered to have it corrected. Packages shuffled inside the duffle bag, and the friction between the garment bags made them hiss and whistle. Ophelia was barely able to get in two raps on the door, almost dropping Mynah's present in the process. The door shuddered for a moment. The doorknob's latch bolt was not completely nestled in the lock but threatened to seek its home.

Ophelia began to tap her foot. Clearly, five seconds was three seconds too long of a wait. Clarence knew of her lack of patience and occasionally tested its limits. The door seemed to sense her agitated mood and swung back on its own to open a crack. She could hear the clinking of dishes among other things on the other side of the door.

"Cheese it! It's the fuzz!" a voice clicked on and off.

"This is the police! Come out with your hands up!" another distant voice echoed.

"Yous'll never take me alive, you dirty cat!"

"Stool, it's rat," a third voice corrected. "Come on in!"

Ophelia entered unfazed to what sounded like a questionable impression of gunfire.

Two African Greys were perched on top of a large cage in the center of the apartment.

"Ahh! Ya got me!" Stool shrieked, flapping his wings.

"Talk, scum!" Pigeon, yelled back.

"Never!" Stool said, his head rolling in figure eights.

"All right, all right. Stoo. Pidge," Clarence said in a firm tone. His back was turned away from the door, dealing with emptying a boiling pot of spaghetti. "Make yourself comfortable, Ophelia. Tea?" A kettle on the back left burner started to shriek.

"Yes, please. Green. No sugar. No milk. Thanks." Ophelia described her preferences slowly and clearly enunciated each syllable.

Clarence nodded along with each detail of her order. "The usual," he replied. "You forget one time…" he muttered and laughed to himself.

There was a loud clatter, a mixture of Ophelia shedding the bags, and Stool and Pigeon clamoring to get inside the cage and running their beaks against the bars — their way of telling Clarence it was time to eat. Ophelia carried Mynah's gift over to the coffee table, setting it down gently.

"Be there in a minute," Clarence said, replacing the pasta back into the pot and ladling a little marinara sauce over it so the noodles wouldn't clump together. He bustled about his tiny kitchen pulling dishes from the cabinet over the sink, collecting a cutting board from behind the bread box, and making no more than two trips to the fridge to retrieve what was needed to prep the bird's dinner and the tea for Ophelia and himself. "Almost done," Clarence said over the furious chatter of his knife slicing through an orange pepper.

He loaded up a tray of the food and beverages, carrying it over expertly balanced on one hand.

"Will I get out for good behavior?" Stool asked as Clarence placed two stoneware ramekins inside, one full of sweet potatoes, cucumbers, and peppers and the other with apples and melon.

"We'll see," Clarence said as he locked the cage.

Ophelia leaned over the arm of the forest green plaid sofa, head in hand, unsure of what level of entertainment this should be categorized at.

"I'm not crazy," Clarence said with a devilish half-smile, flashing only a few of his pearly white teeth. He picked up a teacup off the tray and handed it to Ophelia. The saucer was a bright hibiscus red and the cup itself was a delicate porcelain outlined in silver vines and flowers. There was a tiny candy cane hooked to the inside of the cup.

"I know," Ophelia said. "You're more eclectic, which is easily confused with crazy." She sipped at the tea. It had been brewed at the perfect temperature of one hundred seventy degrees Fahrenheit and only steeped for three minutes. "So, something weird happened today." Ophelia gritted her teeth, unsure if she should share her gossip.

"Yeah?" Clarence asked.

"I *saw* today."

"Wha—?" Clarence exhaled his surprise, dissipating a puff of vapor off his mug.

Ophelia bobbed her head up and down. "It wasn't as clear as before, but when I looked at Fulgencia Wick, I saw her getting flattened by a sheet of ice."

"Is she—"

"I stopped it. She's safe."

Clarence took a seat next to Ophelia, setting his mug on the coffee table. "What does this mean, Ophie?"

"I don't…" she paused, drinking in the excitement that lit up her friend's face. "I don't think it means anything has changed, Clare. At least, it doesn't feel like anything has changed. I tried to see again when I met with Delaney, but nothing happened. Maybe it was a fluke." She frowned.

Clarence placed his hand on top of Ophelia's and gave it a pat. He attempted twice to say something comforting but never got past the initial inhale to start his sentence until he finally managed to say, "I wish I knew." More specifically, Clarence wished he knew if Ophelia would, indeed, remain Ophelia O'Leary indefinitely, until, that is, her life came to a definite end as all mortal life must. Neither of them fully comprehended the consequences that came with the loss of Ophelia's powers, and it was this lack of clarification that made them both uneasy whenever the topic of conversation presented itself.

"It's okay. I'm okay." Ophelia said, breaking the somber mood and changing the subject. "I have something for you." She set down her tea and reached for the black suit bag.

Clarence eyed the bag for a moment, his eyebrows raising as he tried to deduce its contents. "You didn't seriously…" he trailed, running his hand through his slick light brown hair.

"Oooh, yes, I did." She unzipped the suit bag.

Inside was a navy-blue sport coat.

"I know you don't like gold," Ophelia said, indicating the bright blue buttons. But the true surprise was in the details of the coat. The lining was made of a familiar soft cerulean material. Clarence took the jacket from Ophelia and stroked the lining, his childhood blanket.

"Fantastic," Clarence said with such gusto it actually made Ophelia blush.

"You're welcome," she replied, not taking her eyes off his large grin.

"I'll wear it tonight at the Christmas party. I actually don't have to work this year!" Clarence had worked Christmas Eve ever since he had joined the Nollage police force. For many, this would be elating news, but Ophelia knew that Clarence had always volunteered to take other people's shifts on that night. This year, however, he had a very particular reason to attend.

"Wear it with the navy pants, your textured black lace ups, navy vest, red tie, the chambray one, and the red gingham shirt."

"You decide yet if you're coming, Ophie?"

"Uh…" she started, mentally noting that the idea of attending the party had gained three point six percentage points from the idea of going home. Going to Delaney's had donated one percentage point, too.

"Unless…you're going to Delaney's?" He winced at his own question.

Ophelia shook her head in reply. "I honestly thought about it, but I can't. I want to, but let's be honest, Clare, she doesn't really want to see me." Her voice became low and somber. "And I wouldn't know how the whole thing would play out. And we're— you're leaving soon…." Her shoulders slumped, and her thumb and index finger stroked the pinkie of the other hand. She tried to console herself with the thought that Clarence, even after he moved on to assume another life, would come back and visit her. Of this, she was certain. Yet, she could not overlook the fear that with this major change, their friendship, too, would become the worse for wear. With enough time, it seemed inevitable that this life alteration would cause one of them to pull away from the other.

Clarence fidgeted in place, wresting with his own thoughts, wishing his foresight would help him, but it didn't work with those like himself and Ophelia. Try as he might, he could not definitively see what the future held for his friend. "Well…the party's at 7:00 at Brailin's Brewery and Pub. I figure maybe you'd like to admire your handiwork. Plus, you know, it would be great if you came out. I feel like you've kind of fallen off the face of the Earth."

"Our handiwork," Ophelia said, ignoring the last bit of what Clarence said. She took another sip of the now peppermint-infused green tea. "I am but an accomplice."

"As am I," Clarence chuckled.

"Speaking of which," Ophelia said with no intention of completing the statement. She indicated the golden gift in front of her with a grand flourish of her hand, then leaned forward to remove the lid.

"Whoa," Clarence said, mouth hanging open in awe. He stooped down to pick up the box to get a closer look at the details of the gown. "Oof! It's heavy," he said incredulously. His eyes gazed up to the ceiling as he tried to guess the weight. *Twelve pounds, six ounces*, he guessed before setting the box back down.

"It's not heavy. It's really fabulous," Ophelia grinned back at him as she replaced the lid.

Stool picked at the latch of the cage while Pigeon looked the other way.

"All right, well this fabulous—ous—ness," Clarence stumbled over the word, "will make its way across town in about thirty minutes or less." He flashed a straight smile so perfect Ophelia felt compelled to take a snapshot, if only she had a camera.

"Don't make it sound like a pizza," Ophelia retorted as she swigged the last bit of her tea. The candy cane made a lap around the circumference of the cup as she replaced it on its saucer. "Fabulous and pizza are usually mutually exclusive."

"Uh-huh. Well, speak for yourself. I think pizza is fabulous," he replied as he picked up his suitcoat, walked down the small hall, and deposited it in his room.

"Clarence," Ophelia called after him as she walked into the kitchen. "It's that—I'm not sure—maybe I shouldn't go…to the party tonight. I could change things. Mess things up for Copper and Mynah."

"How so?" he called back. There was concern in his tone, the specific variety used between friends when one is about to make a decision for all the wrong reasons.

"You know," she replied, placing her teacup into the sink, "the delicate fabric of events and how my certainty in it all is uncertain now."

There was a pause from the bedroom. Ophelia could only assume Clarence was gathering his thoughts and carefully stringing them together like popcorn on thread.

While she waited for his response, she moved to the stove to sample the pasta sauce.

"The silver is behind the cookies," Stool said almost with a laugh.

"Mook," Pigeon replied from under his wing.

"You won't," Ophelia finally heard Clarence say, his voice coming in loud and clear with one hundred percent certainty as he returned to the living room. "There are no other outcomes other than the one we had planned and worked toward for Copper. The fabric has been reinforced with triple stitching."

Ophelia smiled in appreciation of her friend's carefully chosen sewing reference. "I gotta go," Ophelia said to Clarence, almost tripping over one of the small green kitchen chairs on her way to the door.

"You okay?"

"Fine. Fabulous, even," she said with dripping sarcasm. "I'll see you later." Ophelia bent down to scoop up the rest of her things.

"Gotta ask. What's in there?" He indicated the taupe garment bag.

Ophelia thought about her response. Should she tell him the truth or maybe say something cute like "Get a warrant"? She decided to go the cryptic route. "My decision."

He smiled back, knowing that he would see her later that night, making a mental note to act surprised when Ophelia made her appearance.

And with that, she gave him a hug and pecked him on the right cheek and was on her way.

"Oh, you may want to re-hide the silver," she said before closing the door to apartment 9C. Well, C9, presently.

"Again?" Clarence said with a perturbed expression directed at Stool. The bird stretched his wings back as if to shrug.

*   *   *

Who could it be? Gin wondered to herself only to have Olive ask her the same question from the baby's room as she changed Dalton's diaper. "Ophelia," Gin said brightly.

"Hey," Ophelia replied gratefully, slipping into the apartment with bags in tow.

"Come in," Gin said with a giggle after the fact.

"I decided that I'm going to go to the party." She grinned. "Mind if I get ready here?"

"Not at all!" Gin offered to hang up the garment bag.

"If you thought the yellow dress was stunning…hold that thought," Ophelia said more to herself than Gin. "Can I use your phone?"

"Sure thing," Gin said, already beginning to open the garment bag to have a look at the dress.

Chapter 15

In Which Pretty Petunia Enters the Story and Grey Turns Up Looking Rather Gruesome

To some, Petunia Perkins was in a constant state of Halloween. Her self-presentation was unconventional to say the least. But growing up will do that to you, and college tends to either expedite or snuff out one's true self.

Delaney eagerly ran to open the door to welcome her best friend to her home. "Hello, friend," she said to her, cocking her head quizzically to one side and wearing an uneven smile in the silly way friends do. "Let me take your stuff."

"Hello, friend," Petunia lyrically repeated back, equally as happy. She handed over her silver-gray motorcycle jacket with thick hat, mittens, and scarf, all in a deep purple with small spots of lavender woven through them; that and a bottle of wine, a merlot from the year Delaney and Petunia became friends.

Petunia had a full face with sparkling narrow eyes. Her broad smile almost made it appear as if her eyes were shut tight. Her face was framed by an asymmetrical haircut, most was a short choppy cut, save for the front, which cascaded down the left side of her face. The onyx hair faded to a deep purple at the tip.

"I love your dress."

"Thank you!" Petunia said excitedly, twirling and letting the sequins and crystals that dripped from the dusty lavender flapper dress catch the light and rap against the midnight blue skinny jeans she wore beneath them. With her left hand firmly planted on her hip and a swelled chest, she struck a powerful pose, drawing herself up to her full height of five foot ten and swinging her long sweeping strand of knotted pearls in her right hand.

"Cal, Petunia's here…and she brought wine," Delaney called up the stairs.

Calum's footfalls against the thick oak steps nearly muted his salutation. "Hey, Petunia! How's that Ph.D. program been treating ya?"

It didn't take long for Petunia to consider her answer. "It's been amazing! So fun."

"I can't wait for the day I get to officially say I know a doctor of fairy tales," Calum added.

"Right? It's going to be wicked awesome." Petunia did a little jig.

"I want a copy of the dissertation," Calum grinned.

"So you can put me in one of your columns? Congratulations on the new job by the by."

"Maybe, and thank you," Calum said with a nod of his head and a point of his index finger in Petunia's general direction.

"Shall we all proceed to the drawing room?" Delaney said with a theatrical bow.

"We shall," Calum said. The trio locked arms and strolled into the living room, each somehow managing to keep a straight face.

Delaney was the first to break character when the doorbell bellowed and boomed in a frantic mess of colliding notes with some frantic knocking for percussion.

"Coming!" Delaney looked back at Calum and Petunia, indicating she found this rather odd.

"That's not Greg is it?" Calum asked checking his wristwatch. "He's early. Like by twenty minutes."

Delaney shrugged in reply as she scooted to the hall and opened the door.

The chilling wind seemed to spit the man across the threshold, his knees still knocking together, causing the icicles attached to the bottoms of his wool trousers to chatter.

"Grey?" A flummoxed Delaney stepped aside to welcome her sister's boss into the home.

The man only managed to squelch out an "uh-huh." For warmth, he only wore his tweed suitcoat, the one capped with leather at the elbows.

"Uh, Grey, Ophelia's not here, if you're looking for her—"

"Good," he replied flatly. His eyes slightly bulged from his head, and his face thawed enough so that he could work his mouth into a frown. Grey Terne was a very, very unhappy man that Christmas Eve night at the residence of Delaney O'Leary and Calum Dooley on One Partridge Parkway.

Chapter 16

In Which Ophelia's Alleged Loose Lips Cause an Unraveling of Grey's Sanity

"Ophelia blabbed," Grey said, hysteria running rampant in his tone. His chest heaved up and down as if he had run a marathon.

Delaney, on the other hand, held onto her breath in her throat behind the uvula. *Blabbed? She wouldn't do that to Grey... would she?* This was, after all, only one side of the story. Snap judgements only led to more snap judgements and troubles, like a lit string of firecrackers.

Regardless, Delaney's doubts offered their two cents on the situation. *Then again, Ophelia is not known for keeping her nose out of other people's business, be they stranger, acquaintance, friend, or family.*

Petunia and Calum entered the hall. They moved three steps forward and immediately took one full step and a shuffle back after seeing the crazed look on Grey's face, which was similar to a drenched cat's.

"Grey, what's the matter?" Petunia asked. She brought her hands to clasp her bare arms, imagining how miserably cold Grey must be feeling.

"Ophelia blabbed," he repeated. The small mounds of snow from his salt-stained boots began to shudder off and collect into a small wet mess.

Delaney took Grey by the arm and pulled him to the fire. "Okay. All right," she said slowly in between each of his inhales and exhales. "First, we need to get you warm. No sense in being upset and sick."

"Although Ophelia has that effect on people," Petunia said with half-lidded eyes. Delaney shot her a glance that was both knowing and ever-so-slightly hurt.

"Uh, second," Delaney continued, "you'll tell us what happened…if you want."

"Jus—just blabbed," Grey muttered absently. He remained in this catatonic state as he was wrapped in Delaney's beloved yellow, white, and gold knitted blanket, plopped into Delaney's denim chair, and handed a mug of brandy. After his first swig of the drink, he let out a slow wheezing noise and began to blink away some of the shock to join the rest of the group.

"Grey, what did Ophelia blab?" Delaney clasped his boney fingers, her thumb reassuringly stroked the back of his hand.

"My secret," he gulped, trying to steady his voice. "Not a secret anymore," he said under his breath.

"Start from the beginning," Calum added, rocking on his heels, cradling the bottle of brandy.

Grey remained silent, not hearing Calum.

"Oh," Calum said, realizing he was speaking into Grey's bad ear. He moved over to Grey's left and repeated his request.

Grey took in a shuddering breath and began. "Well, I was at the shop. Finishing up some alterations and counting out the safe, and they...My parents came in." He looked back to blank stares. It hadn't dawned on him until then that the trio hadn't the vaguest thought of what exactly Ophelia had leaked. Each of them, to varying degrees, however, could not deny that whatever the news was, so long as its tidbits were slightly juicy, Ophelia was prone to divulge it to any an open ear. "They didn't know about the shop," he confessed. "I mean, they knew I had *a* shop, but not *this* shop. Dresses. Not suits."

"Couldn't they have come on their own? What makes you think Ophelia had anything to do with it?" Calum offered.

"I was supposed to go to Glory, like I always do." The panic began to creep into his voice, driving it up one full decibel. "Ow," he said when Delaney clamped down on his hand.

"Sorry," she said, making a wincing face. "Continue with the story, Grey. What did they say?"

"'So, this is your shop?' my father says. He kept looking it up and down. My mother kinda stood there like a deer in the headlights clutching at her coat. I think she might have started to cry." He removed his hand from Delaney's and chewed on his thumbnail, which was swapped out for a cracker with cheese by Petunia.

"What else?" Petunia sat down on the sofa.

"That dress is beautiful on you," Grey said, really seeing Petunia for the first time since he got in. He pulled his eyes off the beadwork and got back on topic. "I'm not exactly sure. I panicked and fled the shop."

"You left your parents? In the shop? Alone?"

"No. Kitty was still there. She'll close up."

"Then you came here?"

"I went to your sister's first…when I figured out what to say— really cutting stuff—and…and got up the nerve to say something to her. I was seeing red at that point…uh, figuratively, of course," he laughed softly at his own joke. "When no one answered, I came here. You're her emergency contact." Grey paused to shove the cracker and cheese in his mouth, muttering to himself as he chewed, "Lost my courage and my words by that time, though."

"Grey, not that I'm discounting you, but I still don't see how you know Ophelia was the one who let the cat out of the bag." Calum carefully monitored Grey's reaction to each uttered syllable.

"Could this all be a coincidence?" Delaney wondered. "Maybe they came to surprise you?"

"And maybe," Calum offered, "your parents were the good kind of shocked when they saw your shop."

Petunia remained quiet, finding it futile to attempt a positive spin on any situation where Ophelia was concerned.

Grey Terne shook his head vigorously, unable to allow an alternate theory to buzz around his head in between his good ear and his bad ear. "She said to me today, 'You know it will come out.' Like she was warning me what was coming. She told them to come here," he said with his thumb lodged between his teeth again. "She did. She didn't agree how I was handling things, so she took it into her own hands. This is more than just a fluke."

Petunia raised her eyebrows in agreement.

Grey took another gulp of the brandy and gagged. Spitting out the thought, "It's her fault I even opened up the shop." His eyes widened as his mind fabricated a conspiracy theory at his mental loom that even all those years ago, when they met in college, Ophelia had lulled him into a false sense of security by spinning her own web of deceit. She had convinced him to open up a dress shop, granted a dream of his, all the while waiting to have the whole thing come crashing down around him in the form of an unexpected visit from Mom and Dad. The plot was all for her own sick entertainment. (Grey Terne was not wrong…about the first part, at least.)

Everyone in that room had been a victim of her schemes, but they all had managed to survive them. Had Ophelia been there, however, she would have opted to use the word 'grow.'

Delaney knew the right thing to do was to defend her sister and try to present more reasonable doubt. This conviction wavered and flickered like a waning light bulb. She reflected back on last year, and a smoldering, messy feeling putrefied in the bottom of her stomach.

She was finding herself feeling slightly upset. Not because her sister's boss was bashing her and would most likely fire her. No, that was not it, but the very clear decision that she could not defend her sister. She felt horrible. Because of Ophelia's tomfoolery, Delaney had found herself in the awkward position of having to hear about her sister's deeds, usually in tones that somehow made her feel responsible for her sister's actions.

She played with the charms on her bracelet, her thumb and index finger settling on a tarnished gold-plated pewter heart engraved with a message on the inside. Her then nine-year-old father had scrimped and saved weekly allowance after weekly allowance to purchase the locket for Mother's Day, which his father would acquire on his behalf. Edwin had told him the charm, plus engraving, was twenty dollars. In reality, with the inscription of 'Infinite — EO,' it came to thirty-five. Edwin covered the difference.

The doorbell rang out once more, breaking the silence and bringing life and movement back into the room.

"I'll get it," Calum announced. "Maybe this is Greg." He checked at his wristwatch again. Greg wasn't due for another twelve minutes. "Please let this be Greg," he muttered to himself, walking toward the front door.

"Grey, don't worry about this," Petunia said sympathetically.

He looked back at her with a chummy smile. The sort of one he sported when he was receiving advice he had no intention of taking.

"You'll get past it." She mirrored his expression.

"Mm-hm," Delaney said absentmindedly watching the flames dance from red to orange to yellow. *Do you? Get over it?*

"Time for wine," Petunia said, jumping from the sofa and clapping her hands together in anticipation.

Chapter 17

In Which the "Pity Party" Has Officially Assembled

Gregory McGregor had one of those booming voices, the sort that could make the walls vibrate, and a laugh that would have the cautious bracing themselves in a doorway.

The trio could hear his jovial salutations from the living room, followed by a bang and a short cough. "Hellohohoho! Merry Christmas to all!" Gregory boomed, arms spanning six feet and five inches wide. His coal black eyes sparkled behind the longish dark hair that fell haphazardly about his face. Calum ducked under his arm clutching at his side, unable to reach the spot where Gregory had clapped him on the back. He attempted a smile, but it looked pained.

"Oh," Gregory said, taking note of the pensive stares looking back at him. "Sigh. What has Ophelia done now?" His heavy-footed steps caused the furniture to scooch a sixty-fourth of an inch against the hardwood floor. The sofa cushion flattened to the thickness of cardboard as he took a seat next to Petunia. He nodded at Petunia cordially, who raised her glass in salutation, before turning to look at Grey intently. "Well, Grey, out with it."

"Wow, detective," Delaney said incredulously, "nothing gets by you."

"Eh, it's all in the details. The disheveled appearance, the lack of color in the face…the almost empty mug of," Gregory sniffed, "apricot brandy, is it? Telltale signs of the Ophelia-kind." A crooked smile formed as memories recounted themselves in Gregory's head.

"You dated Ophelia." Petunia said. "I have to ask, what was that like?" she inquired into her glass of wine.

"Hey," he shrugged, "it wasn't so bad. We lasted for about three years."

Calum noticed that Gregory kept his gaze fixed on the fringe of the area rug as he said this. Delaney squinted her eyes at his response. Now that she thought of it, she never knew the story behind what happened between Gregory and her sister. Some questions had a 'No Peeking and No Prying' label covering the answer.

One day, the two of them were fine. The next…like they never had known one another. Ophelia never mentioned Gregory after that New Year's Eve night almost three years ago, and Ophelia never ever passed up an opportunity to include someone in on the inner workings of her life…at least that was Delaney's impression.

Petunia continued to wear a peculiar expression on her face, her mouth working into a wry smile. Gregory could see the

218

skepticism radiating from her. Calum grimaced at the cold front that was moving into the living room from the northeast.

"What?" Gregory worked out through laughs. "I take it you've had a less than pleasurable run-in with Ophelia?" He wore his best interrogator face, unflinching eyes locked on Petunia's.

Squirming in her seat, Petunia dissected Gregory's words. "Well, to be honest—mmm—one time was enough. She almost— it felt like she tried to ruin my life." She winced at the truth of her own words. There was no coating that in sugar and passing it off as pure unadulterated holiday cheer.

Grey made a noise into his mug as if what Petunia said was funny and, sadly, true.

"I get it, Petunia," Gregory said reassuringly. "If it's the truth, it is what it is." He punctuated his thought with a frown, making his face appear one and a quarter centimeters longer than it actually was. "Hey, maybe Cal can get an article out of this…with a couple name and detail changes to protect the innocent, of course."

Calum's mouth quivered into a fleeting uncomfortable smile as he turned to look out the window to stare at the cold punctuated with bright glowing dots of green, red, blue, yellow, purple, and orange. He was not as quick to write Ophelia off or write about her for that matter. That's saying something since she was the one who halted his impending engagement last year. There was more to the story, and the chapter that followed after, he rationalized, was pretty darn good.

Petunia gave a sideways glance to Delaney, and there she let it hang like an icicle precariously pointed over her head. It was a look that seemed to ask, *Can I?*

What was the big deal? Families talked behind each other's backs all the time, right? But why the suffocating sense of guilt? Delaney twirled the charms of the bracelet between her fingers again, each igniting a flash of a memory and story. Her thumb grazed the back of the large gold-plated heart, feeling the uneven scratches that rand the width of the locket. With that, the guilt and the icicle evaporated into thin air.

"It's okay," said Delaney. She nodded to Petunia, giving her permission to share her tale.

Petunia took a deep breath as she pulled her tragic tale from the back of her mind. Grey, now fully defrosted, was able to bend forward and clutched the meager sip left in his mug. Gregory folded his large hands in his lap as he settled himself into the sofa. Calum only ticked his left ear in their general direction but made no move from his place by the window.

Chapter 18

In Which We Hear the Story of the Princess and the Pink Guilded Cage

The tale about to unfurl occurred on the Eve of Christmas, four years before, give or take an hour here and a sprinkling of minutes there. Both O'Leary sisters were attending the University of Nollag. Delaney was in her sophomore year, and Ophelia was completing her senior year.

Delaney chose to make the trip to Glory with her grandfather to see her parents. Ophelia had opted to stay behind to help with the Christmas pageant the university was hosting for the children of Mother Mary Claire Brog's Haven for Tiddlers, Toddlers, Tykes, and Children, a project obviously very near and dear to her heart.

"You'll love the play," Ophelia said, with three pins held between her perfectly aligned teeth. She was trying to reinforce the stitching of an overstuffed Santa Claus belly.

"I'm sure I will," Mynah said. "The costumes alone are breathtaking. Did you do them all?"

"Ptu! Excuse me. Yes, well, myself and Grey." She nodded to the knobby kneed young man currently giving his undivided attention to an emerald green dress. "He did all the girls costumes, and I did all the boys. Don't ask," Ophelia said in reply to Mynah's puzzled expression. "The kids will love the play. Never before seen! In fact, here comes the playwright now. Petunia!"

A slight looking girl of above average height jumped, dropping her script with such a clatter. The noise startled a spindly looking stagehand by the name of Windom Twonee. The chain reaction continued when Windom bumped into Grey. Grey then stabbed his own thumb instead of the dress's sleeve with the needle.

"Oh!" Petunia gasped over the muted whimpers in the background. She scooped up her script, along with a wrinkled green flyer, and toddled over to the two women.

"I'd like you to meet Ms. Mynah Moriel. She was, uh, kinda like a mother when I was at Mary Claire's," Ophelia said, indicating the woman next to her with a nod of her flaming hair.

"Nice to meet you," Petunia said from behind her long straight hair, holding up her hand to wave sheepishly.

"It's a pleasure," Mynah said. "I'm so excited to watch your play. I'm sure it will be fantastic."

Petunia sputtered at the attention, turning a deep pink, not used to the spotlight settling squarely on her. "I—uh, it. Ha. Th—thank you. Thank you—Ophelia, look. Did you see I'm wearing color?"

Ophelia looked up once again from the Santa belly and gave Petunia the up-down. Amidst the almost full-length khaki skirt, clunky worn black slip-ons, and paper bag brown wool sweater that was two sizes too big, Ophelia could see a glimmer of a fuchsia t-shirt peaking over the collar of the sweater. She regarded Petunia's attempt to change the subject of her impending theatrical success with a polite smile. "I see. A vast improvement. There's hope."

Petunia blushed again and bowed out of the presence of the two women as she went to find the director to convince him that a child's Christmas pageant was hardly the place to make Gossamer the elf demand union representation during the toyshop scenes. She would be unsuccessful as she always was when she firmly, but quietly, put her foot down.

Mynah's smile was quickly snuffed out as the corners of her mouth pulled her lips into a straight line. Ophelia was thoroughly familiar with the expression. It made its way into many of her fondest memories at the orphanage, like the time she organized the fruitcake fight when she was four, during which there were no casualties but many a black eye due to a candied cherry. Then there was the time she had dyed all the bathroom towels yellow. It being her first time, she had used too much dye. The outcome was some very jaundiced looking orphans post-bath time.

"Ophelia, you be nice to that sweet girl."

"Don't worry, I have been nothing but. Any sweeter and I'd put her into a diabetic coma."

Mynah still looked rather sour but kept her tone mellow. "It's just...I know that unsolicited criticism can backfire."

"I'll be careful," Ophelia said a little crossly as if Mynah had already known of her intentions toward Petunia Perkins.

"Please," was all Mynah said in reply, laying her hand on Ophelia's shoulder. Mynah knew there was no standing in her way. She had already conceded this, but even when the chips were down and the fruitcake was flying, Ophelia usually emerged sitting pretty. Still, Mynah couldn't help but worry it might catch up to her.

*   *   *

The burgundy velvet curtain fell, muffling the boisterous clapping that had erupted on the other side of it. "They're doing the final curtain call," Ophelia said to Petunia. "Go out there."

Petunia's response was to turn very pink yet again and make a nervous humming sound. She quickly backed farther into the shadows, stepping on Grey's foot in the process. He hopped back into Gregory whose fall was broken by some fake shrubs from the second act. "Oh, I'm so, so sorry!" she gasped.

"Suit yourself," Ophelia said over her shoulder, taking her place on the stage, Grey hobbling behind her for the curtain call. With a grand sweep, Ophelia bowed deeply, radiating from the attention of all the children who were engaged in a competition to see whose clapping and cheering could be heard above the rest.

"—But seriously," Ophelia said once she had left the stage, picking up the very one-sided conversation once again. "You should've gone out there. You wrote the play."

"Yes," Petunia agreed, "but it wouldn't have happened without everyone else's help."

"Beautiful words. Hollow, but beautiful. We all crave some level of attention. That's being human. Did your parents come see the play?"

"Wha—uh, no. No. Did yours?"

"No, they're in Glory. Dee's there, too." Ophelia moved a rolling rack of costumes.

Petunia followed to stand next to her.

"Oh, sorry." Petunia momentarily looked down to stare at the floor, ashamed her social anxiety had made her forget. She tried to think of something more to say. Small talk was not her strong suit. Twirling her finger in her hair did not appear to crank out any new words of comfort. "Um, ar—are you going out to see them?"

Ophelia busied herself with chasing the wrinkles from the garments. "No, I'm behind on my portfolio. I think it's best that I work on it. No distractions this way," she said, doing her best to look forlorn and knowing that Petunia could not resist the urge to offer a happier alternative.

"But on Christmas?" Petunia said sadly. This simply was not viable. While Ophelia was not Petunia's friend, per se, Delaney was. What sort of friend would she be to Delaney if she didn't step in to give Ophelia a happy Christmas? Yes, she decided, rescuing Ophelia from a blue Christmas was fated to be so. "Why don't you spend Christmas with my family and me? We'd love to host you."

Of course, while Petunia's perceived motives appeared to be wrapped up in a fine paper of charity and tied with a curly bouquet of bows and goodwill, there was something else wrapped among the tissue paper of warm fuzzy feelings.

Rory Wort, a family friend, was coming to spend Christmas morning with her and her parents. Actually, Mr. and Mrs. Wort were friends with the Perkinses, and Rory was more like a gift with purchase. He was an overly obedient boy that complemented their equally docile daughter, making what they hoped to be a complete set.

Mr. and Mrs. Perkins had sprung the news on Petunia that morning at the same time she had scrounged up the courage to leave a flyer for her play on the table. Both the news and the courage were a bitter pill to swallow. So bitter, in fact, she opted to only handle the news, immediately crumpling and tossing the flyer in her trashcan, and then retrieving it before departing to the university.

"Of course, I would love to spend Christmas with you," said Ophelia point two seconds after Petunia vocalized the invitation. "When would you like me by? Who will be there?"

"You know, why don't you spend the night?" Petunia offered.

"Great. I'll run to the apartment and pack a suitcase. What will the dress code be? Casual? Semi-casual? Business casual? Formal? Is there a theme? Color scheme?"

"You know…whatever. Um, causal, no color scheme, I think," Petunia quickly amended after looking at Ophelia's perturbed expression.

"Time?"

Petunia looked over her shoulder at the clock. "3:32."

"No, Petunia, what time do you want me to be there tonight?"

The poor girl sputtered, willing to let the words come out. They were mixing with the speech she was reviewing to give to her parents regarding their unexpected guest. Petunia was locked in her mental panic room, climbing the walls and sorting through an ever-rising deluge of explanations, excuses, and answers, along with that nagging feeling that she left the iron on at home this morning.

Ophelia interjected into Petunia's silent deliberations after a full minute and fifteen seconds without a reply to her query. "Why don't you come with me to the apartment, and you can call your parents there?" Ophelia offered, pulling the plug and letting all of

Petunia's frantic thoughts circle the drain. The only thought that remained stuck on the corner of her mouth was an "Okay."

As the two young women collected their coats, Petunia caught Ophelia's arm. Her grip felt like she had the strength of ten Petunias, which still wasn't all that much, honestly. "Ophelia," Petunia said gravely, "don't tell my parents about the play, okay? They're…let's say it's not what they would expect…of me."

Ophelia looked back into eyes that had doubled in size. "Won't say a word, sweetie."

*   *   *

The two stood at the doorstep of 1234 Straight Street, one of eight uniformly built white houses on the block. As Petunia fumbled for her keys with mittened hands, Ophelia could not help but notice the eerily perfect placement of the lights festooned about the gutters and shrubbery. All the bulbs pointed straight out, and not a kink or twist could be detected in the cords or wires.

"Sorry," Petunia said in a puff of white breath. "Here we a—"

The door gently opened before Petunia could insert the key. A pleasant-faced man stood on the other side.

"Welcome!" he said with a great, wide smile.

"Do come in out of the cold," a neat looking woman said from behind the man.

Ophelia found the sight of Mr. and Mrs. Lem and Ming Perkins quite amusing. Lem was a tall six feet without an ounce of fat on him. His face was still unlined in his forty-fourth year, making him look seven years younger. Not a stitch of clothing was wrinkled, nor was a strand of hair out of place, locked securely with an industrial strength pomade.

Ming was a short woman, her body mostly sharp angles save for her round rosy cheeks, the same her daughter sported. Like her husband, her attire was crisp and tailored impeccably to reflect her modest ways. Her black hair, cut into a sharp and sleek shoulder-length bob, was only blemished by a line of gray on the left side. Ophelia noticed the strands had all been carefully collected to not intermingle amidst the black.

Petunia had explained on their way that her parents were both professional organizers. Their consulting business, Dignified Digs, had many a Nollag citizen flocking to them, begging for their expertise to find a place for everything and to put everything in its place.

Clearly, the Perkins practiced what they preached. Ophelia was both blinded and underwhelmed by the inside of the Perkins' home. Everything was white and clean lined. It came as no surprise that Mrs. Perkins politely yet firmly urged the girls to leave their shoes at the door and replace them with little baby blue booties, which, of course, were all wrong with what Ophelia had chosen to wear. Of course, devising an outfit with even the slightest shred of taste *and* that would pair well with paper shoes would have been an exercise in futility.

Ophelia had pulled her sunglasses halfway out of her bag, her eyes still adjusting to the home's brightness, but dropped them back in when she and Petunia were promptly ushered into the kitchen. It, too, was all white.

Mrs. Perkins directed everyone to take a seat at the table while she continued to bustle about the room. There was no question as to which seat was Ophelia's as a nametag had been placed in front of each chair.

Ophelia chose to focus on a photo across the room from her, squinting and blinking four times in rapid succession. Eventually, the softened edges of the photo revealed themselves to be of a six-year-old Petunia, sans her two front teeth. Ophelia chuckled to herself, imagining the outcome were she to slide the perfectly hung photo a half of a degree clockwise. The thought would have to move to the back of the line, though. Her newest musing was why there were name tags at the table. Sinking suspicions, falling at a constant and even rate, she was on some sort of schedule were confirmed by fleeting apologetic glances from Petunia.

What have I gotten myself into? She glanced over to Petunia, who returned a look that was the sweaty palms version of facial expressions. *It's all part of the plan, Ophelia,* she reminded herself. *You have your own agenda. Speaking of agendas, the Q&A should be coming around the corner in 3…2…1….*

"So, Ophelia, what are you studying?" Mr. Perkins asked.

And there it is, Ophelia thought, smiling a subtle smile to herself. *What? No notecards? Not even a clipboard?* She was slightly surprised there wasn't a questionnaire in front of him. Then again, the possibility that Mr. Perkins had already memorized it was not out of the question.

After getting a saucepan of milk on the stove over low heat, Mrs. Perkins came from behind the counter and placed on the table a delicate looking glass platter with snowflake cookies on them. Amazingly, they were all unique in design and perfectly symmetrical, not a crumb out of place.

"Well," Ophelia said, sweeping her red curls behind her shoulders and flashing a smile. "I'm doing fashion design."

Mrs. Perkins disingenuously cooed on cue before returning to the stove to stir the milk.

"Very good. What made you decide on design?"

Judging by the faint twitch of Mr. Perkins' perfectly arched up eyebrow, he had already come to the conclusion this was not a very stable career path.

Placing her feet squarely on the floor, straightening her back against the chair, and locking an unwavering stare, Ophelia simply replied, "It's what I'm passionate about. Have been since I was little. I love the mix of creativity and precision that's involved in it. And I say if you have the talent, and, more importantly, you enjoy the doing of it, why squander it?

"My friend Grey and I—you should see his work. Fabulous gowns. He used to only design them as a hobby. I'm trying to convince him to open a shop after we graduate. Anyway, I start my internship after the holiday. I'm really excited for it." She beamed at the Perkinses.

With that, Ophelia waited three seconds, picked up a cookie, and complimented Mrs. Perkins on how scrumptious its frosting was. Mrs. Perkins stopped pouring milk into white mugs to bat the praise away, blushing and covering her tiny smile with her hand. Petunia's attention was playing a tennis match with itself as it bounced from her father to Ophelia and back. Mr. Perkins, not wanting to be rude, simply smiled a bit too broadly, responding with a "Mm-hm. That's wonderful. Best of luck to you." The sentiment was the appropriate thing to say but was also riddled with judgement.

Ophelia noticed another little white card at one of the two empty seats, almost camouflaged next to the white cloth napkin on the white placemat on the white tablecloth, just like the others. The cursive name appeared to be suspended in midair.

"Who's Rory?" Ophelia asked, going off topic. At 7:35 p.m., everyone was to enjoy a warm glass of milk, "was" being the operative word.

"Oh," Mrs. Perkins sang, distributing the mugs of milk around the table. Her round cheeks becoming rounder and red, unable to hide her glee. "Rory is Petunia's boyfriend."

Petunia's face was now a near perfect match to the bright white tablescape.

"You didn't tell me you had a boyfriend," Ophelia said, nudging Petunia. "We'll dish later, slumber-party style, when we stay up past our bedtimes."

Mr. Perkins both hoped and assumed she was joking. Sarcasm was not a language he spoke fluently.

"In fact," Mrs. Perkins mentioned, checking her mental itinerary, "he will be here at 8:00." The clock ticked 7:36 p.m., and she kicked herself for not budgeting more conversation time and silently fretted that Ophelia had not touched her milk.

At that moment, Ophelia learned that a person could turn a lighter shade of white. *That's right. Petunia missed the part where they said Rory'd be spending the night.*

Petunia quickly picked herself back up into the chair she felt herself slipping from. "What?" she coughed out.

"Yes, sweetie, Rory wasn't able to go on his family's holiday trip this year. Inner ear infection. So, your father and I decided to invite him over a little bit sooner. We told you this morning."

"Oh," Petunia said inaudibly, slowly rotating her mug clockwise on the table. "I thought you had said Christmas. Must have missed the

Eve part." She wanted to be out of the room that instant, schedule be damned. *Rory didn't even celebrate Christmas*, she whimpered to herself. *Couldn't he handle one night alone?*

"No one should be alone on Christmas Eve." Mrs. Perkins punctuated her statement with a protruding lower lip for the right amount of effect.

"Touching," Ophelia commented only half paying attention. "Petunia, why don't you show me to my room."

When the young women made it upstairs and were out of earshot, Mr. Perkins leaned over to his wife, asking her in a hushed tone, "What do you think of Petunia's friend?"

Mrs. Perkins set aside her mangled schedule that indicated the girls were supposed to be singing a carefully selected list of carols. She shrugged, "I'm not exactly sure how I feel about her. She doesn't strike me as someone our little princess would socialize with. Ophelia is so…so…."

"Unstructured?" Mr. Perkins offered.

"Yes," Mrs. Perkins said trying harder to examine her feelings a little more closely. "And Petunia is more…hmmm…."

"Practical?"

"I'm not sure that's quite right," Mrs. Perkins patted her husband's forearm as she got up from the table with the platter of perfect cookies. "Oh, dear," she gasped. "How long has that picture been lopsided?" This was odd, seeing as she had checked each picture with her box level that morning. It wasn't like her to miss one. She quickly rushed over to the stairway to move the framed picture half a degree counterclockwise, hoping Ophelia hadn't noticed.

Everything had its place, and nothing should be out of sorts. This was not only how the Perkins had felt about possessions, theirs and others alike, but about their daughter, as well. Her place was where they deemed best. That best place was learning their trade and committing to heart their carefully crafted rules of success.

Petunia would become engaged to a sensible young man, Rory, who had already been interviewed and vetted, three months after graduating with a bachelor's degree in Business. She would marry after completing a one-and-a-half-year MBA program, after which she would run Dignified Digs. The grandchildren still needed to be plotted on the timeline, but that was a talking point on next year's agenda. This plan was the same one they had used to get ahead in life and, by their logic, was first-rate. Of course, what Mr. and Mrs. Perkins failed to consider was that exact results were not typical.

*   *   *

This is different but not surprising.

Ophelia stepped into a very pink and frilly looking room. The furniture was ornately carved from a heavy wood and painted white with gold leaf pressed into the deep curves. There wasn't a pillow in sight that did not have a ruffle or lace border. Ophelia also noted that she may have actually seen her first tuffet. The footstool was overstuffed and upholstered in a bold rose pink cotton.

"I'll put your suitcase over here," Petunia grunted as she hefted it over by a bay window, framed in light pink drapes, which were pulled back by white ropes. There was another fluffy looking cushion laid out on the window seat. The windowpanes were curved with the glass separated by thin white wooden slats. Ophelia imagined this must be what a bird sees when they look out of their cage.

"Phew! What do you have in here?" Petunia collapsed into a rocking chair, huffing and puffing.

Ophelia took the bed closer to the window. "You know, enough things so I'm prepared for any occasion. That and some light reading. But, yeah, let's talk about this room." She gestured to all the pink.

"I know," Petunia groaned. "My parents still think of me as their little princess."

Ophelia spied a crushed red velvet dress that Petunia's mother had hung up on her closet door. "They certainly dress you like one," she should have said under her breath, choosing instead to say it at a more detectable volume.

"Ugh. I don't want to talk about it." Petunia kicked herself for not having the forethought to stow the dress away before Ophelia had entered the room.

"Okay. We could talk about this boy toy of yours instead. Spill."

My lunch. Petunia could feel her stomach threaten to do so. "He's not my boy toy. If I can be honest," she whispered, "I have no desire to remove him from the box." She unsuccessfully tried to keep from smiling at her own joke. "'Cause, you see, if he's a toy, he'd most likely come in a box…or some kind of packaging."

"Sooooo…not a fun boy toy?" Ophelia pretended to be confused.

"He's…." Petunia let out an exhale and frowned in defeat, unwilling to say the words that were on her mind, which included "dull," "limp-wristed," and "hypochondriac." "You'll see when he gets here tonight. He's no prince charming, let's just say, but very nice. He's a very nice person. Very, very kind," she quickly tacked on.

"Understood. He's a very nice someone, but he is not 'The One.' You are allowed to judge others. It's healthy. Sometimes it can't be helped."

Petunia's mind transformed the third to last statement from a declarative to a query. Was she really able to pass judgement on someone even if it did not arrive at a very nice conclusion? Her parents had always told her to find the inherent goodness in others. The situation with Rory was different, though. She was asked not only to find what she liked about the young man-child, but she was also pressured to like-like him, and she found she did not like that, or him, one bit.

Rory was, in fact, another sore spot Petunia lumped into the silent tension that was becoming more and more prominent between herself and her parents, at least to her. She was their little princess. At this very point of the story, she was locked in her tower with an asthmatic prince with a slight allergy to horsehair to look forward to. However, happily riding off into the sunset, after liberally applying SPF 100, of course, seemed improbable.

Petunia kept a question close to her heart, one that had formulated itself when she was six and one fifth years old. She had been placed into the advanced reading group around that time, and, not wanting to let herself get rusty, she clamored to read and analyze anything that was up to her standards.

She started with the classics, a collection of fairy tales her Aunt Bernadine had purchased for her first birthday. Story after story, young Petunia could not help but to notice a theme developing. It seemed almost every princess was helpless. Each always managed to tick off a sorceress or enchantress or was simply a door prize for any prince or boy with gumption. It puzzled the girl that there were no conversations where the princess ever voiced her wishes, dreams, and professional goals, or, for that matter, talked at all; nor did the books even contain an appendix containing such profiles. These girls were simply, Petunia had surmised, an unattainable level of pretty with no concern of where their lives would lead because there was a godmother or hero to take care of that sort of thinking for them.

Picking up her favorite pencil, the one with the star charm at the end of it, Petunia had scrawled within the book's margin the question: "Why do princesses always have to be saved by someone else?"

Her daughter's question proved to be a little disturbing to Mrs. Perkins, discovering her daughter's scribbled note one night when reading Sleeping Beauty before bedtime. So bothered was she, in fact, that she gave the book away, citing to the young child that books were not for writing in, and the book in question was ruined as a result.

Being young and impressionable, Petunia took a lesson from the outcome of questioning, specifically the questions that made her parents look uncomfortable, furrow their brows, and bite their lower lips. It made them sad, which, in turn, made her sad. Petunia's learning to please her parents by fitting within the organizational structure they had constructed became paramount, and the idea to challenge was overshadowed by this. She tried her best to banish the conundrum of princesses and their constant situations of distress to a faraway part of her brain where it remained for many, many years, but it did not remain entirely locked away in a tower or under a spell of slumber. When not in the presence of her parents, she could still hear these thoughts whisper to her.

Petunia blinked as if she had fallen asleep, her thoughts pulling away to let the noise of reality inch back to her ears. Ophelia had her hand on Petunia's forearm, gently shaking it.

"Huh?" Petunia croaked out.

"The doorbell, sweetie. I think Rory's here." Ophelia admired her nails and then gently blew on them.

Petunia noticed the polish on them had changed from red to clear. She grimaced when she checked the time; her thoughts having kept her preoccupied for sixteen minutes. "Oh. Sorry. I must have drifted off." Taking a deep breath, she pushed herself from the rocking chair and stood up with perfect posture. "We should go downstairs." She was unable to disguise the melancholy in her voice.

"I suppose," Ophelia shrugged. "You okay?"

"Fine." Petunia wore a weary and pained smile. She did not realize how "not fine" the expression made her look.

It'll all be over soon, Petunia, Ophelia thought as they exited the room.

*   *   *

A knobby-kneed and pigeon-toed Rory Wort looked like a fish out of water, or more appropriately a hypochondriac out of his bubble, as he sat in the Perkins' sterile living room clutching a cup of hot water. He had requested it to help take away the chill from outside, and also in case he spilled, there would be no stain. Mrs. Perkins was pleased as punch.

"H—hi, Petunia," Rory had huffed as if to suppress a sneeze. "How are you this evening?"

"I'm fine, Rory. Thank you for asking." She withheld the question "How are you doing?" knowing full well it would result in a fifteen-minute laundry list of supposed illnesses he had contracted since their last meeting. Mr. Perkins beamed from ear to ear at what he thought was a love connection transpiring. "Rory, this is my friend Ophelia O'Leary," Petunia quickly added on, stepping aside to allow Ophelia to make her grand entrance, and that she did.

Ophelia coyly looked up from the floor, tucking her curtain of red locks behind her right ear to reveal her perfect smile, framed by full pink lips, and winking emerald green eyes that one could argue twinkled on command. "It's very nice to meet you, Rory," Ophelia said, her voice a little lighter in tone than usual. She gently shook Rory's hand, discretely noting his limp grip and then wiping the sweat that now coated her palm on a decorative pillow. Rory only gulped air for ten seconds before realizing he needed to fish in his oversized puffer coat, the one with the reflective tape, for his inhaler.

"Are you all right, dear?" Mrs. Perkins asked.

"Yes," Rory coughed, finally getting the inhaler out of his pocket and using it. "Just lost my breath."

"Probably from seeing Petunia again, right?" chuckled Mr. Perkins as he leaned over to give Rory a hearty pat on the back. He thought twice about it, though. He didn't want to break the boy on Christmas Eve of all days.

Rory dopily smiled back at Petunia, his overbite accentuated.

"So, Rory, I haven't seen you at school before," Ophelia said. She needed him to stop staring at Petunia like that. The word disconcerting came to mind.

"Oh, I'm usually in a lab," the boy said, the phlegm in the back of his throat vibrated nervously. "I'm working on a degree in microbiology. Germs and such…."

"Really?" Ophelia said, feigning interest. "Would have never guessed. Well, my, my, look at the time," she said, gesturing to the clock on the end table that read 8:02 p.m. "I must be getting off to bed. I'm sure we have a full and festive day all lined up for tomorrow." She capped things off with a sweet, little smile to Mrs. and Mr. Perkins. "My nighttime ritual takes twenty-five minutes," she added. "But I wanted to make sure I came downstairs to meet Rory. Wouldn't want to be rude."

While Mrs. Perkins still had an hour's worth of activities planned, she did not protest as she too enjoyed a good routine.

"We open gifts at 6:30 a.m., sharp," Mrs. Perkins said, her excitement for a fresh start and a fresh schedule unable to be contained.

"I'll be sure to set my alarm," Ophelia said, her sarcasm imperceptible to the Perkinses. "Come on, Petunia, us girls need to get our beauty sleep."

Petunia was now perched at the edge of the love seat, fingers absentmindedly twisting the fringe off the strategically placed throw. Her eyes darted over to Rory and his unwavering googly-eyed gaze. She was a third of the way up the stairs before Ophelia could finish saying to Mr. and Mrs. Perkins, "Thank you for inviting me into your home."

Despite it being a silent night, the dreams that raged in Petunia's head banged and clattered about like a mouse inside the walls. Her recurring nightmare of dancing with Rory at their wedding was the late, late horror movie for that night. It would replay itself twice, each ending with chapped puckered lips leaning in for a kiss as the clanging of butter knives against frosted champagne flutes screeched in the background. Petunia would wake up before the kiss took purchase and then proceeded to toss and turn before exhaustion would settle her down once again.

*   *   *

As the second showing of *It Came from the Hypoallergenic Lagoon* was beginning, Ophelia made her way downstairs. The moonlight seemed to make the first-floor glow as it reflected and refracted against the shiny white surfaces. *Easier to get to work*, Ophelia thought.

Entering the living room, she took but a moment to admire the glistening white tree in all its symmetrical beauty before she quickly collected every package that had been carefully laid out not two hours and forty-three minutes ago. Each nine and seven-sixteenths inch by fourteen and one-half inch by one and seven-eighths inch box was either wrapped in white, silver, or opal-esque paper.

For the time being, the gifts were haphazardly piled on the kitchen table, camouflaging the white canvas bag containing several reams of paper and a small hairdryer. But first….

"Hm," she purred, "let's see what's on tomorrow's menu." Trash can in place, Ophelia rolled up her red silk pajamas, exposing the lime green lining on the inside, and opened the refrigerator door.

Examining the contents, the first thing to go was the roast of prime rib - much too fatty. The hash browns for breakfast were second. Why have such a heavy starch at all, let alone to start off the day? No one would be running any marathons tomorrow. The dinner rolls were not far behind. The over sauced green bean casserole and jellied cranberry sauce would soon meet a similar fate. After the revelation they would receive tomorrow morning, Ophelia had decided they deserved something a little fancier.

"What are you doing?" a voice wheezed behind Ophelia, who, as a result, was caught off guard, but only for a mere moment.

"Why I'm simply looking out for your best interest," she crooned to Rory.

"By throwing out the rolls?"

"They weren't gluten-free," she lied.

"The cranberry sauce?" He indicated the bowl Ophelia held suspended over the trash, spoon at the ready to help empty its contents.

"High fructose corn syrup. May as well be spoon fed arsenic. Am I right?" She held a teaspoon of the sauce in front of Rory's face, but he didn't have the moxie to taste test it. His lips becoming pursed and ultimately disappearing inside his mouth.

"The green beans?" he queried when the questionable cranberries were removed from sight. "I really like them."

"Made with non-organic cream," Ophelia frowned.

"Oh." Rory exhaled looking rather down. "Mrs. Perkins must not have gotten the list of allergies from Mama," he rationalized to himself.

"I've got it covered," Ophelia winked back at Rory. "You needn't worry." In a flash, she had a glass of warm soy milk in Rory's hand and was sliding him back toward the stairs; easy enough

241

as he was in footy pajamas, which offered very little traction. His mother had stitched the footies onto the pants four nights ago, as well as monogramed *Mama's Little Bed Bug* on the right chest pocket.

"Wait," Rory said applying the breaks, "why aren't the gifts under the tree?"

"Mrs. Perkins asked me to make sure all the corners and edges on the wrapping paper were filed down. No one wants to get a paper cut on Christmas of all days," Ophelia explained.

For most, this would have been an absurd response, but Rory knew the Perkinses were a meticulous family and no expense to detail would or could be spared. He would take and swallow the lie, chasing it down with a gulp of plant-based milk.

Once Rory was safely back in bed, Ophelia returned to the table, slinging the bag over her right shoulder, stacking the gifts in her arms, and shuffling herself into the garage. With the door shut behind her, she spread everything out on the spotless workbench. She selected a gift wrapped in pearl white paper. "You'll be the first," she muttered, plugging in the hairdryer, setting it to high heat, and pointing it towards the taped edges of the present. Fishing in her pocket for a pair of tweezers, she began to pull back the tape. *This shouldn't take too long*, she thought with certainty, and began to swap out each gift's contents with those from her bag.

*   *   *

The holiday enthusiasm was not evenly distributed amongst all who resided under the roof of 1234 Straight Street. Petunia Perkins and Ophelia O'Leary were roused from dreams of slumber and slumbering dreams respectively by a nasty rasping

242

noise that emanated from Rory as he hovered nervously over the threshold of Petunia's bedroom.

"Mrs. Perkins says it's time to get up to open presents," he whispered apologetically.

Ophelia poked one eye open and mumbled into her pillow they would be down in a mere moment.

"That means we have to be downstairs in forty-five seconds." Petunia rubbed the sleep from her eyes.

Ophelia looked at Petunia quizzically as she threw her robe on to chase the chill that clung to her shoulders and ran down her body.

"You don't know my mother," Petunia winced as she sat up straight. Her head spun slightly as her dreams spilled out of her ears.

"We're going to need an extra ten seconds," Ophelia said, picking up a heavy brush and turning a wide-eyed gaze at Petunia's hair.

"Then you should have said we needed a mere moment and one lickety-split."

Mrs. Perkins tapped her foot impatiently; the girls were ten seconds behind schedule. *What could be keeping them?* she wondered as she estimated the family should be two gifts in by now. Her stomach summersaulted and agitated its acids on a cycle much like the color setting on a washing machine.

"So sorry to hold things up. The alarm didn't go off," Ophelia said, arriving downstairs and taking a seat next to the tree, her blazing red robe becoming the centerpiece of the room, contrasting the pale blue pinstripe his and hers pajama set Mr. and Mrs. Perkins wore. Mrs. Perkins' eyes seemed to frown at the robe while Mr. Perkins wore his actual frown across his mouth. "Shall I pass out the presents?" Ophelia offered.

"Yes, dear, that would be wonderful. There's a little something there for you, too. It's not much, but I hope you like it."

"You didn't have to do that, Mrs. Perkins. It's a pleasure to be able to get to spend the holiday with the Perkins family, presently speaking." Ophelia punctuated her gratitude with a giggle and a wide smile. "This one's for you," she said, handing a silver package to Mrs. Perkins, followed by a white box with a recessed stripe patter for Mr. Perkins and opal boxes for both Petunia and Rory.

Of the four of them, Mrs. Perkins was the only one who paused before carefully opening her gift. She puzzled over how the one-inch strip of tape that held down the upper corner of the left side of her package had a crease in it. Knowing her husband's high standards for giftwrapping, she doubted he would have missed this flaw.

A cacophony of ripping and crackling of paper slipped away as if it exited the room single file in an orderly fashion as each of them finished opening their presents. Anything would in the Perkins' home.

"How," was all Petunia managed to squelch out. Her throat spasmed. Her face wore a shocked expression as her wide eyes took in the content of the box.

If nothing had been in the box, it would have made Petunia all the happier, especially knowing the alternative. But the alternative was what was presently nestled within the practically unblemished tissue paper, a thick stack of three-hole punched paper held together with three-inch brass fasteners. *Stepford Princess: An Introspective Analysis on the Fairy Tale Princess and the Search for the Female Heroine* was typed across its cover page.

"What is this?" Mr. Perkins wondered, immediately looking to Ophelia.

"It says Petunia wrote it," Rory noted.

"How," Petunia hiccupped again, only able to pick a point on the wall and focus on it. Her entire being quaked and quavered. Her research was supposed to have been a secret that only a few knew about. Yet it somehow had made it under the tree giftwrapped.

"There are three hundred and eighty-seven pages," Mrs. Perkins said, thumbing through the bundle, "and that's not including the references."

"Petunia, what is this?" Mr. Perkins said urgently.

The schedule flew up the chimney without a racket or a hullaballoo at that precise moment.

Mr. and Mrs. Perkins had a similar tick they shared when they got nervous. Their left eyes would twitch in perfect unison as neurons fired and struggled to pick up the pieces of the dashed reality they had built up for themselves. This was a non sequitur since, quite honestly, it clearly had never truly existed. Gone were the visions of their obedient little girl who was not unlike a carbon copy of themselves, replaced with questions of how Petunia had time to write this book. Why had she kept this from them? When had their daughter learned to question? Questions were messy and tricky things, especially when it came to life choices, and even more especially so when those life choices were made without the carefully researched input from one's parents.

"Petunia," Mr. Perkins stated again with a little more firmness to his tone, "what is this?"

Ophelia discretely looked over in the girl's direction, waiting with bated breath, hoping that Petunia would give the right answer, but knowing its delivery would be delayed.

Petunia could feel the heat of embarrassment, fear, and anger boil in her cheeks, so hot it could have made her teeth pop like chestnuts. Droplets formed at the corners of her eyes. "It's a paper," she began, pausing to swallow an urge to scream, "that I wrote." The young woman braced herself. What for, she was not absolutely sure.

"Why?" Mrs. Perkins coaxed.

"Because...." She was not precisely sure how to explain it partly because her mother's question lacked proper context. Fairy tales, their mythologies, and their countless spinoffs had always been with her, despite trying to turn a blind eye to them in an effort to please her parents. There was constantly something new to discover from them and ponder over. They lived in her dreams, moved to take residence in her thoughts, and persisted in helping to create some of her most cherished memories. She loved them, and they had become a part of who she was. They were her escape to a land of all possibility and a way out of a place where the plotlines of her life had been planned down to the minutest of details. Not to mention, the tales offered glimpses of happy endings, whereas the life that she currently knew did not. How does one succinctly wrap that explanation up in one to two sentences so as to dispel any lingering confusions or disbeliefs? It became crystal clear what she needed to do. "You need to leave," Petunia piped up looking in Ophelia's general direction.

"What?" Ophelia said on cue, her delivery containing two parts shock and one part hurt. She garnished it with a "Petunia, I—"

"No!" she raised her voice, this time locking a death stare on Ophelia's angelic face. "How could you do this? HOW did you get this? HOW? This was private." She was on her feet now. The boxed copy of her paper rattled and scratched against the tissue, hissing menacingly.

"I'm all packed and ready to go," Ophelia said with a sweet and suppressed smile etched across her pink lips. "Oh," she said, stooping down to collect her unopened gift from under the tree, a fruitcake. Then, stepping over Rory's unhinged jaw, Ophelia was out of the room, shortly clattering back down the stairs, luggage in tow.

"Thank you for inviting me into your home."

"Are you serious right now? Leave!" Petunia yelled.

"Dinner will be delivered promptly at 4:30," was all Ophelia said as the front door clicked shut behind her.

Mrs. Perkins eyebrows collapsed and pulled together. "I wonder what she meant by that," she said perplexed to Mr. Perkins, who only shrugged, still bewildered by the book in his lap.

Before he could even take a quarter of a breath, Petunia spun around with a mad rage in her eyes. Tears hung along her eyelashes, evaporating into curling wisps of steam as they crept down to make contact with her red hot cheeks.

"That is mine," she said with a rigid arm trembling and pointing at the paper in her parents' laps. "I wrote it! No sense in denying it. I know you want this designed life for me, but, Mom, Dad, I don't fit in that mold. I don't *want* to fit in that mold." Her face went blank, eyes daring to look over at Rory for a fleeting second.

"What do you want to do?" her father asked in a small voice. He clearly took his daughter to be possessed.

"I want—I want," she huffed puffs of frustration that bubbled and burped to the surface. "I want to be able to figure out what I want. And I want it to be okay for me to want what I want." She gave her head a resolute nod. "Yes, that's what I want." What she actually meant to say was need.

Four seconds later, the courage had drained from her body, and Petunia Perkins made a swift retreat, all copies of her works piled precariously in her arms, which left Mr. and Mrs. Perkins with much mental baggage to sort through, not that they minded. Sorting, after all, was their specialty.

Rory Wort simply sat in silence with his hunger pangs. The whole episode had postponed breakfast by eleven minutes and thirty-two seconds.

Mr. and Mrs. Perkins did not speak to their daughter for two weeks, partly because Petunia avoided them. In that time, Mr. Perkins had found another copy of Petunia's work stowed away in his workbench. Over tea and perfectly symmetrical cookies, Lem and Ming poured over its words, feeling their daughter's curiosity and passion shine through. When the final page was turned, they were able to come to the rightful conclusion that the best laid plans they had made for their daughter were best packed up in the attic, far behind the Christmas decorations they no longer used and that would eventually be passed on to someone better suited for them.

Their daughter had become someone they had not expected, and they had chosen, for however long, to try and put her in a neatly organized box, complete with label and color coding. That would have to change. But there was one thing that had and would remain unchanged: their undying love for Petunia and the desire to see her happy…even if it did not involve a hennin and being swept off her feet by a sensible prince charming of their choosing.

On that Christmas day, they began to realize their daughter was not a project, and that in order for their little girl to grow, a mess here and there would be expected, possibly even, dare it be uttered, encouraged.

*   *   *

"I didn't speak to you for, what, a month?" Petunia said, looking to Delaney for confirmation. "I got it in my head that Delaney had left the copy I lent her out in the open or something for Ophelia to get her hands on. It wasn't until later I realized Ophelia had stolen the paper out of my bag." Petunia elaborated she had a few copies of the paper and didn't realize one had gone missing. She would later find the original pilfered paper hidden under the lumpy mattress Ophelia had slept on that Christmas Eve night with a pea green sticky note saying "Thank you" punctuated with a winky face. She knew it to be hers because it still contained some grammatical errors, unlike the edited one she had shared with Delaney.

"I'm never not going to be sorry for blaming you," Petunia apologized to her friend.

"S'okay," Delaney shrugged. "It was forever ago, and you were upset."

Petunia's lips sported a crooked smile, her face ablaze, realizing she had resurrected some old trust issues that had nearly cost a friendship with a now dear friend. She tried to pacify her uneasiness by stuffing a sugar cookie into her mouth and prayed someone would say something before she swallowed...or she choked – whichever came the quickest.

"Uh, where's your bathroom?" Gregory answering Petunia's silent plea.

"Go back into the front hall and make a left. It'll be the first door on the right," Delaney answered.

Silence settled into the room once more, no one quite sure what to say next. Petunia continued to thoroughly chew her sugar cookie, trying to pin down its tangy flavor. Looking about the room at nothing in particular, she accidentally locked eyes with Grey. Both offered the other an awkward smile and slow, deliberate head nods before breaking eye contact. Petunia swiped another sugar cookie.

Reentering the living room, Gregory looked to have a question buzzing behind perplexed eyes. "Say, Delaney, where is your sister?"

Delaney, in turn, tilted her head to the side, gazing at a spot on the floor as if something interesting was transpiring amidst the design of the flat-weave rug, or as if the ghost of Christmas Present had knelt beside her with an Ophelia related newsflash. On the contrary, though, there was nothing worth noting about the carpet's pattern, and Present was of no use at the moment. Delaney shrugged.

"You know, I saw her this afternoon," he added.

Three sets of eyes locked on Gregory, and he could not help but recall the moment in fifth grade when he had a starring role as the father figure for the Christmas pageant. Back then, with all eyes on him, and a pause that lasted seven and three-quarter seconds too long, fear had gotten the best of him, and it literally scared the—

"Lemonade!" Petunia spat out absentmindedly, breaking her gaze as she rapidly ran her tongue against the roof of her mouth, calling forth the fading taste of her sugar cookie.

Everyone turned toward her with various looks of shock on their faces.

"Did—did you put lemonade mix in these cookies?" Petunia asked Delaney in a small voice. "It's good."

"Uh, yeah," Delaney replied, still a little startled.

Gregory momentarily celebrated he had recently used the bathroom. He was a grown man now, he reminded himself. He needn't be concerned with the events that transpired from that play. History was not likely to repeat itself...well...not until he turned eighty-seven. He made this assumption based on the fact this was the age when his grandfather returned to wearing diapers.

"And? What did you guys talk about?" Calum pressed.

"Nothing," Gregory said conjuring up afternoon memories. "I bumped into her outside of the Fabulously Festooned Frocks and Alterations Dress Shoppe."

Grey glowered.

"She took one look at me, quickly chattered something, and proceeded to skitter off in the opposite direction."

Petunia frowned, feeling glum for the saddened expression Gregory wore on his face. She then offered him a Cranberry and Hazelnut Chocolate Popper as one does to remedy such situations.

"Hm. I never understood her phobia of being near you. Cause she was the one who—" Delaney's words halted there.

Gregory flashed a knowing, toothy grin and finished Delaney's sentence. "Who broke up with me."

"Can I—" Petunia began to raise the plate of confections.

Gregory laughed, pushing back his cowlicked hair from his face. "Yeah," he said brightly, mistaking her cut-short request to serve him a treat to be one asking for his tragedy. "You shared your war story. It's only fair I share mine."

Petunia thought to correct him, but her curiosity squashed the intention.

"Are you sure?" Delaney winced.

"It wasn't all that bad," Gregory half lied. To be frank, the actual breakup was uneventful. The after effect of said breakup, however, was actually akin to ripping off a bandage only to have the nerves wake up screaming after a brief delay.

Chapter 19

In Which We Try to Answer the Question: Who Is Gregory McGregor, Really?

Gregory McGregor's less than fond memory happened two years, eleven months, three weeks, two days, and twenty-three hours ago on New Year's Eve. At that very moment, he could see his twenty-year plan neatly laid out before him. The ideal image of himself that he had constructed and held in high regard was finally that much closer to reality. It would fit like a glove, much like the ones he tugged at as he made his way into Vermont Village to apartment 7H, the one he affectionately referred to as 7th Heaven.

The proverbial horizon glimmered and gleamed as the new year approached with a slew of polished brass rings – resolutions of regular gym attendance, squashing cravings for all things overly sweet and/or salty, and the promise of going to bed at a reasonable hour so as to rise early as all the healthy, wealthy, and wise purport to have done.

Gregory had held the door for Mrs. Wikershamson, who was toting two bags of groceries. "How're things going with you two?" Mrs. Wikershamson asked Gregory as she passed under his tall and impressive form. He noted one of the bags clanged with two bottles of champagne. The other contained chocolate covered strawberries and the latest work of Mrs. Fulgencia Wick, *It Happened One Night…At Least It Think It Did – Short Stories of Sensuous Seniors.*

"Couldn't be any better," he replied, happily realizing there was nothing on the mental docket to make mention of, which was true, in this case, and not due to Gregory being obtuse.

"Oh! Wonderful," she said in reply, batting her eyelashes and puckering her lips as if unable to contain her always sweet smile.

Yes, thought Gregory, *it is wonderful. Perfect, even.*

But everything was not, and would not be, wonderful. Instances such as these tested the theory of happily ever after. Overly confident conclusions caused Reality to rear its ugly head and shake the fairy tale from its blissful daydreams, usually around the stroke of midnight.

Given that nothing of particular interest transpired until after Gregory and Ophelia dined, let's skip ahead. You don't mind, do you?

The confetti had settled to the ground, the noise makers had been blown, and Gregory had given Ophelia the customary New Year's kiss. The young couple was leaving Muffet's Tuffets and Muffulettas, a new-to-them diner that had opened in Nollag about eight years ago, Gregory beaming with the exciting prospects of the next three hundred and sixty-five days, and Ophelia planning to clean house.

"Dinner was good," she said sort of quietly.

"I'm stuffed! You know, Ms. Muffet was initially planning on doing a curds and whey bar before? Given it didn't sit well with the focus group…."

"You don't say."

"That's what the little story on the back of the menu said."

Ophelia had a screwed-up expression on her face. One eye twitched, her lips were folded in, and her nose was wrinkled as if the smell of something rancid had passed under it. She slowed, only taking one step for every one and a half that Gregory took. He came to a halt when he felt a tug from his hand that was interlaced with Ophelia's. He looked down at their clasped hands, puzzled; he was even more so when Ophelia let go.

Ophelia gently shook her head in reply to his silent query. "This isn't working out, Gregory." She winced when she said his name.

"You're…breaking up with me?" He said the last four words quietly and slowly, worried that his uttering those words might speak his fear into reality. He hoped Ophelia would have interjected at some point with a different reason for why she said what she had said. Maybe the scarf she was wearing was too itchy, or she was bothered that the left heel of Gregory's shoe squeaked with each step on the pavement.

"Yes. I am." Her eyes flitted to the other exiting restaurant patrons, some of whom were looking over their shoulder at them.

He waited for an explanation, but Ophelia was unwilling to oblige. She just stood there with her arms crossed, either in obstinance or to keep warm. Perhaps both.

What could it be? His job as a police officer? Had she silently been fearing for his safety this whole time? Could it be something more trivial? Perhaps his fondness of limburger cheese or love of sci-fi movies? But no answer came forward. It had been issued a gag order and scuttled off into witness protection.

"Won't you at least tell me why?" he begged.

Ophelia took a deep breath. "You're the detective. You have the deductive reasoning skills to figure that out." Her gaze did not waver from his own.

"I'm no detective. Not yet…will you at least give me a hint? Even the best and greatest need a clue to start." Gregory shivered in the late-night air.

"Take a good long look in the mirror. Who's looking back?" was all Ophelia offered, a little pain slipping into her tone…but only a smidgeon.

"Huh?" His chin comically protruded out more so than usual. "I—I…don't. I jus—" A long line of questions demanding answers and rationalization immobilized Gregory McGregor into a stupor.

Gregory's mouth struggled to work out what he should say to get Ophelia to stay. He was so focused on this task, he barely noticed the frigid temperatures and the fact that the top button of his coat was undone. Ophelia uncrossed her arms and stepped toward Gregory to button his coat for him.

"Gregory?" Ophelia asked. She stroked his arm.

"What?" Gregory drew in a deep breath and blinked his eyes at Ophelia, coming out of his bewilderment.

"You're not listening," she said impatiently. "Even the best have figured out mysteries with less. Gregory, I'm—I'm going to go home. Uh, I think you should do the same." She resisted the urge to kiss him one last time. Instead, she turned to look over her shoulder into the darkened front windows of the now almost vacant restaurant, save for one person still inside. *I'm sorry, Gregory*, she thought as she stepped past him, momentarily pausing before resolutely picking up her pace.

Gregory continued to hold to one spot as if the soles of his shoes were frozen to the concrete. His breath came out in puffs. On the inhale, he could feel the frozen air cut at his throat, while his exhaled breath formed ice crystals on the tip of his flat nose. He hummed to himself, marveling at the blank slate that was his mind. *How to solve this mystery?*

The front door to Muffet's Tuffets and Muffulettas chimed open and a short woman with large brown, black curls stuck her head into the night, looking up and down the street before looking back at Gregory. She had large, expressive, amber colored eyes that matched the freckles sprinkled about the light, olive tones of her face. "You okay, sweetheart?" she asked. Her lower lip protruded in sympathy.

Pulling from his stock of generic pleasantries, Gregory replied with an "I'm fine."

Ms. Muffet, however, could clearly see that the young man was definitively the opposite of fine. "You're not fine," Ms. Muffet said. "You're cold. Come in and warm up."

To Gregory's own surprise, he did not put up a fight. Instead, he ushered himself back into the now empty restaurant and took a seat on a tuffet that was much too low to the ground for his six-foot five stature. His elbows rested directly on his knees, and his head lay lopsided in his hands.

Ms. Muffet disappeared into the glow of the kitchen light for a minute, returning with two mugs, one red, one purple, and a large, heavy-looking copper tea kettle. Tendrils of steam curled from the spout. Not a word was said nor silently exchanged as Ms. Muffet handed Gregory the purple mug. He saw that it contained a scoop of cocoa powder and seven mini-marshmallows.

"Times like these call for chocolate." Ms. Muffet smiled and leaned over to pour hot water into the cup. "Here," she said, pulling from her apron a small pewter spoon decorated with a rose on the handle.

"Usually, people abstain from the sweet stuff this time of year," Gregory mused, watching the powder swirl in the hot liquid and the marshmallows melt about their edges.

"I resolved never to make resolutions nearly twenty-three years ago," Ms. Muffet said.

"Why's that?" Gregory wondered out loud without taking his eyes off his own mug.

Ms. Muffet studied the grain of the wood tabletop. She suppressed a smile, stifled a giggle, and slowly shook her head, loose curls bouncing to and fro. "We're not here for me," she chuckled.

Gregory grimaced and took a sip of his hot chocolate, singeing the top of his tongue and the hard palate of his mouth. "I'm fine."

"You got dumped, and, from the look on your face, by someone you cared for a lot. A broken heart...it stays with you. It lingers." She said this last part more to herself.

Gregory swallowed hard. The prognosis was right on the money. "How did you know?"

Ms. Muffet leaned forward, the waning light gathering over the lines around her eyes and mouth, and a few silver strands woven through her dark hair could now be seen winking back at Gregory. She waved a hand around the perimeter of her face, her left eyebrow arching up as if she had presented a most convincing argument and won the case. "Been around," she finally tacked on.

"I wouldn't have guessed," Gregory lied. He was an astute observer. That was, after all, what put him at the top of the list of candidates for detective. He had acquired his eye for detail from his adoptive parents. Mr. McGregor was an illusionist and had taught Gregory to see the unseen and to no longer allow his eyes to be hoodwinked. The skill was handy to have as a police officer, but not so much when he made Adadadoodi Skippadoodi the Astounding openly weep at Rodney Saurbaughni's eighth birthday party. A magician may never reveal his secrets, but it was no skin off Gregory's nose to do so for him.

Mrs. McGregor was an improvisation artist and helped to fuel Gregory's imagination. "Don't limit yourself," she would repeat to him almost every day at six forty-five in the morning before he went off to school. "Possibilities are endless." This one phrase would open the young boy's mind, never taking anything at face value and always following up an observation with a "Yes, and…."

Gregory's willingness to consider every scenario helped him earn As on all his research papers and science projects all through middle and high school. His unmatched eye for even the most miniscule of details afforded him the ability to create elaborate set designs for his mother's theater troupe. All the same, these skills were also what would eventually put him in the running for a position as a Nollag detective.

"You're gonna be fine, kid," Ms. Muffet said, looking Gregory squarely in the eyes. "And if you ever want to talk, need to talk, come on by…I won't even charge ya," she said with a wink.

"Thank you," Gregory replied, appreciating the warmth and sweetness he received, not only from the hot chocolate, but from his new friend.

"You're quite welcome. Now, hurry up and chug your hot chocolate. It's past midnight, and I've got a threesome to get to… me, my favorite pillow, and my electric heated blanket."

Gregory stared back, unsure what to say at first. "I guess I'm not sure what to do with myself. Sounds a bit pathetic," he said to himself.

"No. Not pathetic. Human," Ms. Muffet replied. "Get a good night's sleep and take a good look at yourself in the mirror tomorrow morning."

"What did you say?"

Some coincidences are not accidental, such as the words that Ophelia may have intentionally plucked from this eventual moment.

* * *

The next day, Gregory McGregor did exactly what Ophelia and Ms. Muffet had recommended. After his shower, he stood in front of his bathroom mirror, wiped away the condensation, and took a good long look at himself, but he saw nothing out of the ordinary. He saw the same man, at least on the outside, that had always been on the opposite side of the glass.

He didn't get it. What was the clue? What was he missing? What did Ophelia want him to find? What did *Gregory* intend to get out of this?

Gregory paused, stringing the last two queries together, rearranging words and mashing new ones together, snipping here and adding there.

What do I want to find? No. What do I want? Wait. Who am I?

He pulled himself from his thoughts, back to his reflection that slowly blurred and then disappeared, shrouded again by the steam from his shower.

No one individual makes it through their developmental years without an issue here or a slight trauma there. For all the good qualities his parents had passed on to him, there was also a catch with their approach. In viewing life as a trick of the eye or an act to move the story along, Gregory had never truly defined who he was, his role in it all.

He slumped onto the bed and took stock of himself in the full-length mirror across the room. The turquoise pants and knitted yellow, purple, and red-orange fair isle were never really his style. Ophelia had always said they were much better than his wardrobe of blacks, beiges, and grays. The haircut he had was the cut Ophelia said was best to highlight his high cheekbones, or something to that effect. He never quite understood what she meant but did it anyway.

But it went further than that…so down a rabbit hole Gregory plummeted. He had initially wanted to be a policeman because Copper Lawson was one, and people seemed to admire and love him for all his good deeds. Before he was adopted at eight, he could recall Copper had made frequent visits to the orphanage to visit the kids and, mostly, Mynah, sometimes sharing age-appropriate stories from old cases. Even the sci-fi poster that hung over his bed was a gift from Clarence, who was a big fan, while Gregory's passion for the genre was more on the lukewarm side of things. As the pieces of the puzzle came together, first the corner pieces, then the border, and, lastly, the oddly shaped solid-colored pieces, Gregory's mind churned over the evidence, which was very little and only brought about more questions.

His favorite color was the result of his best friend from third grade. Did he *really* like yellow orange? Was his favorite flavor of ice cream really cookies and cream with sprinkles, or was it because he never ventured beyond the suggestion from the ice cream scooper at Sugar and Spice and Everything Nice Ice Cream Parlor? How could he be sure? The only thing Gregory knew for certain was that he was unsure about preferred colors and cold treats, along with any other aspect of his identity. Gregory, it should come as no surprise, was feeling less convinced about everything on that New Year's Day.

*   *   *

Later that morning, Gregory sat in Mother Mary Claire's office and nervously twisted the fingers of the brown leather gloves in his hands. *This will fix everything*, he thought, watching Mary Claire flip through the red, blue, and green file folders in the top drawer of the filing cabinet.

Mary Claire let out a low pensive hum when she reached the end of the drawer. She proceeded to comb through the files once again, this time a little slower. She tsked and stooped down to peer deeper into the cabinet, probably hoping the file had fallen behind the drawer. "Uh…" Mary Claire began.

But Gregory did not need to hear the rest of her answer. He could feel his heart crack with disappointment. His brain tried to cut the sound off from his ears to spare him the bad news but had started a little too late.

"I'm sorry, Gregory. I—I can't find the file. It should have been in there. I don't understand," Mary Claire explained, her tone apologetic.

Gregory slowly took in a breath, shifting uneasily in his seat. He blinked twice to scatter the disappointment from his eyes, focusing his gaze on a rainbow mug full of pencils instead of on Mary Claire. "It's okay," he said. "Thank you for trying."

"I'm sorry, Gregory. If it—when it turns up, I'll call you immediately." Mary Claire looked back at the filing cabinet completely befuddled. "I'll keep searching. It has to be here somewhere."

Gregory couldn't help but wonder if there was more to Mary Claire's confusion. Did she know more than she was letting on, or was his disappointment conjuring up hopeful speculations? Regardless, he decided he needed a distraction of the baked good variety.

After a dejected Gregory left her office, and she heard the front door close, Mary Claire made a phone call.

∗　　　∗　　　∗

"Hello!" Ms. Muffet boomed over the crowds of people sitting on their overstuffed tuffets enjoying their portly muffulettas. "How're ya doin', sweetheart?" she asked, pulling Gregory over to the counter.

"Gregory. You can call me Greg," he said, knowing they hadn't properly introduced themselves the other night.

"Catrice. Cat," she said sweetly. "It's good to see you again, kid. Can I get you something?"

"Maybe a muffin, uh, banana-chocolate chip, and a coffee…please?"

"Absolutely. Cream? Sugar? Milk?"

"Cream." Though a part of him second guessed his choice.

"Back in a jiffy," she said with a smile and wink.

Gregory sat amongst the murmurs and chatter of the other patrons, remarking to himself how the overlapping unintelligible babble was not unlike the conversations percolating in his head. His fingers fiddled with the menus on the counter, reading them, yet not really. When he had finished doing that, he looked at those around him, extending the obligatory smile and nod whenever his eyes met with someone else's.

"I think I figured it out," Gregory said once Catrice had brought him his banana-chocolate chip muffin, a cup of French roast coffee, and a small pitcher of cream.

"Figured what out, hon?" she asked sweetly and started to wipe down the counter with a tad too much gusto.

"I have no idea who I am."

Catrice stopped mid-scrub, a little perplexed. "Didn't you just say you're Greg?"

"No. I mean, well, I am Greg. What I mean is—I was adopted at age eight. So, what I'm trying to say is that I have no idea who I am—where I come from."

"Oh, honey…."

"I tried to get my file, but…."

"Your birth parents said they wanted the file sealed?" she asked.

"I don't know. I went by Mother Mary Claire's on my way here, and she told me my file had gone missing!"

Catrice bounced back from the counter, comically groping for the edge of the counter with a funny cross-eyed look on her face, clearly gobsmacked by Gregory's findings. "What?" she finally squelched out, hoping her being overly dramatic would bring some levity to the compounding mystery.

Gregory shrugged, wearing an equally stupid look on his face. The two were silent, each one engrossed with the puzzle. Eventually, matching conspiracy theories about secret agent parents and the dangerous life that forced them to give up their son bubbled to the top. Perhaps the detail of the missing file was more so a means to keep Gregory safe than maintaining his parents' anonymity. Each of them eyed it hungrily like a dog with a fresh beef bone, desperate to crack it and get to the center.

Gregory sat there, his left hand cupping the right as if praying. For what, even he was not sure. On the one hand, specifically the right one if one must know, knowing who his parents were, he was convinced, would offer him a profound sense of relief.

He would finally know where he came from; an identity of himself would finally be neatly wrapped up — bow optional. Plus, knowing if there were any medical red flags, such as a hereditary disease, would also be nice. He was particularly interested to find out if he had a nut allergy. His parents had never let him have anything peanut-based, just to be on the safe side.

On the left hand, should Gregory finally meet his biological family, and again, possibly try peanut butter for the first time, would it really be worth it? Would it magically present a personal identity he so desperately craved?

He couldn't bring himself to answer the question, his mind unable to choose between "yes" and "no". Convincing himself that his true desires had evaded him gave Gregory permission to wrap himself up in the comforts of his insecurities and sympathies. Instead, he just took a bite of the muffin and stared into the off-black coffee.

The answer that Gregory was looking for, but was right outside his line of periphery, was that an identity was not a gift. It's something one makes for oneself. After all, he had seen many of his friends who had their biological families still struggle with the question of who they were. He had been too busy, however, to see he had the same problem. He had been too engrossed in figuring out how they would solve their trials and tribulations. He never had paid much attention to the finer details of his own life, as ironic as that may sound. Gregory's stomach sank a notch. The muffin suddenly lost its scrumptious taste, feeling like a heavy, wet mess in his mouth. He was starting from square one again. Who was Gregory McGregor?

Catrice leaned over to look at the entranced young man, studying the left corner of his mouth, which seemed to be perpetually downturned except when he smiled. "Listen, darlin'," she began, concern crowding along the corners of her eyes, her hands wringing themselves. He looked up at her, a few crumbs of banana-chocolate chip muffin stuck in his stubble. "You can't change the past, so don't throw this guy out. You have some good raw material you're workin' with. So…iron yourself out and take a second glance."

"What if I don't like what I see, Cat?"

The woman shrugged and stuck out her lower lip. "Isn't it obvious? Change it."

The young man and the not-so-young woman sat in silence, the chorus of customer babble, clinking dishes, and slurping of coffee filled their awkward pause once again.

"It's gonna be okay, you know," Catrice said. "No one says you have to have it all figured out right now."

Gregory allowed himself his first smile, which was more of a smirk, as he felt a fleeting sense of reassurance. "There is something I know about myself for certain," Gregory said, fingers absentmindedly rotating the coffee mug along the slick countertop. "I love your banana-chocolate chip muffins."

"And that is the reason you're taking some home on the house." Catrice beamed, and so did Gregory.

*   *   *

Gregory made several morning visits to Muffet's after that time, mostly under the guise of a banana-chocolate chip muffin craving, but really he was there for the good company and the advice.

Before Catrice's eyes, she watched Gregory shed the armor he had collected from his friends and family and don one that he forged himself. His hair was now a small mess of waves and curls; his clothes were predominantly neutral colors. The occasional pop of color, usually a canary yellow, still managed to sneak its way in on the random occasion because Gregory still liked to "shake things up." He pursued his dream of becoming a detective because he realized he could not do anything else happily. He traded away his "love" of sci-fi and replaced it with his previously closeted fascination of animated films and a budding interest for the non-formulaic romantic comedy. He found he did not have a favorite ice cream flavor, more that frozen lactose of any variety had a welcomed home in his bowl or cone. Lastly, regarding a potential peanut butter allergy, he simply went to the doctor to have the question answered. He was not and has since developed a preference for crunchy over creamy.

With every new decision, Catrice would ask, "Who are you doing this for?"

And Gregory would respond "Me" most of the time as he still sometimes struggled with his habit of people pleasing.

Gregory could finally see who was looking back at him beyond the superficial details. He liked what he saw, who he saw, even the mysterious parts because he still knew this person better.

*   *   *

"It's funny," Gregory reflected over his one hundredth and sixty-eighth muffin.

Catrice tilted her head to the left and tossed an aqua colored tea towel over her right shoulder, eyebrows raised in anticipation for the second half of her friend's thought.

"Before I really looked at myself, I was…blindly complacent with my life. Wasn't a bad life, but it was barren. I was afraid to like the things I liked," Gregory admitted, "because, I guess, I wanted to be liked, included. But since I started to listen to myself, I've tried new things, made new friends, and found people accept me."

"Not to get all sappy, dear, but they love you because you love being yourself. You stopped walking on eggshells, and you became happy. Who wouldn't love that? They envy it. They want to know your secret." She clasped her hand on top of Gregory's and gave it a gentle shake.

"Ophelia didn't."

"The girl that dumped you?" Catrice snapped a hand over her mouth. "Sorry, that was crass. Here, have another muffin on the house. Shoot! I'm out of banana-chocolate chip."

Gregory waved the offer away. "It's fine," he chuckled.

"Well, forget her," Catrice said with a huff, hands firmly placed on her hips.

Gregory continued to laugh. "I ran into her today. First time in three years. She looked like she saw a ghost and fled the premises before I could get word one out."

"Clearly, she realized what she lost," Catrice said a tad too sternly.

"Mm, I don't think so, Cat. Who Ophelia dumped then is not the same Gregory occupying this stool right now." He sat up a bit straighter, throwing his shoulders back, his almost black eyes reflecting flecks of gold from the fading afternoon light.

"I'm going to be a gossip," Catrice proclaimed. "If she wanted to get back together…would you?"

Gregory opened his mouth to answer, but stopped short of the word, "I." He looked toward the clock as if to check the time, furrowing his brow and rubbing his chin as he considered the scenario. "No," he replied after eight seconds. "Don't get me wrong, but…I don't know how to explain it. I don't get that—that umph in my heart. Does that make sense?"

"Hm." Catrice slowly nodded her head. "I had that umph once."

"What happened?" Gregory inquired, easily detecting the sadness that clung to Catrice's last statement.

"Aw, thanks for asking, sweetie, but sad stories shouldn't be told on Christmas Eve. It's bad luck."

"Don't they tell ghost stories in that one Christmas carol? You can tell me."

"Another time, Gregory." She had never addressed him by his full first name before.

Gregory's heart began to sink as he watched his friend dab her eyes on the tea towel, and what he was about to say, he hoped, would chase away her aqua tinged blues.

"Hey, Cat, you're good at giving good advice. Oops, that was redundant, wasn't it?" He made a face as he scrutinized his compliment. "Because who would want to be told they're good at giving bad advice? Although, I'm sure some people have heard that one before."

Catrice stared at Gregory, mid-sniffle.

"Okay, listen, um, would you disagree with the statement you can only have one best friend?"

Catrice nodded.

"Well," he cleared his throat, "along the same lines, I think it's silly to say you can only have one mom. I mean, look at me, I have a biological mom and my mom-mom. So, I'd like you to be my third mom…if you'll have me." He smiled at her, and Catrice saw an adorable four-year-old version of Gregory looking back.

Really, this was not a query for advice, that much was clear, but rather a heartfelt invitation. Again, Catrice was unable to speak as emotions and words of gratitude lodged in her throat behind where her wisdom teeth used to be. She leaned over the counter, pulled Gregory into a hug, and sobbed into his left shoulder.

"Great," Gregory said. "I'll see you for Christmas tomorrow then."

While Gregory was unable to hear the apparent tragic story about Catrice's one true love, he did know another one of her unspoken tales. Catrice was alone and had been ever since he had met her those two years, eleven months, three weeks, two days, and eighteen hours ago. She had no family to speak of, constantly working around the clock at her restaurant and, therefore, had never made room for any friends, save for Gregory and three of her regulars.

"Ugh, you gotta get going, honey. You'll be late for your friend's party." She wiped at her eyes, trying to pull her composure back into place.

"I can show up late."

"Don't be rude," she wagged a finger at him. "You get going. I have some cleaning up to do. Listen to your 'mother.'"

"Okay," he laughed. "I'll see you tomorrow. Here's the address." Gregory handed her a small Christmas card of an evergreen tree decked out in holly berries, cardinals, and glitter taking the form of sparkling snow collected on the branches. Two reindeer nestled together at the base of the tree.

As the front door to Muffet's jangled open, but had not jingled shut yet, Catrice called back to Gregory.

"Yeah?"

"Thank you," she said.

He flashed a smile in reply.

After Gregory had disappeared, Catrice took to the pantry of Muffet's. She read over the card and took in every detail of it before finally placing it in the left breast pocket of her blouse and pressing it closer to her heart.

Chapter 20

In Which Two Friends Have a Conversation on a Frigid Curb

There was more to Gregory's tale that not even he was made explicitly aware of. Every effect has its cause just as every gift has its reason for being given.

Ophelia sat on the curb of Bitter right before the intersection with Sweet on that New Year's night exactly two years, eleven months, three weeks, two days, and eighteen hours ago from this present moment. Heaving a great sigh, she gazed absentmindedly over the tops of her boots completely unaware of the plummeting temperature.

What she was aware of was the almost inaudible footfalls of someone approaching from up the street, only to stop and take a seat next to her.

"How're you doing?" asked Clarence, shuddering as his posterior made contact with the frosted concrete.

Ophelia gave a small shrug in reply before digging her face into Clarence's shoulder. He put an arm around his downtrodden friend and gently rocked her. He could not help but notice the city seemed to be mourning with Ophelia, everything appearing to be shrouded in black and gray. The sparkle and buzz of New Year's potential was muted in the deepening shadows of what the two knew was looming in the not-too-distant future. The details of this future were still sketchy, but all were leading to a mess.

"Oh, Ophie," Clarence exhaled into the sharp night air. "If you're this upset, you could tell him or drop off his file. Maybe mail it to him?"

Ophelia wrinkled her nose at the suggestion as if it were served up to her like canned cheese on a cracker. "Mm…no, he needs to find his own way first. The lesson has to stick, and that takes time." Her rationale bolstered her resolve to her plans, and the sadness, unlike anything else on that night, began to melt away. She sat up a little straighter, and a smile began to spark about the corners of her lips. "Besides, you know he's meant to find Catrice. Or is it Heather? It's Heather."

"He did. Mission accomplished," Clarence said, pointing his thumb in the direction he had come.

"Good," was all she said. Ophelia's smile came forward in full force before it faded away again. She knew how events beyond this one were to play out: happy endings for all at the expense of her own, which was barely visible.

This was not her first time ending a romantic relationship. She sincerely loved Gregory, but had also, at times, intentionally kept him at arm's length. Little things that would serve as "evidence" when Gregory would eventually go back and review their relationship to see where things went wrong.

Not every variety of love comes with a guaranteed happily ever after. Admittedly, Ophelia was having trouble seeing anything beyond the moment she finished helping Delaney, which would be coming up on the Christmas Eve after next. Due to this lack of foresight, she operated under the assumption that, now that Gregory was on his path to true happiness, he didn't need her anymore. In fact, her presence could hinder his progress, which she could not allow to happen.

It never got easier for Ophelia. Each time she had to break a heart, hers would fracture, too, and when you've lived as many lives as she had....

The two sat without speaking, only listening to the sound of the still air freezing as the darkness deepened in preparation for the dawn.

"You know, I'm sure there are other ways to go about helping Delaney."

Ophelia lifted her head from Clarence's jacket. She looked at him blankly for a moment, sweeping her hair from her face and then shaking her head. "You're wrong, Clarence. Well, not about there being an alternative path. There are plenty of those. I need to do this in this specific way. This is how the dominoes have to be set up to give the greatest payoff for her...for them, too. Petunia's already on the right path. Gregory's on his way now. It's just Dee and Calum left to go. I've come this far. I can't believe that Dee is the only one that I'm supposed to help."

"Best guess—I can't believe we're actually guessing—is that you and I would have come back to help Petunia, Gregory, and Calum."

Ophelia curled her upper lip, almost as if to snarl at the theory. "Why wait, though?"

"I know," her friend sang back.

"Why wait to help them when I can help them now? Spare them years of not living up to the potential they have. Potential gets better with use, not left on a shelf to age."

"I know," Clarence agreed again. "Except…helping that many people at the same time—that many fates all at once…it bends the rules." He was stating the obvious, he knew. "And I'm worried," he continued with a strain in his vocal cords, "what that means. It's uncharted territory for the both of us. I mean there's the real possibility I could lose you. What am I going to do without my best friend?" His lower lip quivered, or it possibly could have been his teeth chattering.

To this, Ophelia did not have an answer, just a hug. The two friends held on to each other tightly, both unsure if the embrace was one of reassurance or one of resignation. They stayed that way for seven minutes and forty-two seconds.

"Okay, I'm going to go home," she said. "I still have three hundred twenty-four more letters from Santa that need to be addressed and a bedazzling project to tackle."

Clarence did not question her.

Ophelia pulled her friend from his seat and helped to dust the frost that had settled in the folds of his herringbone car coat.

"Happy New Year, Clare," she said.

"Happy New Year, Ophie," Clarence replied.

Chapter 21

In Which Mynah Moriel Receives a Gift That is Decidedly Not Socks

The memory of that New Year's night shared almost three years ago by the two friends crept back into Clarence's mind as he continued down Sweet Street.

He resettled the cumbersome golden box under his left arm. It caused his side to ache as the box pressed against his ribcage.

What time is it anyway? he wondered, vigorously jiggling the loose-fitting watch back down to his wrist. *4:45. I knew that*, he reassured himself.

And Clarence did, in fact, know that. He also knew how the events tied to the gold box would unravel practically to a T now that the moment in question was two hours and forty-three minutes away.

Nothing surprised Clarence, a fact that bothered him to no end as of late. The amazement was gone; the magic of the reveal evaporated and was unable to be put back and experienced in exactly the same way.

Stepping into the lives of others, simultaneously becoming a part of their stories and working behind the scenes to fix, replace, or build from scratch a destiny for bliss, was what he and Ophelia actually did for a living. He would continue to do this as someone new after he finished helping Copper and Mynah. This next time around, he feared, he would have to make do without Ophelia working her own case by his side. Every time he attempted to picture this, it was unfathomable, partly because he could not comprehend it and partly because he *would* not.

Ophelia had gone off the beaten path by helping more than two souls at once, and it had cost Ophelia her foresight. There was an order to these things that his friend chose to treat as loose suggestions. After tonight, when it came to what would come next, neither could be sure. *I take it back*, he thought, *some surprises are better spoiled.*

"Jiminy!" Clarence called to a young bespectacled boy in an oversized and garish red coat with an orange and green stripped hat and bright blue mittens. Magnified hazel eyes blinked in wonderment; the rest of the boy's face was buried in a navy scarf that trailed behind him. "Your boot's untied."

Jiminy muffled what was most likely a "thank you" as he struggled to bend down to find the stray laces before giving up and sitting on the ground with an exhausted huff.

A couple of stray snowballs flew over Jiminy's head and crashed to the ground. Two heads popped around the corner, grinchy smiles curled across rosy cheeks only to vanish upon seeing a very unscathed Jiminy assuming the downward dog position as he hefted himself back to a standing position…well…that and a pair of snowballs flying back at them.

Without missing a beat, and paying no mind to the cries of defeat behind him, Jiminy waddled over to Clarence, who was dusting the snow off his gloves and stooping down to collect his cargo. With a firm tug on his coat and a muffled sound that was, once again, a "thank you," Jiminy was off toward home with a little spring in his step, concealed by his oversized and clumsy boots. Clarence smiled after the boy.

*   *   *

Five and a half blocks more, and Clarence was only two porch steps away from the front door of Mother Mary Claire Brog's Haven for Tiddlers, Toddlers, Tykes, and Children – his first home in this life.

A short woman answered the door. She only opened the door a crack at first, leering out into the dusk, squinting like a ground hog. She had tiny tight curls of dark gray and pearl white hair turned a fluorescent orange by the setting sun. Her face was heavily lined, and her mouth was tightly drawn into a pucker as if she were tasting something familiar that she couldn't put her finger on. This was Mother Mary Claire.

"And what do you want?" the old woman asked dryly, pretending to be annoyed. She opened the door all the way to stand in front of Clarence, impatiently tapping the ground with a fuzzy slipper that was beginning to go bald at the toes. Her eyes drifted to the very large, gold present Clarence held. "Is that it?" she whispered excitedly, breaking character.

He nodded in reply.

"Wonderful," she squealed, unable to contain her joy. "She's in the other room with the kiddos. I'll go fetch her. It's about time this girl had a bit of fun." That last thought was meant for no one in particular.

The hurried shuffling of Mary Claire's feet faded away down the hall. Clarence set the gift down on the table in the middle of the front room. He took in the familiar sights of the scuffed wooden floors and the tiny smudges of fingerprints and chocolate that clung to the walls at approximate heights of three to four feet tall. The air smelled of boiled macaroni and sugar cookies, punctuated with the laughter and shouts of the children running all through the house.

Of all the homes Clarence had had, this had been the warmest of them all. There was a love and innocence here that could never be replicated.

He sauntered over to the north wall in the entryway and ran his hand along the eight-foot-long curtain. He gleefully recalled the memory of his wild red-headed friend during a time when she was at her most certain and happiest and wished she would make it back to that state of mind.

Clarence was one of the few to leave Mother Mary Claire's to live with a less than desirable family, but he had planned it that way. Richard and Bethelda Smith were not very nice people. Yes, they were doting parents to the young Clarence by day, living out a quiet existence in a small apartment tucked away in an even quieter part of the city. By night, however, they were an infamous cat burglar duo, stealing from the rich and ever so slightly well-off and giving only to themselves.

They were naïve to believe their young son, who had been procured to keep up appearances and who would hopefully be useful in literal tight spaces, would be mum about their nightlife. Oh, how mistaken they were, very much so.

Clarence had reached his quota of bad deeds by the age of eight, almost nine, and, instead, began to collect evidence against his delinquent parents, delivering both the evidence and the Smiths into the hands of the police…specifically the reindeer mittened hands of Copper Lawson.

Not a full two years later and Clarence found refuge, once again, within the walls of the orphanage where he would remain until he was eighteen. The hearts of the people of Nollag cracked and crumpled, unleashing a flood of emotion for the orphan boy with a doubly sad story and also shed a light on the orphanage's own financial woes.

An outpouring of donations inundated the orphanage, which, at the time, was operating on a budget with tightly cinched purse strings. Mary Claire would never admit it, but a part of her was glad for the Smiths and their foiled dastardly deeds. The extra money she received would help with the food, repairs to the roof, clothes, and keep a certain Ms. Mynah Muriel on the payroll.

Clarence would never admit that he could not have planned the whole thing any better, literally. Had Mynah been let go, then she would have most likely left Nollag, making his best laid plans for her and Copper all for naught, or, at the very least, that much more challenging to pull off.

"Hey!" Mary Claire hissed at Clarence. "Can't you read?" She pointed a crooked arthritic finger to a sign scrawled on yellowed notebook paper that read "BACK OFF! DON'T TOUCH!" in harsh capital letters.

"Oh, leave him alone. It's Christmas," Mynah said in a calm and soothing tone.

"Honey, that can't be your excuse for everything," Mary Claire said with a deep chuckle.

Clarence slowly backed away from the shrouded wall, hands up and clearly visible, as he made his way over to take Mynah into a big hug.

Mary Claire wore a broad smile across her face, deepening her laugh lines around her mouth. "He's still your little boy," she said adoringly. She was actually addressing the fact Clarence was two inches shorter than Mynah.

"I can take you downtown, you know," Clarence said, giving Mary Claire the stink eye and unwittingly adjusting his posture in an attempt to add another quarter of an inch to his height.

"But…it's Christmas," she retorted theatrically.

Mynah rolled her eyes, specks of gold winking in the light. "What brings you by?"

"This," Mary Claire answered for him, pointing at the box clad in gold paper.

Mynah focused her attention on the box, a look of humble surprise upon her soft features. She turned back to Clarence. "For me?" she inquired, sounding like one of her four-year-old orphans. "But—but…why? You shouldn't have gotten me anything. Oh, don't think I'm not appreciative, Clarence, I…" she trailed as he reached into his coat pocket and deposited a small white envelope into the palm of her hand.

Mynah immediately recognized the small, neat, boxy lettering. Her mouth silently worked the name "Copper" from her now smiling lips.

282

"Before the New Year, darling," Mary Claire coaxed. She waved her hand in a circular motion.

"Um," Mynah said, voice shaking as she simultaneously worked the note open and wiped the mist from her eyes. "To my darling and loving lovely, you have been a spot of bright magic in my otherwise mundane life, and I wanted to return some of the fairy tale back to you."

She handed the note back to Clarence as she proceeded over to the present.

"Whatcha got in the box, Ms. M?"

"You got a Christmas present!?"

"Is Mother lettin' you open it early?"

"How come you get to open your present early, but we gotta wait 'til tomorrow?"

The children had torn themselves away from their Christmas television special and were now beginning to pour into the entryway.

"Isn't it obvious," Grinelda scoffed. "She gets to open her gift now because she's older. Duh," she punctuated her conclusion overdramatically, the "duh" hitting the absolute bottom of her vocal range. She looked to Mary Claire for confirmation.

"Sure, we'll go with that. Now go on, dear, open it up. Open it up!" The children joined in the chant with Mary Claire.

"All right, all right," Mynah said. She glanced sideways at Clarence, searching for a hint of what laid inside, but, as always, Clarence never exhibited a tell…which was a little aggravating back when he was five years old, and she was being stonewalled during interrogations whenever some mischief went down in the house. Presently, she found his mute expression to be equal part annoying and nostalgic.

"To my One," Mynah said, reading the gift tag's message aloud. She set aside the top of the gift and pushed the tissue paper back. Mynah gently reached into the box and carefully lifted its contents up for all to see. A dress of yellow and gold spilled from the box as Mynah held it in front of her. Some of the little children "oohed" and "ahhed" while others wore expressions of disappointment and sympathy that almost said, "Aw, she might as well have gotten underwear and tube socks."

"Scoot! Scoot!" Mary Claire said to the children, who shuffled out of the way.

Mynah walked over to the mirror to admire the gown. "Oh, my," she exhaled.

"The prophecy has finally come true!" Mary Claire said with a giggle much too young for someone her age, approximately fifty-eight years, six months, and two days too young.

"Whatever do you mean, Mary Claire?"

"Honey," Mary Claire chastised, surprised the woman was still not on the same page. "Even after all this time. Even when the evidence is screaming the answer at you…" she trailed off as she shuffled through the sea of kids to the wall hidden behind the curtain. "Don't you see?" With that, Mary Claire tugged at the beige shroud to reveal a very large painting of the woman in a gold and yellow gown. "It's you," she pointed from the painting to Mynah.

It's not as if Mynah was unaware of the painting. She was the one who had caught Ophelia in the act of adding the final brushstrokes to it those eighteen years or so ago.

She squinted at the painting, cocking her head to the right and then to the left. She held up and took away the dress in a side-by-side comparison.

"Did Ophelia make this? The dress?"

"Ophelia always said you would look good in yellow…well, her exact word was 'fabulous.'" Clarence smirked and raised his middle and index fingers to make air quotes. "Copper commissioned her to sew it. He got the idea from…." He gestured back to the mural. "He wanted you to have it for the holiday party tonight," he confessed.

Mynah looked back at Clarence gobsmacked. "Tonight? But Copper's working tonight, isn't he? That's what he told me. Mary, you said you needed me here…" She fished her memories for any hints she might have missed leading up to this moment. She came up with an empty line.

Clarence smiled mischievously and shook his head. "He's actually on his way. Should be here in about an hour."

"I bet that Ophelia and Clarence are the Angels of Nollag," five-year-old Jaxon said in a low whisper to Grinelda, using his hands to funnel the words to her right ear.

"Pfft! Everyone knows that there's only one Angel of Nollag," she said dismissively, drawing on her more seasoned seven-year-old knowledge base about the angel, a being who would do good deeds for the citizens of the city needing a boost in the luck department.

Mynah held the gown close to her. Her smile fell but once when she realized, "I can't go and leave you alone to take care of everyone else," she said to Mary Claire, worry crowding her eyes.

"Psh," Mary Claire said, waving away the concern like a fly. "You think Copper didn't clue me in months ago? Mrs. Wick will be by in a matter of moments. Yes, we'll all watch a Christmas movie, except not one of those stupid how to land a man on Christmas ones…I'm sick of those," she growled. "After that, we each get to open up ONE gift—"

"It's socks," Gaylord said sullenly, sweeping his thin black hair from his face. Having been at the house for his third year, he knew the drill. A choir of whining began to rise in volume.

"—and then it's off to bed," Mary Claire finished with a scowl across her face.

Gaylord wasn't too far from the truth. Imagine his surprise when he opened his gift of a brand-new package of tighty-whities, bonus pair included.

Clarence matched Mynah's smile as the realization that she was living out an actual fairy tale was coming true. The apples of her cheeks flushed pink. Copper really did care for her, so much he employed the most romantic ploy out of the entire lot: deception.

"You should probably get ready, Ms. Moriel," Grinelda chirped, unable to peel her eyes from the gown.

"My goodness, you're right." Mynah blinked the stardust from her eyes.

Grinelda wore a smug smile, pleased with her burgeoning time management skills.

"Come on, kids. Who wants to decorate me like a Christmas tree!?" Mary Claire said in very high spirits. The response was unanimous and deafening. "Good job, young man," she called over to Clarence. "Operation complete. Go have a beer for me. Actually, make it a glass of wine. Red. Cabernet Sauvignon. I'm feeling classy tonight. I'm caring for the kiddos so even though I will be decked to the nines, I can't get lit like a tree." The joke sailed over the children's heads. Mynah appeared to have swallowed her tongue in shock.

"We have some extra lights," a boy with straight platinum blond hair and full lips said. Sweet baby Bricen always made Mary Claire smile.

"I stand corrected," she said sweetly to him.

As Clarence slipped out the door, he could hear Mynah say, "Mary, make sure Mrs. Wick doesn't read the children any of her bedtime stories."

"She can tell 'em to me, though, right?" Mary Claire asked.

Chapter 22

In Which Ophelia Demonstrates How to Properly Pop a Santa

Delaney checked the time. It would be seven o'clock in five minutes and forty-nine seconds. Something had nestled itself in the pit of her stomach, and it seemed to disagree with the stories that had dominated the conversation. It did, however, agree with the cheese ball with pralines and diced green olives she had sampled.

Despite the ache she felt that slowly crept toward her heart, she wished to continue, unwilling to acknowledge she had reached her fill of the topic of her sister and her track record of ruined Christmases — like a child wishing to stay blissfully unaware that one more sugar cookie will inevitably lead the previously consumed baker's dozen to be tossed in the most unsatisfying of ways.

Calum, recognizing Delaney's emotional queasiness, decided to step in and quell this potential stomachache with a story of his own that, fittingly enough, started with a bit of peppermint....

*   *   *

Two years, plus three days, one hour, and thirteen minutes ago, Calum was in a bit of his own emotional turmoil, so accustomed to life tossing him here and there, luring him down routes of potential happiness only to find two-thirds of the way through his journey that the proverbial path had been overgrown with thorns or had a bridge that was currently out of service. Each false start had become an affirmation that his father was right about him — Calum Cornelius Dooley had no future.

This apparent fact had led him to work at Gingerbread Man's Snappy Service Stop at the mall. Despite the name, this was where his road had dead ended, and Calum knew it from the moment he had gotten the job.

He had finished serving a short man wearing mittens with little reindeers crocheted on them when he heard someone say, "You're too good to be working *here*" with disgust dripping off that last word.

Calum looked over his shoulder to give a disapproving glance to his heckler.

Emerald eyes looked up at him. They mimicked the impish smile that subtly graced Ophelia's lips. She rested her chin gently on the back of one gloved hand, the other holding a candy cane, the end of which had been worn down to a fine point.

Calum's annoyance sprinted behind the dirty dishes and spoons, sporting imaginary incognito sunglasses. This was an O'Leary girl, both of whom had the effect of making the bile roil about, causing his tummy to ache and his underarms to perspire at an unnatural rate. Of course, in the case of Delaney, these symptoms also came with an induced feeling of fluttering butterflies, which did, in fact, soothe some of his gastrointestinal discomfort.

In the case of Ophelia, however, Calum didn't know the reason. It could have been that her smile wasn't screwed on just right and instead was more of a lopsided smirk. Or, perhaps, the justification was her fear of failure was three sizes too small compared to the national average, while his own outlook on potential victories would have negatively skewed the distribution. What it could have been, actually, was her knowing look. Ophelia O'Leary seemed to know everyone better than they knew themselves.

"What're you doing here?" he blurted out.

"Mm, doing a little shopping," Ophelia answered, placing a small paper bag on the counter of the snack stand.

The purchase came from Retellings, a used bookstore whose motto was "Where Every Ending is a New Beginning."

But Calum really did not care what her answer was, still hung up on her commentary on his current employment. So, he asked, "Why? Why do you say that? That I'm too good to work here?"

Ophelia frowned at the question. The answer was evident, was it not?

"Uh," she began, "it's blatantly obvious that you don't belong here."

"Then where do I belong?" Calum replied in a hushed tone, keeping his eye on Windom Twonee, his manager, who appeared to be intent on the Santa at the front door.

It may be, like many a patron of the mall, Windom noticed how this Santa looked fatter than the other impersonators. This specific Father Christmas had a belt that was unable to wrap around the overstuffed belly, forcing it to be fastened up near his chest.

"Ugh, I wish that incessant bell ringing would stop." Ophelia curled the upper right portion of her lip and dotted it with a stink eye. "The fact there is a bearded fat man in red polyester and rayon should be sign enough he's asking for charity. Gimmie a cookie. One of the snowflake ones. Friends of employees get discounts, right?"

By discount, Calum knew that translated to him paying for the treat out of his pocket. He heaved a heavy sigh but said nothing in reply as he reached into the case to pick up the cookie with a square of bakery tissue. He handed her the treat.

Ophelia started in on one of the points of the cookie while Calum fished in his pocket for another five cents. He was careful to pay in exact change. Windom preferred it that way and had an uncanny ability to tell how much was in the cash register, to the penny, by simply listening to the drawer slam shut. This was one of the reasons Bannock Kolobok, the owner of the little eatery, had appointed Windom as manager...well, that and nepotism.

"Listen, Cal," Ophelia said, rapidly shaking the little white and baby blue crumbs from her fingers, "you already know where you belong. You already know what you want. The last thing you need is another person giving you their two cents on what's best for you. If you did, you'd probably have enough to buy everyone in here a round of rum raisin clusters and," she paused to take a look at the menu, "a cranberry and sugar plum shake." She paused, discretely working the snowflake cookie from in between her teeth.

Calum applauded Ophelia for her skills of stealthy ordering and excused himself to make her shake. His stomach gurgled back at him in protest; meanwhile, his backbone was out on break.

"Calum!" Windom yelled. He jerked his head over to the cash register where a plump woman along with her five rambunctious children bounded and tottered around the stand and counter, after which he went back to staring at the shabby Santa Clause 'ho-ho-ho'-ing off key. Windom gave off a slight shiver, crossing his arms and pressing them tightly against him, even though the mall was holding at a comfortable seventy degrees.

"You don't know what you're talking about," Calum muttered without making eye contact with Ophelia, briefly returning to their conversation before setting the timer on the drink mixer and scuttling to the opposite end of the counter to take the woman's order.

"You can leave," Windom declared to Ophelia without breaking his steeled gaze on Kringle.

"Are you sure you really want me to do that?" Ophelia replied almost threateningly as she returned to her candy cane, twirling it about her fingers.

Windom nodded his head almost in unison with the now jiggling belly of St. Nick. "When you're not working your mouth on my employees, you only seem to be working it on the food you've been siphoning."

Ophelia raised a single eyebrow.

Calum returned six minutes and forty-three seconds later, shake in hand, now sporting a splotch of pumpkin spice icing in the upper left-hand corner of his apron, one of the five children's way of paying their compliments to the chef. At least, that's what the red-faced mother, clearly outnumbered by her five sugar-crazed ruffians, had quipped, trying to make light of the food-based assault. Calum had momentarily smiled at the feeble joke, not so much due to its comedic value, but more so because he was feeling passive aggressive.

"Do you want some advice?" Ophelia stated more than asked.

Calum shrugged and braced his arms against the counter. What was having something else catapulted at him really going to do? "You're not going to go until you tell me," he said, stone-faced.

"You've been talking to Dee."

Calum looked back at her, defeated, through half-lidded eyes. "Ready. Aim. Fire."

"Grow a pair. He is not you. Time to cut the strings, step out of dad's shadow, and be a real boy."

Calum's eyes bugged out of his head for three hundredths of a second. *How did she know?*

"Just because someone has known you your entire life, doesn't mean they have *your* best interests at heart." She stated this in a sweet greeting card tone before taking a sip of her shake and casting her knowing look that made Calum feel queasy once again. "Eh, this is okay," she shrugged, smacking her lips.

"Cal!" Windom roared in a feeble crackling voice, swinging spindly arms about. A boney finger jabbed at the air, pointing in the vicinity of a now forming que. "I've had it! What are you being paid for? Do I need to babysit you like the witless toddler you are? Because I'm not gonna do it! You're fired!"

Shoulders slumped and posture well below subpar, Calum swung his gaze back to the young woman now working on the candy cane in an effort to get the taste of shake off her tastebuds.

"Thanks for the favor." The words were glazed in dark syrupy sarcasm.

"Oh, you don't have to thank me," Ophelia said with a smile. "Tell you what," she said, twirling on the stool, "I'm in a giving kind of mood. I'll do you another favor. No cookie required."

"You're leaving?" Windom said at the most predictable of times.

Ophelia smiled back at the wisp of a man, her expression icy, almost cruel, as her eyes scanned over his knobby form, from his pigeon-toed feet to his barely noticeable under bite.

Without a word, Ophelia collected her candy cane and bag and spun off her seat with such finesse that it must had been choreographed. Her steps fell in sync with the Christmas bells that signaled the six o'clock hour. Calum glanced under discretely lidded eyes to watch as Windom's left eye grew large with surprise while the right narrowed skeptically.

"How exactly does one learn to play a bell off-key?" Ophelia queried in an acidic tone to the faux fat man at the mall entrance.

"Buzz off, lady," the Santa said, a little more than put off.

"I guess it could be a play of the sympathy card," she continued between licks of her candy cane. "You know? A poor shlub in an ill-fitting sweat stained Santa costume desperately ringing his heart out for scraps of loose change to help the poor. Still…I bet it adds up."

The Santa boiled underneath his polyester beard. "Get outta here, b—" he caught himself remembering the children that had finished depositing two dollars and eighty-three cents into the bucket not five and three-quarter seconds ago.

"What was that?" Ophelia batted her eyelashes.

"You're bothering me," the man said, this time in a hushed tone.

"What were you going to say?" Ophelia raised her voice. The mall patrons started to look in their direction.

"You don't wanna know, lady. Now get out of my face!"

"Go on and say it, Nick," Ophelia pressed. "Say it," she enunciated each word.

Little six-year-old Tilda Timson pulled away from her mother, walking over toward the commotion with purpose; a look of concern weighed heavily on her brow and mouth. She tugged on Santa's coat. Some of the red fur rubbing off and clinging to her navy-blue mittens. "Santa, what were you going to say to her?" she asked innocently.

"Uh," the man stammered, letting the bell hang limply by his side as he searched the dimly lit stores of his mind. Truth be told, there was very little in there to work with. "Um, that she is being very naughty," he finally cooked up.

"Oh," Tilda said, feeling rather sorry for Ophelia now as she was sure the woman would receive nothing but coal dust and ash in her stocking.

"Hmm. You're pretty full of it, and *it* most certainly is not holiday cheer, Nick," Ophelia said, moving closer to the Santa Claus, brandishing the sharpened tip of her candy cane.

"Get away from me! Security!" He added a nervous "Ho, ho, ho," still seeing that Tilda had not retreated back to her mother.

"You should be ashamed of yourself," Ophelia chastised the man. "For the lousy bell ringing, for this cheap, threadbare atrocity you call a suit and beard, but most of all…this," she said.

With one deft jab, Ophelia slipped the point of her candy cane between the buttons of the jacket into the prosthetic tummy and pulled it downward. The sounds of the belly ripping and the candy cane snapping reverberated off the walls and columns of the shopping establishment.

Tink! Clang! Tink, TANG!

The entrance filled with the tinkling of pennies, quarters, nickels, and dimes hitting and then rolling across the floor, one hundred forty-nine dollars and eighty-three cents to be precise.

Wait....

The final penny slipped through the deflated, ratty, and thin fabric of the eviscerated tummy of Santa's little felon, making the total one hundred forty-nine dollars and eighty-four cents. The coin bounded against the floor, its copper exterior winking in the light. It rolled over to little Esmerelda Mircle, a girl with tight black braids that framed her circular face.

Esmerelda struggled to pick up the penny. It proved to be quite a feat, what with her small pudgy fingers encased in fuchsia fuzzy mittens. By the fourth attempt, she was successful. She made her way through the still and shocked crowd to the little red bucket that hung on a hook. A sign framed in holly and ivy that read "Give to the Poor" had been slapped across it, angled at approximately thirty degrees.

She looked up at the bucket, and then turned to stare up at the gentleman who had made his way up to the Santa, handcuffs in hand. Eyes large and pleading, she placed the penny in Copper Lawson's hand. "Will you please put this in the bucket, mister? I'm too short."

"Sure, sweetheart," Copper said. The penny hit the bottom of the charity bucket with a loud resonating clank.

Esmerelda turned to the imposter Santa, who was now flanked by Copper and a mall security guard. She was breathing heavily, biting on her lower lip, choosing her words carefully. She was only four years and nine months old. She did not know many of them at this age yet.

"Make sure it stays in there," she finally said angrily before remembering her manners and adding, "please."

The girl ambled back to her mother, pulling her close to her round, little face. She whispered something to her mother at a frequency high enough that it managed to shatter every heart within the lobby, much like an opera singer with perfect pitch and a delicate crystal goblet. "I don't believe anymore" was all she said, each word dripping with sorrow. She looked back at the deflated Santa and over at Ophelia. She decided right then and there that she would commission her father, because he had the better handwriting of her parents, to write a letter to the Angel of Nollag. At least *she* still existed, Esmerelda consoled herself, already composing her request to the angel to help both the debunked Santa and Ophelia be nicer. She debated whether she should spring for express mail.

Mrs. Mircle's forlorn gaze and long face only settled on the now pathetic Santa before a much harsher glare was turned on Ophelia, followed by equally sharp looks from the rest of the congregated crowd. Because of her, they would have to hastily switch out the gift tags that read "From Santa" in their distinguishable handwriting. Yes, this putz of a man was stealing charity, but Ophelia had done something much worse. She not only stole that certain magic in the air that really only lasts until one is around ten years old, she had obliterated it.

Ophelia had known all of this well before, which was why she did not stand before them with a head hung low from copious amounts of shame. Never mind that she would not stand for bad posture. Knowing what would come after, she had it all taken care of.

"You," Copper yelled over toward the Gingerbread Man's Snappy Service Stop. He locked eyes on a quaking Windom. "You're coming with me, too."

Windom and Calum looked somewhat stupefied as the short but intimidating detective power-walked towards them…or perhaps they were blown back by the gust of wind generated by all the mall patrons turning their heads in unison to look at them. This was true for all but one particular woman who took it as her chance to quietly slip through the main entrance doors.

Windom stammered, sputtered, and stuttered making a soggy mess of saliva down the front of his shirt as he unsuccessfully tried to plant the blame for the, up to this point, unknown reason Copper Lawson had feigned interest in the Gingerbread employees.

"I—he—uh—he did it. It was all Cal's doing."

Calum's vocal cords double knotted themselves, permitting him to emit only a faint squeak.

Copper's eyes slid from one boy to the other. "So, you're the culprit," he said to Calum flatly.

A sound similar to a yellow-bellied warbler squawked and gurgled in the back of the petrified Calum's throat.

"Yes, yes it was him," Windom said breathlessly. Unable to bear all eyes upon him, Windom's explanation was off and running, with some poetic license. "He's been talking to Hamish Slight!"

"Who?" Cooper pressed.

"Him." Windom hastily pointed to the man resembling an extreme weight loss version of St. Nick, who also wore a dark expression on his mug. He pressed on before Hamish could get in a word. "Hamish would collect the money in the bucket. It has a false bottom. When no one was looking, Calum would signal to Hamish to perform his magic trick of turning charity into loot." Windom's voice rose higher and higher with each panicked breath. "He did it through a clever system of blinks and socially acceptable ticks. Like, uh, a double blink meant the coast was clear to empty the bucket, or—or a shiver meant to wait...which is odd since it is so toasty in here. It's hot in here, right? Are you warm? I'm warm." His smile became pained as he logically deduced that a shiver was not the smartest of signals to have used.

"Now, this is a guess," he continued to blather, "but I think Hamish would stoop down and then feed the money down the sleeve that fed into the belly in seconds flat. Every hour on the hour, Hamish would jiggle the belly, and somehow, *somehow*, Calum could ascertain the profit they had collected. Yeah, that's how they did it. Yes, indeed, officer." He finally stopped to refill his severely depleted lungs with the oxygen his word vomiting had caused him to expel.

Copper nodded slowly, carefully cataloguing the evidence with hypothetical latex gloves and tweezers and neatly placing them in imagined evidence bags. "Able to count the money in the belly, huh? Sounds like Calum is a sort of savant. Calum, how much change do I have in my pocket?" Copper jostled his pocket three times, making sure the clinking and clanging of coins was more than audible.

"Uh, I don't know," Calum replied.

"Don't lie, Cal. Windom gave you up in extremely detailed testimonial. Now, I want the amount," he said sternly. He jingled his pocket once more.

Calum considered the sound of the pocket change. His eyes rolled up into his head as he asked himself if the sound of a quarter against a penny was any different than that between a nickel and a dime. Also, what if he guessed correctly? This was not a game he wanted to win.

"Come on, Calum."

"Uh, ninety cents?"

"Wrong. Seventy-seven." Copper suppressed a smile.

"Actually, it's seventy-six," Windom spat out. His hands were not fast enough to hold the words in his mouth.

Copper no longer held back his toothy grin. "You're free to go, Calum."

Calum did not hesitate. Before stepping out of earshot, he overheard Copper say something about a little girl calling in the tip about the Claus Caper.

As gifted as Windom Twonee was at counting, his street smarts and common sense had never truly gained their sense of direction.

Hard-pressed for cash to fund his addiction to exotic teas and homemade jams, he had enlisted the help of Hamish Slight, a down-and-out illusionist who was, for lack of a better term, a one-trick pony and, like Windom, was a theic. Thankfully, Hamish's one trick would, well, do the trick when it came to pilfering the charity bucket undetected.

Stealing the Santa belly from the University of Nollag had been easy as Windom had volunteered as a stagehand two years prior and had neglected to return the key to the costume department. From there, the two set their scam in motion during charitable times of the year just as Windom had overshared.

What Windom had failed to realize was that no plan was ever airtight, especially when it came to the unsavory matters of greed and theft. Ophelia, on the other hand, knew this quite well. If one looks hard enough, one can always expose a hole in even the tautest of plots. In this case, it came in the form of a Santa belly Ophelia had constructed with flimsy fabric and "shoddy" stitchwork back when she had helped Petunia put on her Christmas play.

*   *   *

Three…two…one…aaand….

"How did you know?" Calum said, bursting outside of the mall, nearly sliding into a mound of freshly shoveled snow.

"Windom has his abilities, and I have my own. I can recognize my work even if it's covered by some decayed polyester Santa coat."

"That's how you knew where to poke the belly…."

"I was never able to reinforce the stitching properly," she laughed at her own inside joke.

"It still doesn't answer my question."

Ophelia looked at Calum expectantly.

"How did you know Copper was going to be there? You see, in these instances, one would think you were working undercover.

But Copper mentioned he was there because of a tip from what sounded to be a little kid hours earlier."

(It should be mentioned that earlier that day, Nigella had learned the art of prank calling when she had paid a visit to Ophelia. Ophelia was kind enough to have even provided her a script detailing the whereabouts of a rogue Santa's helper.)

Ophelia made room for silence because she knew it would make Calum feel awkward.

"By the way, Copper wants to talk to you about something when you get a free moment." Calum shook his head, realizing he had taken himself off track. "So, how did you know? You can't tell me all of this was coincidence."

Ophelia was indiscernibly impressed by his discovery. "You're perceptive," was all she said. "But you better get back in there. The Gingerbread Man is probably going to be swamped with parents buying their kids consolatory treats after the spectacle they witnessed. You may want to put on a pot of pumpkin spice Earl Grey and have two raspberry cherry tarts and one chocolate chip cookie at the ready."

Calum took this all in, still befuddled.

"It's a gift," she tacked on, before sealing her lips in a tight smile.

Calum knew better than to press her for what this meant. If she hadn't answered his question by now, she wasn't going to at all.

"Before I go, I know you and Delaney are in town this Christmas."

"We'll be there," she half-lied.

"Great. Dinner will be at around 5:30," he replied as he ran back into the mall. To his not-so-great surprise, the first order he took was for a tall pumpkin spice Earl Grey, two raspberry cherry tarts, and one 'I'm sorry the truth hurts' chocolate chip cookie for Ms. Esmerelda Mircle.

*   *   *

Of course, not every tragic story necessarily must remain in that state. The children of Nollag received a Christmas Miracle of sorts two days after Santa's Little Klepto had been shanked when they each received a postmarked letter from the holly jolly man from up North himself.

Dear Esmerelda,

It has come to my attention that one of my little helpers went AWOL in a rather big way. Please be aware that he has been turned over to the proper authorities, and my Human Resources Director and I have decided to terminate his employment at this point in time.

Mr. Slight had been released into the field on my behalf that day as I had a doctor's appointment that I couldn't reschedule. I won't bother you with unnecessary detail. Again, my profuse apologies for having deceived you. I'm sure you understand the weight of responsibilities of my position.

Rest assured that I do exist, that I know you exist, as well, and that you have been a very good girl to boot.

If you don't leave me milk and cookies this year, I entirely understand, but I do hope you can find it in your heart to forgive me.

Best regards and warmest holiday wishes from mine to yours,

SANTA

Young Esmerelda, being a precocious child, was flattered but slightly skeptical. She enlisted the help of her friend, Mortimer Page, an aspiring handwriting analyst, to compare and review each letter from their kindergarten class of thirty-three and a half students. (Little Jesse Blitzer adamantly declared he was half werewolf.)

Mortimer's conclusion of the analysis was most definite. Each letter was written by the same hand. Whether the author was Santa Claus, or someone else, was still up for debate. Mortimer told Esmerelda they would need additional handwriting samples for further investigation.

However, based on the timeline of the incident and the reception of the letters, coupled with the fact every child in the city had received a letter, which was "a whole bunch more than thirty-three and a half, plus another, I don't know, fifty?" according to Esmerelda, the two friends considered the case closed on the letters. Santa must be real. Esmerelda wasted little to no time in alerting all media outlets. With that, another miracle manifested itself for every child and every parent. Apparently, innocence, once lost, can be found again...or at least coaxed to come out of the cold for one more cup of cocoa.

Chapter 23

In Which We Get a Glimpse at a Traditional Christmas at the Dooley's...It's...Um...Wonderful...ly Uncomfortable

With that, Calum concluded his tale, drinking in the perplexed faces that gapped back at him on that present Christmas Eve night at One Partridge Parkway. The fire cracked and crackled as if to politely applaud his storytelling skills.

"Do you still think Ophelia wrote all those letters?" asked Gregory, already suspicious of the answer to come.

Calum nodded his head in reply. He truly did believe, which would have to do in lieu of any hard evidence.

"She'd be crazy enough to pull something like that off," Delaney chimed in, referencing a lifetime of memories to back her up.

"So, she actually uses her powers for good," Petunia theorized as she sported a broad grin and raised her eyebrows in astonishment, none of which actually indicated she believed it to be true. "Sometimes...."

Grey made a snoring sound. During Calum's story, he had given Delaney her chair back and moved to the loveseat where he was curled up in a ball, sleeping off his brandy from earlier.

"Well…" Delaney trailed, a bitter memory creeping forward, "we've only gotten halfway through the story." Her eyes swept up to meet with Calum's. He gave an almost inaudible sigh, for he had known his turn to share his memorable Christmas catastrophe with Ophelia O'Leary was not over, but he also hoped to avoid the second half of that past Christmas, like the gaudy handmade sweater he had gotten from his Aunt Wendy at age seven. Why could he not stuff the memory in the back of a dresser drawer with that itchy brown and purple stripped gift?

Under other circumstances, the young man would have had no problem spinning this particularly interesting yarn, but as Delaney, Petunia, and Gregory leaned in to listen, it became undeniably clear to Calum the tale about to be told was not for pure entertainment; rather, this was to be used as testimony of Ophelia's character. This, he had confirmed with his insides, both real and metaphorical, was something that did not sit well with him.

Still, from his experience, every retelling of a story revealed something new. Perhaps there was more to the debacle that had unfolded that Christmas night. And so, he, albeit begrudgingly, continued his story….

*　　　　*　　　　*

The doorbell was rung two times before Calum was able to wade through the plethora of Dooleys to answer the door. As the bright red door was swung open to welcome in the frigid night air and his guests, Calum's own beaming smile flickered and faltered for a count of one point two-five seconds exactly. Two crossed the threshold, but not the exact two he had been expecting – Ophelia instead ushering in the heavy wet snow that had accumulated on her shoulders and hat and in her hair. "Ophelia. Uh, welcome. Please, come it," Calum said in greeting. "It's really coming down out there." He quickly scanned the stoop for the other O'Leary.

Ophelia said nothing at first while Calum took her hat and coat. His vocal cords were too incapacitated, unable to ask the query of the whereabouts of Delaney O'Leary. Finally, a couple of false starts later, Calum was able to hiccup the question out from the back of his throat.

Ophelia took a break from surveying the Dooley home long enough to look over her shoulder, past her bright red curls to say, "Dee came down with a touch of the flu a couple days ago. Still sick, unfortunately. Ew."

Calum allowed himself to look crestfallen for another three-quarters of a second so as not to seem ungrateful for his guest who was able to make it. That would be rude and uncouth, especially given the weather turning cold and overly generous with a wintry mix of snow and freezing rain. Still, he had to admit to himself that Delaney would have been a shining star amidst the smog that was his family, most of whom, he had harbored the unfounded belief, hated him. When he got down to the brass tacks of things, most of his family barely said two words to him. At times, it seemed they were not completely aware he was in the room. It had happened on more than one occasion that his grandmother had sat in a chair that he was already occupying. True, she was legally blind, but that was beside the point, wasn't it?

He had only assumed Delaney would have called to decline the invitation. *Would it have killed her to have picked up the phone?* He immediately felt bad for thinking such thoughts.

Ophelia left the young man with his over analysis and made her way into the kitchen. Martina Dooley, Calum's mother, recognizing that one of these things was not like the other, quickly set down her green bean and fried onion casserole she had removed from the oven and made her way over to the young woman, picking up a tray of hors d'oeuvres on the way.

"You must be…" she trailed. "De—lay—ney?"

"Ophelia," the young woman corrected, picking up a cocktail weenie in puff pastry. "Delaney is ill." The corners of Ophelia's mouth turned down; her eyes fixed on the over-processed snack at the end of the toothpick before replacing it back on the cardboard tray. She was all too aware of the effects food like this had on one's arteries. Martina, always the gracious hostess, pretended not to notice.

"Aw. I'm so sorry, but it's wonderful that you were able to make it," she lied. Martina allowed herself to wade into her own mental quandary as to whether she pitied Delaney for being abandoned by her sister or envied her instead. She picked up the rejected hors d'oeuvre, popped it into her mouth, and chewed vigorously.

A raucous noise, best described as the sound of testosterone, erupted in a wave of red, navy, and evergreen plaid as the Dooley men and Aunt Corina screamed, "TOUCHDOWN! WHOO!" Ophelia noted that the look of the approaching Calum was similar to hers in this instance, emotionally detached with a smidge of disinterest.

310

"They won!" Martin Dooley Jr., Calum's father, practically sang as he fell back into the brown and green plaid recliner. The group performed the requisite series of chest bumps, high-fives, and fist bumps.

"Who won?" Ophelia asked.

The Dooley clan swiveled their heads, in unison, in Ophelia's direction, each wearing the same befuddled expression: eyebrows knitted together and the corners of their mouths dragging down. The family resemblance was uncanny.

"Who wo—the Nollag Finaglers," Martin said, waiting for a look of embarrassment to wash over Ophelia's face. It did not. "You need to educate your friend there," Martin said to his son. His jovial tone disguised his annoyance. Barely.

Calum stammered but was cut short by his father correcting himself. "Wait. You can't."

"Doesn't interest me," Calum said, trying to convey a sense of personal resolve and security. Instead, his affirmed rebuttal sounded more like a whine.

Martin merely responded with a slow shake of his head.

"Dinner!" Martina called from the dining room.

Ophelia stiffened from the tension in the air. She reminded herself that the dinner would only take twenty minutes, but first, she reminded herself, as Dooleys young and old exited the room, she needed to make a phone call.

*   *   *

"Pass the sweet potatoes," Martin said to Mitchell, Calum's brother. With a great slapping sound, Martin piled a massive spoonful of the orange mush, marshmallows dripping all over it.

311

"Are you sure you don't want anything else? Not even a bit of gravy?" Calum asked Ophelia, regarding her sparse plate containing two of the thinnest slices of ham she could find and a small serving of undressed iceberg lettuce.

"No," she smiled sweetly. "I'll not have anything else to ease your unease."

Calum blushed, hoping no one else heard Ophelia.

"So, Ophelia, what is it you do?" Martina asked the stock question between the sounds of her husband's gnashing teeth as they tore into chunks of honey baked ham with canned cranberry relish. The sound made Ophelia squeamish.

"I design dresses at the Fabulously Festooned Frocks and Alterations Dress Shoppe," she said in a practiced way as this was usually the first or second question that was asked in polite, contrite conversation. Either that or the question, "Are you Delaney's older sister?"

"That's the new shop on Twin Street, right? I've been meaning to come by there. It looks darling," Martina complimented.

"Yes, we opened about nine months ago."

"Lovely," Martina replied. "Please pass the butter. Thank you. And are you Delaney's older sister?" She looked up from her roll at Ophelia.

"Yes, I am. I'm her older, adopted sister."

This did not register a reaction from the Dooleys, whose attention was fixated on chowing down.

Huh, Ophelia thought. Usually, the follow-up question was how that happened. Many expected a heartfelt yarn about an infertile O'Leary couple, desperately wanting to give their love to a child – in this case a chubby cheeked, red-headed orphan girl named Ophelia – only to be blessed with a child of their own years later. The classic "oopsie-baby" story as Ophelia liked to call it.

"And what is she going to school for?"

"Um...she's doing a liberal arts degree." Ophelia paused. She could feel Calum stiffen his posture mid-chew of his dinner roll as if about to brace for impact. "I'm not sure what she will do with it," she concluded. Her eyes covertly moved in the direction of Martin.

"Humph," Martin grunted, taking a deep breath, and pushing the over-salted holiday meal down his gullet. "Liberal arts," he muttered to himself. The very idea rolled from left hemisphere to right as he slowly shook his head, appraising it. "She should do something practical, like pharmaceuticals or accounting." The other Dooleys, most of whom were pharmacists or accountants (with the exception of Cousin Murdock, the rebel of the clan who held a job in marketing) grunted in agreement, their eyes never leaving their plates piled high with ham, buttery mashed potatoes, and gelatin salad.

"She should do something that makes her happy," Ophelia flatly corrected Martin.

"Happy is having a way of paying your bills. Happy is a savings account with a surplus and a healthy interest rate. Am I right?" Martin directed the question toward those who would agree with him, which was all present company excluding Ophelia. Calum pretended to be on the fence.

The Dooley clan's heads nodded and rattled in agreement, not unlike the bobble head collection of the Nollag Finaglers that lined the shelves of the china cabinet.

"That's something that Calum knows very little about," Martin persisted, pointing a fork at the young man. "Barely out of college, and he's been a teacher and a dog trainer. He's barely dabbled in marketing and, most recently, started slinging cookies at the mall of all places. Now—and now—he wants to be a writer," he chuckled. "Stupid," he grunted.

The word practically punched Calum below the belt, making him grimace. He knew all Dooley eyes were boring into him. It gave him a cramped and sweaty feeling among the usual places one tends to ache and perspire.

"Why is that?" Ophelia asked, taking Calum's staring at the cherry chunks in the gelatin salad as cowardice over appreciation for the jiggly confection.

"Because it's not practical."

"Conventional," Ophelia corrected Martin again.

"Do you know how difficult it is to make a living as a writer?"

"Do you?"

"I know people."

"Who?"

"I know people," Martin repeated a tad more firmly, which Calum knew meant that he actually did not. "Besides, you would have to be really good to make any sort of real money," he sniffed.

"Hm. So, you've read some of Calum's work?"

Calum's eyes bulged open, aghast at the question, and he battened down his hatches, readying himself for the swell of hot air that would be coming across the table in the form of his father's tirade.

"Ha! Don't have to. I know my son. He doesn't have that kind of talent in him." He smiled a self-assured smile.

"I would disagree, Mr. Dooley—"

"All due respect," (of which there was none), "what does a seamstress know about the *lucrative* world of writing?" He did not wait for the woman to answer before continuing. He immediately abandoned his question, redirecting his frustrations back to his son. "Cal's probably going to move on to something else next week anyway." He waved his hand in what seemed an overly dramatic fashion, done with the topic of conversation, and returned to his overloaded plate.

But the exchange was, in fact, not over. Ophelia slowly and carefully replaced her flatware on the tartan covered table and gently pushed her plate away. She took a sip of water, and with that, opened the sky to rain down a deluge of the cold hard truth upon Martin Dooley's head, taking a cue from the frightful weather outside, which was snowing sideways at this point.

"I can't help but ponder and puzzle and even ruminate and marinate over how you must have heard the exact same speech when you were Calum's age."

Martin grimaced and pinched the corners of his eyes at the woman who smiled a little too sweetly back at him as she unfurled a yarn of a tale chock full of drama.

Speaking of which, that was where it all started — the Drama Department at Nollag University. Upon the pages of some mildewed playbills, Ophelia learned of a young man, many years ago, who had honed his craft as a thespian, of a man who had dreams to do it all from Broadway to the screen, of both the small and glittery silver varieties.

Yet, on a particular program of *It's a Wonderful Life*, Ophelia discovered something curious...the word "Curious," twice underlined, followed by three identical looking question marks neatly scrawled across the headshot of the young prodigy that was D.F. — Douglas Fir. The name had also been underlined.

The impeccably perfect handwriting could belong to only Professor Araminta Vanbrugh, who would mend the thread of a clue to a larger tapestry. She had written and underlined the word on the playbill draft to remind herself to ask her student, Martin, about it. You see, Douglas Fir was the stage name of Martin Donald Dooley.

On opening night, Professor Vanbrugh explained to Ophelia, Mr. Dooley Sr. showed up in an agitated state. He was furious at the knowledge that his second oldest son wanted to pursue a dream as a performer. Dreams were to be locked away and only entertained at night behind one's eyelids. They were less lethal that way.

Once his father was able to slip backstage, Martin was subjected to the same monologue about the safety of a nine to five and, without it, the inevitable failure and lack of proper health insurance, including vision and dental, a life in theater would bring. Hiding behind the thick cakey stage make-up, Martin was successfully able to sweep his disappointment deep down within himself. Having heard his father's speech one too many times, he could no longer fight back against the foreboding words about the harsh, cold world. Whether he simply gave up or began to believe in them, no one knows, much like no one is sure how his father came to know about Douglas Fir and his debut performance.

The prodigy that was Douglas Fir vanished that night, leaving an ill-prepared understudy to fill the role of Mr. Potter. Martin Dooley would appear next semester pursuing a double major in Accounting and Business Management to prepare him to work his way up the ladder at the paper mill, just like his father.

Martin Dooley quaked in his seat as he was confronted with the ghosts of what had been and what could have been. It can be surmised that this resurrected secret was all too much for his heart to bear.

For within twelve point two-five seconds after the story of the performer turned miller was concluded, a tremor made the flatware chatter and the slices of canned cranberry sauce tremble, shaking everyone, except for Cousin Murdock, from their shock. Martin had clutched his left arm and proceeded to face plant into his sweet potatoes and marshmallows. Professionals of the health variety would unquestionably conclude the seventy-percent blockage in the coronary artery was to be fingered as the culprit.

Martina screamed, running to her husband's side. Mukonry, Martin's older brother, helped her pull Martin up, so as he did not asphyxiate in the mashed-up mess of heavy holiday food. Calum beat his aunt Marilyn to the phone to call the paramedics. (Had everyone not been distracted by all the chaos, this would have registered as a surprise. Marilyn was a marathon runner, after all, but was hindered by her habit of stretching first before any sort of strenuous activity.) Ophelia quietly made her exit out into the muted night, a stark contrast to the Dooley dining room.

How is the ambulance going to make it? Calum fretted. As he looked out the window, there was at least a good eight or so inches piled on top of the cars lining the curb, here and now known as the Dooley Caravan.

"9-1-1. What is your emergency?" a nasally voice inquired on the other side of the line.

"I need an ambulance to 26-82-9 Ponderosa Promenade presently and promptly!"

"Not possible, ma'am," the operator flubbed. "All our ambulances have been dispatched. It's a mess out there. You see, the weather has it snowing and sleeting not just cats and dogs, but several other varieties found in the animal king—oh."

Oh? Calum wondered. "What?"

"My records show you called about a heart attack twenty minutes ago. The ambulance should be there in—" but Calum did not let the operator finish her statement. A knock at the door had him, and now Marilyn, bolting toward the front of the house where two very wet and weary looking paramedics stood on the Dooley stoop.

They found Martin clasping his chest and vigorously chewing on several aspirin, reminiscent of one of Mrs. Fulgencia Wick's harlequin novels: *I'll See You In the ICU*. Admittedly, not her best work.

*　　　　*　　　　*

Martin Dooley died that Christmas night. Well, died in a figurative manner would be more accurate. Apologies, for the scare.

He interpreted the unfolding of the evening's events as a cosmic sign. Douglas Fir would once again emerge from behind the heavy velvet curtains, if only in community theater. But this particular gift did continue to give as Martin was now able to

318

recollect how much joy pursuing his dreams had brought him. It inspired untapped faith and support in his son to let him delve into his writing, which, in turn, gave Calum hope.

Hope was not all that was on the mind of the young man. Intrigue had supplanted itself quickly with the errant question, *Who called the ambulance exactly twenty minutes prior to Dad's big, dramatic scene?* Followed by, *How did they know?*

The former of these questions withered and blew away almost at the instance of being posed. There was only one person who could possibly have done so.

*   *   *

"Ophelia!" Delaney shouted through one of her sneezes.

Her older sister closed the apartment door behind her and then turned to face Delaney, who was wearing an expectant look on her face.

Delaney clasped her palm over the mouthpiece of the phone. "Whad did you do?" she whispered in a low, groggy tone.

Expectation turned to feigned concern as the phone was handed, albeit hesitantly, over to her.

"Hello?"

"How did you know to call?" Calum's voice came across the line.

"Excuse me?"

"You called the ambulance twenty minutes early so that it would make it in time. You saved my dad. How did you know?" he repeated the question persistently.

Ophelia shook her head, ready with a plausible explanation. "I wasn't the one who called the ambulance. True, I did use your phone, but to call and check on Dee. Your great aunt Millicent, or some other M-named relative, was hanging on the phone squawking to someone about an overbearing scent of burnt toast. Guess she thought she was having a stroke or something." Ophelia could hear the slight clicks and ticks of Calum's brain working out the logic of her story. "I quickly pointed out to her that she was actually smelling the last batch of dinner rolls, took the phone from her, explained the misunderstanding, and hung up."

"The operator said it was a heart attack, not a stroke," Calum said. "I distinctly remember her saying heart attack."

"I don't know, Calum." Ophelia said, not attempting to hide her annoyance. "Maybe your aunt thinks smelling burnt gluten is a sign of a heart attack. Or maybe the operator misspoke? Who knows how many medical emergencies they handled tonight?"

"My dad is okay, by the way," Calum said, changing the subject, not bothering to ask why she had bolted from the Dooley home as he was confident the answer would be along the callous lines of, "I saw no point in staying. The evening had run its course."

"Listen, Calum, while I am happy to hear that he is doing better, I feel this conversation has run its course." Ophelia could see Delaney opening and clasping her hand, silently beckoning for the phone.

"Let me leave you with this," she said. "Start taking control of your life. Do what you want. Don't care what anyone may think. Start dating."

Delaney gave her sister a sour scowl as she took the phone back.

Seeing no reason to stay twiddling her thumbs, Ophelia left to change.

"Calum, whad habbened? Hard addack?" Delaney asked, only having half of the cryptic conversation between him and Ophelia, as well as his worried tone from when he first called. "Whad!? Oh, by word, is—is he okay? Oh, whad a relief. Yeah. Yeah. I understend. Go be wid your dad. Tell him I hobe he feels bedder soond. Bye."

Ophelia heard footsteps come pounding down the hall until Delaney, wrapped in a king-sized beige blanket and pink bunny slippers, halted and darkened her doorway. Her face was now as red as her congested nose.

"A hard addack! Really?"

"Delaney, you can't possibly believe I gave Mr. Dooley a heart attack. That defies medical science."

Delaney swayed and leaned against the doorframe. Her one-hundred-degree fever made her question whether she was giving the stink-eye to Ophelia or the dress form in the room, her Christmas present to her sister a couple years back.

"Doh, I subbose dnot," she conceded with very little resistance. However, a small shred of her being would not put it past her sister. This was the same shred of being that entertained the possibility of elves, flying reindeer, and sugarplum fairies. *Just because you can't explain it, doesn't mean it's not a real thing*, Delaney recalled her sister telling her when they were little. *Go lay down, Delaney. You're starting to listen to your sister.*

Fatigue weighed heavily on Delaney, causing her to drop her anger. "I don'd rebember you callinguh. Whad dime did you callugh?" She pulled the comforter tighter around her.

"You never picked up. Must have been asleep, which is what you should be doing now. Let's get you into bed," Ophelia said, wrapping her arm around Delaney's waist for added support.

"Way ahead odb you," Delaney said drowsily.

The sisters shuffled from the closet, making their way through the kitchen, on the way to Delaney's bedroom.

"So, that's who that guy is," Ophelia exclaimed out loud to herself, taking notice of the plaid clad Murdock Dooley staring back at her from the wrapper on a roll of paper towels on the counter.

"Huh?" Delaney said, now half-asleep.

After Delaney had been zonked out with the appropriate cocktail of cold medicine and chamomile tea and lovingly tucked away for the night, Ophelia stealthily tip-toed back to the phone. Slowly, she picked up the receiver, careful not to let the rotary click too loudly after completing each revolution.

"Hello?" Clarence said on the other end of the line.

"Hey," Ophelia said, her voice slightly above a whisper.

"How'd it go?"

"Calum's back on track. It's going to take a couple years, but the seed for his great writing idea has been planted. Dee is the only one left now."

"The whole point of Ophelia O'Leary herself," her friend chimed in.

"Yeah…s'hard to believe that this will all be done soon." Ophelia bit down on her thumbnail.

"How long, exactly?" Clarence asked.

"In almost a full year. After Bailey, it all gets dark. But it has to be this way, right, Clare?" She nodded her head not waiting for her friend's confirmation. "It has to be this way. It's for the best," she said, answering for him.

There was silence on the other end of the phone at first, then a deep inhalation followed by the question, "But what about you?" Though what he really wanted to ask his friend was, "But what about us?"

"I broke the rules," she admitted, more so to herself. "I guess that means I stay Ophelia O'Leary longer than originally scheduled. It might not be so bad." But what she really wanted to say, after reflecting on the many bridges she had already burned and would burn was, "I'm afraid that you'll have to move on without me." Eventually, all lives reach an end, and perhaps this time Ophelia would not step into a new one once her time as an O'Leary expired.

*   *   **

That's not plausible, thought Calum after he hung up the payphone. Aunt Millicent had no sense of smell due to an addiction to nasal sprays and an unhealthy obsession with strong room deodorizers.

Why would Ophelia lie? One thing Calum did know was that she was the last one to have the phone. *Of course, she very well could have called to check up on Delaney*, he rationalized.

He pondered, walking down the hospital corridor. *She seems the type to always have a plan. First Santa, then dad.* Indeed, it did seem that all of Ophelia's messes were too neat upon closer inspection. *Wait and see what comes to light*, he mentally noted, filing away the information for later. *And maybe check the phone bill when it comes.* The thought, however, would not be committed to memory as Calum would soon find himself distracted.

Bailey Barrymore, the candy striper on duty, locked eyes with Calum Dooley and smiled a sweet and coquettish smile as she passed him at the threshold of his father's room. Calum's stomach plummeted and reeled back up to lodge itself in his throat as he gazed at the young woman in her fitted white and pink dress. His brain fizzled and cracked, managing to send a message to his lips to smile back before he was out of Bailey's peripheral vision.

Chapter 24

In Which We Are Introduced to Bailey Barrymore and Are Reacquainted with Woody Hinklehimeriner

Back in the present moment, Delaney wrinkled her nose at the mention of the name Bailey. "Oh, yeah. That's right. That's how you and Bailey met." She made a comically disgusted face at Calum.

"Don't remind me," Calum lamented.

"I say you're allowed at least one mistake," Petunia said.

"Or four…five tops," Gregory added pitifully under his breath and towards the floor. "It's been a rough few years."

"You figure, though, without my dating her, we may not have gotten together," Calum said, running a finger along Delaney's charm bracelet, making it tinkle and sing.

"Keep telling yourself that dating the criminal was a good call," Gregory said.

Calum frowned his way.

Delaney looked adoringly at the charms. "It was one of the few Christmases Ophelia did something somewhat right," she uttered, her subconscious willing her mind to slip the words past her lips. This thought was the same realization Delaney happened upon a mere two weeks and one day ago, which transformed into her extending an invitation to her sister to meet at Beatrice Clark's Caffeine and Bean Coffee Café earlier that afternoon.

Good feelings were fleeting, however. "And I really do mean 'somewhat.'" An edge returned to Delaney's tone. "Even though she got it back, she was the one who had lost our Grandma's bracelet in the first place." She raised the wrist wearing it as if exhibiting evidence. "And—wh—when did she get her hands on a taser!?"

With exception of the still slumbering Grey, all nodded their heads in unison as they had either been there on that fateful holiday that year or had been immediately filled in on the electrifying details not two hours after its occurrence.

*   *   *

Meanwhile, across town, back at the Wallace and Davis Flats, a large, kilted man stood on the doorstep of Officers Gin and Olive Norp-Polsta. "You look wonderful," Woody Hinklehimeriner said with a broad goofy grin.

"Thank you," Ophelia replied absentmindedly, handing Woody four pristinely wrapped gifts one by one from her duffle bag.

"It's such a pretty shade of crimson. Did you make it yourself?" he inquired about her dress.

"Uh-huh—Woody, I need you to take these over to 61377 Twin Street. Fabulously Festooned Frocks and Alterations Dress Shoppe. Big pink sign. Can't miss it."

"Of course. Anything for you. Especially since you helped me get a job after that little adventure," Woody said, thinking back to earlier that day.

"Don't mention it," Ophelia said in a nervous exhalation.

"Ophelia? There must be something awfully interesting on the floor for you to have been staring at it this whole time. May I ask, does it have something to do with these?" Woody gently shook the packages piled up in his arms.

Ophelia wore a look of concern on her face, but the gifts only shared half of that blame. She rarely wore the vexing expression and mentally noted that, after an extended period of time, one's forehead could, indeed, cramp.

"Ophelia?" Woody gently coaxed, unable to quell his curiosity for, what he hoped, was a good story.

"Does it have something to do with the party tonight?" Olive queried as she emerged from the kitchen, stepping towards the front door. "What? I'm a cop whose partner of late spits up on himself and has a huge fixation with his feet. I'll take whatever investigation I can get. Who're the gifts for?"

"Um," Ophelia blinked from her reverie, "Delaney, Calum, Petunia, and Gregory. Oh! I almost forgot. Woody, ask for a Kitty Cloissone and tell her to take these over to One Partridge Way. It's close to where she lives."

"Huh," Olive laughed. "Are they Christmas gifts or belated apologies? I'm sorry that didn't sound as passive aggressive in my head as it did out loud, Ophelia."

"Who's Delaney?" Woody's eyes ping-ponged between the two women.

"My sister."

"Well, forgive me, but why aren't *you* taking these to her?" Woody said with concern in his tone…along with a bit of eagerness for the story.

"I don't know if she really wants me around. I mean, she did invite me to spend Christmas with her, but I don't know if she really meant it. For once, I don't know." And, yet again, Ophelia felt something that she was still struggling to get used to: a sense of loneliness. Her surroundings faded away, leaving her only with a feeling of isolation to keep her company. Ironic, if one thinks about it.

Olive walked over and took Ophelia in her arms, gently swayed her back and forth, and whispered, "It's okay, honey." Her motherly touch pulled Ophelia back to reality, and she reciprocated the embrace with a silent thank you.

Woody's broad grin shrunk into a gentle smile. His usual booming voice folded in on itself to a soft rumble. "I'm sure there's a story behind these," he gestured to the boxes in silver, blue, green, and red, all tied up in thick ribbons. "You'll have to tell me sometime if and when you're willing."

Ophelia was warmed by the oversized elf's goodwill and sympathy. It made her smile and her eyes shimmer. A thought sparked in her mind, a contrast to her gloomy worries. Maybe the unforeseen changes that were coming wouldn't have to be faced completely alone. Maybe she could entertain hope.

"Maybe I can tell you at the party tonight," she sniffled.

Chapter 25

In Which Ophelia's Charm Begins to Wear Off

Now seems about the right time to clue you in to that fateful night everyone has been alluding to throughout this story. You've been patient and have refrained from creasing the pages and cracking the spine. For that, you deserve a treat.

The events that played a pivotal role in creating the youngest O'Leary's emotional quagmire transpired one year, one hour, and fifty-three minutes ago. Delaney O'Leary frantically moved about apartment 7H at the Vermont Village, making sure everything was in its place. Not a speck of dust could be seen perched upon the tabletops. Not a smudge could be found on any pane of glass. Not a pillow was left untouched. Each was fluffed to its optimum cushion. The food—

"—is fine. Delaney, you need to calm down," Petunia said, watching her friend turn a small platter of pumpkin pie spiced nut cups thirty-eight degrees counterclockwise.

Delaney chose to ignore her friend. The copper plate the nut cups were set on needed to catch the light just so.

"Ahem, stop stressing yourself out." Still no response. "Delaney," Petunia cautioned, her tone dropping in a sympathetic way. "He's—"

"I know, Petunia…. It's just nice not to think about things the way they really are and, instead, ponder over the way—the way things could be," Delaney said, not looking forward to the fact that *he* would finally be introducing them all to his new girlfriend.

"That could get you into trouble," Petunia surveyed, intentionally dancing around the specifics of what exactly 'that' was. "Sooo…?" She sang the vowel, filling in the awkward silence while Delaney staged the throw blanket over the right arm of the sofa in such a way to make it look like it was placed there casually, folding it here and tucking it there. Her eyes traveled down the hall to Ophelia's bedroom. "So," she repeated, "um, is…?"

"Of course, she is. She's my sister," Delaney grumbled.

"Technically…" Petunia began, stopping to chew her Christmas tree cookie and using it to mark the air with imaginary ellipses before she continued her thought, bright green sprinkles and crumbs speckled everywhere.

"Technically, it's her apartment, and she *is* my sister." Delaney's eyes locked on the little mess than now dotted the table.

Petunia grimaced at the recollection of her story from three Christmases ago, the last time she had willingly been in a room with the oldest O'Leary sister. Then, catching her friend's silent hint, she stuffed the rest of the cookie into her mouth and swept up the crumbs with her hand.

But if Delaney had it her way, Ophelia would not be in attendance. Her sister had proven to her over and over again that she was incapable of remorse for any of the wrongdoings she had committed in the past. Her sister's sins, in the eyes of some, had rubbed off on her to the point of chafing. She was finding her stock of tolerance and forgiveness had run significantly low, and she didn't want to face any of it, not right now or the day after. Perhaps she could squeeze it in next week, but that wasn't looking too good either.

The anxiety she felt, and failed to avoid, was a heartache of sorts. *It's silly to miss someone who you still see every day, isn't it?* Delaney wondered. She missed the Ophelia from when they were growing up — the sister that sparked her imagination, the friend that made her feel it was okay to be a little less Type-A and a little braver in facing the unknown that life would conjure. The creativity and the courage that Ophelia had helped Delaney cultivate over her formative years was now crowded by resentment and trust issues.

"How's your first year in the doctorate program going, by the way?" Delaney reminded her friend, lobbing the awkward conversation to Petunia's side of the court. Petunia responded by clearing the decorative holiday plate that had been teeming with Santas, trees, and lightbulb shaped confections. A mouthful of cookies would buy her some time. Plus, sugar helped her to think.

The program was going just fine, by the way. Still, a part of Petunia was not ready to face down the "what-ifs" that threatened to jinx the dream she had finally found the courage and support to pursue. Not talking about school, meant she could blissfully save uncovering the cons, barriers, and challenges of her academic quest for a later date.

"The cookies are delicious," Petunia commented, choosing a safer topic. "Have you had any luck in drumming up business with them? These are really good. I mean it. What's in them?"

Delaney did not want to tell her friend that she hadn't started to showcase her goods to any of the local shops in the city. A part of her, about sixty-one percent, did not wish to hear any rejection that she had convinced herself would happen one hundred percent of the time should she try. The daydream was safe, and it made her happy enough. Instead, all she said was, "A little vanilla and—" Her answer was cut short when she heard a knock at the front door. Guests started to arrive, and holiday cheer managed to outshine Delaney's neurosis over the boy she could not be with and the sister she quietly and begrudgingly had to keep.

Among the chitter and chatter of Delaney's guests, most of whom were gushing over the cranberry tarts and the Thanksgiving empanadas, there came a loud clatter, followed by the sound of heavy stomps coming down the hall outside, increasing in volume.

The apartment conversation had died down to a murmur as they heard a key inserted into the lock. The knob turned, and Ophelia peered into the room, grinning behind fiery red bangs, like a child who had arisen early to take account of all the gifts stashed under the tree. "Hello, everyone," she sang, quietly pressing herself against the door and following its quarter-circular path.

The room echoed with salutations with a faint undertone of a groan. Ophelia was more than aware that the greetings were passive aggressive at their most polite. Being disliked by some, she had learned a long time ago, was a part of life. Being disliked by those who you cared for, well....

For the sake of her sister, on this particular night (specifically when the clock reached 9:12 p.m.), Ophelia would make the greatest of sacrifices to ensure Delaney was securely placed on her path to happiness. She tried to shake off the troubled feeling cautioning her the certainty of events that would follow after tonight would not be so certain.

She was experiencing a new sensation within her gut, giving her the collywobbles. She knew this sinking feeling was her mind attempting to attribute a physical symptom to her fear of the unknown. She would later describe it as simply unpleasant as no other word could be found that was more befitting this, until now, underutilized sensitivity.

"Did you slip?" Delaney asked her sister.

"No, the snow is so thick and heavy. I swear, it clung to my boots all the way to the top step."

"Well, be careful, Ophie."

Ophelia could tell the care had left her sister's tone. She was simply saying what was expected to be said. "You should save that concern for Mom and Dad. Did you know they were planning to drive in yesterday? They got halfway and had to turn around," Ophelia explained in a pained and dramatic tone. She only allowed herself a mere moment to wish they had made it, so the O'Leary family might celebrate one more Christmas together. A freak snowstorm continued to bluster within the Nollag city limits, strangely leaving everywhere else untouched.

No matter, Ophelia attempted to reassure herself. Somehow, happy times were bound to happen in the future, even if only few and far between. *How anyone managed the unknown without going mad...,* she wondered. The sheer number of outcomes that could unfurl, transpire, result, turn up, or shake out should have been enough to render most astounded. Don't even get her started on the intricate web of variables that played into the events in a day, an hour, or even a minute. They would not sit still!

"Yeah, you'd have thought they would have known better, what with them practically sending fan mail to the Glory meteorologist," Delaney said, pulling Ophelia from her spiraling musings.

"Don't you remember? Glory Bea actually read their names during one of her forecasts. It was Dad's birthday present," Ophelia added. She grimaced at the realization that such an act made her parents approximately twenty-six percent less hip than she had initially calculated.

Delaney exhaled a tiny laugh through her nostrils and smiled at the recollection of her parents trading off and telling the story, gushing over their, albeit secondary, star struck encounter. Interwoven between the breaks of the edited memory was a realization. Despite the (ahem) challenge her older sister could be at times, Delaney felt a certain comfort and warmth knowing she had Ophelia to share in these memories in such a way that only siblings could.

Ophelia noted the genuine smile gently curving Delaney's lips. She shut her eyes as if to hold this image in her mind, to commit it to memory. Just as she was stitching the finer details into place, there came a loud THUMP from out in the hall. All those in attendance momentarily looked to the door before returning to the party's conversations and delectable spread.

Ophelia recognized the mysterious sound as a new arrival to the festivities. She excused herself from her sister and went to the door. Upon opening up the door and looking out into the hall, her eyes widened and her jaw dropped in practiced shock.

"Oh, my! Are you okay? Come in," she said to Calum as he crossed the threshold with a hobbling Bailey Barrymore, her arm slung around his shoulder. Ophelia suppressed a look of pleasure at the girl's pain while her sister worked to hold together her faltering smile as she gazed upon the young man.

Calum shot Delaney a friendly smile, but she dodged it deftly and made her way over to greet the couple. Calum and Bailey had been going out for a year, ever since the candy striper had been assigned to the hospital room Calum's father was placed in on that fateful Christmas night last year. At least, that's how Bailey would explain it in gushy and exaggerated tones.

"Our eyes met, and it was fate," she would say, making sure to put extra emphasis on the last word, believing it really drove the story home and tucked it into bed. People loved the idea of Fate, how it seemed to do all the heavy lifting in constructing Happy Endings for others. Fate would like you to know orchestrating these blissful outcomes can be a thankless job at times, but that's a discussion for later.

"Oh! What happened?" Ophelia asked, helping Bailey to the nearest chair.

"It's fine," Bailey replied, a bit exasperated. Getting a good look at Ophelia, her expression faltered. Had she met Ophelia before? She couldn't recall. "Uh, there was a huge clump of snow at the top of the stairs, and I took a spill." She offered a pained smile to everyone in the room, as Calum helped her make her way to a freshly vacated seat.

Delaney swore she saw Ophelia shoot her a glance that seemed to say, "You're welcome." Delaney was not sure exactly what for.

"Let me get you some ice for your ankle." Delaney only took a fleeting glance at Calum, wishing the glance had the power to convey her wishes for circumstances to have arranged themselves in a more convenient order.

No words would properly construct the feeling that caused a tingling sensation all the way from her fingertips to all four ventricles of her heart. But unlike the decidedly "unpleasant" feeling Ophelia was experiencing that night, Delaney's was a mix of emotions that made her heart jump and sink in an exhilarating and sickening fashion. Unrequited fantasies for the affections of another can have that effect on a person.

Of course, this burning fire was quelled by the reality that in order for this fantasy to be a reality, Bailey Barrymore would have to be no more. The lighthearted tingling degraded to a slow smoldering as guilt settled in upon the realization that wishing someone to be bumped out of the picture, or, at the very least, to the outer edges of the frame, was in poor taste. Now only a small part of Delaney, no more than one point two percent, wished this fantasy to fruition.

"Here is your ice, Bailey," Delaney said with a pained smile, this time avoiding looking at Calum.

Ironic that ice was what put her in this situation, Ophelia wanted to quip. Instead, she opted to say, "My, what a lovely charm bracelet!" She gasped, appraising the golden trinkets that jingled and jangled delicately on Bailey's wrist. Calum silently noted how rehearsed Ophelia's fawning over the jewelry seemed to be. Ophelia held a charm resembling a tiny rattle between her index finger and thumb as she absentmindedly touched the poinsettia broach on the lapel of her red velvet blazer. "They say that each charm has a story behind it. What's this one?"

Bailey's face was blank as she looked down at the charms. "Oh, um, I—I don't remember," she said with a tinge of annoyance at the question. She tended to a bruise that was forming below the knee of the same leg with the sprained ankle, a terrible two-for-one special, really.

"My grandma used to have one just like it," Delaney said, more to herself than to anyone else. Her expression grew somber, and she excused herself to restock the low sodium pita chips and the smoky cheese spread.

The party wore on but showed very few signs of excessive use, in spite of the call the police paid on behalf of Mrs. Beezle, whose patience had worn very thin. There were carolers and movies and grab bags and an exorbitant amount of calories dressed up as hors d'oeuvres or decked out in brightly colored crystalized sugar. The night, by all in attendance, including Delaney, would be declared a success. It would be the main topic of discussion by the Ghost of Holiday Parties Future for years to come.

Of course, by 9:12 p.m., all recollection of the soiree would be for an entirely different reason.

Chapter 26

In Which Ophelia Forgets to Warn Bailey Barrymore That She is Armed and Bedazzled

At 9:04 p.m., Bailey asked where she might find the bathroom, and Ophelia was all too happy to help her hobble down the dark hallway to it. "It's no problem at all," Ophelia said, before Bailey, who seemed unsure if she wanted to be alone with Ophelia, could object.

She pretended not to notice that Bailey's attention was momentarily held by light pouring out of the first door on the right, Ophelia's closet, and the mounds of jewelry and baubles set atop her dressers framed by the doorway.

"Oh, that won't be necessary," Bailey sweetly replied to Ophelia's offer to help bring her back to the party after she was done. "I can manage back. It's actually feeling better." She stood on one foot while rotating the other in midair.

"All right," was all Ophelia said. She waited until she heard the lock of the door click before quietly slipping into her closet to enter her tiny bedroom to retrieve a box from under her bed. Setting it on the mattress and lifting the lid, she stared at its contents. She grimaced at it before turning to her left to check the time on her alarm clock. 9:07 p.m. *Five minutes*, she thought. She waited and listened for the quiet rummaging sounds that would come from her closet.

At 9:11 p.m., at the top of the minute, she grabbed the contents of the box. Taking four steps back into the closet, she planted her feet, inhaled a breath, and pulled the trigger to release two wires from her taser as someone departed from the chest of drawers by the door.

At 9:12 p.m., Bailey Barrymore came crashing down upon the carpet in a crumpled and twitching mess. A very large bauble, a padmaraga yellow sapphire cocktail ring, rolled from her hand to stop at the tip of Calum's boot. The air escaped from the room as the partygoers gasped at such a rate that should Rory Wort have been invited, he almost certainly would have passed out from a perceived loss of cabin pressure.

Ophelia stood over the mess of a girl holding a purple bedazzled taser.

Questions and exclamations spewed free-flowing from Delaney's mouth. "Wh—what are you doing, Ophelia? Give me that! Are you crazy? Why is this purple!?" Delaney pinched the taser between her thumb and index finger, gingerly placing it on a table next to the platter of mushroom caps stuffed with garlicy breadcrumbs, red pepper, and burrata on top. She reached for the kitchen towel that rested on her shoulder and wiped her fingers as if the taser had somehow stained them.

"She's fine," Ophelia said coolly, barely batting an eyelash in Bailey's direction.

"No. No. No. I—I am so sorry, Bailey. Are you okay?" Delaney asked. She held her breath and began to nervously wring the towel.

The young woman, still fidgeting from a spasm here and there, slowly pulled herself upright. "Ow!" Bailey shrieked when the nerves closest to her wrist finally got around to sending the message that it had sustained a break from the fall.

"Ooo…yeah, we need to get you to the hospital, Bae. Up you go." Calum helped his girlfriend to her feet. Coats were thrown on in a rush, scarves wrapped around necks haphazardly, and hats sat askew. Once gloves were pulled on, well, except for Bailey's right one for obvious reasons, the couple was almost out the door when….

"I'm coming with you. Bailey, I feel somewhat responsible," Ophelia said, this time without even a trace of false remorse.

"Get away from me," Bailey said with acidic words. "Follow me—come near me again, and I will press charges!" She cradled her wrist in her left hand, working her face into a wince, and limped out of the apartment for what some, actually only Ophelia, perceived as dramatic effect.

Without missing a beat, Ophelia had draped herself in an emerald green cashmere coat and slung a large fire engine red bag across her shoulder. The bag connected with the open front door, and its contents gave an odd and heavy "thunk."

"Where are you going?" Delaney asked incredulously.

"After Calum and Bailey," Ophelia said matter-of-factly. "Didn't you hear me a couple of seconds ago?"

341

Before Delaney could voice her dissatisfaction with this course of action and reiterate Bailey's legal threats, Ophelia was two and a half flights below.

Delaney stood at the threshold of the apartment, her temper boiling to a dangerously high heat. She found her patience was all but completely evaporated. She immediately released the choke hold she had on the kitchen towel, folded it along its faded creases, and looked to Petunia for a ride, the party be damned.

Chapter 27

In Which There Are Hefty Fruitcakes and Harsh Words Thrown About

"Sit," Ophelia commanded Calum as she approached Hospital Room 3.

"She doesn't want to see you," Calum said, rooted to his seat. He could feel his knees begin to quake from her authority.

"Aw. Why ever not?" Ophelia asked in a saddened tone, ripe with sarcasm. She did not wait for the lapdog to speak as she passed by and was met with a bitter glower.

"I ought to press charges," Bailey threatened.

"I could say the same," Ophelia said with a smile, having a seat on the bed, placing her satchel at the foot of the mattress. Bailey was thrown by Ophelia's placid demeanor. Threats of arrest usually left people…um…well, threatened, really.

"You broke my wrist."

"Sweetie, I didn't break your wrist. The floor did."

"You tased me!"

"You had it coming," she shrugged. There was a new edge to Ophelia's voice. "And seeing as this is the second time you've stolen from me...."

"Wha—"

Ophelia snatched the girl's good wrist, easily unlatching the charm bracelet that adorned it. Bailey swallowed her words of shock and protest, choosing instead to stare back at the collection of charms that dangled between Ophelia's thumb and index finger.

"They say that charm bracelets harbor a collection of stories within them, and this one has a doozy. Would you care to hear it? You see, once upon a time, a dear woman by the name of Mildred O'Leary, on her deathbed, wished to pass it along to her granddaughter. As it turns out, tragedy came too soon, and the gift became lost in the shuffle. No. Not lost, but stolen. But by who and why?

"The culprit had wormed her way into Mildred's life. She pretended to be nice to her, knowing her sweet demeanor would bring Mildred's usually guarded walls crumbling down. Impressive, by the way, she was a tough nut to crack. Then, one day, in her ill and dying state, Mildred shared with the candy striper the final gifts she was going to will to her granddaughters: a poinsettia broach and *this* charm bracelet.

"I'm not done yet." Ophelia held up a hand to silence Bailey, who now stared back, mouth agape, a protest at the back of her throat halting and going cold. Ophelia imagined the head of a goldfish looking back at her. "Let's see here," she said, resting a large pewter heart charm on her fingertips, a little gold still clung to its edges. She regarded it for a moment before unlatching it. The charm was a locket. "Strange, Bailey. Why have a locket with no pictures? Not even one of the boyfriend?" She turned the open heart to face the girl and tapped a fingernail against the blank cardstock inside.

"That *is* my locket," Bailey said with what sounded, at best, like lukewarm conviction.

"What's your proof? Finders Keepers?"

"What's *your* proof?"

A smile pulled at the corners of Ophelia's mouth. She took a fingernail and began to pull at the white cardstock within the heart. Inside were two etchings: 'Infinite' on the left and '–EO' on the right, followed by a newer etching of '& MO' beneath the first set of initials.

"Hm. Look at that. EO, Éamon O'Leary. MO, Mildred O'Leary. You outta be cracked in the face with a three-year-old fruitcake for lying."

"I'm sorry—"

"That you got caught. Bold choice, by the way, wearing it to my sister Delaney's party tonight."

Mildred O'Leary. She chastised herself as realization slowly filled in the details that Delaney was Delaney O'Leary, the sad girl from five years ago she'd seen as she passed by the waiting room, and that she had lifted the charm bracelet from her grandmother. *But she had never gone into the room!* Her mind spun and sputtered. Getting caught caused her guilt to overwhelm any flimsy justifications she tried to wield. A lack of vindication turned her mood sour. "All right, you have the bracelet back. You win," she said in a snit.

Ophelia replied, "You, Bailey Barrymore, are going to change your life for the better…with a little help from me and a little bit of blackmail for good measure."

Bailey's brow furrowed. "What do you want me to do?"

"You're going to fix everything. Specifically, you're going to return all of the items you've ever stolen, including those collectible mallard salt and pepper shakers from Mr. and Mrs. Dooley."

"How did you—"

"I know things." Ophelia paused as if to consider something, when really she was relishing in Bailey's shock, watching the wheels and cogs turn in her head, picking up on the slight panic as Bailey wondered what else Ophelia knew. "Ooo! While we're at it, you're going to break it off with Calum. Let the dog off the leash."

"You can't tell me who I can and cannot see! That's—"

"Blackmail," Ophelia finished Bailey's sentence in a condescending tone. "We already checked that box. Besides, you don't love him. You love the fact he's a pushover, but you don't love *him*. In the brief seven minutes that I bothered to watch you two at Delaney's party, six minutes and forty-five seconds were devoted to a whole lot of avoiding eye contact and you pulling away every time Cal so much as touched your hand. You're trying to keep a heart that doesn't belong with you."

"Set it free." Bailey said back sarcastically.

"Okay, I see we may need to knock some sense into you. I'm not going to bother wasting my breath any longer." Ophelia pulled her purse over her shoulder and took a step closer to face Bailey. She said nothing, only smiled, before she swiftly turned on her heels, letting her bag swing outward. It connected squarely with the side of Bailey's face.

Before Bailey's cry of pain, Ophelia caught the beginning of Calum's involuntary gasp. She knew that he had been standing right outside the doorway and had been doing so long enough to hear the more shocking parts of the conversation. Ophelia also knew that he would be in a state of shock, which would work in her favor for the next step in her plan.

"Ow!" Bailey shrieked, holding her right cheek. "What is in that bag?"

"Didn't I mention that earlier?" Ophelia asked. "It's a three-year-old fruitcake." She dug in her bag to reveal the cellophane wrapped confection. Having finished her last piece of business, she exited Hospital Room 3, knowing full well common sense would settle in the mind of Bailey Barrymore and leave a permanent dent, not unlike the noticeable impression that the fruitcake had left in the bottom right corner of the hospital bed's mattress where Ophelia's bag had sat.

Not two clicks of Ophelia's shoes along the maroon and salmon linoleum floor, and she was met with a stern finger wagging, or what Calum intended to be a stern finger wagging. Mostly, his index finger somehow remained stationary while the rest of him quavered. His expression was hard to place, somewhere between anger and stupefaction, which translated to a look of constipation. He was struggling to make sense of how a simple holiday party had turned into an interrogation and confession.

Ophelia stopped in her tracks and met Calum's gaze. Despite his wading through discombobulated thoughts and newly forming theories, he would be the first to see the uncertainty winking into existence within her emerald green eyes.

"I—uh. I don't have time for this," she said in a manner of someone who was late for something imperative. She looked at the bracelet in her hand and gave a sad but brief smile and walked past him. "Ask your girlfriend about it. Oh, and…you can do better."

She abruptly stopped in her path toward the elevators as if realizing she forgot something and returned back to Calum. Without looking at him, she quickly snatched the engagement ring from inside of his jacket pocket and deftly replaced it with the charm bracelet. She held up the tiny box with the crunched ruby red bow that was affixed to the top. "You're not going to need this. Trust me. And you're welcome."

Calum worked his lips to form words, but no sound came forth, his mind pleading with the questions that crowded his thoughts to politely take a number and queue up. One of the more pressing questions was what she planned to do with the ring. It had not been a trivial expense.

Ophelia's usual certainty had begun to shrink to a gut feeling that Calum's soon-to-be relationship with Delaney would distract him from such immediate queries. She knew enough that she was to hold onto it for the time being.

The elevator doors shut before Calum's first question stepped forward.

*   *   *

Delaney could no longer control the frustration that itched under her skin. The pressure built as Petunia drove her to the hospital, and it showed no signs of dissipating after she got out of the car while Petunia looked for parking. Seeing her sister turn the corner was the tipping point, and it all began to pour out.

"Don't. How could you? How could you do it again!? You do whatever you want and disregard how it affects everyone around you—how it affects me. It's embarrassing. You should be ashamed of yourself!"

Delaney called forward all the ghosts of Christmases past: how she almost lost her friend when Ophelia stole and photocopied Petunia's thesis; how, it seemed, the entire city of Nollag shunned her after Ophelia had physically eviscerated Santa Claus in front of a packed mall; how Ophelia managed to almost kill Calum's father by sheer wit, and how that had cost her the chance for her and Calum to be something a bit more than awkward acquaintances.

Ophelia was a villain who caused messy troubles and left supposed loved ones to clean it up in her wake. She broke hearts and tested the limits of bonds where she had no business doing so. This rang truest regarding that fateful night in the hospital lobby. Because for all the things Ophelia had done and would do, for the life of Delaney, she admitted she could never answer the question that still lived comfortably in a far corner of her mental junk drawer: Why was Ophelia allowed in *that* room? Why was Ophelia allowed to say goodbye to Mildred, and Delaney was left always to wonder? The unknown eclipsed any shred of good Ophelia had ever done.

"There are days I wish that I—" wide-eyed and gulping at the air, Delaney steadied herself as she tried to force her rage-filled words back into her lower stomach where they would hopefully be disintegrated and digested.

It truly is the thought that counts, however, and Ophelia knew the rest of that sentence. This exact moment in time had run through her head the first time she met Delaney. (Unbeknownst to Delaney, their first encounter was not on the day a sweet, introverted, little girl came to Mother Mary Claire Brog's Haven for Tiddlers, Toddlers, Tykes, and Children to claim a friend.)

With those stifled words left undisclosed, a panic set in beneath Ophelia's impenetrable placid façade. For you see, Ophelia prided herself on being anywhere between a step and a third to two and three-quarter steps ahead in this dance called life. That was until, at 10:06 p.m., right on the thirteenth second, she lost count, and the choreography flicked out of her mind. *What now?*

"Um, Dee, what I did—all of it—I. You see—the reason—" But it was no use. Her words fidgeted and tripped over themselves as Ophelia tried to find the correct string of 'magic words' that would ease her sister's anger and pain. Alas, her mind was now clouded with the fact this incantation was buried and tangled amidst an innumerable list of replies that would only make things worse. "D—Delaney." *Stop. You have to stop. If you want her to have happiness, you have to stop.*

"What is it, Ophelia? What justification can you possibly offer?" Delaney sounded sick, as if her words tasted of cod liver oil.

"All I ever was...was me," she said plainly. Her shoulders dropped in defeat. She made to raise her hand and place it on Delaney's arm, but she changed her mind, letting it fall away. As Ophelia passed her sister, for the first time, neither knew what would come next for them.

But what Delaney did know was she couldn't stay with her sister anymore. She would make plans to move out immediately. Perhaps move in with her parents in Glory? The idea did not comfortably settle in her mind. Nollag was her home, and she couldn't bear to leave it.

An idea came to her then as she made her way to the fifth floor and stormed down the hallway to where Calum was. Ophelia wasn't the only O'Leary who was allowed to pursue 'unconventional' and 'risky' dreams. She wanted a piece of that pie, too.

Her thoughts jumped to the chia spiced maple pumpkin pie she had figured out the recipe to earlier that day. Maybe she should seriously do something with her grandmother's and her own recipes. She set the idea on the back burner of her mind, carefully setting the heat to low and cracking the lid to let the steam escape so as to not let the idea boil over into a burned and sticky mess.

Chapter 28

In Which Things Come to a Close, but Opportunity Opens New Doors...and Possibly Cracks a Window

Ophelia could not help but feel a sense of déjà vu. Walking toward the exit of the hospital, away from Bailey Barrymore, away from Delaney, she had the same tightness in her throat as the night Mildred had left them, altogether an unpleasant and unwelcomed sensation. *How can it be the faster I walk, the longer this hall seems to get?* The hospital exit taunted her as she chased after it. She hated that door. Truthfully, her loathing was misplaced, but it made it easier to manage. She would eventually pass over the threshold of the exit, but she would never be able to escape from herself.

"Hey," Clarence said as he came in through the entrance, stepping into his friend's path. Where many would see a cool exterior, Clarence knew never to take Ophelia at face value. He saw the pain she carried on her shoulders, the sadness that made her hands tremble, and the fear that constricted her throat.

"What's—"

"No. Clarence, I'm fine."

The cop knew better than to argue. No amount of huffing and puffing words of sympathy and concern would blow down Ophelia's obstinate walls. There were no assurances that everything would be okay, at least not certain ones.

Ophelia opened her mouth to speak, but she was unsuccessful.

"Oh," Clarence knowingly said, as if the whole scene had transpired right before his eyes in excruciating and explicit detail. His heart sank to meet with his friend's. "Listen, Ophie, you weighed these risks for years, and you did what you knew was right. You didn't stick to the rules, but you did help *all* of them."

"Did I? Do we know for sure? Do you? Because I don't know. It's all gone." She waved her fingers in the air about the temples of her head. She could no longer conjure events to come.

"No. I don't know for sure. You have to trust—you have to believe—"

Ophelia wrapped her arms around her friend as she felt her hard candy heart begin to crack and finally break. It hurt. Hearts were not supposed to hurt. "I don't know if I really know how to, Clare. It's all gone," she said, referring to her ability to peek at fate's plans and intentions. "I'm scared."

The two friends stood at the opening of the hospital, holding each other. The world passed them by. People worked, lived, died, cried, and smiled, but in their small piece of the world, time had politely paused.

Clarence pulled away to face Ophelia. He gave a soft smile and firmly squeezed the hand she had placed on his shoulder. With that, Ophelia's world began to spin once again and sync up with the rest of reality.

"You did it to save them."

"I did it to save them," she repeated, nodding.

*   *   *

Delaney caught Calum as he left hospital Room 3. He had a sullen expression that pulled dangerously at the corners of his mouth as he stared at something in his hand.

"How is she doing?" Delaney went to touch his arm but reconsidered it mid-raise and moved to push her hair behind her right ear instead.

"Her jaw hurts," he said, absentmindedly turning the trinkets on the charm bracelet over. It had somehow found its way off of Bailey's wrist and had taken up residence in his coat pocket out of which Ophelia had plucked the engagement ring.

"She hit her jaw when she fell?"

Calum ignored the question. His fingers moving back to a heart-shaped locket. It had been partially opened when he had found the bracelet.

"Calum." Delaney sat down and gestured for him to do the same. "Um...I am so, so, so sorry that my sister tased your girlfr— Bailey. To be honest, I never thought I would have to make an apology like this one."

"It's okay," he said.

Delaney's mind could not compute the simple reply of forgiveness. She cast aside her awkward fear to look at the young man. As she had guessed, the half-hearted response was due, in part, to the fact Calum was half listening and was engrossed in something etched inside of the heart-shaped locket. Delaney laid a hand on his forearm to bring him back to the reality that was the two of them sitting on a deflated deep sea foam green love seat speckled with salmon colored tulips.

Still, the young man did not speak, instead handing the charm bracelet to Delaney and giving into his thoughts.

Delaney wasn't sure why Calum had handed over his girlfriend's charm bracelet. She tried to meet his gaze, which was fixated on the wall in front of him. Not entirely convinced he was enamored with the faded print of wilted daisies, she prodded him. Still, he did not respond. Perhaps he was bothered that the picture was situated at an awkward eighty-eight degree angle and not a perfect ninety degrees?

She went back to admiring the charms, now able to take the time to notice each trinket. *Wait*, she thought, noticing a pewter heart with most of its gold plating rubbed off.

The travesty of the evening was muted by the simple and soothing memories of Christmases past when the holiday was distilled down to anticipation, cookies, and presents, in that order. She allowed a split second of sadness for the fact those specific happy times would remain in the past. After all, the best memories are unplanned and can never be truly replicated as they always start out as unexpected. That's why the fondest and cherished of recollections are special. They are, in essence, pleasant surprises.

Amidst the turmoil of this Christmas present, a new memory was about to spring around the corner, blaring a horn and tossing confetti…with Petunia pulling up the rear carefully shuffling over to the pair with two brimming cups of cocoa.

"Read the etching inside the locket," Calum said cryptically.

This time, when Delaney turned to look at Calum, their eyes met. She was taken aback by the sense of urgency his deep blue eyes communicated.

She opened the pewter heart to find the message 'Infinite — EO & MO' inside. Her brown eyes widened with shock. The thought that the charms cradled in her fingertips were those lost five years ago stepped out of the murky shadows of fantasy into the light of reality.

"How—you mean these are—this isn't Bai—" Delaney shook her head to reset. "How did Bailey get this?"

Calum pursed his lips and stuck them out as he exhaled. "I think you need to talk to Bailey about that."

Petunia finally made it to the little table next to Calum and Delaney. "What's happening?" she asked casually, blowing on one of the molten hot cocoas.

"I'll fill you in," Calum said.

When Delaney eventually made her way into the room, Bailey would recount the factual story to her. How the bracelet came into her possession an hour after Mildred's passing when no one would be looking or missing the treasure. She even added how she had done this to other people and how those knickknacks and baubles made their way to the Deal and Steal. For some reason, the bracelet did not meet a similar fate. Chalk it up to a Christmas miracle maybe. There was something beautiful about it — special. Try as she might, Bailey Barrymore could not clearly articulate her reason, especially since her love of money trumped that of her fancy for things that shined and glittered.

One thing Bailey Barrymore knew for certain was she detested the very existence of fruitcake, and that the pain in her right cheek would persist well into New Year's Eve. The former would add to the discomfort she would feel when she picked up the phone to call the Nollag Police Department and make her confession.

*   *   *

That same night, returning from the hospital, Ophelia found herself pausing at her front door for a moment after placing the key in the lock but before turning the doorknob. Her mind sputtered and skipped, not wishing to feel what she felt in the present moment and not wanting to dwell on the evening's earlier events. Memory and emotion clashed, deteriorating Ophelia's usual crystal-clear reasoning to something grainy and illegible.

She closed her eyes, shut them tight in an attempt to see. Images flickered in and out of sight just past her eyelids. She gritted her teeth, held her breath, and clutched her hand around the engagement ring in her pocket. She willed herself to see one last time.

A hand gently rested upon another. A frown slowly pulled into a kind smile.

And then the image was gone.

Good, Ophelia exhaled, glad that her visions were able to hold out long enough to confirm Delaney was now on the right path.

For the first time in a long time, or perhaps for the first time in all of her existence, she picked up on a sadness of a particular kind. Not the sadness one experiences receiving a dolly or board game as a Christmas present at the ripe old age of a very practical nine-year-old when all was desired was real estate or, at the very least, white tube socks with extra cushioning in the soles. Nor a melancholy felt when oversleeping the biggest holiday sale of the year for the latest doodad that seemed to be in a perpetual state of low inventory. This was a sense of loss, a grieving for no longer knowing what would come to pass. Without this foresight, who was Ophelia?

"Who?" Ophelia echoed her thoughts.

If that weren't enough for one to be muttering to oneself and lurking in doorways, it certainly was enough to have Mrs. Beezle peering out from a crack in her doorway.

Ophelia jumped upon catching the old woman's scowl out of the corner of her eye. She promptly remembered how doors worked, turning the knob and stepping inside, away from the frigid look of judgement.

"I should have seen that coming," she groaned.

The apartment was empty now. Ophelia instinctively raised a hand to flip the light on, but decided against it, letting her arm flop back to her side. With her back pressed against the door, her legs protested for her to sit, and so the sound of her wool coat hissed against the heavily painted door as she slid down.

Deep shadows shrouded the remnants of the gathering from roughly one hour and fifty-one minutes earlier. The starlight offered the slightest peek at the sequined ornaments that hung on the tree, each carefully spaced two to three inches apart from one another, and the pile of presents, no doubt white elephants that would have been redressed in new brightly colored paper and exchanged again next year.

Slipping the little box from her pocket, she popped open its lid to look at the ring. It glittered and glinted in what little light the diamonds could catch, but this was the sort of things engagement rings did. Except it really could not be called an *engagement ring*, not anymore.

She removed the ring from the box, tilting it to look at the inside of the band. *No engraving*, she noted. Ophelia thought about returning the ring to Calum, so long as it wasn't used when he proposed to Delaney. For now, it would return to its box, which would reside in her bag, next to the fruitcake, until she decided what to do with it.

As she exhaled, she hoisted herself up to her feet by propping an elbow against the little table by the door that contained the dish for her keys and loose change alongside the tiny Christmas tree. The flimsy table gave a shudder, and the little jingle bell that had come from her first Christmas gift as an O'Leary gave a gentle tinkle, its ball bearing swaying back and forth within the sphere.

No sooner had Ophelia turned the corner, heading to her bed and the loving embrace of her pillow and down comforter, than a knock on the door of apartment 7H came low, almost a mumble as it were. Then it became more urgent, the knocking rising in speed and volume. Most could have categorized it as a rapping.

"Officer Lawson," Ophelia said as she peered from around her door. She guessed Copper had come by to bring her in for assault and battery. In this instance, it seemed wrong to be informal and address him in her usual way, using his first name.

He looked back at the formality not totally aware as to why it had emerged from the figurative left field. "Uh, hi, Ophelia. I heard about what you did to Bailey Barrymore. Can I come in?" Copper rolled his eyes to the end of the hall to silently indicate that Mrs. Beezle was hanging over her threshold, listening in.

The young woman nodded and opened her home up to her friend. "So, she must be pressing charges?"

"No," Copper answered flatly. "Shocking, isn't it?" he smirked.

The joke evaded Ophelia as it dawned on her that the answer, any answer that Copper would have given, would have registered as a surprise. *So, this is what it feels like,* she thought, noting how her stomach yo-yoed from throat to diaphragm all in eight-tenths of a second. She casually sat down in a chair, trying not to give away that the room faded out of her consciousness for a split second.

"I'm sorry, Officer—Copper, then why are you here?"

"To thank you. Bailey Barrymore's confession was a missing link to a case we've been investigating for a while now," Copper trailed, allowing for a flashback to insert itself comfortably into the story.

*   *   *

Bailey had first met Adele Swinde suspiciously eyeing a therapy parakeet with a sign that read "I bite" next to her hospital bed. Adele had admitted herself into the hospital to have a doll's crown removed from her nasal cavity. Truthfully, the crown had been lodged there since she was six years old, shoved up her nose by her older sister, Imogene, and had posed no health risk. Upon hearing the crown belonged to Gorgeous Georgina, a rare find since the princess was evolved to also be a warrior scientist after an extensive focus group of Nollag's girls ages four to eight, Adele jumped at the chance to have the accessory removed. It would easily sell for a grand or two. She could practically smell it…and it had faint notes of polystyrene.

The two recognized kindred spirits within each other. In this case, very literal partners in crime. Bailey Barrymore was a candy striper with an innocent face who carried a touch of truth serum in her smile. This fact, and these traits, gave her access to befriend the ill, who also, at times, were rich. Adele was a pawnbroker whose shop had seen better days. At the time, the most valuable thing in her shop was the rock salt kept by the front door to ensure the icy sidewalks out front did not cause a lawsuit to skid into her. With only little Houdini, the therapy parakeet, to witness, a partnership was struck with the expressed goal of lining the shelves of the Deal and Steal with valuables, which, in turn, would line their pockets with cash.

*   *   *

"It's usually been little things," Copper explained, "like of things the vics don't think to check on every day. Bailey would make house calls to 'catch up' on her favorite patients, but mostly she was there to pilfer what Adele told her would sell for the most and the quickest."

"But best laid plans still have their slip-ups," Ophelia chimed in.

Copper paused and gave one heavy nod. Small town or big city, people talk. "Imagine the shock of the vics when they saw friends with similar, if not identical, knickknacks, baubles, and what-nots, only to find theirs missing when the thought came into their heads to check on them. Coincidence goes to the wayside when these stories enter the double digits," Copper continued. "Investigations revealed two common threads…."

"Uh-huh," Ophelia agreed, "Bailey and the Deal and Steal."

"Right."

"So, you have evidence. Case closed."

"Not exactly. Bailey admits to stealing and selling to the Deal and Steal. I, uh, I only suspect that Adele advised her on what to take," he sheepishly amended.

"Oh," Ophelia said, somewhat annoyed, "the way you explained it, you made it sound like she confessed that part." Ophelia immediately regretted not hitting the young woman with the fruitcake a smidge harder. "Wait, then how do you presume this Adele is the brains?"

"I have a gut feeling."

Ophelia blinked through her confusion. Not only did that sound disgusting, it sounded highly unreliable. "So, your hard evidence of the real guilty party is an assumption?"

"That," Copper added, "and some evidence she's been cooking her books."

Ophelia decided to get the conversation back on track again. "Why are you here, Copper?" Ophelia repeated.

"The Deal and Steal's inventory currently includes a cat lamp and a book — *Alice's Adventures in Wonderland*. First edition. Gold binding. Fancy," he explained, not trusting that his young friend appreciated why a children's book would be so valuable beyond sentiment. "Bailey lifted them from two retired agents we had pose as patients a couple of months back."

"Hm—sounds involved," Ophelia stated flatly.

Copper agreed. "I want you to pick them up. Adele won't know you, and, for all I know, she has the faces of every officer on the force memorized. She might not make the sale otherwise or stash the merchandise in the back. My ma wants her lamp back.

"We'll put a wire on you to monitor your conversations and make sure you're not in any danger. You're also going to sell something. We'll round out that part of your backstory later. When she makes the sale, most likely grossly undervaluing your item, we ride in and take her down." Copper always enjoyed the dramatic effect with his busts.

Ophelia considered the cop's plot. "Firstly," Ophelia said, "I'll do it." She got up and walked to her red bag, which still sat beside the door, pulling out the small, black box, its bow barely hanging on now. "Secondly," she tossed the box to Copper, "I know what I'll be selling. I can tell you that ring is worth $2,178 exactly. Thirdly, why didn't you bug the lamp and catch Adele leaking her plans after store hours?"

"Best laid plans." Copper smiled sheepishly. "We tried, but without any luck. Adele hasn't said anything that would implicate her, even when it's only been her and her new employee. She's being mum around him, which makes me think he doesn't have a clue about her side business."

Ophelia smiled back. Even though somewhat artificial in nature, she was grateful to once again have a sense of foresight.

Copper then explained, when Bailey stopped showing up, it wouldn't take long for Adele to put two and two together that her business partner had either been nabbed or skipped town. If she was as careful as Copper assumed, she would likely stow away her special "merchandise" until any speck of suspicion had been thoroughly scrubbed, becoming virtually imperceptible under the magnifying glass of the Nollag Police Department.

"Clarence thinks we should give it about a year before Adele starts moving the stolen merchandise back out onto the floor."

"He would know," Ophelia chortled under her breath.

Copper continued with his plan, how Ophelia would find a key in the back of the book, how the key would open the hidden drawer of his mother's lamp, which contained $200 worth of two-dollar bills, and how he had even placed an envelope sealed with wax with a special message for Adele, which was "Gotcha."

Chapter 29

In Which the Holiday Party Takes a Couple More Ternes

That's the thing about stories, you see. It's all about perspective. Where some would find hilarity, others can only manage to find the tragedy. A win in one's book is a loss in another's. A savior can be mistaken for a villain. The omission of one crucial detail, and you can have a completely different tale.

Back in the present, Delaney found herself momentarily out of her body, observing a scene of what many would consider a holiday get together of friends. Still, she felt nothing remotely close to cheer. Why?

The doorbell rang as Delaney wrapped up her recount of last year's failed Christmas, but before she could stand, Calum was halfway out of the room and mumbling something about not losing his words. The party could hear the door carelessly swung open as Calum bleated out, "Come in!" before charging up the stairs to his study.

Grey perked up in his seat as the voices of the new visitors wafted into the living room. His lips pulled together to work the word "No" out of his mouth.

"That was rather odd—Grey?" Mrs. Terne said as she and her husband stepped from around the corner.

"So, this is where you ran off to," Mr. Terne chimed in with a smile. The couple were laden down with brightly wrapped gifts bedecked in metallic blue, green, red, and silver.

"What are you doing here?" Grey spat out, immediately clapping his hand over his mouth at his curt question.

"You know it's a strange story," Mrs. Terne began. "Um, your father," she indicated the impeccably tailored Mr. Terne, who had just set the gifts down onto the coffee table to help himself to a treat, "and I were leaving your shop, by the by it was all lovely, when we ran into a rather large man…both tall and wide."

"We thought we were about to be mugged," Mr. Terne said through a mouthful of butter cookie. "B—but we weren't. Mm—do you have any more of these?" he asked Delaney, Gregory, and Petunia. He shifted his gaze to each of their faces, unsure of who had the answer.

Petunia answered Mr. Terne by pointing a finger at Delaney.

"Yes," Delaney replied, getting up to retrieve the cookies from the kitchen.

"As it turns out," Mrs. Terne said, picking up where her husband left off, "this gentleman, a Mr. Winklemer? Hinkmeyer? To tell you the truth, I'm not sure. Do you know who I'm talking about, dear?"

Grey shook his head in response. He was still processing her compliment.

"Well, anyway, this man was going to be late for his new job and needed to have these packages delivered. Your father and I had some free time on our hands, so we decided to do our good deed for the day. Goodwill. Reason for the season and all. Funny how it brought us here!"

"Who are they for?" Petunia asked.

"They're for us," Gregory answered as he poured over the tags, "and they're from Ophelia."

The room fell silent, save for the sound of Mr. Terne chowing down on another butter cookie.

"Grey, dear, there was an absolutely breathtaking dress in your front window. You know the one? Little off the shoulder sequined number? Do you think you could get me a discount?"

In Grey's case, he had missed a crucial plot point in his own life story. True, he came from a long line of talented tailors in menswear and suiting, but what he failed to realize was the only person placing the hefty expectations to continue this legacy was himself.

Since first picking up a needle and thread, Mr. Turne could not conceive of doing anything outside of the tailoring profession and thought it natural that his son would likely do the same. Grey, after all, had never said anything to him on the contrary. That being said, this did not preclude that Mr. and Mrs. Terne could not fathom the possibility their son's passions would lie somewhere beyond lapels, vents, and waistcoats. They genuinely wanted to see him happy.

Grey wished for the same, for both his parents and himself, which is why he thought up the lie that allowed him to create his gowns in secret while needlessly appeasing his parents. If only he had replaced his suppositions with an honest conversation from the get-go. And in the end, he would do that on the way home from that night's gathering.

Despite the hullabaloo his thoughts and worries spun into a convincing knock-off of reality, at the very least Grey did get a story out of it, albeit with an ending of the anticlimactic variety.

Chapter 30

In Which Pauline Brailin Perpetuates the Reputation of the Angel of Nollag

Ophelia stepped out of the cold into the cozy atmosphere of Brailin's Brewery and Pub. The pub was alive with the roar of reminiscent conversation punctuated by boisterous laughter. With the exception of a few who were on patrol, Brailin's harbored the entire Nollag Police Force and their families.

Lochlan Brailin, owner of the brewery, sang a little off key at the piano in the back. All one could see was a tangled mess of faded blond hair bouncing to the tune of the piano as he pounded on the keys. Pauline Brailin sat in a rocking chair surrounded by a captive audience of children. She had stopped to take a sip of her scotch, festively adorned with a cinnamon stick in the glass, when she caught sight of the latest visitor. Immediately, she beckoned to Ophelia to join her.

"This, children, though she will probably never admit it, is the Angel of Nollag herself." The children looked back at her gape-mouthed, and all Ophelia could do was blush and shake her head "no" in reply.

"Ya see! Told ya," Pauline teased, a sweet smile on her lips. She winked at Ophelia in a not-so-conspicuous way. She didn't actually believe that Ophelia was the Angel of Nollag. The very idea was impossible in her mind since she had known Ophelia as a child, having been over to the orphanage to visit with her friend, Mary Claire. Besides, she found it immensely fun to get a rise out of the children. On the other hand, there was a small part of Pauline, about two percent, that couldn't ignore the fact that Ophelia reminded her of someone from her past, Rae Cuddy, if only because her drink of choice was an Earl Grey Vodka Cocktail, the same as Rae's.

"But didn't she stab one of Santa's helpers one time?" Dalbert Teller inquired a little too audibly. Being only five years old, he was still working on his socially acceptable voice volume, along with how to filter his thoughts when in public.

Nine-year-old Amanda Winthrop spoke next. "My dad says the Angel of Nollag comes around every generation and gives a miracle to the person that needs the most help and disappears when they're done. Miracles," she defined, "are good deeds that make your life *better*." By "better," Amanda emphatically meant not worse.

"Yeah! An-angels are only supposed to do good things," little Amoura Oakleigh corroborated. She closed her statement with a firm nod of her head and returned to sucking her thumb.

"I don't know," Pauline sang back to the children, her words acting like a seed of doubt now planted between the hemispheres of their brains.

The Angel of Nollag had almost begun to rival Santa Clause thanks to Pauline. The angel had gotten so much notoriety because of the sheer amount of passion and certainty Pauline put behind telling the tale. The fact that it happened to her didn't hurt either.

*   *   *

Forty-seven years, six months, one week, and three days ago, life was going as Pauline had anticipated, with a margin of error of point nine percent. She had her health, her artistic abilities, and a good head squarely set on her shoulders. But Pauline knew that while life had been kind, love and romance were still not guaranteed. Her younger self accepted this and closed her heart toward that hypothetical outcome relegated to children's storybooks.

Every Friday, Pauline would make her way down to Brailin's for a scotch (although some poetic licensing modified it to cream soda when the audience was under the drinking age). Lochlan gave her a free one each week as a thank you to Pauline for doing the artwork for the pub's ads, an idea put forward by Lochlan's fiancée and co-owner of the bar, Rae. Pauline would recall Rae as having a fiery personality and as someone who seemed to be two steps ahead of everyone else. She was both loved and misunderstood, sometimes even hated. (Sound like anyone you've ever met? If not, please kindly proceed back to page one.)

One evening, Pauline noticed something off about her friend. Lochlan had lost the spring in his step, his smile was lopsided, and his hair drooped like a wilting begonia that hadn't been watered for three and a half days. She prodded her friend in order to find out what could be troubling him. At closing time, he relinquished that Rae had left...and not to restock the bar. She had left without warning, practically vanished. Along with the engagement ring, Rae did leave a note, only saying that she was sorry and she was needed elsewhere. No forwarding address was provided, and no date to indicate when, or if, she might return. With her departure, Pauline saw that Rae left behind a confusion and sadness that stole away Lochlan's happiness and light.

The very next day, blindly hoping she was still in Nollag, Pauline stomped over to Rae's place to see if she might find a lead. Upon her arrival, the property manager handed over an envelope and a key to her apartment, explaining that he had found them pushed under his door two mornings ago. The envelope was addressed to Pauline, its note asking her to please donate the possessions inside the apartment.

She proceeded to the second floor to apartment 204. Once inside, Pauline noted that everything had been left behind as she went through the cupboards, drawers, and closets, save for a few empty hangers. She checked the note again, really studied it this time. Maybe she overlooked something, perhaps a postscript. But nothing was missed as she scrutinized the neatly written note.

Pauline wondered where Rae could have gotten off to, the mystery replacing her anger. She found a small fuchsia address book in the back of the top left desk drawer. Hoping for a lead, she flipped through its pages, only to find three contacts inside: a gentleman by the name of Linus Lewin, Lochlan Brailin, and a woman named Mary Claire.

She phoned Linus first. The voice that greeted her on the other end of the receiver sounded old and hoarse. Pauline introduced herself several times, having to raise her voice a little each time she repeated herself. Linus, apparently, was hard of hearing. Pauline explained she was a friend of Rae's, but before she could get to Rae's disappearing act, Linus beat her to the punch.

"So, she left, huh?" (Pauline recalled he chuckled when he said this.) "Well, don't worry, young lady. I've known Rae for a veerrrrrry long time. She'll be fine."

This reassurance did anything but allay Pauline's unease. Before Pauline could press for more details, Linus had hung up the phone.

She tried Mary Claire next.

"Hello?" a woman said, her voice sounding tired.

"Hello. Is this…" Pauline paused to make sure she read the smudged name in the address book correctly, "Mary Claire?"

"Yes, this is."

"Hi, Mary. My name is Pauline Neese. I'm a friend of Rae's. Um, this may sound strange, but Rae seems to have vanished. Possibly skipped town? Uh, I found your name in her address book, and—well, do you know where she might have gone?"

Pauline could hear Mary Claire take in a breath as she tried to place the name. "Who?" was her reply.

"Rae. Rae Cuddy. She's part owner of Brailin's Brewery and Pub."

"I'm sorry, Pauline, that name doesn't sound familiar. You said my name was in her address book?"

"Uh, ye-yeah. I'm looking at it right now." She placed an index finger on the name as if to hold it down, fearing it might get up and walk away when she wasn't looking.

"How strange," Mary Claire exhaled. "Do I?" she pondered to herself. "No. Nothing is coming to me."

"She wasn't, by chance, planning on making a donation to you?" Pauline asked, pinning the phone to her ear with her right shoulder and flattening out the note on the desk. If not Mary Claire, then Pauline would have to phone Linus again.

"No, but it's funny you mention that. I just bought a home. I'm opening up an orphanage, you see. Like Old Mother Hubbard's cupboard, it is quite bare at the moment."

"Oh," Pauline said, the hand that had smoothed out the note now took the phone. She twisted in her seat to survey the little living room and kitchen. "Could you, perhaps, do anything with a loveseat, a kitchen table with four mismatched chairs, a writing desk, and a sewing machine? Rae left a note asking me to donate everything." (This is the same sewing machine, by the way, that now sits in Ophelia's closet at the Vermont Village. Mary Claire would bequeath it to Ophelia on her eleventh birthday.)

"Uh—well, I mean—huh," Mary Claire sputtered. "That— that's very generous. Are you absolutely sure she wanted you to donate everything?"

"To be honest, Mary, your guess is as good as mine, but it seems that Rae isn't planning on coming back anytime soon. So, if you would like to come take a look at everything, maybe this afternoon? I'll even throw in the two unopened boxes of Peppermint Cookie Crumblies I found in the cabinet."

Mary Claire happily agreed, and with that, the door to a new friendship was nudged ajar.

After hanging up the phone, Pauline left the apartment and locked it, making her way back to the brewery and pub to console her heartbroken friend. Being the person she was, and still is to this day, Pauline helped her friend for years on end to find his happiness within himself and not in faded memories. With that time came new memories. Lochlan and Pauline would fall in love and respect with each other. They realized they were cut from the same cloth. Both needed someone to complement them and not complete them. Both saw in one another not a savior but something more, something inexplicable and beautiful, something that glittered brighter than gold.

*   *   *

"Many saw what Rae did as awful, to break someone's heart, children. But lest we forget, hearts are resilient and some need to be broken, to be opened up to all kinds of new possibilities and friendships. Understand sometimes the painful actions people do can maybe lead us down much happier paths." Pauline concluded, smiling sweetly at Ophelia. The children were silent, trying Pauline's theory on for size.

"Is that why you popped Santa?" Amanda blurted out to Ophelia.

"Can I go now?" Ophelia asked Pauline.

"Eat, drink, and be merry. First one's on the house, my dear," Pauline added with another wink and raised her glass of her sco— erm—cream soda on the rocks.

Chapter 31

In Which We Request You Please Forgive the Rough Draft...

Calum had left the group, charging upstairs. Inspiration had finally struck, and he could not risk the chance that the words would remain intact until morning. Really good words sometimes risked a very short shelf-life.

Within the small den, he pulled the little cord on the desk lamp. It bathed the room and the countless first editions contained on the shelves in a vibrant green light. Almost completely submitting to the words inside his head, he allowed them to take new life on paper. (Please forgive his rough draft.)

Every year, we all yearn for the perfect holiday. Everyone is happy to be with family, the one you're born into or the one you fashion yourself, some of whom, redacting specific names, we can barely stand when the magic of a winter's snow and the glow of flickering multi-colored lights have faded away.

We all have that one perfect, memorable holiday. The one where you got exactly what you wanted, that hard to come by toy. The one when you ate an excessive amount of stuffing, perfectly crisped on all the edges. That one time Mom let you taste test the cookies that would go out for Santa. That moment you caught yourself looking at the tree in wonderment during a silent night, only rivaled by the glittering, unblemished blanket of snow outside.

We love this one moment above all else because it happened as we wished, and we barely did a thing to make it come to fruition. It inspires a warm feeling because it's almost like a gift from the universe.

We love it so much that every year we try to recreate the spontaneity of that day, to invoke again that joyful surprise. Therein lies the rub. How does one successfully relive a day of surprise by making sure each detail from a year or more ago is meticulously set back into its original place? Why not welcome change? Why say, "Thanks, but I'm pretty sure this is as good as it gets?"

We prefer to trick ourselves into believing one moment in time is enough to satisfy and sustain our happiness. We fearfully cling to it. But even the best of memories fade and fray and alter. What once was can never be recreated. Not exactly.

Let's move to the other side of the spectrum, away from the impeccably wrapped presents and unhealthy amount of tinsel. Have you ever considered the good that can come from the not-so-illustrious holidays?

380

Dear readers, here is a thought...Now pay close attention to these words. Read them twice, if not more, if you must: The perfect holiday may not be where the most cherished memories reside.

Unpleasant events have their role in the grand scheme of things, don't they? They create opportunities for us to lose control of our pristinely set scene, walk off stage right, and reassess our motivation.

Usually, in instances of holiday mishap, we look for someone to blame. We can all think of our own personal grinch who allegedly purloined or razed our chance to recapture a time from Christmas past.

Being that I am writing this in the season of magic and miracles, I'll do my best to adhere to that theme. Mayhap that grinch in your life is not so much an anarchist, but an angel. Perchance they're the Angel of Nollag?

(Note: Pauline Brailin would receive a credit for the Angel of Nollag rumor in the updated version of the article. Sorry to interrupt.)

Think back. Have you had this special brand of angel? Maybe they made you question your identity. Maybe they made you pull yourself out of a dark situation on your own because they made it that much more intolerable to simply "go through the motions." Maybe they made you think for yourself (heaven forbid). Maybe they broke your trust and told your secrets. Maybe they constantly gave you unsolicited advice that you didn't want to hear but needed. I bet you hated them for it, or, at the very least, really disliked them. What if, though, you never let that person into your life? Where would you be without their chaos?

Presently, I spent an evening with three of the greatest people I count myself amazingly lucky to have in my life. It turns out we all have a certain "angel" in common. From where I sat, as everyone took turns trading war stories, I saw unimagined success and self-assurance in that room. But none of us started there.

These recounted tales made it very clear we all came from some dark or troubled places where we were at risk of losing ourselves. Our angel in common tipped the scales in our favor, albeit by throwing us in the deep end, shocking our systems, waking us up to remind us we could make a change and save ourselves. There was no guiding light on this journey. No one told us we had a wonderful life after all. Sometimes, the opposite.

So, the point—I should probably get to one—is that our particular angel did a very brave thing to set us on these better tracks, to pull some of us back or push the others forward to places where passion and meaning exist even if we went kicking and screaming along that particular path. This is a thank you of sorts to that guardian angel here in Nollag. Thank you for saving me. Thank you for making me find myself.

As we fall forward into the New Year, consider thanking your own angel, especially the ones that didn't make it easy on you. I'm not saying you have to forgive them, but consider, for a moment, that what they did for you, or to you, might have been done for a reason. Then ask yourself: Are you better off than you were?

Best wishes to you all, guardian angels included, in this New Year.

Calum paused for a moment, letting his fingertips touch the scrawled words noting the yellowed edges of the paper. He scribbled a few notes in the margins and then thumbed through the preceding pages of the little 4x6 brown book. He had carried this book with him since he had received it as a Christmas gift when he was four. He had affectionately titled it 'Calum's Idea Book' in green marker across its front cover. Only his best and most important thoughts would grace its pages.

In a way, his life flashed before his eyes going backwards. It started with what would become his first published piece. He found youthful musings of unrequited love from his high school days about a shy girl named Delaney who would never in her right mind agree to spend time with an awkward, oily-skinned, tubby geek. The histories of alleged Angel of Nollag miracles and theories of the angel's identity were dogeared throughout the book. (Calum had been chronicling them since he had first learned to spell at age six; the first few entries were recorded as the Angle of Nollag.) Until, finally, the first page of the journal slipped past his left thumb. The illustration on the front of the page was of a little boy painting a picture. Every color had been used in its creation, and, to a now grown-up Calum, it could be viewed as overly detailed. But four-year-old Calum wanted this book to be special, and to be special, its contents must be perfect, so even the finest detail could not be spared. A true artist would not have it any other way. That was what young Calum decided he would be in this life. Grown Calum was finally in a place to make good on this wish made so long ago.

He smiled to himself. He had a good feeling about the article he would submit to his boss at the *Nollag Blow-by-Blow Bugle*.

Without wasting any more time, and, admittedly, his deadline beginning to overshadow the fact there were guests downstairs, he uncovered the typewriter, threaded a crisp sheet of paper through the roller, and set to typing.

Chapter 32

In Which We Examine the Idea of Identities and True Selves

The ticking and pinging from upstairs told Delaney that Calum would not be making an appearance anytime soon. If she were being honest, she was a tad jealous Calum was able to maneuver so suddenly around his writer's block. Delaney was wedged between hers and her own self-doubt, not one of the most comfortable places to be.

Mr. Terne leaned into the group, looking at each of them with slight bewilderment. "Um," he sputtered, "so you will not be opening the gifts from this Ms. Ophelia, then?"

The group, consisting of Petunia Perkins, Gregory McGregor, and Delaney O'Leary, along with Grey Terne and his parents, had spent the time since Calum had sped upstairs eyeing the pristinely wrapped gifts.

"I guess we could?" Gregory said, wincing at the possibility he had landed on the wrong choice.

"Of course, dear," Mrs. Terne chimed in between chews of her cinnamon and salt caramel chew. "'Tis the season. Go on! I'm dying to know what's inside, myself. Mm. Delaney, you must share this recipe."

"Thank you, Mrs. Terne. I'll have it for you before you leave."

"You—you know, Mom, um, Delaney will be releasing a cookbook in a few months," Grey offered. He hoped to steer her away from revisiting the topic of his shop as he was not entirely sure he could allow himself to believe her pleasure to be genuine.

Mrs. Terne perked up and made a guttural noise as she sucked in the air in her general vicinity. "Really? Absolutely wonderful. Will it contain goodies such as these?" she asked, pointing to the picked over spread.

Delaney, remaining silent, nodded and withdrew further into her turtleneck. Over exuberance had that effect on her.

"Grey," she said, turning to her son, "I hope you offer complementary alterations; I may plan on plumping up a bit." She gave him a playful wink, puckering and puffing out her cheeks. Mrs. Terne's smile broadened. "Delicious! I'll have to tell all my friends. Darling," she said to Mr. Terne, "you're going to be very busy letting everyone's pants out…yours included," she chortled, picking up an orange infused sugar cookie. "Absolutely delectable. Mm-mm!"

Grey laughed uncomfortably. His cheeks became rosy.

"Gifts! Gifts!" Mrs. Terne clapped her hands in anticipation for what lay inside each package. She picked up a small box in metallic green tied with a red bow. The tag simply read *To My Sister*. "Who's the sister?" she asked.

"That would be me," Delaney said.

"Ah," Mrs. Terne replied with a smile. She stood up and brought the gift over. The box fit in the palm of Delaney's hand and gave away no rattling hint as to what was inside.

What was inside was a charm shaped like that of a doll. It had been carefully wrapped in crisp white tissue paper, its polished gold a striking contrast against the matte finishes of the rest. Though approximately one half the length of her thumb, Delaney could pick out the fine details of the doll. Its hair had been made to look like yarn, and its dress was painted a metallic red. The charm was like Corlis, the doll a seven-year-old Ophelia had offered to her back at Mother Mary Claire Brog's Home for Tiddlers, Toddlers, Tykes, and Children. Whether intended or not, it served as a reminder of a host of other memories Delaney kept of her sister...of the more sentimental variety: The tape recorder. Their sleepovers when the summer thunderstorms would roll in. The time Ophelia ate Delaney's first cake in its entirety to prove its irrefutable delectability when Delaney had convinced herself even before the oven timer went off that it would be, at best, mediocre. The time Ophelia had done up her spare room at apartment 7H, complete with a welcome home banner, when Delaney first moved in. "I've got you, sis," she had said, giving her a tour of her new room.

And just like that, Delaney found the scales evening out on her feelings toward her sister, possibly even tipping in her favor, even if only by one gram. To purchase some time to take these resurrected memories into consideration, and to work through the shame of not remembering them sooner, Delaney paid with a "Your turn" to Petunia.

Mrs. Terne found the gift and handed it over to Gregory, who, in turn, passed it to Petunia.

Beneath glittery blue paper and a white and silver stripped bow, and buried underneath gobs of tissue paper, was a mirror. Petunia lifted it by its handle to examine the detail on the frame, a smooth rounded frame etched with silver ivy, which curled in and out of sight. It took the young woman a moment, but Petunia also noticed lettering intertwined amongst the ivy. "Strength is more than skin deep," she read to herself. As she looked back at her reflection, coupled with how drastically different her life was now compared to four years ago, the true meaning of those words sunk into her mind and took a firmer root. No longer a damsel in distress, Petunia saw the true hero was within herself.

"It's absolutely lovely," Mrs. Terne remarked.

"There's got to be something else in there," Gregory said, looking back into the box. "It felt way too heavy to be holding only a mirror."

Petunia dug further within the folds of tissue paper to uncover a small hardbound book of fairy tales. It looked familiar. She cracked the book open to a page that had been marked by a pink ribbon. The page contained the ending of Sleeping Beauty. Within its margin, in pencil, was scrawled the question, "Why do princesses always have to be saved by someone else?" Petunia smiled to herself, gently laying the book and mirror back in their box. She caressed the words on the mirror's frame with her fingertips before carefully swaddling them in the tissue paper again.

Sensing Petunia needed a moment to herself, Mrs. Terne returned to the last two presents. "Who's next? You?" she said, looking at Gregory. She leaned forward to read the tags on the last two gifts. "Um…so sorry. I seem to have forgotten your name. Are you Calum or Greg?" she asked with a strained smile that did little if anything to mask her embarrassment.

"That's Greg," replied Grey.

"Thank you, dear," she said to her son, finding a box with icy silver paper, and placing it into Gregory's hands.

Gregory told himself that whatever the contents were, it felt nearly weightless as it shifted and knocked against the sides of the box. The scene seemed to unfurl in slowed time, yet all at once.

As the lid came off the box, he found a red file folder inside. The edges of the folder were boxed, showing its age. Parts of the pages were yellowed with time while the others were bleached from being left in direct sunlight for too long.

The air of mystery had thickened in the room.

"What…?" Gregory wondered to himself, pulling at the twine that held the threadbare file together. The name *William* "*Billy*" *Croi*, which meant nothing to him, was handwritten on the folder tab. The pages were brittle, rough to the touch. Gregory carefully scanned the information, noting the file was a little over twenty-six years old. He continued to thumb through the documents until he was no longer doing so and, instead, was out the door in a flash.

"What do you suppose that was all about?" Mrs. Terne asked. "Does he not appreciate white elephant gifts?"

Delaney and Petunia stared intently at one another, a serious and silent conversation bounding back and forth between them. "I don't think that was a gag gift," Petunia said. "The file had a stamp from the orphanage, not to mention the word CONFIDENTIAL across the front."

Delaney laid back against her armchair, affixing the new charm to her bracelet and feeling rather warm. The fire aside, this warmth bubbled from within. Her memories, and then an idea, began to play a rousing game of hide and seek. Their giggling bounded and reverberated off the walls of her mind, which made Delaney smile. She was convinced a type of Christmas miracle had transpired.

"Care to catch us up?" Grey asked, reading Delaney's face.

Chapter 33

In Which Clarence Declares He and Ophelia Will be Soulmates Always

The party at Brailin's Brewery and Pub was losing steam but was about to regain its second wind. The door swung open with a clattering of jingle bells and a gasp of frozen night air as Copper Lawson and Mynah Morial stepped in. Mynah was decked out in a festive yellow gown, and Copper was beaming from ear to ear.

"I told her yellow was her color," Ophelia muttered under her breath as she found a seat at the bar.

"She is a vision," a jovial and booming voiced added. A very large figure stood across from Ophelia, hand on his hip, showcasing a fetching kilt and rocking back and forth with little bells on his socks keeping time. "How're you doing, Ms. Ophelia?"

Ophelia considered the question and shrugged. "I'm doing okay." She nodded as if to agree with her assessment.

"Thank you so much for gettin' me this job." He beamed with joy.

A small, surprised smile pressed across the woman's face. Downcast eyes almost made her appear bashful. "You're very welcome, Mr. Hinklehimeriner. I guess I felt a tad responsible for you losing your last job."

"Ah," he batted the apology away like a gnat. "It didn't really pay that well, anyway," he lied. Being an accessory to a crime, even an oblivious one, tended to pay fairly well. While Adele thought she had been buying Woody's silence, he had assumed the extra padding in his paycheck was compensation for her lackluster attitude.

"Still…I hope you are treated better here. Besides, I think this is a better fit for you. Imagine all the stories you'll hear."

Woody nodded in agreement at the thought. "Can I get you something to drink, miss?"

"I would absolutely love an Earl Grey Vodka Cocktail." Reading Woody's blank expression, she added, "I think Lochlan keeps it written down under the Earl Gray infused vodka over there." She indicated a small dusty bottle at the end of the shelf that contained the house made liquor, a card sticking out from under it.

After briefly scanning the card, Woody whipped up the drink with surprisingly dexterous hands. "The charge will be one story," he said, amending Pauline's original 'on the house' offer. He placed the drink down in front of Ophelia. "How about the one behind the golden gown over there?" He nodded in the direction of Mynah.

"Can I have everyone's attention?" the little man named Copper bellowed from the center of the pub.

"Well, Mr. Hinklehimeriner, I believe you are about to find out, but I will offer you the prequel at a later time," Ophelia said, taking a sip of her drink and smiling over the fresh orange slice that garnished the top of the glass. "Very good, by the way."

"Copper, are you okay?" Mynah whispered to him as he had begun to shake noticeably.

But he let her concern go unattended. His heart was too focused on the task at hand as it implored his brain to work his vocal cords to recite the speech that he, still at that very moment, was editing to near perfection. "Uh, Mynah, you've always been a wonderful friend and more to me. You've been there for everything, every case. You gave me your shoulder, your ear, your—your hand. Oh…." Copper took her hand in his. He grinned a nervous smile, and, beyond the slight lines of his face, Mynah wondered if she could see what Copper used to look like as a young boy. Her heart tingled, which made her eyes glitter.

"Mynah, I want to—I want to tell you that you deserve," he paused and swallowed, "everything, even though you'd never ask for something so grand. Know that I still want to try. Uh," he swallowed again, "I'm, um, rambling. I'm sorry."

Mynah pressed his hand. "It's okay," was all she said in reply, both to the apology and Copper's jittery nerves.

"I want you to know, Mynah, how special you are to me, a—and I should have done this sooner—wanted to do this sooner, but silly fears got in the way." Copper looked crestfallen for a moment as he ruminated on the past, and then, without allowing his gaze to waver from Mynah's, Copper got down on bended knee.

Copper held a delicate ring of rose gold and opal; its many iridescent colors swirled and mingled atop the stone.

He did not speak at first, momentarily becoming preoccupied with the pounding in his chest. His heart clumsily tried to spell out "I love you" in Morse Code.

"Mynah, since the day we met, I've been infatuated with you. I'm still in awe of you. Suffice it to say, there hasn't been a moment where I haven't been in love with you."

Mynah smiled her trademark sweet smile that made Copper's heart stop beating one second and thump harder the next to catch up for lost time. She knelt down to meet him face to face. (Ophelia held her breath, praying the floor of Brailin's Brewery and Pub had received a thorough scrubbing and mopping prior to the party.) With a deep breath, she fell forward, wrapping her arms around the man's small frame, her fingers grasping at the back of his coat as if she never wished to part from him again.

Mynah Morial whispered, "Yes."

The pub burst out into roaring applause and cheers. Lochlan began to pound the piano keys in a congratulatory song. The neighbors upstairs would have called the police about the noise, but…well…all things considered….

"Hey! Copper!" Ophelia shouted from the bar, "way to put Mynah on the spot there!" She smiled her mischievous smile, punctuating it with a crooked eyebrow.

"We practiced in the car on the way over," he joked, playfully sticking his tongue out at her.

Ophelia simply laughed, a wide smile stretched across her face. Raising her glass to the couple, she yelled, "That's fair. To

Copper and Mynah, you two deserve each other, and I mean that in the most loving and genuine of ways. You two are like my first parents. Because of you, I know what real love is. Thank you."

The rest of the Nollag Police Force joined in agreement, although they were taken a tad aback. Heartfelt words were normally not heard from Ophelia without a sarcastic slant to them.

*   *   *

By half past midnight, give or take a minute to a minute and three seconds, very few remained in the pub. Most sat at tables, a low hum of chatter filling the room as people discussed holiday plans and swapped war stories from last year's respective family festivities and how one was almost forced into committing unethical acts to acquire the latest and supposedly greatest toy to put under the tree.

Ophelia smiled sweetly over at Woody, silently declining an offer for another Earl Gray Vodka Cocktail. She pulled out a fifty-dollar bill and placed it on the bar, knowing full well her bill was exactly nineteen dollars and sixty-nine cents.

"We did it," Ophelia heard a quiet voice gently state. Clarence set his empty glass, which contained the last few drops of a whiskey Old Fashioned sweet and the stems of four cherries, on the bar and took a seat next to Ophelia. He placed his head on her shoulder, allowing his own shoulders to slump from exhaustion. Ophelia smiled to keep from frowning and looked at her hands.

Clarence's mission was over. *Now what?*

"Yeah," she said with an exhaled laugh. "Everyone who was supposed to have a happy ending got one."

"And then some," Clarence reminded her, showing Ophelia four fingers.

The smile she returned to him this time was noticeably bittersweet. She thought of Delaney, Petunia, Calum, and Gregory as she recited one of Mynah's reminders from their childhood at Mother Mary Clair's: "Reminder number five: Fun is not necessarily found in rules. Sometimes the fun is found in breaking the rules…I added that last part." Her smile was now more sly and less forlorn. "So…what's next?"

Clarence had turned his head to look past the bar. Thoughts had percolated to the top of his brain, but they were not done cooking, and no rumination stews for the same amount of time as another.

Ophelia shrugged Clarence off her shoulder. "Come on now, Clare. Don't hold out. Is it time for you to start over again? Can you stay until New Years? I'm—" her voice caught. "I'm not ready."

Clarence said nothing at first, appearing to suppress a smile.

"*Come on*, Clare, you know how I hate not knowing."

For anyone around them, it sounded like an overly melodramatic conversation about how life was arduous and unfair. Older generations would reminisce how they had the exact same conversations with their peers when they were in their twenties. The good bits of life were fleeting and scattered amongst eight-hour plus workdays and too-short weekends. "They'll learn," they would laugh to themselves. In actuality, Ophelia was not kidding about starting all over again. It was her and Clarence's cosmic destiny. Well, just his now, it seemed.

During that evening, Ophelia had taken the opportunity to scan the pub in hopes of finding a new soul to redirect onto a path toward happiness but had come up empty. Either no one was in need of help, or her ability to review their destinies and fates was still on the fritz in the indefinite sort of way. Her money was on the latter. There was no need to shed her identity of Ophelia O'Leary to become someone new, not that that was an option either.

There was an understanding that handling more than two fates at once came with risks. As much as she wanted to lament her decision to break the rule by taking on four charges, those sour feelings were dwarfed by a sense of sweet peace that their fates were sealed with joy. Delaney, Calum, Gregory, and Petunia may never understand the why behind Ophelia's calamitous actions or the sacrifice she made, but that didn't matter. They didn't need to know. They just needed to live their lives.

"Oh, I do indeed," Clarence laughed. "I know of your disdain for the not knowing, Ophie, but I got nothing." He knew the smile stretched across his face was misleading Ophelia into thinking this was a devious trick. He was, however, tickled for other reasons.

Ophelia looked away, back at her hands that were now clenching her drink; her brow furrowed as her mind tried to find its footing again and allowed itself to believe what was beginning to unfurl. "Wha…?"

"I…" Clarence trailed as he quickly sorted his thoughts in order, "I'm off the clock. Clarence Smith isn't going anywhere, Ophelia O'Leary."

"For how long?" Ophelia quickly followed up.

Clarence shrugged. There were other ways to forfeit one's powers. The game that was meddling in the fates of others required a delicate balance. Just as helping too many people at one time had caused Ophelia's abilities to go on the blink, deciding to help no one at all held the same consequence. To remain with his friend as a mortal, like her, Clarence opted not to find someone in need of a life tune-up. Within the week, his glimpses into the future would, likewise, fade to little more than static, and the capability to assume another identity would become a thing of fiction. Simply put, there was a use it or lose it clause. In either case, the friends had no guarantee that their respective choices could be undone.

Ophelia looked back at her friend. She drew a breath to say something but found that she had no words readily available.

Clarence did the same, a goofy looking smile on his face. He made the decision right then and there that he liked surprises, and, at least in this instance, he could tell his friend liked them, too.

"But...but," she finally sputtered, "but it still begs the question: What do we do now?" Ophelia halted her panic right then; a thought soothed her anxieties. Clarence had done the same thing that Ophelia had done for her sister and her three friends: He ensured that she would not be alone in this life. His decision made her heart swell with gratitude.

"I think we enjoy the lives that we've built." Clarence smiled back, for he truly adored this identity much more than the ones he had in previous generations.

The pair each stared off at nothing in particular, maybe taking in their reflections or admiring the collection of bottles that lined the counter and shelves. Neither said a word, simply existing and taking in their new reality.

Clarence moved his left hand to rest on his best friend's and gave it a sentimental pat. He rested his head on his right hand to lazily look back at Ophelia. In that moment, Ophelia saw that mischievous boy from Mother Mary Claire Brog's Haven for Tiddlers, Toddlers, Tykes, and Children, and it made the wild haired sassy young girl inside of her bare a toothy grin.

"I think after all the years I have known and worked with you," Clarence began, "I know you fairly well." He lifted the hand he had laid on hers and waggled a finger from side to side jokingly. "I can't tell you what will happen now as we enter the unknown." He stopped, blinking, a perplexed expression contorting his face, "Uh, for obvious reasons."

Ophelia exhaled a slight chuckle but tried her best to recompose herself for what appeared to be a very serious moment.

"You, my friend, like to have a constant to hold onto. Because that constant will ground all the other variables, like, 'Do I turn left or right? Or 'Do I have a lemon poppy seed bagel or bacon and eggs for breakfast?' Watching what happened tonight, what we helped do tonight," Clarence said covertly, "it got me thinking. Copper said he regretted waiting so long to tell Mynah exactly how he felt. I want you to know, Ophie, you have always been my best friend. I see you, and you remind me that the world is fixable, that sometimes happy endings have to come from broken dreams. I love you, Ophelia, for the fact that you are you.

"What I'm trying to get at is, well, I can be your constant. No matter what life potentially brings – be it heartache or euphoric happiness, just as we are sitting on these barstools now, I want to be sitting with you on a park bench, wrinkly and blue haired, swapping inappropriate jokes about adult diapers and laughing until we pee a little…testing the absorbency of said diapers…."

Ophelia squinted as if to try and glimpse this future and laughed.

"You're my soulmate, Ophelia. Not in the strict fairy tale sense…no, something better, stronger. No matter where we are, no matter what lives we end up leading, we've always been there for each other, and we always will be," Clarence said resolutely.

Ophelia blinked away the wisps of tears that had collected on her eyelashes. She coyly looked over her shoulder, a roguish look in her eye. "Thank you, Clarence," she said in a tone not unlike the times when she was eight and her mother would prompt her with a 'Now what do we say, Ophelia?' after having received a lackluster, although practical, gift of a savings bond for her birthday.

"You always seem to know exactly what to say," he replied sarcastically to lighten the moment.

"It's my gift. You know that, and I mean every word of it."

He leaned over to put his arm around Ophelia, giving her a hug. Right then, Ophelia felt true love. True love in the sense that there was no agenda behind it. There was no sacrifice in this decision, no question to give pause, not really. The world went away into that quiet good night as the two best friends sat at the bar.

"Are you all set, Ms. Ophelia?" Woody asked.

Ophelia simply nodded in reply as Woody came by to collect his tip and her empty glass. "You can keep the change. No buts," she said, pointing her right index finger at him.

Woody stared at the fifty-dollar bill, fingers hovering over it as if unsure it might singe his fingers. "Oh, na—I mean—this is very generous," he faltered before finally getting a "thank you" out. "Anything else for you, Mr. Clarence? Can I refresh your drink?"

"No thank you, Woody." Clarence slipped his empty glass over to him.

Before Woody turned away, he could not help himself but to appraise them. "You two look like a pair of old souls," he said. "I bet you have some good stories to tell." With a twinkle in his eye, he stepped away, jingling with each step. He made a mental note to learn their stories, which he was sure were seventy-five percent shenanigans, twenty-four point three percent side aching laughter, and perhaps zero point seven percent tear-jerker.

"So, are you liking the suitcoat?"

"Of course. The pocket square was a nice touch, too," Clarence said. The handkerchief was the same soft cerulean blanket material as the jacket lining. "Like wearing a hug. I must say, you're looking classy tonight. Red is your color."

"You have no idea how challenging this was to make. The bodice nearly was my undoing."

Clarence wore a comically unimpressed expression. "I'm sure."

The two friends continued their conversation late into the frigid night, taking a brisk walk back to Ophelia's apartment after the brewery and pub had closed, speaking on topics that ranged from the absolutely absurdly random to the introspectively deep. Past troubles melted away and future worries no longer seemed insurmountable. But really, isn't that what soulmates are for?

Chapter 34

In Which Delaney Is Given Something to Chew on Aside from the Butter Cookies... Which Are Practically Gone Anyway

Delaney was puzzled. The gears and cogs within the deeper recesses of her mind were running hot and were in severe need of maintenance. Unfortunately, the current thoughts they were helping to process did not indicate a definite end time, barring an emergency shutdown.

Reading the rough draft of Calum's article was not helping. The exquisitely written piece made valid points. And that was just it. Valid points only spurred thoughts, which were now compounding on top of Delaney's other reflections from earlier that night, the lot of them pressing on the forefront of her mind, like ravenous Black Friday shoppers trying to force open a shop's doors before midnight. Her mind was a cacophony of confusion.

The wadded-up ball of thoughts began to swell inside Delaney's head. Things were beginning to smoke, and the emergency shutoff was looking all the more appealing.

The sound of soft footsteps could be heard approaching across the floor until they were not. Calum took a seat on the other end of the couch to face the woman he loved unconditionally. Reading her face, Calum could sense the unease Delaney felt and was about to offer an ear, but he barely got a vowel out.

"A—"

"Do you really think she knew what she was doing?" Delaney asked. "Do you believe that somehow Ophelia had some divine plan?"

"What do you mean?" Calum cautiously asked. Discussions involving the other O'Leary sister rarely led to pleasant trips down memory lane unless, that is, one is fond of soggy paths lined by brambly bushes on either side. Given what was told earlier this evening, this made all the more sense.

"I guess…" Delaney trailed, trying to unstick a thought from her ball of messy musings. "Hm, I guess all of this time it—she did all this stuff that was not so great, you know? And she didn't even bat an eyelash. Things could have gone very badly, and yet none of it did—for anyone. Not really."

"How do you mean, Del?"

"Okay, take Petunia. Ophelia practically stepped in and ran her life. Ophelia stole Petunia's paper. She ran off those copies, and then swapped out an entire household's worth of gifts for them. That's insane. People don't do that, but *she did*."

"So, you're saying Ophelia isn't a person?" Calum could not help the sarcastic question.

Delaney ignored him. "Petunia was being kind when she was telling her story. If you had heard her tell it a few years ago…her

404

parents almost kicked her out. She actually hid out at our apartment for a couple weeks, not that she could stand Ophelia at that point, and not that she even wanted to trust me. But she had no other place to go.

"She wouldn't speak to either of us. She just sat on our couch and poured over books of fairy tales with this conflicted look on her face. Looking back on it, I wonder if she was actually in a bigger moment of crisis than she was letting on. I remember her gripping the books so tightly. They were the reason, well one of them at least, why she felt unwanted. Yet they are very much a part of who she was — is. A part that not many were allowed to know about.

"But if she continued to hide this passion of hers, how would that have worked out? How would any of what *she* wanted ever come true?" Delaney considered her question. She sucked at the butter cookie that somehow had made it from the plate on the coffee table to rest in between her teeth. She looked at the faded footprints in the area rug as if they would lead her to the exact answer. Instead, she found a clue within her own experiences. "Maybe it was easier to keep the passion alive as a dream instead of pursuing the reality of it."

"To an extent," Calum added, referencing his meandering life-journey. "It's scary to actually commit to something that isn't a sure thing."

Delaney nodded, and then added, "You know, even when Petunia was rooted to our couch, even though she probably hated Ophelia, or at least something in close proximity to hate, Ophelia still intervened. She would always check on Petunia with grilled cheese sandwiches and another book of fairy tales or folklore. But now I wonder if she did it for another reason other than guilt."

Calum only raised his eyebrows in reply.

Delaney bit down on the tip of her thumb as the butter cookie was long gone. "Hm. So do I forgive her? And I mean forgive, forgive, not that premature type of forgiveness where you say you've let go of the bad feelings, but really you're still chewing on them. Can I even decide to forgive her? Is it as easy as flipping a switch? I'd like to believe I can." She sat in her quandary, uttering an "I don't know," to buy herself some more time to think, unsure which choice she was afraid of more.

"Del," Calum said moving a bit closer. "Do you really need an answer? I mean, we could talk about Ophelia's actions and motives behind those actions from sunup tomorrow until sundown next year and still not have any resolution. I think you're right, though. To forgive doesn't always come from a black and white decision. Forgiveness…it comes more so from that emotional gray area, dappled in shattered prismatic light." With that, Calum gave Delaney a sympathetic smile and stood up to leave her to add his reflection on the matter to her tightly compacted clod of thoughts. She decided to apply some more pressure to it in hopes that it would result in a diamond of a truth. But before she did….

"Here," Delaney said handing Calum a small five by nine rectangular box before he could take a step from the couch.

"What's this?" Calum asked, giving the small candy-striped box a look over. "Aren't we opening gifts tomorrow?"

"It's from Ophelia," Delaney replied absentmindedly as she retreated further into her thoughts.

Calum waited until he was upstairs before opening the box. Beneath crinkled navy-blue tissue paper, he found a thick looking envelope. Within that contained a healthy stack of one-hundred-dollar bills, Ophelia's reward money for helping to catch Adele Swinde in the act of her dirty dealings plus the value of the ring. On top of the bills was a scrawled out note:

I did you a favor and sold that eyesore of a ring. Here're the profits, plus a little extra. If you're gonna marry my sister, you better get her a nice ring. One that she really wants.

See Baojin at THE DIAMOND MINE on Cut Street and Clarity Avenue.

-O

Speaking of always intervening, Calum thought laughing to himself.

Chapter 35

In Which Catrice Muffet Is Unmasked

Gregory sat in his car across the street from Muffet's Tuffets and Muffulettas. He hadn't slept a wink but didn't feel any of the effects.

A beat-up file folder laid in his lap. Gregory had read its contents five and a half times, exactly how many times he needed to commit it all to memory.

The contents of the file told a story about an infant boy given up for adoption by a Ms. Heather Croí. True, most of the contents were legal forms Ms. Croí needed to fill in to give her little boy, Billy, up. He could tell that she had not wanted to let go of Billy, as noted by the warped tear-stained spots on the page. One marked an empty space where the name of the boy's father should have been.

Gregory needed more details and was unable to sleep. While libraries and city records were closed that evening for the Christmas holiday, Gregory had a hunch that Mary Claire would surely have a lead. So, at 2 a.m. on Christmas morning, he phoned her. Upon learning his discovery of the missing adoption file, she obliged to give him answers but thought it best done face-to-face. She invited him over to the orphanage where she would start off by sharing Ms. Croí had been in love with a Mr. William Krad.

*   *   *

At 2:18 in the morning, Mary Claire turned on the desk lamp in her office. Taking her seat, she gestured toward a chair on the other side of the desk for Gregory. "They were very much in love," began Mary Claire as she unsuccessfully chased the sleep from her eyes.

"Heather and William?"

Mary Claire nodded. "Yes," she paused, her next few words catching in her throat. "You're…mother and father."

Gregory swallowed hard but didn't say anything. He had his suspicions the moment he laid eyes on the folder back at the house, but hearing the truth that this was *his* file, that *he* was Billy, a sense of relief washed over him. He had waited for so long and needed to hear more.

Getting nothing more than a blink and a shudder of his Adam's apple in reply, Mary Claire continued. "And with every love story, there must be some heartache, I suppose. You see, Gregory, your grandfather, Nathaniel Krad, was a heartless man. He was incapable of compassion, and since that energy had to go somewhere, he directed it toward the love and acquisition of money and property. Business was logical. Emotion was…a messy expense with a negligible dividend.

"William was supposed to take over the family business and all the strings that came with it. It wasn't solely about owning big buildings. It was about assembling an empire with the right players. And Heather wasn't the right, uh, pedigree." Her pinched smile soured to a bitter frown as she ruminated. "Sort of a cruel joke that William and Heather found each other. When William told your grandfather his intentions to marry Heather, well, you probably already can guess how that whole idea unfurled into a tangled heap."

"Where is my dad? Where's my mom?" Gregory implored, wishing to skip to the hopefully, but unlikely, happy ending.

Mary Claire's gaze fell away from Gregory's face. She had wished this moment in time could be skipped over, too, but for different reasons. "Um, when your father was denied his wishes to be with your mother...his...his heart broke quite literally. He was torn between earning, at the very least, the approval of his father, an all but impossible endeavor, and keeping the love of your mother. His heart gave out, son. They say, mind you I don't know who 'they' are, but they say his heart just stopped. He collapsed leaving his family home on his way to see your mother. We'll never know his intentions."

"Did...did he know about me? My dad?"

Mary Claire frowned and shrugged her shoulders, wishing she had the answer he needed. "I'm sorry, sweetheart. I—I don't know. She carefully appraised Gregory's expression, unsure whether she should press on with the story. Gregory recognized her apprehension, the same look many wore when they were in interrogation with him. He nodded gently to let Mary Claire know to continue.

"Uh, yes, well, I'm afraid the story doesn't get much better. Nathaniel banished any memory of William from his life. Some people, again, I'm not sure who exactly, but they believe that Nathaniel was devastated over the loss of his son, as would any parent, cold or not. It's rumored that weak hearts run in the Krad family, and Nathaniel feared embracing the grief over his departed son would take him, too. This banishment extended to poor Heather. He made a promise that if she did not leave Nollag, he would be sure to make life very difficult for her. He had decided she was the one who took his son from him. She would be refused work and shelter. Nollag would never be her home so long as he lived." Mary Claire frowned and shook her head in a slow disappointed tempo.

"What was she to do, Gregory?" But Mary Claire did not pause for him to answer. "Because of all that, Heather did her best to ensure your grandfather never knew of you. As far as I know, he never did. She feared you would only be a reminder of the son he had decided to embrace too late. Probably would have groomed you to be a copy of himself." She paused, looking a little embarrassed before composing her solemn expression again. "I'm sorry to speak ill of your grandfather, but he wasn't a very nice man."

Gregory didn't care about the gossip. He wanted answers. "What happened to my mom, Mary Claire? Why was I put into an orphanage? She could have taken me with her."

Mary Claire slowly nodded her head. This was a question that every child (with the exceptions of Ophelia and Clarence) at the orphanage would ask her at some point during their residence.

412

The instances where she knew the answers, especially the difficult answers, caused her the most pain. She chose time and time again to take on that pain herself, fearing the burden of the truth would be soul-crushing for any of her children.

When she looked back at Gregory, her memory flashed to the six-year-old boy who would storm into her office, almost daily, to report on yet another shenanigan Clarence had gotten up to. She wanted to hug him.

"Appreciate the fact that your mother's only constant was this city. Everything outside of Nollag was uncertain. With Mr. Krad's words, suddenly the unknown offered more security for her, but she wasn't sure she could give you a stable life out there.

"Before Heather had met William, she was pretty much alone in this world. After he died, well, she was without any sort of family or financial support again. Add in a baby that would depend on her for everything, and…." Mary Claire let her thought trail off, stopping to choose her next words with care. "She couldn't fathom putting you into a difficult situation."

"She would have been all I needed," Gregory said to himself resolutely and a little hurt.

"You say that now, sweetie, but understand she did not abandon you to fulfill some selfish needs. Nor could she look into a crystal ball to peek at the ending. Heather left you with me because she knew I could give you a happy home."

Gregory allowed the words to sink in. He opened his adoption file that he still held in his hands and placed it on the desk. A small wallet sized photo of a young woman, thick curls framing her round cheeks, smiled up at him.

413

"Heather left that picture on purpose," Mary Claire chimed in. Gregory pulled his stare away from the black and white photo, giving his undivided attention back to Mary Claire. "She wanted you to have that picture. Should she ever be able to return, you would have a way of finding her." She paused, her gaze shifted between Gregory's face and the photo of Heather. "You have her eyes," she said. All at once, the young man that sat across from her was no more, now replaced by the memory of a young woman. Her face was tear stained and obscured by those dark brown curls of hers.

"I'm sorry, Gregory. I'm sorry that I was never able to give you the photo, but like I said, the file somehow went missing."

*   *   *

The day the file was compiled was approximately twenty-six years, three months, and nine days ago. The room was silent as Heather filled out the paperwork, save for the scratch of the pen, the plop of two tears striking the paper, and the coo of her newborn son, barely a week old.

"Do you want the adoption sealed?" Mary Claire asked the young woman.

"I, uh," Heather paused to sniffle, "I never thought about it. I suppose he might want to know who I am, assuming he'll forgive me for leaving. Can we seal it until he grows up?" she asked, her tone on the edge of begging.

"For you..." Mary Claire trailed, stamping the word CONFIDENTIAL across the front of the file.

A tiny Gregory, then named Billy, stirred in his basinet. Heather gently laid her hand on his chest, and his small digits hooked around her pinky.

"Um, uh, here. Please keep this in the file for Billy for…when he turns eighteen or something." Heather slid a small 2.5x3.5 photograph of herself to Mary Claire. "In case I can't come back, maybe this will help him find me."

"Heather," Mary Claire said with a caution to her voice.

"I've already told you, and please don't try to change my mind. I'm his momma. I have to do what's best for him. This—this is what is best."

"But you can stay."

"He'll figure out a way to destroy you, Mary. The man broke his own son's heart. Do you think he's above closing down an orphanage? If I go, there is no risk of those hypotheticals becoming factual. If I go…Billy can hide in plain sight and be guaranteed a home." She paused for a moment, an idea coming to her. "Do me a favor?"

"Of course," Mary Claire replied. "What?"

"Give him a new name. If Krad really does have eyes and ears everywhere, well, he might already know about Billy. It's not much, but a new name could make all the difference in keeping him hidden. It'll be sorta like a fresh start."

Mary Claire nodded in agreement. "I can do that."

"Thank you." Heather took a deep breath. "I know I'm taking a chance. I know I'm holding onto a miracle. This option, what I'm about to do—" she gritted her teeth and swallowed the urge to cry, "is going to hurt like the dickens." She patted her heart as her voice constricted again with sorrow. "But it's the soundest decision to make. It must be the right decision, too…why else would my heart be cracking?"

*   *   *

"Gregory, I'm curious. How did you get the file?" Mary Claire asked.

"It was a gift from Ophelia," Gregory tattled in reply, but he was no longer invested in his interrogation. *How'd she get it?* was his final thought before filing that mystery away for another day. His mind was now piecing together what he had learned. The picture and the contents of the file did not necessarily offer much, at least not at the moment, but the name Krad spoke volumes.

"Nathaniel Krad…passed away." He squinted at Heather's photo, blurring the image of the woman. If he didn't know better, she kind of looked like….

"Yes," replied Mary Claire, "last week."

Gregory's face pinched as he struggled to form his theory.

A broken heart. It lingers, a memory whispered.

He let out an audible exhale, as his mind connected the dots.

"You think she's here. You think she's been here." Mary Claire said astonished. She could read all her children clearly, like open picture books.

"I have to go," Gregory said, a touch of urgency in his tone.

"Before you do…" Mary Claire said, holding her left index finger in the air. "Although, it's apparent you've already figured it out, just in case, there's something I need to tell you."

*   *   *

Gregory watched as his "mother" Catrice Muffet opened the front door of Muffet's Tuffets and Muffulettas and turned the sign from "Sorry, We're Closed" to "Yes, We're Open! Come and See for Yourself!" He stepped out of his car, stowing the file inside his jacket, making sure the photograph was on top. Mary Claire was right; he did have her eyes, and a bit of her smile, too. How had he not seen it before?

His knees buckled underneath him as feet met pavement. Perhaps he had been sitting too long, or there was some black ice. It most certainly could not be due to his nerves, could it? He refused to answer the question as he began to take jittery steps toward the very thing that he both hoped and feared would be life changing.

To any regular at Muffet's Tuffets, the day would appear to be formulaic. Gregory McGregor always came in two minutes past the hour and took a seat at the second to last barstool on the right as he had done ever since his first night on that frozen New Year's Day almost three years ago. As always, he would order the vanilla curds and whey, served with warm apples, cinnamon, and all spice, plus a banana-chocolate chip muffin for later. The similarities halted there, for, usually, Gregory wore a smile on his face, rubbing his palms together as if to warm them up for the task of eating. This time, the young man appeared nervous, his back hunched over, and he was painfully wringing his hands at double jointed angles.

"Cat," Gregory said, "I have a question for you."

"Your breakfast will be up in a moment, sweetheart," she gave her reply oblivious to his actual query. Gregory's heart performed two beats in rapid succession as there was new meaning placed on Catrice's final word. *Sweetheart.*

"Uh, no, does—does the name Nathaniel Krad mean anything to you?"

"Hm?" she hummed, beginning to come out of her morning fog. "I believe I read his name in the paper. Such a shame. Dying as close to the holiday as he did. His poor family." She ran back to the kitchen to collect Gregory's breakfast.

Gregory noted that Catrice's expression and body language became eerily neutral after he asked his question.

"Catrice," Gregory began again when she returned. "May I ask you another question?"

"Fire away," she answered.

"Well…you see…It's not so much a question as it is your opinion. You know how I told you I was adopted? Some information recently came into my possession, information that could lead me to my mother." He paused to see if she picked up on his clue. Her expression remained unchanged.

"There's no hint as to who my father was, at least that was the case until I spoke with Mother Mary Claire. My father is William Krad. He was a gentle soul, I'm told, who had possessed a very fragile heart. My mother—my mom is Heather Croí. She's this brave woman who sacrificed her happiness with me in order to guarantee a happy childhood and life for me."

Catrice had stopped her hustling and bustling. Her mind slowed to a low whirr. She only listened, hanging on every word and nodding…a little more agreeably with each syllable uttered by the young man.

"Do you think," Gregory said, nervously eyeing Catrice's expression, "that if I ever found Heather, she might want to see me?"

Catrice was unable to offer up her opinion as she realized that Gregory had his father's nose and jawline. How had she not noticed those details before? Her brain convinced her that what was transpiring could only be appropriately identified as magic.

"Catrice," Gregory began again, "can I ask you another question?"

Catrice nodded her head fervently.

Laying the file marked CONFIDENTIAL on the counter and slipping the photo from its collection of papers, Gregory extended it to her. "Is this you?"

Catrice gently and shakily took the photo between her fingers, appraising it. Truthfully, she no longer resembled the woman who she once was, save for the eyes. Her curves were more pronounced; her face was deeply lined from time and worry and sadness; her hair was threaded with silver. "You can't see, but I was five months pregnant with you in this photo. Well, I guess I never really showed."

A gentle smile momentarily flickered across her face. Her eyes stayed trained to the photo. "I was almost certain it was you" She tapped the left corner of her mouth. "One corner of your mouth is perpetually turned down, just like his, Will's, your dad's, especially when you're deep in thought.

"I wanted to tell you who I was," she confessed, "but I—I wasn't sure if you would be mad at me. I mean…I would be mad at me. I—I don't know—wanted to skip the potentially hard parts. I wasn't thinking." She paused to take a gulp of air. "Mary Claire knew, a few years after I came back, but I swore her to secrecy. I should have just—I know it sounds—uh, what does it sound like? Crazy? Stupid? I don't have the words. When I realized it was you, you were here, and I was so afraid. I was so afraid that the truth might disrupt what we had. Sort of a careful-what-you-wish-for kinda thing, where the reality of finding out I'm your mom wouldn't live up to the fantasy. And then you would go away...." Her rambling turned to tears.

She wanted to confess it all to him. How, during her time away, she had scrimped and saved and developed a compelling business plan complete with a market analysis and financial projections. How she had timed her return to Nollag to fall on Gregory's eighteenth birthday in hopes that he would stumble into Muffet's Tuffets and Muffulettas. How she adopted the name Catrice Muffet to remain inconspicuous from Nathaniel Krad.

Gregory made his way to the other side of the counter to sweep his mother in a hug. This embrace was different from the others that Gregory and Catrice—er—Heather had shared over the years. In that moment, Catrice melted away, and Heather held her son along with all the missed memories the two of them could have had. It simultaneously crushed her heart with sadness and overfilled it with joy. For Gregory, the man who spent so long fitting his true self together, he was elated that he could now add another piece to his personal puzzle. He now knew who he came from. In this instance, knowing his past would let him move forward.

*　　　*　　　*

But how had Gregory's file come into Ophelia's possession, you might wonder, and why had it come to him now? Ophelia clearly had it since before he had sought it from Mother Mary Claire those three or so years ago. What was her motive for relinquishing its secrets now?

To put it simply, Gregory was not ready for the truth until this particular holiday. Without a strong sense of self, the young man would have continued to exist as a shell, which he would require his mother to fill with her own definition of who he was or should be. This would only lead to resentment due to the sheer impossibility and impracticality of the task, for answers about oneself should only come from within.

This was why, many years ago, Ophelia took on that role, helping to bury Gregory under false identities until finally cutting him loose with the query of who he really was. If one considered it, her intentions were actually poetic: In order to save the true self, one must learn their self-worth amidst complete identity annihilation. This was a task that had left Ophelia only slightly tickled to undertake, not for reasons of existential crisis, but because Gregory's was a soul that deserved true happiness.

*   *   *

Our story returns to that day at the orphanage now eighteen years, twelve days, and eighteen hours ago, to moments before the O'Leary family came to meet Ophelia.

"Why do you need me to steal Greg's file?" Clarence prodded. "If I'm gonna do a job, I need full disclosure," he said, using words much too big for a child of seven.

Ophelia let out an over emphatic sigh and rolled her eyes back into her head. "Because, Clare, if we don't, he's going to be sad… forever. I can't let him be a lost soul."

"Okay," Clarence said, not fully satisfied with the explanation, "but you know how dangerous this could be, Ophie. You should just help Gregory. You can help the others after." He again spoke

421

with an authority beyond his apparent years. Yes, two souls were the limit, but something nagged at him that his friend wouldn't be able to stop herself. One was safest.

"You know I can't, Clarence. I explained my reasons before." Ophelia let the silent argument hang in the air as if to let Clarence reread it.

"Yeah, fine. It was more convincing when you were older. It's just—I think you're overachieving, which comes with its own consequences."

She shrugged his cryptic warning off and hopped onto the bed to place Corlis on the windowsill. "No one lives in absolute isolation, or no one should. That's the whole point! And, um, aren't you planning on saving the entire orphanage?" She gestured, indicating their home. "Doesn't that mean you're helping more than two people?"

"Correction," Clarence countered. "I'm actually helping Mary Claire. The kiddos just reap the aftereffect. You're planning to rearrange multiple fates. Fate doesn't like that." His expression became cringy as he uttered those last few words, similar to the nights when Mary Claire served creamed spinach with dinner. Both left an unpleasant taste in his mouth.

"If I can save Gregory, Petunia, Calum, and Delaney, then so be it. It's the right thing to do." She dismounted off the bed, landing with a loud "bang."

"Delaney..." he said as if the name took on new meaning. "That's the girl who's coming—"

"In about two minutes," Ophelia finished his sentence as she fished a small cardboard box labeled "Fabric" from under the bed.

422

"Remember, you're gonna act like you don't like Delaney when you meet her, giving me a chance to show her I can be the protective big sister she needs. Also, it wouldn't hurt to cry a little when you find out I'm getting adopted. Now," she said, returning to the plan, "in three days, at 1:16, you're going to sneak into the office to—" She sat on her bed and pulled a small red dress for her doll from the box; its hem still required some attention.

"—Get the Billy Croí file located in the top file drawer. It's closer to the front of the drawer between Paulianna Baffin and Umberto Crill because Mary Claire isn't the greatest at alphabetizing," Clarence finished with a smile. "I'm not a child, Ophie. When have I ever done a job halfheartedly? I'll even do a dry run when the O'Learys get here."

"I know," she said as she slipped a magenta thread through the eye of her needle. She took a breath deciding to address what was bothering her friend. "You're right, Clare. There's no telling what will happen if I bend the rules…all right, break," she amended reading Clarence's half-lidded expression. "What if I do lose the ability to see what's coming next?"

"You mean like you almost did back when you jilted Lochlan Brailin?"

"You have to admit, him and Pauline were meant for each other." Ophelia's smile waned thinking about how deeply Rae had hurt Lochlan when she left. She still carried both the love and pain with her; the two feelings were sometimes indistinguishable from each other.

"Yeah, but they were supposed to make that realization nine years, four months, and six and a half days later than they actually did."

"If it's true love, then why waste time? Now they don't have to say, 'If only we'd managed to get together sooner,'" she said in a mocking tone.

"They still say that."

"Yes," agreed the little girl, "but they say it with less regret. Specifically, nine years, four months, and six and a half days' worth." She smiled triumphantly.

The two children heard the doorbell ring. "Well, I guess I'll go do a practice run for the file now. Maybe get my blanket back. I'll see you in a few, Ophie," Clarence said, knowing Ophelia had made up her mind. He turned around and took determined little steps out of the room, pausing in the doorway. In a flash, he quickly ran back to Ophelia, hopped up on the bed, and threw his arms around his friend. "Be brave," he said before bounding from the mattress and tearing around the corner.

Funny, thought the girl as she continued with her project, *I should have said the same to him.*

Chapter 36

In Which Ophelia Is Still Not Used to Unexpected Surprises...but at Least This One Is Pleasant

Sometimes, the solutions to one's greatest troubles appear disguised in the most un-profound of ways. For Ophelia O'Leary, hers would come in the form of a knock at 6:11 a.m. on the door of apartment 7H.

Ophelia shuffled from her bedroom, bleary eyed. She instinctively tamed her mess of curls and covered her wrinkled oversized sweats with a more flattering royal purple robe with a quilting detail about the plush collar. She exhaled a sigh of relief, realizing the apartment was still tidy, save for a passed-out Clarence on the sofa, which was rectified with a crème-colored blanket thrown over him.

Who could it be? Ophelia wondered as she drew herself closer to the peephole. She still had not accustomed herself to lacking the luxury of being two and three-quarter steps ahead. In this instance, however, the person on the other side was a pleasant surprise.

Delaney stood in the hallway with a befuddled look on her face. Her confusion from the previous night had not fallen away like the sleep from her eyes that morning. She looked entirely lost and not altogether sure how she found herself at the doorstep of her adopted sister.

"Delaney," Ophelia said blandly, after deciding in a split second that she was not sure if she should sound surprised or quizzical in tone.

"I needed to come by," Delaney blurted out, her thought being interrupted as Clarence turned himself from his right side to his left to face the back of the couch, grumbling in his sleep. "Uh, sorry," she said, turning her attention back to her sister. "Something has been weighing on my mind."

"Something heavy? Or something simply weighing in? Everything okay?" Ophelia asked, her concern genuine as this time she hadn't the foggiest idea as to what could be troubling Delaney.

"Yes, but no?" A thought had slipped through Delaney's fingers, only leaving fragmented traces of what she truly felt instead of the exact words she needed to articulate herself. Like pinpointing the secret ingredient in a recipe, the remaining notes of the thought taunted her.

She took a deep breath and started again. "I need us to go down a familiar road again. For the longest time, Ophelia, Christmas has been an epic debacle. And…and usually you seem to have been behind it."

Ophelia's hopeful surprise began to sink into fear.

"I mean, you put people in awkward—and I mean a*wkward*—predicaments. Some even ended up in the hospital. It's a bit

426

bothersome that it's happened more than once. You shanked Santa with a candy cane! Petunia, Gregory, Calum, even Grey…what you did to each of them, it seems like you were out to get them."

"Delaney—"

Delaney gently raised her hand up to stop her sister. "I don't need you to explain, Ophelia."

Ophelia was relieved that her sister had interrupted her. If she didn't, Ophelia would have offered up an explanation, and she would have wanted it to be an honest one. That being the case, now that she had a moment, she became unsure if honesty would necessarily translate to believable.

"I mean, I could," Delaney continued. "I don't know. I could ask you why you were so sneaky and mean and crass, but I suppose you weren't, actually. You were as you always were, blunt and honest to a fault." Her words preached acceptance. Her tone did not. The fact of the matter was not how one always wished it to be. Be that as it may, the fact of the matter was still, well, a fact.

"Maybe none of that matters." Delaney threw her hands up. "Considering all things, everything has turned out fine. Everyone seems to be happier. It just seems more than serendipitous that from all this chaos everyone got a happy end—outcome," she amended her last words as the logical side of her brain instructed her that everyone's stories were still in progress. An ending was presumptuous. "Perhaps there actually was some order to it all. And maybe I don't need to know how it exactly fits together."

Ophelia stepped out into the hall, gently closing the door behind her. She swallowed hard, her mind whirring away. Then it dawned on her, who she was. She was more than the adopted

427

daughter of Éamon and Alicia O'Leary, sister to Delaney, in this life. She was more than an accomplished designer at the Fabulously Festooned Frocks and Alterations Dress Shoppe. She was someone that helped those souls of a particular variety who had an inclination to fit into a prescribed life but not actually live it. Her methods were extreme, true, but sometimes one had to take drastic measures, even taking things right down to the studs or totally burning it all to the ground, to get at the core of what it meant to do more than merely survive in this world. Foresight or not, the woman that was currently Ophelia O'Leary was a force to be reckoned because of all that she had been and would still become. She recalled reminder number thirteen Mynah had taught her: When you know who you are, fear isn't necessary.

Ophelia's rediscovered confidence cooled her words. "You're doing it again. Overthinking."

"I know. I've already constructed about thirty-eight possible ways this conversation could go," Delaney replied in an unapologetic monotone.

"Do any of them end well?" Ophelia asked. Her subtle, yet confident, smirk shrouded her remaining feelings of trepidation that quaked past her expectant eyes.

Delaney considered the question. "I think I finally figured it out, or at least came to a conclusion that I can live with, but not in a defeatist settling kind of way."

"Good. I taught you better than that…the whole settling thing."

"Yes, yes you did. While your approach was, um, unorthodox, you did teach me to never box myself in or make a home inside a mold made from other's expectations." Delaney paused as a new thought sprung to life from her own words.

Ophelia watched her sister's pinched eyebrows begin to ease only for them to pull together once again.

Delaney shook her head, pushing back the many different theories and postulates she had concocted from the previous evening to make room for a new, itty-bitty idea to ponder. "It doesn't matter," she said to herself. But the words were neither flippant nor frigid. On the contrary, with these uttered words, a warm light of realization shone through, and a tingling sensation moved over the surface of her skin.

It didn't really matter, indeed. If Delaney gave forgiveness or a piece of her mind to Ophelia, it wouldn't undo the past. Bailey would have still swiped her grandmother's bracelet. Martin would have still needed a triple bypass and a change of heart on the meaning of life. Calum would have still lived under his father's shadow, trying again and again to seek out his passion in places where it did not lie. Gregory would still have questioned his place in the world as all do at some point in time. Petunia would still have awoken from her spell of routine and people pleasing to rediscover her true passion in folklore and tales, secreting it away from her parents. Delaney…Delaney was not sure about herself. She was never good at understanding her own troubles.

"It doesn't matter," Delaney repeated. "Look, Ophelia, I really don't know why I came here. Maybe to forgive you. Maybe to yell. Maybe to come stand on your welcome mat and blather on and on…."

"Sometimes you just need a sounding board."

"I do. I do…" she trailed off, absentmindedly touching the charms on her bracelet. She felt her heart warm and tingle, which triggered the corners of her mouth to pull upward and smile. With that, Delaney willingly misplaced her tightly held animosity toward her sister. Her shoulders and lower back thanked her for the lightened load.

"Soooo...then you're not here to lecture me? Still on the fence?" Ophelia pondered, not confident which of the thirty-eight scenarios her sister revisited and played out in her head was taking place in the hallway. She did not realize Delaney was not mentally filing the remaining thirty-seven away for a rainy day but shredding them from her thoughts.

"No. No yelling today," Delaney groaned, the tension leaving her furrowed brow and her jaw finally unclenching, "so long as you don't push Grandpa toward a three-quarter life crisis or something."

"Were you trying to make a joke?" Ophelia sported a grimace that threatened to turn up at the corners into a smile.

"I would have said something along the lines of not tasing him, but...."

Ophelia smirked back. "Hm. I see. This is how it's going to be from now on? We're never going to let that one go?"

"Kinda the point of the holidays, sis. So, yeah."

"How's that book intro you've been stewing over?"

"Two can play at this game. Mrs. Wickershamson wants to know what you and Clarence were up to last night? Hm? On my way up, she informed that she hasn't see him come down yet."

Ophelia didn't bat an eyelash. "He spent the night. Fell asleep after a hardcore marathon of Christmas movies. Not like this is the first time. You know this."

Delaney, ignoring the facts, puckered her lips to the left side of her face and batted her eyelashes, embracing the childish mannerisms she had deprived her younger self, before she had met Ophelia, that is. "Uh, huh," she giggled. "Mrs. Wikershamson said otherwise. She said she saw, and I quote, 'sparks flying left and right' off you two."

Ophelia shook her head. "Ugh. First, of all, Violet was clearly inebriated. That woman loves a holiday party."

"I know," Delaney interjected. "She and Mr. Wikershamson are still waltzing in the lobby. You and Clarence are invited for French toast and mimosas, by the way."

"Aw, that's so sweet of her...but, second," Ophelia said, regaining her train of thought, "the tipsy librarian aside, people have no problem believing a man who gallivants around the world breaking and entering to commit charity, yet still find it inconceivable that two people of the opposite sex can be platonic. It's a sad overly simplistic world we live in."

"Are you done being overdramatic?" Delaney wore an expression that included half-lidded eyes and pursed lips.

"Are you done avoiding my question?"

"Wha—oh," Delaney paused. "You know, I think I may have an idea or two percolating in the background for the introduction."

"Hm," Ophelia grunted. "Then you're welcome." Her smirk now rested a little more securely on her mouth.

"We all know it is undeniable you've had a strong influence on my life. I mean, a big one, you know?" Delaney stretched out her arms and spread her fingers through still mittened hands. "So enormously gargantuan tha—"

431

"Maybe save your words for that introduction."

Delaney let her arms flop to her sides. "All right," she said, slightly defeated. "I've got go get on that. Who knows, maybe inspiration will strike on my way home, and something magical will come out on the page," she laughed.

Ophelia looked back at her sister thoughtfully. Delaney had never been one to believe in anything that existed outside the realm of sound logic.

"I'll see you at 8:00…or 8:22, knowing you. You're coming over, by the way," Delaney added, noting the look of confusion on her sister's face

"Oh? Then I'm looking forward to it."

Then, Delaney surprised her sister with a hug. "Don't forget," she said, "French toast and mimosas downstairs." She could feel her sister reciprocate and hold her closely in a secure embrace.

Ophelia wore a smile on her face, the broad genuine kind one dons right before a blissful cry. She squeezed her eyes tight and focused on the tingly feeling that spread over her.

Something caught Ophelia's eye as the two pulled apart, the small rattle charm of Delaney's bracelet had snagged on the sleeve of her robe. "That reminds me," she said, thinking back to that night in the hospital with Mildred. "What's the story behind the rattle charm? I remember Gramma telling me you would know."

Delaney considered the charm, sorting through each as if it were a different key to help unlock her memories. "This one…" she began, "Grandma bought this one to remind her of that first Christmas we welcomed you into the family."

"She wanted to be reminded of that day?" Ophelia laughed uncomfortably. "I don't recall it being one for the Christmas cards. I'm pretty sure I wrecked Gramma's Christmas. Broke one of her favorite ornaments…ate my weight in cookie dough…ruined the dress she and Grampa bought me…wasn't three to six months old, like she was expecting…."

Delaney agreed with everything her sister listed and more. "Yeah…" she shrugged, "it wasn't perfect, but you made it memorable." She smiled to herself, recollecting the shocked faces her grandparents had made when Ophelia pulled the rattle from her gift. "Classic," she said to herself. And then she paused, a thought creeping into her mind. She puckered lips, pulling them to the left side of her face. *She broke every rule of a "perfect" Christmas…Rule? Or guideline?*

"Whatcha thinkin' about there, Dee?" Ophelia finally chimed in, breaking twenty-three seconds of silence.

"Hm?"

"You had the thinking face on." Ophelia, without thinking, mirrored Delaney's thinking face, a quirk the pair shared. Neither were exactly sure how they both came to exhibit it, if they had developed it separately or if one influenced the other.

"I, uh, think I got something, uh, for the intro." She dug in her purse for a pen and a scrap of paper, quickly scrawling something down. "I gotta go!" Delaney said with a bright smile as her mind combined several of her fragmented ideas for the introduction to her cookbook with a new thought and would let the whole thing proof for at least an hour.

"See you at 8:22" was all Ophelia said, waving goodbye to her sister before slipping back into the apartment.

"You okay, Ophie?" Clarence asked groggily from underneath the blanket. Despite the sleep in his eyes, he caught the tears starting to collect at the corners of her eyes and wink in the morning light.

"I'm fine," she gasped, wiping furiously at the tears. "I got a glimpse. When—when Dee hugged me. She hugged me."

"A glimpse." Clarence straightened. "You mean you can see again?"

"Only a brief moment, I think," she said somewhat uncertain.

"Wh—What did you see?"

"I saw…." She blinked furiously to conjure up the image again, willing it to be burned into her mind's eye so that she could look upon it whenever she wished. Alas, the effort was for naught. "Ugh," she exhaled as the image was both foggy and fuzzy, an undesired combination for visibility and clarity. "I can't recall the specifics. Just a feeling."

"And?" Clarence prodded apprehensively, still not certain about the meaning of the tears.

"Everything's going to be okay…it's all going to be okay." She smiled as she recollected the feeling. It could be likened to a sense of security, a sense of finding home.

"Okay, we also need to backtrack," Clarence said, interrupting Ophelia's reverie. "Delaney hugged you?"

Ophelia beamed.

"So…then, you two are okay?"

"We're gonna go with yes? I mean, she invited me over to the house tonight. Wanna join me for some Christmas festivities, Clare?" She wore a look of giddy anticipation as she waited for her friend's reply.

"I'll wear my new sport coat," he said with a laugh.

Chapter 37

In Which Readers are Encouraged to Try the Salted Caramel Sweet Potatoes

So much more goes into a recipe than just a cup of sugar, a teaspoon of nutmeg, or a pinch of sea salt. Although, you will find a recipe or two in here that do call for this exact combination.

In learning these recipes by heart, and in compiling them, they all call for the spice of life. If you'll indulge me, before indulging in the Walnut Mint Fudge (pg. 43), most of you are probably recalling warm memories as children. Maybe it's watching your grandfather carve the turkey and him saving the crispy skin for you. Mayhap it's one of you licking the cookie batter off the beaters before picking the best cutouts of candy canes and stockings to be put out for Santa that night.

Understand that the best recipes are both sweet and bitter. Not every December holiday, Christmas, Hanukah, Kwanza, or Solstice, will be a keepsake. Some are most definitely savored more than others. This goes for cooking, as well. Not every recipe will come out perfectly. Not everyone will love it. However, appreciate the fact you may get a good story out of it, which could turn into a treasured memory.

I sincerely hope that the food you create from these pages of *Seasons Servings* will act as a wonderful garnish for all your holidays to come, from the truly warm and magical to the downright shocking and chaotic.

Admittedly, it can take some time to embrace the mayhem of the holidays. It certainly took me a while, but I can't deny those moments have yielded some flavorful tales.

I hope you like what you see and what you taste.

I'll finish this introduction with a saying my sister, Ophelia, taught me when we were kids: "Appearances can be deceiving. The rules you find in games (or recipes) are guidelines."

These recipes are suggestions. Feel free to get imaginative. Heck, make a mess! (But don't get too wild, especially when baking! Leveled measures and sifted flour are your friend.) Jot down some notes about your delicious discoveries in the margins and crease the pages. There are even some blank pages in the back of this book for you to add brand new culinary creations. Conjure up your own unique magic in the kitchen and enjoy.

P.S. I highly recommend the Salted Caramel Sweet Potatoes on page 33. They were my grandmother's specialty and are my sister's absolute favorite.

-Delaney O'Leary

Epilogue
(That Is Actually a Prologue)

In Which Two Friends Plotted on a Park Bench

Looking back nineteen years, two months, sixteen days, and eighteen hours to a brisk October day when thoughts of tricks and treats were just beginning to haunt the minds of the citizens of Nollag young and old, Ophelia, who was Jucinda Jorgenson at the time, had finished working her own spell with her latest charge, Fulgencia Wick.

At that very moment, Ophelia knew Mrs. Wick was sitting at her kitchen table with a glass of Moscato, feverishly writing down the details for what would become her debut novel, *Senile and Still Nubile: An Amorous Elders Erotica*, on the back of her shopping list. She didn't know it at the time, but the words "monotonous" and "humdrum" would no longer require a prominent place in her vocabulary. This was as much a victory for Mrs. Wick as it was for Ophelia.

Mrs. Wick had required a lot of convincing, leaving Ophelia feeling spent and in need of a bit of fresh air. Ophelia made her way through the park, past the organizers who were setting up for the Nollag Harvest Festival coming up that weekend, until reaching her destination, a park bench within earshot of the playground.

From her seat, Ophelia took in the splendors of autumn, the high noon sun providing a fantastic lightshow with the red-orange leaves that danced in the chilly breeze. Ophelia flexed her fingers to chase the arthritic ache from them and rolled her neck. One vertebra cracked, which gave her a small sense of satisfaction and relief. Reaching into her purse, the leather a lovely shade of lavender, she pulled out a piece of toffee, unwrapped the treat, and popped it into her mouth. She scanned the park wondering if any of the parkgoers were her friend, Clarence. She didn't expect this day to be any different from the others, but that didn't stop her shoulders from drooping and her lower lip from pouting when she realized no one looked back at her in a familiar way. It was coming up on six years, one month, and two whole days in her role as Jucinda Jorgenson, and she, unfortunately, had yet to bump into Clarence.

Before vacating her life as Rae Cuddy, Ophelia had forgotten to give Clarence a heads up that she would be returning to Nollag as Jucinda, by which time Clarence had moved on from his role as Linus Lewin.

It frustrated her to no end, knowing her best friend was out there, and she had no way of knowing where, or who, he could be. The facts were these: Ophelia and Clarence always returned to Nollag as someone new. Clarence always seemed to come back with an entirely different set of quirks, which only proved to complicate matters.

He was usually the one to find her, perhaps due to her always having something purple either on her or with her. When Clarence was fairly certain he had found Ophelia, he would always pose the question to her, "Are you allergic to nutmeg?"

While she had access to the potential futures and fates of most of the citizens of the city, things worked differently for herself and Clarence. Sometimes she liked to use the term "angel," borrowed from the city's Angel of Nollag mythology. Angel or not, neither was privy to the other's whereabouts as they jumped from life to life, appearing to the other as someone who did not require any assistance.

She resigned herself to the hope they might find each other on her next assignment. For that hope to waltz into the realm of possibility, Ophelia needed someone to help, either as Jucinda or someone else. Admittedly, Ophelia was tired of Jucinda. She was a little too suppressed for her taste, only taking on this persona to aggravate Fulgencia to step out of her own carefully crafted and unexamined personal restrictions. *That settles it*, Ophelia mentally noted. *Jucinda is going into retirement.*

Ophelia set to work and began to appraise the parkgoers. *Maybe someone younger this time*, she mused, surveying the children out for a stroll with their parents.

She observed Mr. Perkins pushing a stroller that appeared to be full of pink taffeta, which was actually a napping four-year-old Petunia. When they passed, she was able to see her little legs poking out, dressed in tights and shoes the same shade of pink as the oversized tutu. Mrs. Perkins toted a thick bubblegum pink binder under her right arm, its pages containing the milestones little Petunia was expected to achieve during her sixteenth year. In their pursuit of her "full potential," Petunia's parents were running the risk of squandering her actual full potential. Ophelia put a pin in this thought, deciding Petunia could be a good case to take on.

"Calum!" a voice cried out further down the path. Ophelia turned toward the commotion, past the Perkinses, to see a little boy making a beeline to the playground, hugging an electric blue rubber ball against his chest. He ignored the protests of his father, Martin, to return. The boy only slowed when he approached another little boy and a woman, Gregory and Mynah Moriel, who were sitting on the swings.

"Hi!" Calum exclaimed, flashing a big smile at Gregory and setting down his ball to push back the sleeves of his red and black checkered flannel shirt. "My name's Calum. What's your name?"

Before Gregory could share his name, and before Calum could offer an invitation to play, Martin caught up to his son. "Don't run off on your own," he said, trying to sound stern, but Ophelia picked up on the thread of underlying fear in his tone. "So sorry." He smiled at Mynah.

"It's no problem at all," Mynah offered. "Uh, would Calum like to play with Gregory?" Gregory waved to Calum.

"Yeah!" Calum shouted.

Gregory beamed, only to dim when Martin said, "I'm sorry. Clearly, he'd love to, but we're running late for a dentist appointment."

Calum began to protest, upset his plans of an impromptu playdate did not save him from a teeth cleaning.

"I'm sorry, son, but we have to go," Martin pressed.

"Sorry, Gregory," Calum apologized, picking up his ball and moping away with his father, who continued to reprimand him.

Ophelia could feel her heart fracture watching a crestfallen Gregory gently swing back and forth, staring at his sneakered feet.

"I'm sorry, Gregory," Ophelia overheard Mynah say.

"It's okay," Gregory glumly replied, exhaling the words. He began to pump his little legs harder, wanting to swing higher, so he didn't have to dwell on his sadness.

Poor lost boys. Ophelia turned away, resting against the bench and reviewing the prospects of Calum and Gregory. When she had looked at Calum, she saw his potential future of one constantly trying to find his place in the world, yet always seeming to be in the wrong place at the wrong time by everyone else's standards but his own. Gregory would wander in metaphorical circles in search of himself. *Which boy needed the help most?*

Before she could dissect the question, weighing the pros and cons of their futures, something tapped her shoe. A piece of orange chalk, Ophelia deduced, had rolled down the gentle slope of the path. She stooped to pick it up.

Delaney, four years old, pulled her grandmother over to Ophelia, stopping six feet and ten inches away from the bench. Delaney eyed Ophelia warily while Mildred gave a polite wave before kneeling down for a hushed conversation at the behest of her granddaughter.

"Grandma, can you ask for my chalk back, please?" Ophelia eavesdropped on the little girl's imploration. She watched as the child gently petted the cowl neck of her grandmother's sweater.

"No, Delaney, you can ask for it back."

Delaney replied with wide eyes and momentarily forgot how to breathe.

"You're a big girl. Go on. I'm right here, sweetie." Mildred straightened up, then smoothed the creases from her slacks and showcased proper posture.

Taking five and a quarter tentative steps that included one glance over her shoulder to get a reassuring nod from Mildred, Delaney stood in front of Ophelia. She kept her gaze trained to her white canvas shoes and nervously played with her fingers. "Excuse me, miss?"

"Yes?" Ophelia smiled sweetly.

As Delaney took a breath to muster her courage and make her plea for the chalk, Ophelia saw where Delaney's life would be headed. Her life wouldn't be littered with soul-crushing hardships and insurmountable challenges, but it also wouldn't know personal joy and triumph. In fact, there was very little that Ophelia could see at all. It appeared Delaney would live a lonely life, an unfulfilled life. Yet, as Ophelia ran through alternate scenarios her intervention might allow, the outcome perplexed her.

"Um, may I have my chalk back?" Delaney paused, playing back her words in her head before adding a "please."

"Certainly," Ophelia replied after a beat, the images of Delaney's altered life still playing in the peripheries of her mind. She handed the chalk back to Delaney, who took it in her little hand.

"Thank you." Delaney smiled and wiped the strands of her black hair from her face that had been displaced by the breeze.

Even though she knew the answer, Ophelia asked, "What are you drawing?"

Delaney gave a chummy smile. "Linear equations."

"Ah," Ophelia replied. "Well, I won't keep you. It was nice to meet youuuu...?"

"Delaney," Delaney said, finishing Ophelia's sentence.

"It's a very pretty name, Delaney. I'm Jucinda."

Delaney hummed a shy reply, not sure what words would politely, and expeditiously, excuse her to return to solving for the variable x.

"Thank you, Jucinda," Mildred said, walking up and extending her hand to shake Ophelia's. "I'm Mildred."

Ophelia leaned forward to take Mildred's hand. "Pleasure," was all she said in return, preoccupied with the life of Delaney that was yet to be. *I can't quite see what happens next.*

"Well, have a nice day, Jucinda," Mildred said, reading Ophelia's silence and slight look of concern that had settled around her eyes as a hint that she wanted to be left alone. Delaney silently waved as they departed.

"Oh, yes. Nice to meet you both." Ophelia awkwardly flexed her fingers giving them a wilted wave before returning to her ruminations. "Curiouser and curiouser," she muttered to herself. She blinked through the potential future of Delaney, the one that would include her. They were all there: Petunia Perkins, Calum Dooley, even Gregory, who would become a McGregor, but whose actual surname was Croí.

"What's curious?" a small boy with wispy platinum blond hair asked, popping up from behind Ophelia's seat and startling her.

"Something I was thinking about."

"Oooh," the boy said knowingly, as he, too, had a quandary of his own to untangle. He took the cerulean blanket he held in his left

445

hand and wrapped it around his neck like a scarf. "Hey, can I ask you something?"

"I don't see why not," Ophelia answered.

He stood on his tiptoes, cupping his hand to the side of his face. She tilted her ear to the boy to meet him halfway. Apparently, the question was of a sensitive nature, Ophelia deduced.

"Are you allergic to nutmeg?"

A smiled danced on Ophelia's face. Clarence had found her. "Only on Tuesdays and every third Wednesday of the month," she chortled. "I've missed you! Uh, what are you going by these days?"

"Clarence," he answered, coming around the bench to take a seat, positioning himself close so Ophelia's body would block Mynah's view of him.

"You're using your real name this time?" Ophelia inquired. She moved her purse from her lap and placed it between them as she shifted in her seat to face him.

Clarence shrugged. "Yeah. It's been a while since it's been in rotation. Who are you this time, Ophie?"

"Jucinda Jorgenson. Fulgencia Wick needed a little reminder that life doesn't *have* to be bland once you turn sixty, especially since she's got many years ahead of her. So, I helped her find the gumption she needed to jumpstart her writing career. We should be seeing her first novel on the shelf in…" she her squinted eyes and puckered her lips, "three years, four months, and thirteen days."

"What's she working on?"

Ophelia looked back at Clarence, who appeared approximately five years, ten months, and twenty-eight days old, and suddenly she felt a little uneasy telling him Mrs. Wick would become a prolific

author of over-the-hill erotica. "Uh, I'll tell you when you're older."
She quickly changed the subject. "How long have you been here?"

"Almost six years. I'm here to save the orphanage. It's going
to hit some hard times in five years. I take it you're done helping
Fulgencia, or do you still have some loose strings to tie up?"

"All done," Ophelia said, propping her left arm on the back
of the bench.

"Who's next?"

"Now that you mention it..." she trailed and looked up the
little hill. "That little girl up over by the picnic table. For once, I
can't explain it, which makes it strange."

"What?" Clarence pressed, windshield wiping his feet back
and forth.

"She's connected to three other kids in this park," Ophelia said,
excitement creeping into her voice, "all with their own potential
sad stories." She pointed out Petunia, who now sat on a gingham
blanket between her parents, looking anywhere but at her life plan
as Mrs. Perkins penciled in addendums to the binder's pages, and
Gregory, who had abandoned the swings to collect dandelions.

"That snitch?" Clarence spat.

Ophelia was taken aback.

"Sorry," Clarence apologized. "Greg's a good kid, but such a
big mouth."

"Makes sense," Ophelia said, now watching Gregory hand
over a bouquet of the yellow weeds to Mynah and move over to the
slide. She flipped through images of the numerous times Gregory
informed Mynah or Mary Claire about Clarence's antics. She would
have to ask him what was up with all the schemes.

"But four, Ophie?" Clarence returned to the matter at hand. "Simultaneously? That's unheard of! I mean, two, okay, but—"

"That's not the strangest part of it. If I help Delaney, I can't see anything beyond that—like, nothing. It's all a blank."

"Could be handling that many fates at once puts the powers on the fritz? Did I mention that four is a lot?"

Ophelia slowly shook her head, her shoulders slowing rising to shrug. "I think I should do it, Clare. There's this sadness in there. If I don't fix it, well, I don't know if I could live with that."

"But if you can't see anything beyond Delaney, is it worth it? What about after? You might not be able to help anyone else." Clarence's hands wrung one end of the blanket.

Ophelia considered this and the fates of the four children. "Clarence, I have to do this. They all have destinies where they end up alone or lonely. Delaney will get the worst of it."

The two sat in silence for a minute, listening to the faint chirps of the birds above.

Ophelia was the first to speak. "Can you do me a favor, Clare?"

"You know you don't have to ask, Ophie."

"It's a big ask, though. Will you stay with me if it does all go away? For a little while, at least?"

"Of course, my friend," Clarence said immediately. He pulled the blanket from around his neck and began to pull its edge between his thumb and index finger, all the while unable to keep his anxieties for his friend at bay. "So, you're doing this? You don't want to take more time to think about it?"

Ophelia ignored her friend's questions. "The blankness won't be for nineteen years," Ophelia added. Her eyebrows knitted together, and she gritted her teeth in the anticipation of Clarence changing his mind based off this new information. If Clarence went too long without helping someone, he would run the same risk as Ophelia and be powerless.

"I'm sure there's something I can do to keep myself busy." Clarence bit his lip and considered Mynah and Copper, both dancing around their relationship with cold feet. Perhaps Clarence could pick up the tempo.

"You're sure? I shouldn't have asked."

"No, Ophie, you absolutely should have." Clarence offered her a smile to let her know he was sincere. "Mynah is coming over," he said, looking in the direction of the playground. He hopped down from his seat. "Will I be seeing you soon?"

"Expect to see me at the end of the harvest festival in three days. Mother Mary Claire Brog's Haven for Nippers, Toddlers, Tykes, and Children will be getting a new resident — a little girl with curly red hair…" She looked over her shoulder to see Mynah coming to collect Clarence, Gregory held in her arms. "… named Ophelia. I'll see you soon," she whispered to Clarence, a mischievous smile stretched across her lips.

"Sooner than you think." Clarence waved emphatically before running over to Mynah.

"Where'd you go?" Gregory prodded Clarence once he met up with him and Mynah.

"Talking to that lady," he pointed over to Ophelia, who offered a sweet smile and a wave to the group before collecting her things.

"Uh-oh. Pockets, Clarence," Mynah said, worry creased across her brow.

Ophelia found this an odd thing to say but ignored it. Buttoning the top of her olive-green cocoon coat, she stood to head up the slight hill when she heard Mynah call out, "Miss! Miss, please wait." Ophelia turned back to see Mynah and the two boys coming over to her.

"Did you give Clarence some candy?" The bewildered look on Ophelia's face was answer enough for Mynah. "I believe these are your toffies," she continued, opening her left hand to show four individually wrapped hard candies.

Ophelia opened her purse to take a quick inventory. "Oh, so they are, but it's all right. He can have them if he likes." She smiled back at Clarence.

"That's very kind of you, Ms. Jorgenson, but I'm afraid he can't accept them."

Ophelia collected the sweets, returning them to her bag. She paused for a second before affixing the clasp on the purse. "Um, how did you know my name?"

"Ah," Mynah said, handing over a small card she held in her right hand, Jucinda Jorgenson's bus pass. "Clarence, unfortunately, is going through a little kleptomania phase."

"I see," Ophelia said, pretending to sound perturbed.

Clarence shrugged. "Sooner than you think," he muttered. He winked at his best friend.

Acknowledgements

There are many people that helped to make *Christmas Bitch* a possibility. Writing can be hard at times, and these friends and loved ones encouraged me to start, reminded me to keep going, and cheered me on as I trudged through the editing process.

Kevin, without you, Ophelia O'Leary would never have existed. That one winter night, back in 2012, you had posited, "What if you wrote a story about someone who ruined everyone's Christmas? There could be a taser involved." The very idea of writing a whole novel about a series of ruined Christmases seemed impossible until it wasn't.

Ami, one of my favorite humans and my favorite editor. You tackled a developmental and line-edit job with love and care. Thank you for loving *Christmas Bitch* and wanting it to succeed as much as I do. Thank you for the text conversations and late-night FaceTime brainstorm sessions while I excitedly shared the details of Nollag. Thank you for reminding me that this is my story, and that I should stay true to it. Also, thank you for fixing all my comma errors. I think the world of Nollag is richer because of you.

Cris, I appreciate your taking on the task of proofreading *Christmas Bitch* after getting only the briefest of synopses, and doing so amidst an unbearable heatwave to boot. Hopefully, the story conjured cooling thoughts.

Moriah, I am so glad that *Christmas Bitch* found a fan in you, friend. You were there to refute any negative thoughts I started to believe and pushed me to continue to edit each chapter so that you could find out what happened next. That meant, and still means, so much to me.

Mom and Dad, even though I didn't become the Disney animator I had hoped to be when I was a kid, I still managed to put my creativity to good use. Thank you both for reading my earlier works and for giving me honest feedback so that I could improve. Thank you, Dad, for instilling within me a solid work ethic. Mom, I will forever be grateful for your undying support and your believing in my special brand of magic.

To Butler, my best friend of over thirty years. You were with me from the very beginning of my writing journey, back when I attempted to do my own version of Rapunzel in a little 3.5"x5.5" notebook on a train ride to and from Chicago. Thank you for reading my first novel. (Although, going back and re-reading it, maybe I should apologize instead.) Thank you for your continued encouragement to not give up on this creative path.

Thank you to everyone who played a part in making *Christmas Bitch* a reality. Those tiny check-ins gifted me with significant motivation to keep writing, editing, and designing. Thank you Alexis, Grace, and Jenny for asking me, "How's the book coming?" To Candis and David, I appreciate you encouraging me to get

Christmas Bitch out there already. To Melissa (Twin!), Pat, and Marjory, thank you for letting me spam you with story and cover art updates. To Isaac, Mary, and Rich, thank you for your insights and resources when it came to the actual publishing and marketing side of the writing process. These acts all mattered because you all matter to me.

About the Author

Lisa Monet Photography

Jack Lelko has been drawing and coming up with story ideas since he was single digits. He has a penchant for writing complicated plots and putting twists on fairy tales. His friend, Butler, would like to add, "He has a sixth sense, a sight for the story, if you will...he pulls inspiration from nearly every crevice of his world and spins it into another for the pleasure of his readers." Jack lives in the Pacific Northwest with his cat, Natasha Jane Nodognik. This blurb would have been longer, but she was demanding snacks at the time.

Website: Neurdotically.Wordpress.com
Instagram: @neurdotically_writes
Twitter: @neurdotically
TikTok: @neurdotically
Store: Society6.com/Neurdotically

Made in the USA
Middletown, DE
06 August 2022

70385498R00279